"Speculative fiction without HARLAN ELLISON would be the Fourth of July without fireworks."

—*URSULA K. LEGUIN*

"SHATTERDAY should be banned from all science fiction shelves. HARLAN ELLISON no longer belongs there. Do Jonathan Swift, Edgar Allan Poe, Rimbaud, or Kafka? Occasionally, there's a writer with the mind, passion, and audacity to create a one-man revolution in his field. HARLAN ELLISON is such a writer."

—*ROGER CORMAN*

"HARLAN ELLISON'S prose has a remarkable vitality. Adrenalin seems to drive him to the type-writer where, for our entertainment, he produces crackling and powerful tales."

—*STEVE ALLEN*

"HARLAN ELLISON has a supersonic mind, and SHATTERDAY is its flagship, a streak of literary light across a mythological sky."

—*WILLIAM KOTZWINKLE*

"You have to read SHATTERDAY, feel it, experience it.... It is an event."

—*SCIENCE FICTION REVIEW*

"Because HARLAN ELLISON pretends that he is just a nice guy who has dropped in to read you his latest tale, you drop your defenses and wham—you discover he is a horror-story writer in disguise. Things do not go bump in Ellison's tales. That would be too easy. Instead, his heroes crash into the night en route to final, fatal meetings."

—*SATURDAY REVIEW*

"ELLISON, that feisty, unreasonable, prevaricating, megalomaniacal and revanchist monster...the quintessential SF short story writer of his time..."

—*FANTASY & SCIENCE FICTION*

"Whatever the genre or blend of genres, ELLISON delivers."

—*PUBLISHERS WEEKLY*

"One of the few masters of the short story. Maturing, refining his art, aging like a fine, strange wine."

—*LOCUS*

"HARLAN ELLISON's short stories have already won high praise in his native America, and the sixteen recent specimens collected in SHATTERDAY are impressively various and accomplished....An authentic writer."

—*Robert Nye, THE GUARDIAN*
(England)

HARLAN ELLISON

SHATTERDAY

B

BERKLEY BOOKS, NEW YORK

The quotation on page 163 from POE POE POE POE POE POE POE by Daniel Hoffman (Garden City, New York: Doubleday & Company, Inc., Copyright © 1972 by Daniel Hoffman), is used by permission of the author.

This Berkley book contains the complete
text of the original hardcover edition.
It has been completely reset in a typeface
designed for easy reading, and was printed
from new film.

SHATTERDAY

A Berkley Book / published by arrangement with
Houghton Mifflin Company

PRINTING HISTORY
Houghton Mifflin edition / November 1980
Berkley edition / October 1982

ISBN: 0-425-05370-9

A BERKLEY BOOK ® TM 757,375
Berkley Books are published by Berkley Publishing Corporation,
200 Madison Avenue, New York, New York 10016.
PRINTED IN THE UNITED STATES OF AMERICA

Acknowledgments

When the time comes to assemble the indicia matter for one of my books I am invariably astonished at how many dear friends, wise sources and dedicated readers have lent their encouragement, store of obscure facts, concern and, sometimes, homes in aid of the creation. To sum them without naming them, to say, "You know who you are," would be to demean their invaluable gifts at precisely the moment I needed them. And so, with your indulgence, a compendium of worthy heurists, with love and thanks: Isaac Asimov; Haskell Barkin; Keith Berwick; Victoria Bolles; Ben Bova; Jacques Brel; Ed Bryant; Ms. Marty Clark; John Clute; Arthur Byron Cover; Jack Danon; Richard Delap; Bill Desmond; Leo & Diane Dillon; George Alec Effinger; Lori Ellison; Audrey & Ed Ferman; Stacey Franchild; Kelly Freas; Kenneth L. Gross; Jim Harmon; Fred Harris & Carole Hemingway of KABC-AM, Los Angeles; Gary Hoppenstand; the Iguanacon committee of the 36th World Science Fiction Convention; Walter Koenig; Shelley Levinson; Edward London; Barry Malzberg; Lydia Marano; Sheryl Dichter Martin; Terry Martin; Vincent McCaffrey & the staff of the Avenue Victor Hugo Bookstore, Boston; Thomas F. Monteleone; Michael Moorcock; Jonathan Ostrowsky; Tom Owen; Ms. Eusona Parker; Sue Pounds & the staff of The Portobello Hotel, London; Charles Ryan; Mary David Sheiner; Robert Silverberg; Julie Simmons; Linda M. Steele; Leslie Kay Swigart; and with greater sense of loss than I can convey, to the memory of Victoria Chen Haider, my editor at *Playboy,* who died on 25 May 1979 in the crash of a DC-10 in Chicago.

Jim Blish once dedicated a book to me.

He did other things for me:
He introduced me to the music of Charles Ives, to the taste of Vander Flip, to the urgency of avoiding the said-bookism, to the concept of the watershed, to the pleasures of Indo-Ceylonese food.

He taught me the value of uncompromising literary criticism and the absolute necessity for perfect grammar, and I try, Jim, God knows I try. But the most indispensable lessons he taught were how badly I could write when I wasn't paying attention, and how I could be king of the world when I did the work with love and courage.

Jim is gone now, but for all that, and for much more, this progress report, this book, with respect and friendship, for

JAMES BLISH

Contents

Fear is implanted in us as a preservative from evil; but its duty, like that of other passions, is not to overbear reason, but to assist it. It should not be suffered to tyrannize in the imagination, to raise phantoms of horror, or to beset life with super-numerary distresses.

—DR. JOHNSON

Introduction

MORTAL DREADS

WITH A TOUCH of quiet pride the Author states that he has watched the Johnny Carson Show only once in his life. (The single blot on an otherwise exemplary record occurred when I was pressed, one night, into sitting through consummate dreariness to reach the moment when Robert Blake, a friend of many years even though he's an actor, was to sit and talk to Orson Welles, one of my heroes despite his hawking of inferior commercial wines. It was a moment I wish had been denied me. Bob, a good and decent and talented man, clever, witty and articulate, perhaps driven mad by the fame and cheap notoriety of having become a television cult hero for several seasons, proceeded to insult Mr. Welles in a manner I suppose he thought was bright badinage. It was a maleficent spectacle in overwhelming bad taste, culminating in Bob's passing a remark about Mr. Welles's girth.

(Welles sat silently for a moment as the audience—and I— winced in disbelief and horror. Then he said, very softly, very softly, "My weight is correctable only with enormous difficulty at my age, but I live with it comfortably; as opposed to your bad manners.")

There should be benign deities who would send ravens to pluck out one's eyes so such sights could be avoided.

I did not need to see my friend make an ass of himself. And I sat there thinking, for a wonder, is *this* what a vast segment of the American viewing public truly accepts as "the rebirth of conversation"? This endless babble and confluence of self-serving "celebrities" who warm studio sets with the indispensable intelligence that they'll be doing *Pal Joey* at the Country Squire Dinner Theatre in Lubbock, Texas from June 12th to 18th?

And I could not contain my sorrow that my friend had been driven mad by television, to sit there having been gulled into thinking he was having a "conversation" before so many millions of moon-white eyes in darkened bedrooms. But this time I will not inveigh against the Monster Video; that was the fulmination that served to introduce my previous collection of stories, *Strange Wine*.

No, this time I would speak of conversation; of speaking to the true and universal darkness that fills so much of our souls. Of mortal dreads and the value of such terrors as I present here.

I do a considerable number of college lectures every year. It helps pay the freight so I don't have to write television ever again. From my lips to the ear of god . . . or whoever's in charge. And frequently I will say something about the human condition that seems perfectly rational and proper to me, because I know we all share the same thoughts. Invariably, some feep in the audience will attempt to pillory me with the stunning accusation, "You only said that to shock!"

My response is always the same:

"You bet your ass, slushface. Of course I said it to shock you (or *wrote* it to shock you). I don't know how *you* perceive my mission as a writer, but for me it is not a responsibility to reaffirm your concretized myths and provincial prejudices. It is not my job to lull you with a false sense of the rightness of the universe. This wonderful and terrible occupation of re-creating the world in a different way, each time fresh and strange, is an act of revolutionary guerrilla warfare. I stir up the soup. I inconvenience you. I make your nose run and your eyes water. I spend my life and miles of visceral material in a glorious and painful series of midnight raids against complacency. It is my lot to wake with anger every morning, to lie down at night even angrier. All in pursuit of one truth that lies at the core of every jot of fiction ever written: we are all in the same skin . . . but for the time it takes to read these stories I merely have the mouth. You see before you a child who never grew up, who does not know it's socially unacceptable to ask, 'Who farted?'"

Thus I try to codify in noble terms the obsession with Art and the inability of the writer to stop writing, to get along with others, to view without rancor the world as a gem, at once pure and perfect. But that's flapdoodle, of course. I write because I write. I can do no other.

It is the love of conversation.

I am anti-entropy. My work is foursquare for chaos. I spend my life personally, and my work professionally, keeping that soup boiling. *Gadfly* is what they call you when you are no longer dangerous, when the right magazines publish your work and you don't have to seek out obscure publications as homes for the really mean stuff, when they ask you to come and discuss matters of import with "celebrities" on the Johnny Carson Show. I much prefer troublemaker, malcontent, pain in the ass, desperado. As I've said elsewhere, I see myself as a combination of Jiminy Cricket and Zorro. *Thus* do I ennoble myself in the times when all the simple joys I've forsworn rush back on me as chances lost, and I'm left with only the work and something Irwin Shaw said: "Since I am not particularly devout, my chances for salvation lie in a place sometime in the future on a library shelf."

Why is he telling me all this?

He's telling you all this because the feeps thought they were getting off a hot one when they accused him of merely writing to shock.

That's my job. To stir the soup, to bite your thigh, to get you angry so you keep the conversation going. Don't invite me to parties for pleasant chat. I want to hear the sound of your soul. Then I can translate it into the mortal dreads we all share and fire them back at you transmogrified, reshaped as amusing or frightening fables.

Look, it's like this: I was in Utah doing some work for the Equal Rights Amendment late last year, and I said some things like this during a radio interview. So the interviewer, who was a very bright guy, pushed at it a little. He asked me to explicate some of these "mortal dreads" that we all share, that I thought I was illuminating by writing such weird and troubling stories. I thought about it a moment, and then in a fit of confession that passes for honesty I told him about writing the title story of this book, "Shatterday."

"I was sitting in a hotel room in New York in the middle of a January snowstorm in 1975," I said. "I had to have the story finished by 7:00 that night so I could present it at a reading uptown at 7:30, allowing myself time to get a cab and find the auditorium . . . and I was writing furiously, hardly thinking about how the story was creating itself—"

The interviewer looked at me oddly.

"It was *creating itself?*"

"Yeah," I said. "I was just the machine that was putting it on paper. That story came out of secret places in my head and ran at the paper without regard for my breaking back or the deadline. It created itself. Well, I finished it barely in time, got downstairs, shoved an old lady out of the way to grab her cab in the snow, and just got uptown in time for the reading. I didn't even have time to proofread the copy.

"So when I was in the middle of the lecture, reading the section where the lead character is having the argument with his alter ego about his mother, I realized for the first time that I wanted *my* mother to die."

The interviewer looked uncomfortable.

"No, wait, listen," I said hurriedly. "I didn't mean that I wanted her to *die,* just to be gone. See, my mother was quite old at that time, she'd been extremely ill off-and-on for years, and in that eerie way we have of exchanging places with our parents when they grow old, I'd become the parent and she'd become the child; and *I* was responsible for *her.* I supported her, and tried to keep her comfortable down in Miami Beach where she was living, and that gave me pleasure, to play at being a real grownup son, and like that. But she was just a shadow. She hadn't been happy in a long time, she was just marking out her days, and I wanted to be free of that constant realization that *she was out there.* I loved her, she was a nice woman. I didn't have any rancor or meanness in me . . . I just had to admit that I wanted her gone."

The interviewer looked *really* uncomfortable now.

"Well, oh boy, that was some helluva thing to have to admit to myself. 'You slimy sonofabitch,' I thought, and I was still reading aloud to the audience that had no tiniest idea what monstrous and hellish thoughts were tearing me up. 'You evil, ungrateful, selfish prick! How the hell could you even *consider* something as awful as that? She never did anything to you, she raised you, put up with your craziness and always had faith in you when everyone else said you'd wind up in some penal colony or the chipmunk factory! You sleazy, vomitous crud, how can you even *think* of her being dead?' And it was terrible, just terrible. I thought I was scum unfit to walk with decent human beings, to harbor these secret feelings about a perfectly innocent old woman. And I remembered what Eric Hoffer once wrote: 'What monstrosities would walk the streets were some people's faces as unfinished as their minds.'

"But there it was, in the story. I'd written it and had to confront it and learn to live with it." It was like the line out of another story in this book, "All the Lies That Are My Life," where I mention the ugliness of simply being human. But I hadn't thought of that line then. And the interviewer didn't quite know what to say to me. What the hell can you say to some dude sitting there copping to wanting his mother to pass away?

Well, it was one of those call-in radio shows, and we started taking calls from Salt Lake citizens who were pissed off at an "outsider" coming in to tell them that Utah's not ratifying the ERA was a sinful and mischievous act. And then, suddenly, there was a woman on the line, coming over the headphones to me in that soundproof booth, with tears in her voice, saying to me, "Thank you. Thank you for telling that about your mother. My mother was dying of cancer and I had *the same thoughts* and I hated myself for it. I thought I was the only person in the world who ever thought such an awful thing, and I couldn't bear it. Thank you. Oh, thank you."

And I thought of that heartrending scene in Jack Gelber's play, *The Connection,* where the old Salvation Army sister who has been turned into a medical junkie by inept doctors says to this apartment full of stone-righteous street hypes, "You are not alone. You are not alone."

I damned near started to cry myself. I wanted to hug that nameless woman out there in Salt Lake City somewhere, hug her and say *you are not alone.*

That's why I tell you all this.

You are not alone. We are all the same, all in this fragile skin, suffering the ugliness of simply being human, all prey to the same mortal dreads.

When I lecture I try to say this, to say most of the fears you invent—atomic war, multinational conspiracies, assassination paranoias, fear of ethnic types, flying saucers from Mars—

those are all bullshit. I inveigh against illogical beliefs and say that the mortal dreads are the ones that drive you to crazy beliefs in Scientology, est, the power of dope, hatred of elitism and intellectual pursuits, astrology, messiahs like Sun Myung Moon or Jim Jones, fundamentalist religions. I try to tell you that fear is okay if you understand that what you fear is the same for *everyone*.

Not the bogus oogie-boogie scares of Dan O'Bannon and Ridley Scott's *Alien,* slavering creatures in the darkness that want to pierce your flesh with scorpion stinger tails and ripping jaws, but the fear of Gregor Samsa waking to discover he isn't who he was when he went to bed; the fear of Pip in the grave-yard; the fear of Huck finding his dead father on the abandoned houseboat. The fears to which we are all heir to simply because we are tiny creatures in a universe that is neither benign nor ma-lign . . . it is simply enormous and unaware of us save as part of the chain of life.

And all we have to stand between us and the irrational crazy chicken-running-around-squawking terror that those mortal dreads lay on us is wisdom and courage.

That is why I tell you all this, and why I write to shock you and anger you and frighten you. To tell you with love and care that you are not alone.

These stories are about the mortal dreads.

Each one is a little different from all the others because, to fall back on words of Irwin Shaw again, ". . . in a novel or a play you must be a whole man. In a collection of stories you can be all the men or fragments of men, worthy and unworthy, who in different seasons abound in you. It is a luxury not to be scorned."

And so, with the serious warning that you not try to pick out the pieces of the Author that went into the writing of each of these little cautionary tales, I give you another year or two of my life's work, all of which say, with love and care, and the intent to anger, shock and frighten you . . .

Honest to god—or whoever's in charge—you are not alone.

HARLAN ELLISON
Los Angeles
14 February 80

Jeffty is Five

INTRODUCTION

Writers take tours in other people's lives.

The purpose of these introductory notes to each story is to reaffirm that fact, over and over again. It cannot be said too often. A writer cannibalizes his own life, that's true: all we have to relate are the perceptions of ourselves and our experiences that parallel other people's perceptions and experiences. But you are not alone; where you've been, there have I gone; what you've felt, I have also felt. Pain and joy and everything that lies between are universal.

I have taken what you've given me—though you never knew I was watching—and I've run it through the purifier of my imagination for the sole purpose of giving it back to you with, I hope, some clarity. If you would best use these reconstituted snippets and scintillae of your lives, I urge you to hold up the realities portrayed here to the mirror of fantasy. Things often seem clearer in the silver light of the extraordinary. Some call this magic.

Take "Jeffty Is Five" for example.

At the moment, this is one of my half dozen favorite stories. It is both a hard-edged and a romanticized view of the innocence that we all possessed as children. Jeffty has become an image of reverence for the parts of my childhood that were joyous and free of pain.

I suppose what I'm saying is that a large part of myself as an adult is Jeffty. They are parts of my nature I hold very dear. But, sadly, Donny is also a part of me. The part of me that grew up in order to deal with the Real World.

The Real World exists utterly in the Now; in a present time that seems to find the dearly remembered Past abhorrent, unbearable. And so, as this story contends, the Present tries to eradicate the Past. Please note that a distinction is drawn between change and eradication. This is not one of those embalmed adorations of nostalgic sentimentality. It merely suggests for your consideration that there are treasures of the Past that we seem too quickly brutally ready to dump down the incinerator of Progress. At what cost, it suggests, do we pursue the goal of being *au courant*?

There are those who ask me, "Where do you get your ideas?" Of all the silly questions asked of writers, that one, surely, is the silliest. It presupposes there is a *place* or a *method* by which dreams become actualities on paper.

No. There is no such place (though I usually respond with the spine-straightener that I get my stories from an idea service in Poughkeepsie, New York...$25 a week and they send me a fresh six-pack of ideas fifty-two times a year) and there is no universally explicable method (hell, not even Aristotle could codify the act of creation). But you'd be both amazed and appalled at how many people ask me for the address of that idea service in Poughkeepsie.

But this I can tell you of how I came to write "Jeffty Is Five":

My friends Walter and Judy Koenig invited me to a party. I don't like parties. I do like Walter and Judy. I also like their kids. I went to the party.

Mostly I sat near the fireplace, friendly but not overly ebullient. Mostly I talked to Walter and Judy's son, Josh, who is remarkable beyond the telling. And then I overheard a snatch of conversation. An actor named Jack Danon said—I *thought* he said—something like this— "Jeff is five, he's always five." No, not really. He didn't say anything like that at all. What he probably said was, "Jeff is fine, he's always fine." Or perhaps it was something completely different.

But I had been awed and delighted by Josh Koenig, and I instantly thought of just such a child who was arrested in time at the age of five. Jeffty, in no small measure, is Josh: the sweetness of Josh, the intelligence of Josh, the questioning nature of Josh.

Thus from admiration of one wise and innocent child, and from a misheard remark, the process not even Aristotle could codify was triggered. And soon afterward, Jeffty and Donny and the terrible and wonderful thing that happened to them ordered itself on paper.

One more thing about this story.

Despite what seems to be a quality of universality that I attribute to *you* more than to me or to any great genius in the writing of it, the ending of the story somehow escapes the slovenly reader. It's all there, what happened to Jeffty. Very clearly. It's done with what I hope is some subtlety, and you may have to read the last page or so with some careful attention to detail...but it's all there.

As the Past is always there, if you learn from it; treasure the treasures and let the dross go without remorse.

Writers take tours in other people's lives. Jeffty is me; he is also you. This is a short, memory-filled trip through your own life.

Jeffty is Five

WHEN I WAS FIVE YEARS OLD, there was a little kid I played with: Jeffty. His real name was Jeff Kinzer, and everyone who played with him called him Jeffty. We were five years old together, and we had good times playing together.

When I was five, a Clark Bar was as fat around as the gripping end of a Louisville Slugger, and pretty nearly six inches long, and they used real chocolate to coat it, and it crunched very nicely when you bit into the center, and the paper it came wrapped in smelled fresh and good when you peeled off one end to hold the bar so it wouldn't melt onto your fingers. Today, a Clark Bar is as thin as a credit card, they use something artificial and awful-tasting instead of pure chocolate, the thing is soft and soggy, it costs fifteen or twenty cents instead of a decent, correct nickel, and they wrap it so you think it's the same size it was twenty years ago, only it isn't; it's slim and ugly and nasty-tasting and not worth a penny, much less fifteen or twenty cents.

When I was that age, five years old, I was sent away to my Aunt Patricia's home in Buffalo, New York for two years. My father was going through "bad times" and Aunt Patricia was very beautiful, and had married a stockbroker. They took care of me for two years. When I was seven, I came back home and went to find Jeffty, so we could play together.

4

I was seven. Jeffty was still five. I didn't notice any difference. I didn't know: I was only seven.

When I was seven years old I used to lie on my stomach in front of our Atwater-Kent radio and listen to swell stuff. I had tied the ground wire to the radiator, and I would lie there with my coloring books and my Crayolas (when there were only sixteen colors in the big box), and listen to the NBC red network: Jack Benny on the *Jell-O Program, Amos 'n' Andy,* Edgar Bergen and Charlie McCarthy on the *Chase and Sanborn Program, One Man's Family, First Nighter;* the NBC blue network: *Easy Aces,* the *Jergens Program* with Walter Winchell, *Information Please, Death Valley Days;* and best of all, the Mutual Network with *The Green Hornet, The Lone Ranger, The Shadow* and *Quiet Please.* Today, I turn on my car radio and go from one end of the dial to the other and all I get is 100 strings orchestras, banal housewives and insipid truckers discussing their kinky sex lives with arrogant talk show hosts, country and western drivel and rock music so loud it hurts my ears.

When I was ten, my grandfather died of old age and I was "a troublesome kid," and they sent me off to military school, so I could be "taken in hand."

I came back when I was fourteen. Jeffty was still five.

When I was fourteen years old, I used to go to the movies on Saturday afternoons and a matinee was ten cents and they used real butter on the popcorn and I could always be sure of seeing a western like Lash LaRue, or Wild Bill Elliott as Red Ryder with Bobby Blake as Little Beaver, or Roy Rogers, or Johnny Mack Brown; a scary picture like *House of Horrors* with Rondo Hatton as the Strangler, or *The Cat People,* or *The Mummy,* or *I Married a Witch* with Fredric March and Veronica Lake; plus an episode of a great serial like *The Shadow* with Victor Jory, or *Dick Tracy* or *Flash Gordon;* and three cartoons; a James Fitzpatrick TravelTalk; Movietone News; a sing-along and, if I stayed on till evening, Bingo or Keeno; and free dishes. Today, I go to movies and see Clint Eastwood blowing people's heads apart like ripe cantaloupes.

At eighteen, I went to college. Jeffty was still five. I came back during the summers, to work at my Uncle Joe's jewelry store. Jeffty hadn't changed. Now I knew there was something different about him, something wrong, something weird. Jeffty was still five years old, not a day older.

At twenty-two I came home for keeps. To open a Sony television franchise in town, the first one. I saw Jeffty from time to time. He was five.

Things are better in a lot of ways. People don't die from some of the old diseases any more. Cars go faster and get you there more quickly on better roads. Shirts are softer and silkier. We have paperback books even though they cost as much as a good hardcover used to. When I'm running short in the bank I can live off credit cards till things even out. But I still think we've lost a lot of good stuff. Did you know you can't buy linoleum any more, only vinyl floor covering? There's no such thing as oilcloth any more; you'll never again smell that special, sweet smell from your grandmother's kitchen. Furniture isn't made to last thirty years or longer because they took a survey and found that young homemakers like to throw their furniture out and bring in all new, color-coded borax every seven years. Records don't feel right; they're not thick and solid like the old ones, they're thin and you can bend them . . . that doesn't seem right to me. Restaurants don't serve cream in pitchers any more, just that artificial glop in little plastic tubs, and one is never enough to get coffee the right color. You can make a dent in a car fender with only a sneaker. Everywhere you go, all the towns look the same with Burger Kings and McDonald's and 7-Elevens and Taco Bells and motels and shopping centers. Things may be better, but why do I keep thinking about the past?

What I mean by five years old is not that Jeffty was retarded. I don't think that's what it was. Smart as a whip for five years old; very bright, quick, cute, a funny kid.

But he was three feet tall, small for his age, and perfectly formed: no big head, no strange jaw, none of that. A nice, normal-looking five-year-old kid. Except that he was the same age as I was: twenty-two.

When he spoke it was with the squeaking, soprano voice of a five-year-old; when he walked it was with the little hops and shuffles of a five-year-old; when he talked to you it was about the concerns of a five-year-old . . . comic books, playing soldier, using a clothespin to attach a stiff piece of cardboard to the front fork of his bike so the sound it made when the spokes hit was like a motorboat, asking questions like *why does that thing do that like that,* how high is up, how old is old, why is grass green, what's an elephant look like? At twenty-two, he was five.

Jeffty's parents were a sad pair. Because I was still a friend of Jeffty's, still let him hang around with me, sometimes took him to the county fair or miniature golf or the movies, I wound up spending time with *them*. Not that I much cared for them, because they were so awfully depressing. But then, I suppose one couldn't expect much more from the poor devils. They had an alien thing in their home, a child who had grown no older than five in twenty-two years, who provided the treasure of that special childlike state indefinitely, but who also denied them the joys of watching the child grow into a normal adult.

Five is a wonderful time of life for a little kid . . . or it *can* be, if the child is relatively free of the monstrous beastliness other children indulge in. It is a time when the eyes are wide open and the patterns are not yet set; a time when one has not yet been hammered into accepting everything as immutable and hopeless; a time when the hands can not do enough, the mind can not learn enough, the world is infinite and colorful and filled with mysteries. Five is a special time before they take the questing, unquenchable, quixotic soul of the young dreamer and thrust it into dreary schoolroom boxes. A time before they take the trembling hands that want to hold everything, touch everything, figure everything out, and make them lie still on desktops. A time before people begin saying "act your age" and "grow up" or "you're behaving like a baby." It is a time when a child who acts adolescent is still cute and responsive and everyone's pet. A time of delight, of wonder, of innocence.

Jeffty had been stuck in that time, just five, just so.

But for his parents it was an ongoing nightmare from which no one—not social workers, not priests, not child psychologists, not teachers, not friends, not medical wizards, not psychiatrists, no one—could slap or shake them awake. For seventeen years their sorrow had grown through stages of parental dotage to concern, from concern to worry, from worry to fear, from fear to confusion, from confusion to anger, from anger to dislike, from dislike to naked hatred, and finally, from deepest loathing and revulsion to a stolid, depressive acceptance.

John Kinzer was a shift foreman at the Balder Tool & Die

plant. He was a thirty year man. To everyone but the man living it, his was a spectacularly uneventful life. In no way was he remarkable . . . save that he had fathered a twenty-two-year-old five-year-old.

John Kinzer was a small man; soft, with no sharp angles; with pale eyes that never seemed to hold mine for longer than a few seconds. He continually shifted in his chair during conversations, and seemed to see things in the upper corners of the room, things no one else could see . . . or wanted to see. I suppose the word that best suited him was *haunted*. What his life had become . . . well, *haunted* suited him.

Leona Kinzer tried valiantly to compensate. No matter what hour of the day I visited, she always tried to foist food on me. And when Jeffty was in the house she was always at *him* about eating: "Honey, would you like an orange? A nice orange? Or a tangerine? I have tangerines. I could peel a tangerine for you." But there was clearly such fear in her, fear of her own child, that the offers of sustenance always had a faintly ominous tone.

Leona Kinzer had been a tall woman, but the years had bent her. She seemed always to be seeking some area of wallpapered wall or storage niche into which she could fade, adopt some chintz or rose-patterned protective coloration and hide forever in plain sight of the child's big brown eyes, pass her a hundred times a day and never realize she was there, holding her breath, invisible. She always had an apron tied around her waist, and her hands were red from cleaning. As if by maintaining the environment immaculately she could pay off her imagined sin: having given birth to this strange creature.

Neither of them watched television very much. The house was usually dead silent, not even the sibilant whispering of water in the pipes, the creaking of timbers settling, the humming of the refrigerator. Awfully silent, as if time itself had taken a detour around that house.

As for Jeffty, he was inoffensive. He lived in that atmosphere of gentle dread and dulled loathing, and if he understood it, he never remarked in any way. He played, as a child plays, and seemed happy. But he must have sensed, in the way of a five-year-old, just how alien he was in their presence.

Alien. No, that wasn't right. He was *too* human, if anything. But out of phase, out of sync with the world around him, and resonating to a different vibration than his parents, God knows.

Nor would other children play with him. As they grew past him, they found him at first childish, then uninteresting, then simply frightening as their perceptions of aging became clear and they could see he was not affected by time as they were. Even the little ones, his own age, who might wander into the neighborhood, quickly came to shy away from him like a dog in the street when a car backfires.

Thus, I remained his only friend. A friend of many years. Five years. Twenty-two years. I liked him; more than I can say. And never knew exactly why. But I did, without reserve.

But because we spent time together, I found I was also—polite society—spending time with John and Leona Kinzer. Dinner, Saturday afternoons sometimes, an hour or so when I'd bring Jeffty back from a movie. They were grateful: slavishly so. It relieved them of the embarrassing chore of going out with him, of having to pretend before the world that they were loving parents with a perfectly normal, happy, attractive child. And their gratitude extended to hosting me. Hideous, every moment of their depression, hideous.

I felt sorry for the poor devils, but I despised them for their inability to love Jeffty, who was eminently lovable.

I never let on, of course, even during the evenings in their company that were awkward beyond belief.

We would sit there in the darkening living room—*always* dark or darkening, as if kept in shadow to hold back what the light might reveal to the world outside through the bright eyes of the house—we would sit and silently stare at one another. They never knew what to say to me.

"So how are things down at the plant?" I'd say to John Kinzer.

He would shrug. Neither conversation nor life suited him with any ease or grace. "Fine, just fine," he would say, finally.

And we would sit in silence again.

"Would you like a nice piece of coffee cake?" Leona would say. "I made it fresh just this morning." Or deep dish green apple pie. Or milk and tollhouse cookies. Or a brown betty pudding.

"No, no, thank you, Mrs. Kinzer; Jeffty and I grabbed a couple of cheeseburgers on the way home." And again, silence.

Then, when the stillness and the awkwardness became too much even for them (and who knew how long that total silence reigned when they were alone, with that thing they never talked about any more hanging between them), Leona Kinzer would say, "I think he's asleep."

John Kinzer would say, "I don't hear the radio playing."

Just so, it would go on like that, until I could politely find excuse to bolt away on some flimsy pretext. Yes, that was the way it would go on, every time, just the same . . . except once.

"I don't know what to do any more," Leona said. She began crying. "There's no change, not one day of peace."

Her husband managed to drag himself out of the old easy chair and went to her. He bent and tried to soothe her, but it was clear from the graceless way in which he touched her graying hair that the ability to be compassionate had been stunned in him. "Shhh, Leona, it's all right. Shhh." But she continued crying. Her hands scraped gently at the antimacassars on the arms of the chair.

Then she said, "Sometimes I wish he had been stillborn."

John looked up into the corners of the room. For the nameless shadows that were always watching him? Was it God he was seeking in those spaces? "You don't mean that," he said to her, softly, pathetically, urging her with body tension and trembling in his voice to recant before God took notice of the terrible thought. But she meant it; she meant it very much.

I managed to get away quickly that evening. They didn't want witnesses to their shame. I was glad to go.

And for a week I stayed away. From them, from Jeffty, from their street, even from that end of town.

I had my own life. The store, accounts, suppliers' conferences, poker with friends, pretty women I took to well-lit restaurants, my own parents, putting antifreeze in the car, complaining to the laundry about too much starch in the collars and cuffs, working out at the gym, taxes, catching Jan or David (whichever one it was) stealing from the cash register. I had my own life.

But not even *that* evening could keep me from Jeffty. He called me at the store and asked me to take him to the rodeo. We chummed it up as best a twenty-two-year-old with other interests *could* . . . with a five-year-old. I never dwelled on what bound us together; I always thought it was simply the years. That, and affection for a kid who could have been the little brother I never had. (Except I *remembered* when we had played together, when we had both been the same age; I *remembered* that period, and Jeffty was still the same.)

And then, one Saturday afternoon, I came to take him to a double feature, and things I should have noticed so many times before, I first began to notice only that afternoon.

I came walking up to the Kinzer house, expecting Jeffty to be sitting on the front porch steps, or in the porch glider, waiting for me. But he was nowhere in sight.

Going inside, into that darkness and silence, in the midst of May sunshine, was unthinkable. I stood on the front walk for a few moments, then cupped my hands around my mouth and yelled, "Jeffty? Hey, Jeffty, come on out, let's go. We'll be late."

His voice came faintly, as if from under the ground.

"Here I am, Donny."

I could hear him, but I couldn't see him. It was Jeffty, no question about it: as Donald H. Horton, President and Sole Owner of The Horton TV & Sound Center, no one but Jeffty called me Donny. He had never called me anything else.

(Actually, it isn't a lie. I *am*, as far as the public is concerned, Sole Owner of the Center. The partnership with my Aunt Patricia is only to repay the loan she made me, to supplement the money I came into when I was twenty-one, left to me when I was ten by my grandfather. It wasn't a very big loan, only eighteen thousand, but I asked her to be a silent partner, because of when she had taken care of me as a child.)

"Where are you, Jeffty?"

"Under the porch in my secret place."

I walked around the side of the porch, and stooped down and pulled away the wicker grating. Back in there, on the pressed dirt, Jeffty had built himself a secret place. He had comics in orange crates, he had a little table and some pillows, it was lit by big fat candles, and we used to hide there when we were both . . . five.

"What'cha up to?" I asked, crawling in and pulling the grate closed behind me. It was cool under the porch, and the dirt smelled comfortable, the candles smelled clubby and familiar. Any kid would feel at home in such a secret place: there's never been a kid who didn't spend the happiest, most productive, most deliciously mysterious times of his life in such a secret place.

"Playin'," he said. He was holding something golden and round. It filled the palm of his little hand.

"You forget we were going to the movies?"

"Nope. I was just waitin' for you here."

"Your mom and dad home?"

"Momma."

I understood why he was waiting under the porch. I didn't push it any further. "What've you got there?"

"Captain Midnight Secret Decoder Badge," he said, showing it to me on his flattened palm.

I realized I was looking at it without comprehending what it was for a long time. Then it dawned on me what a miracle Jeffty had in his hand. A miracle that simply could *not* exist.

"Jeffty," I said softly, with wonder in my voice, "where'd you get that?"

"Came in the mail today. I sent away for it."

"It must have cost a lot of money."

"Not so much. Ten cents an' two inner wax seals from two jars of Ovaltine."

"May I see it?" My voice was trembling, and so was the hand I extended. He gave it to me and I held the miracle in the palm of my hand. It was *wonderful*.

You remember. *Captain Midnight* went on the radio nationwide in 1940. It was sponsored by Ovaltine. And every year they issued a Secret Squadron Decoder Badge. And every day at the end of the program, they would give you a clue to the next day's installment in a code that only kids with the official badge could decipher. They stopped making those wonderful Decoder Badges in 1949. I remember the one I had in 1945: it was beautiful. It had a magnifying glass in the center of the code dial. *Captain Midnight* went off the air in 1950, and though I understand it was a short-lived television series in the mid-fifties, and though they issued Decoder Badges in 1955 and 1956, as far as the *real* badges were concerned, they never made one after 1949.

The Captain Midnight Code-O-Graph I held in my hand, the one Jeffty said he had gotten in the mail for ten cents (*ten cents!!!*) and two Ovaltine labels, was brand new, shiny gold metal, not a dent or a spot of rust on it like the old ones you can find at exorbitant prices in collectible shoppes from time to time . . . it was a *new* Decoder. And the date on it was *this* year.

But *Captain Midnight* no longer existed. Nothing like it existed on the radio. I'd listened to the one or two weak imitations of old-time radio the networks were currently airing, and the stories were dull, the sound effects bland, the whole feel of it wrong, out of date, cornball. Yet I held a *new* Code-O-Graph.

"Jeffty, tell me about this," I said.

"Tell you what, Donny? It's my new Capt'n Midnight Secret Decoder Badge. I use it to figger out what's gonna happen tomorrow."

"Tomorrow how?"

"On the program."

"What program?!"

He stared at me as if I was being purposely stupid. "On *Capt'n* Mid*night!* Boy!" I was being dumb.

I still couldn't get it straight. It was right there, right out in the open, and I still didn't know what was happening. "You mean one of those records they made of the old-time radio programs? Is that what you mean, Jeffty?"

"What records?" he asked. He didn't know what *I* meant.

We stared at each other, there under the porch. And then I said, very slowly, almost afraid of the answer, "Jeffty, how do you hear *Captain Midnight?"*

"Every day. On the radio. On my radio. Every day at 5:30."

News. Music, dumb music, and news. That's what was on the radio every day at 5:30. Not *Captain Midnight.* The Secret Squadron hadn't been on the air in twenty years.

"Can we hear it tonight?" I asked.

"Boy!" he said. I was being dumb. I knew it from the way he said it; but I didn't know why. Then it dawned on me: this was Saturday. *Captain Midnight* was on Monday through Friday. Not on Saturday or Sunday.

"We goin' to the movies?"

He had to repeat himself twice. My mind was somewhere else. Nothing definite. No conclusions. No wild assumptions leapt to. Just off somewhere trying to figure it out, and concluding—as *you* would have concluded, as *any*one would have concluded rather than accepting the truth, the impossible and wonderful truth—just finally concluding there was a simple explanation I didn't yet perceive. Something mundane and dull, like the passage of time that steals all good, old things from us, packratting trinkets and plastic in exchange. And all in the name of Progress.

"We goin' to the movies, Donny?"

"You bet your boots we are, kiddo," I said. And I smiled. And I handed him the Code-O-Graph. And he put it in his side pants pocket. And we crawled out from under the porch. And we went to the movies. And neither of us said anything about *Captain Midnight* all the rest of that day. And there wasn't a ten-minute stretch, all the rest of that day, that I didn't think about it.

It was inventory all that next week. I didn't see Jeffty till late Thursday. I confess I left the store in the hands of Jan and David, told them I had some errands to run, and left early. At 4:00. I got to the Kinzers' right around 4:45. Leona answered the door, looking exhausted and distant. "Is Jeffty around?" She said he was upstairs in his room...

...listening to the radio.

I climbed the stairs two at a time.

All right, I had finally made that impossible, illogical leap. Had the stretch of belief involved anyone but Jeffty, adult or child, I would have reasoned out more explicable answers. But it *was* Jeffty, clearly another kind of vessel of life, and what he might experience should not be expected to fit into the ordered scheme.

I admit it: I *wanted* to hear what I heard.

Even with the door closed, I recognized the program:

"There he goes, Tennessee! Get him!"

There was the heavy report of a squirrel-rifle shot and the keening whine of the slug ricocheting, and then the same voice yelled triumphantly, *"Got him! D-e-a-a-a-a-d center!"*

He was listening to the American Broadcasting Company, 790 kilohertz, and he was hearing *Tennessee Jed,* one of my most favorite programs from the forties, a western adventure I had not heard in twenty years, because it had not existed for twenty years.

I sat down on the top step of the stairs, there in the upstairs hall of the Kinzer home, and I listened to the show. It wasn't a rerun of an old program; I knew every one of them by heart, had never missed an episode. Further evidence that this was a new installment: there were occasional references during the integrated commercials to current cultural and technological developments, and phrases that had not existed in common usage in the forties: aerosol spray cans, laserasing of tattoos, Tanzania, the word "uptight."

I couldn't ignore it: Jeffty was listening to a *new* segment of *Tennessee Jed*.

I ran downstairs and out the front door to my car. Leona must have been in the kitchen. I turned the key and punched on the radio and spun the dial to 790 kilohertz. The ABC station. Rock music.

I sat there for a few moments, then ran the dial slowly from one end to the other. Music, news, talk shows. No *Tennessee Jed*. And it was a Blaupunkt, the best radio I could get. I wasn't missing some perimeter station. It simply was not there!

After a few moments I turned off the radio and the ignition and went back upstairs quietly. I sat down on the top step and listened to the entire program. It was *wonderful*.

Exciting, imaginative, filled with everything I remembered as being most innovative about radio drama. But it was modern. It wasn't an antique, rebroadcast to assuage the need of that dwindling listenership who longed for the old days. It was a new show, with all the old voices, but still young and bright. Even the commercials were for currently available products, but they weren't as loud or as insulting as the screamer ads one heard on radio these days.

And when *Tennessee Jed* went off at 5:00, I heard Jeffty spin the dial on his radio till I heard the familiar voice of the announcer Glenn Riggs proclaim, *"Presenting Hop Harrigan! America's ace of the airwaves!"* There was the sound of an airplane in flight. It was a prop plane, not a jet! Not the sound kids today have grown up with, but the sound *I* grew up with, the *real* sound of an airplane, the growling, revving, throaty sound of the kind of airplanes G-8 and His Battle Aces flew, the kind Captain Midnight flew, the kind Hop Harrigan flew. And then I heard Hop say, *"CX-4 calling control tower. CX-4 calling control tower. Standing by!"* A pause, then, *"Okay, this is Hop Harrigan . . . coming in!"*

And Jeffty, who had the same problem all of us kids had had in the forties with programming that pitted equal favorites against one another on different stations, having paid his respects to Hop Harrigan and Tank Tinker, spun the dial and went back to ABC where I heard the stroke of a gong, the wild cacophony of nonsense Chinese chatter, and the announcer yelled, *"T-e-e-e-rry and the Pirates!"*

I sat there on the top step and listened to Terry and Connie and Flip Corkin and, so help me God, Agnes Moorehead as the Dragon Lady, all of them in a new adventure that took place in a Red China that had not existed in the days of Milton Caniff's 1937 version of the Orient, with river pirates and Chiang Kai-shek and warlords and the naive Imperialism of American gunboat diplomacy.

Sat, and listened to the whole show, and sat even longer to hear *Superman* and part of *Jack Armstrong, the All-American Boy* and part of *Captain Midnight,* and John Kinzer came home and neither he nor Leona came upstairs to find out what had happened to me, or where Jeffty was, and sat longer, and found I had started crying, and could not stop, just sat there with tears running down my face, into the corners of my mouth, sitting and crying until Jeffty heard me and opened his door and saw me and came out and looked at me in childish confusion as I heard the station break for the Mutual Network and they began the theme music of *Tom Mix,* "When It's Round-up Time in Texas and the Bloom Is on the Sage," and Jeffty touched my shoulder and smiled at me, with his mouth and his big brown eyes, and said, "Hi, Donny. Wanna come in an' listen to the radio with me?"

Hume denied the existence of an absolute space, in which each thing has its place; Borges denies the existence of one single time, in which all events are linked.

Jeffty received radio programs from a place that could not, in logic, in the natural scheme of the space-time universe as conceived by Einstein, exist. But that wasn't all he received. He got mail-order premiums that no one was manufacturing. He read comic books that had been defunct for three decades. He saw movies with actors who had been dead for twenty years. He was the receiving terminal for endless joys and pleasures of the past that the world had dropped along the way. On its headlong suicidal flight toward New Tomorrows, the world had razed its treasurehouse of simple happinesses, had poured concrete over its playgrounds, had abandoned its elfin stragglers, and all of it was being impossibly, miraculously shunted back into the present through Jeffty. Revivified, updated, the traditions maintained but contemporaneous. Jeffty was the un-bidding Aladdin whose very nature formed the magic lampness of his reality.

And he took me into his world with him.

Because he trusted me.

We had breakfast of Quaker Puffed Wheat Sparkies and warm Ovaltine we drank out of *this* year's Little Orphan Annie Shake-Up Mugs. We went to the movies and while everyone else was seeing a comedy starring Goldie Hawn and Ryan O'Neal, Jeffty and I were enjoying Humphrey Bogart as the professional thief Parker in John Huston's brilliant adaptation of the Donald Westlake novel *Slay-ground*. The second feature was Spencer Tracy, Carole Lombard and Laird Cregar in the Val Lewton-produced film of *Leinengen Versus the Ants*.

Twice a month we went down to the newsstand and bought the current pulp issues of *The Shadow, Doc Savage* and *Startling Stories*. Jeffty and I sat together and I read to him from the magazines. He particularly liked the new short novel by Henry Kuttner, "The Dreams of Achilles," and the new Stanley G. Weinbaum series of short stories set in the subatomic particle universe of Redurna. In September we enjoyed the first installment of the new Robert E. Howard Conan novel, *Isle of the Black Ones,* in *Weird Tales;* and in August we were only mildly disappointed by Edgar Rice Burroughs's fourth novella in the Jupiter series featuring John Carter of Barsoom—"Corsairs of Jupiter." But the editor of *Argosy All-Story Weekly* promised there would be two more stories in the series, and it was such an unexpected revelation for Jeffty and me that it dimmed our disappointment at the lessened quality of the current story.

We read comics together, and Jeffty and I both decided—separately, before we came together to discuss it—that our favorite characters were Doll Man, Airboy and The Heap. We also adored the George Carlson strips in *Jingle Jangle Comics,* particularly the Pie-Face Prince of Old Pretzleburg stories, which we read together and laughed over, even though I had to explain some of the esoteric puns to Jeffty, who was too young to have that kind of subtle wit.

How to explain it? I can't. I had enough physics in college to make some offhand guesses, but I'm more likely wrong than right. The laws of the conservation of energy occasionally break. These are laws that physicists call "weakly violated."

Perhaps Jeffty was a catalyst for the weak violation of conservation laws we're only now beginning to realize exist. I tried doing some reading in the area—muon decay of the "forbidden" kind: gamma decay that doesn't include the muon neutrino among its products—but nothing I encountered, not even the latest readings from the Swiss Institute for Nuclear Research near Zurich, gave me an insight. I was thrown back on a vague acceptance of the philosophy that the real name for "science" is *magic*.

No explanations, but enormous good times.

The happiest time of my life.

I had the "real" world, the world of my store and my friends and my family, the world of profit&loss, of taxes and evenings with young women who talked about going shopping or the United Nations, of the rising cost of coffee and microwave ovens. And I had Jeffty's world, in which I existed only when I was with him. The things of the past he knew as fresh and new, I could experience only when in his company. And the membrane between the two worlds grew ever thinner, more luminous and transparent. I had the best of both worlds. And knew, somehow, that I could carry nothing from one to the other.

Forgetting for just a moment, betraying Jeffty by forgetting, brought an end to it all.

Enjoying myself so much, I grew careless and failed to consider how fragile the relationship between Jeffty's world and my world really was. There is a reason why the present begrudges the existence of the past. I never really understood. Nowhere in the beast books, where survival is shown in battles between claw and fang, tentacle and poison sac, is there recognition of the ferocity the present always brings to bear on the past. Nowhere is there a detailed statement of how the Present lies in wait for What-Was, waiting for it to become Now-This-Moment so it can shred it with its merciless jaws.

Who could know such a thing . . . at any age . . . and certainly not at my age . . . who could understand such a thing?

I'm trying to exculpate myself. I can't. It was my fault.

It was another Saturday afternoon.

"What's playing today?" I asked him, in the car, on the way downtown.

He looked up at me from the other side of the front seat and smiled one of his best smiles. "Ken Maynard in *Bullwhip Justice* an' *The Demolished Man*." He kept smiling, as if he'd really put one over on me. I looked at him with disbelief.

"You're *kidding!*," I said, delighted. "Bester's *The Demolished Man?*" He nodded his head, delighted at my being delighted. He knew it was one of my favorite books. "Oh, that's super!"

"Super *duper*," he said.

"Who's in it?"

"Franchot Tone, Evelyn Keyes, Lionel Barrymore and Elisha Cook, Jr." He was much more knowledgeable about movie actors than I'd ever been. He could name the character actors in any movie he'd ever seen. Even the crowd scenes.

"And cartoons?" I asked.

"Three of 'em: a *Little Lulu*, a *Donald Duck* and a *Bugs Bunny*. An' a *Pete Smith Specialty* an' a Lew Lehr *Monkeys is da C-r-r-r-aziest Peoples*."

"Oh boy!" I said. I was grinning from ear to ear. And then I looked down and saw the pad of purchase order forms on the seat. I'd forgotten to drop it off at the store.

"Gotta stop by the Center," I said. "Gotta drop off something. It'll only take a minute."

"Okay," Jeffty said. "But we won't be late, will we?"

"Not on your tintype, kiddo," I said.

When I pulled into the parking lot behind the Center, he decided to come in with me and we'd walk over to the theater. It's not a large town. There are only two movie houses, the Utopia and the Lyric. We were going to the Utopia and it was only three blocks from the Center.

I walked into the store with the pad of forms, and it was bedlam. David and Jan were handling two customers each, and there were people standing around waiting to be helped. Jan turned a look on me and her face was a horror-mask of pleading. David was running from the stockroom to the showroom and all he could murmur as he whipped past was "Help!" and then he was gone.

"Jeffty," I said, crouching down, "listen, give me a few minutes. Jan and David are in trouble with all these people. We won't be late, I promise. Just let me get rid of a couple of these customers." He looked nervous, but nodded okay.

I motioned to a chair and said, "Just sit down for a while and I'll be right with you."

He went to the chair, good as you please, though he knew what was happening, and he sat down.

I started taking care of people who wanted color television sets. This was the first really substantial batch of units we'd gotten in—color television was only now becoming reasonably priced and this was Sony's first promotion—and it was bonanza time for me. I could see paying off the loan and being out in front for the first time with the Center. It was business.

In my world, good business comes first.

Jeffty sat there and stared at the wall. Let me tell you about the wall.

Stanchion and bracket designs had been rigged from floor to within two feet of the ceiling. Television sets had been stacked artfully on the wall. Thirty-three television sets. All playing at the same time. Black and white, color, little ones, big ones, all going at the same time.

Jeffty sat and watched thirty-three television sets, on a Saturday afternoon. We can pick up a total of thirteen channels including the UHF educational stations. Golf was on one channel; baseball was on a second; celebrity bowling was on a third; the fourth channel was a religious seminar; a teenage dance show was on the fifth; the sixth was a rerun of a situation comedy; the seventh was a rerun of a police show; eighth was a nature program showing a man flycasting endlessly; ninth was news and conversation; tenth was a stock car race; eleventh was a man doing logarithms on a blackboard; twelfth was a woman in a leotard doing sitting-up exercises; and on the thirteenth channel was a badly animated cartoon show in Spanish. All but six of the shows were repeated on three sets. Jeffty sat and watched that wall of television on a Saturday afternoon while I sold as fast and as hard as I could, to pay back my Aunt Patricia and stay in touch with my world. It was business.

I should have known better. I should have understood about the present and the way it kills the past. But I was selling with both hands. And when I finally glanced over at Jeffty, half an hour later, he looked like another child.

He was sweating. That terrible fever sweat when you have stomach flu. He was pale, as pasty and pale as a worm, and his little hands were gripping the arms of the chair so tightly

I could see his knuckles in bold relief. I dashed over to him, excusing myself from the middle-aged couple looking at the new 21″ Mediterranean model.

"Jeffty!"

He looked at me, but his eyes didn't track. He was in absolute terror. I pulled him out of the chair and started toward the front door with him, but the customers I'd deserted yelled at me, "Hey!" The middle-aged man said, "You wanna sell this thing or don't you?"

I looked from him to Jeffty and back again. Jeffty was like a zombie. He had come where I'd pulled him. His legs were rubbery and his feet dragged. The past, being eaten by the present, the sound of something in pain.

I clawed some money out of my pants pocket and jammed it into Jeffty's hand. "Kiddo . . . listen to me . . . get out of here right now!" He still couldn't focus properly. *"Jeffty,"* I said as tightly as I could, *"listen* to me!" The middle-aged customer and his wife were walking toward us. "Listen, kiddo, get out of here right this minute. Walk over to the Utopia and buy the tickets. I'll be right behind you." The middle-aged man and his wife were almost on us. I shoved Jeffty through the door and watched him stumble away in the wrong direction, then stop as if gathering his wits, turn and go back past the front of the Center and in the direction of the Utopia. "Yes sir," I said, straightening up and facing them, "yes, ma'am, that is one terrific set with some sen*sa*tional features! If you'll just step back here with me . . ."

There was a terrible sound of something hurting, but I couldn't tell from which channel, or from which set, it was coming.

Most of it I learned later, from the girl in the ticket booth, and from some people I knew who came to me to tell me what had happened. By the time I got to the Utopia, nearly twenty minutes later, Jeffty was already beaten to a pulp and had been taken to the manager's office.

"Did you see a very little boy, about five years old, with big brown eyes and straight brown hair . . . he was waiting for me?"

"Oh, I think that's the little boy those kids beat up?"

"What!?! *Where is he?*"

"They took him to the manager's office. No one knew who he was or where to find his parents—"

A young girl wearing an usher's uniform was kneeling down beside the couch, placing a wet paper towel on his face.

I took the towel away from her and ordered her out of the office. She looked insulted and snorted something rude, but she left. I sat on the edge of the couch and tried to swab away the blood from the lacerations without opening the wounds where the blood had caked. Both his eyes were swollen shut. His mouth was ripped badly. His hair was matted with dried blood.

He had been standing in line behind two kids in their teens. They started selling tickets at 12:30 and the show started at 1:00. The doors weren't opened till 12:45. He had been waiting, and the kids in front of him had had a portable radio. They were listening to the ball game. Jeffty had wanted to hear some program, God knows what it might have been, *Grand Central Station, Let's Pretend, The Land of the Lost,* God only knows which one it might have been.

He had asked if he could borrow their radio to hear the program for a minute, and it had been a commercial break or something, and the kids had given him the radio, probably out of some malicious kind of courtesy that would permit them to take offense and rag the little boy. He had changed the station . . . and they'd been unable to get it to go back to the ball game. It was locked into the past, on a station that was broadcasting a program that didn't exist for anyone but Jeffty.

They had beaten him badly . . . as everyone watched.

And then they had run away.

I had left him alone, left him to fight off the present without sufficient weaponry. I had betrayed him for the sale of a 21″ Mediterranean console television, and now his face was pulped meat. He moaned something inaudible and sobbed softly.

"Shhh, it's okay, kiddo, it's Donny. I'm here. I'll get you home, it'll be okay."

I should have taken him straight to the hospital. I don't know why I didn't. I should have. I should have done that.

When I carried him through the door, John and Leona Kinzer just stared at me. They didn't move to take him from my arms. One of his hands was hanging down. He was conscious, but just barely. They stared, there in the semi-darkness of a Saturday afternoon in the present. I looked at them. "A couple of kids beat him up at the theater." I raised him a few inches in my arms and extended him. They stared at me, at both of us, with nothing in their eyes, without movement. "Jesus Christ," I shouted, "he's been beaten! He's your son! Don't you even want to touch him? What the hell kind of people are you?!"

Then Leona moved toward me very slowly. She stood in front of us for a few seconds, and there was a leaden stoicism in her face that was terrible to see. It said, *I have been in this place before, many times, and I cannot bear to be in it again; but I am here now*.

So I gave him to her. God help me, I gave him over to her.

And she took him upstairs to bathe away his blood and his pain.

John Kinzer and I stood in our separate places in the dim living room of their home, and we stared at each other. He had nothing to say to me.

I shoved past him and fell into a chair. I was shaking.

I heard the bath water running upstairs.

After what seemed a very long time Leona came downstairs, wiping her hands on her apron. She sat down on the sofa and after a moment John sat down beside her. I heard the sound of rock music from upstairs.

"Would you like a piece of nice pound cake?" Leona said.

I didn't answer. I was listening to the sound of the music. Rock music. On the radio. There was a table lamp on the end table beside the sofa. It cast a dim and futile light in the shadowed living room. *Rock music from the present, on a radio upstairs?* I started to say something, and then *knew*... Oh, God... *no!*

I jumped up just as the sound of hideous crackling blotted out the music, and the table lamp dimmed and dimmed and flickered. I screamed something, I don't know what it was, and ran for the stairs.

Jeffty's parents did not move. They sat there with their hands folded, in that place they had been for so many years.

I fell twice rushing up the stairs.

There isn't much on television that can hold my interest. I bought an old cathedral-shaped Philco radio in a second-hand store, and I replaced all the burnt-out parts with the original tubes from old radios I could cannibalize that still worked. I don't use transistors or printed circuits. They wouldn't work. I've sat in front of that set for hours sometimes, running the dial back and forth as slowly as you can imagine, so slowly it doesn't look as if it's moving at all sometimes.

But I can't find *Captain Midnight* or *The Land of the Lost* or *The Shadow* or *Quiet, Please*.

So she did love him, still, a little bit, even after all those years. I can't hate them: they only wanted to live in the present world again. That isn't such a terrible thing.

It's a good world, all things considered. It's much better than it used to be, in a lot of ways. People don't die from the old diseases any more. They die from new ones, but that's Progress, isn't it?

Isn't it?

Tell me.

Somebody please tell me.

How's the Night Life on Cissalda?

INTRODUCTION

Writers take tours in other people's lives.

As I write this, I'm sitting on an American Airlines flight between Toronto and Los Angeles. I've just come back from delivering a lecture at Queen's University in Kingston, Ontario, about 265 kilometers from Toronto and I'm sitting here at 37,000 feet above Bryce Canyon annoying the other passengers with the tippy-tap of my portable Olympia.

I tell you this because it happened again in Kingston:

Some wiseass took a tour through *my* life.

The feep in question is Gary Crawford, an otherwise nice guy who attempted to encapsulate me for a female housemate of his by quoting out of context one line from the introduction to my collection *Love Ain't Nothing but Sex Misspelled.*

Her response to that line, when Gary suggested she attend my lecture, was something akin to this: "Go see that sexist pig asshole? Forget it."

For the introduction to that book, I wrote an essay in which I attempted to summarize everything I thought I knew for sure about love; everything I'd learned in the forty-one years I'd been around at that point, five years ago. It was not a very long essay.

But in that essay I recounted an anecdote concerning

myself and the woman who was to become my fourth wife. We had just met, were just beginning to date, and she asked me how many women I had been with. "Been with": that's one of those phrases we use.

After a few days of hemming and hawing, and avoiding answering the question because I didn't think she really wanted to hear the truth, I was pressured into answering, and I did. It was a substantive number of liaisons.

Gary Crawford read that line about how many women I'd "been with" to this total stranger, this Anne who shares the cost of renting a house up in Kingston; and with a demonstration of provincial audacity that resonated perfectly with the concretized tenets of the Judeo-Christian Ethos, she concluded I was a brutalizer of women, a shallow gigolo or profligate tramp; a womanizer of the most odious sort.

Ah, lady, would that it were so. Too much pain and visceral material expended during the course of my love life ever to garner me such unassailable encomiums. No, kiddo, I'm just a slave of love like you.

The judgment is one, clearly, of geography...not morality.

But there it was happening to me again: some reader taking a tour through *my* life and doing it with considerable ineptitude, and then reporting back to strangers the skewed visions he had had while on his jaunt. And there goes Anne, getting all pruney around the lips and calling me bad names.

I won't run my credentials. Call me what you will. It's your problem and none of my own, friends. Anarchist, rakehell, asshole, monster, pyromaniac, child molester, assassin, lover of the music of Lawrence Welk...the most awful things you or I could think of. What the hell do I care? I'm *still* the one who can write these stories.

And no one ever said Dostoevski was a paragon of the virtues; but I'll bet he bought his way into Heaven with *The Idiot*.

Why does he tell us all this?

I tell you all this because the next story you'll read here is about fucking. No, not lovemaking, or "being with," or anything more meaningful sexually than fucking. And I tell you all this ahead of time so you will understand that I think love and sex are separate and only vaguely similar. Like the word *bear* and the word *bare*. You can get in trouble mistaking one for the other.

The same goes for love and sex.

Writers take tours in other people's lives. This is a hippity-hop through all of yours; even you too, Anne; you who engage in all that deep breathing about love and romance and the intricate pavane of sexual encounter when the truth of the matter is...the whole damn subject is mostly just funny.

How's the Night Life on Cissalda?

WHEN THEY UNSCREWED the time capsule, preparatory to help-
ing temponaut Enoch Mirren to disembark, they found him
doing a disgusting thing with a disgusting thing.

Every head turned away. The word that sprang to mind first
was, *"Feh!"*

They wouldn't tell Enoch Mirren's wife he was back. They
evaded the question when Enoch Mirren's mother demanded
to know the state of her son's health after his having taken the
very first journey into another time/universe. The new President
was given dissembling answers. No one bothered to call San
Clemente. The Chiefs of Staff were kept in the dark. Inquiries
from the CIA and the FBI were met with responses in pig Latin
and the bureaus were subtly diverted into investigating each
other. Walter Cronkite found out, but after all, there are even
limits to how tight security can get.

Their gorges buoyant, every one of them, the rescue crew
and the medical team and the chrono-experts at TimeSep Central did their best, but found it impossible to pry temponaut
Enoch Mirren's penis from the (presumably) warm confines
of the disgusting thing's (presumed) sexual orifice.

A cadre of alien morphologists was assigned to make an
evaluation: to decide if the disgusting thing was male or female.
After a sleepless week they gave up. The head of the group
made a good case for his team's failure. "It'd be a damned

sight easier to decide if we could get that clown out of her ... him ... it ... that thing!"

They tried cajoling, they tried threatening, they tried rational argument, they tried inductive logic, they tried deductive logic, they tried salary incentives, they tried profit sharing, they tried tickling his risibilities, they tried tickling his feet, they tried punching him, they tried shocking him, they tried arresting him, they tried crowbars, they tried hosing him down with cold water, then hot water, then seltzer water, they tried suction devices, they tried sensory deprivation, they tried doping him into unconsciousness. They tried shackling him to a team of Percherons pulling north and the disgusting thing to a team of Clydesdales pulling south. They gave up after three and a half weeks.

The word somehow leaked out that the capsule had come back from time/universe Earth$_2$ and the Russians rattled swords—suggesting that the decadent American filth had brought back a decimating plague that was even now oozing toward Minsk. (TimeSep Central quarantined anyone even remotely privy to the truth.) The OPEC nations announced that the Americans, in league with Zionist Technocrats, had found a way to siphon off crude oil from the time/universe next to our own, and promptly raised the price of gasoline another forty-one cents a gallon. (TimeSep Central moved Enoch Mirren and the disgusting thing to its supersecret bunker headquarters sunk beneath the Painted Desert.) The Pentagon demanded the results of the debriefing and threatened to cut throats; Congress demanded the results and threatened to cut appropriations. (TimeSep Central bit the bullet—they had no other choice, there had been no debriefing—and they stonewalled: *we cannot relay the requested data at this time.*)

Temponaut Enoch Mirren continued coitusing.

The expert from Johns Hopkins, a tall, gray gentleman who wore three-piece suits, and whose security clearance was so stratospherically high the President called *him* on the red phone, sequestered himself with the temponaut and the disgusting thing for three days. When he emerged, he called in the TimeSep Central officials and said, "Ladies and gentlemen, quite simply put, Enoch Mirren has brought back from Earth$_2$ the most perfect fuck in the universe."

After they had revived one of the women and four of the men, the expert from Johns Hopkins, a serious, pale gentleman who wore wing-tip shoes, continued. "As best I can estimate, this creature—clearly an alien life-form from some other planet in that alternate time/universe—has an erotic capacity that, once engaged, cannot be neutralized. Once having begun to enjoy its, uh, favors . . . a man either cannot or *will not* stop having relations."

"But that's impossible!" said one of the women. "Men simply cannot hold an erection that long." She looked around at several of her male compatriots with disdain.

"Apparently the thing secretes some sort of stimulant, a jelly perhaps, that re-engorges the male member," said the expert from Johns Hopkins.

"But is it male or female?" asked one of the men, an administrative assistant who had let it slip in one of their regular encounter sessions that he was concerned about his own sexual preferences.

"It's both, and neither," said the expert from Johns Hopkins. "It seems equipped to handle anything up to and including chickens or kangaroos with double vaginas." He smiled a thin, controlled smile, saying, "You folks have a problem," and then he presented them with a staggering bill for his services. And then he departed, still smiling.

They were little better off than they had been before.

But the women seemed interested.

Two months later, having fed temponaut Enoch Mirren intravenously when they noticed that his weight had been dropping alarmingly, they found an answer to the problem of separating the man and the sex object. By setting up a random sequence sound wave system, pole to pole, with Mirren and his paramour between, they were able to disrupt the flow of energy in the disgusting thing's metabolism. Mirren opened his eyes, blinked several times, murmured, "Oh, that was *good!*" and they pried him loose.

The disgusting thing instantly rolled into a ball and went to sleep.

They immediately hustled Enoch Mirren into an elevator and dropped with him to the deepest, most tightly secured level of the supersecret underground TimeSep Central complex, where a debriefing interrogation cell waited to claim him. It was 10'x10'x20', heavily padded in black Naugahyde, and was honeycombed with sensors and microphones. No lights.

They put him in the cell, let him stew for twelve hours, then fed him, and began the debriefing.

"Mirren, what the hell *is* that disgusting thing?"

The voice came from the ceiling. In the darkness Enoch Mirren belched lightly from the quenelles of red snapper they had served him, and scooted around on the floor where he was sitting, trying to locate the source of the annoyed voice.

"It's a terrific little person from Cissalda," he said.

"Cissalda?" Another voice; a woman's voice.

"A planet in another star-system of that other time/universe," he replied politely. "They call it Cissalda."

"It can talk?" A third voice, more studious.

"Telepathically. Mind-to-mind. When we're making love."

"All right, knock it off, Mirren!" the first voice said.

Enoch Mirren sat in darkness, smiling.

"Then there's life in that other universe, apart from that disgusting thing, is that right?" The third voice.

"Oh, sure," Enoch Mirren said, playing with his toes. He had discovered he was naked.

"How's the night life on Cissalda?" asked the woman's voice, not really seriously.

"Well, there's not much activity during the week," he answered, "but Saturday nights are dynamite, I'm told."

"I said *knock it off,* Mirren!"

"Yes, sir."

The third voice, as if reading from a list of prepared questions, asked, "Describe time/universe Earth$_2$ as fully as you can, will you do that, please?"

"I didn't see that much, to be perfectly frank with you, but it's really nice over there. It's warm and very bright, even when the frenzel smelches. Every nolnek there's a vit, when the cosmish isn't drendeling. But *I* found . . ."

"*Hold it, Mirren!*" the first voice screamed.

There was a gentle click, as if the speakers were cut off while the interrogation team talked things over. Enoch scooted around till he found the soft wall, and sat up against it, whistling happily. He whistled "You and the Night and the Music," seguéing smoothly into "Some Day My Prince Will Come." There was another gentle click and one of the voices returned.

It was the angry voice that spoke first; the impatient one who was clearly unhappy with the temponaut. His tone was soothing, cajoling, as if he were the Recreation Director of the Outpatient Clinic of the Menninger Foundation.

"Enoch . . . may I call you Enoch . . ." Enoch murmured it was lovely to be called Enoch, and the first voice went on, "We're, uh, having a bit of difficulty understanding you."

"How so?"

"Well, we're taping this conversation . . . uh, you don't *mind* if we tape this, do you, Enoch?"

"Huh-uh."

"Yes, well. We find, on the tape, the following words: 'frenzel,' 'smelches,' 'nolneg' . . ."

"That's nol*nek*," Enoch Mirren said. "A nol*neg* is quite another matter. In fact, if you were to refer to a nolnek as a nolneg, one of the tilffs would certainly get highly upset and level a renaq . . ."

"*Hold it!*" The hysterical tone was creeping back into the interrogator's voice. "Nolnek, nolneg, what does it matter—"

"Oh, it matters a lot. See, as I was saying—"

"—it doesn't matter at *all,* Mirren, you asshole! We can't understand a word you're saying!"

The woman's voice interrupted. "Lay back, Bert. Let me talk to him." Bert mumbled something vaguely obscene under his breath. If there was anything Enoch hated, it was vagueness.

"Enoch," said the woman's voice, "this is Dr. Arpin. Inez Arpin? Remember me? I was on your training team before you left?"

Enoch thought about it. "Were you the black lady with the glasses and the ink blots?"

"No. I'm the white lady with the rubber gloves and the rectal thermometer."

"Oh, sure, of course. You have very trim ankles."

"Thank you."

Bert's voice exploded through the speaker. "*Jeezus Keerice,* Inez!"

"Enoch," Dr. Arpin continued, ignoring Bert, "are you speaking in tongues?"

Enoch Mirren was silent for a moment, then said, "Gee, I'm awfully sorry. I guess I've been linked up with the Cissaldan so long, I've absorbed a lot of how it thinks and speaks.

I'm really sorry. I'll try to translate."

The studious voice spoke again. "How did you meet the, uh, Cissaldan?"

"Just appeared. I didn't call it or anything. Didn't even see it arrive. One minute it wasn't there, and the next it was."

Dr. Arpin spoke. "But how did it get from its own planet to Earth$_2$? Some kind of spaceship, perhaps?"

"No, it just . . . came. It can move by will. It told me it felt my presence, and just simply hopped across all the way from its home in that other star-system. I think it was true love that brought it. Isn't that nice?"

All three voices tried speaking at once.

"Teleportation!" Dr. Arpin said, wonderingly.

"Mind-to-mind contact, telepathy, across unfathomable light-years of space," the studious voice said, awesomely.

"And what does it want, Mirren?" Bert demanded, forgetting the conciliatory tone. His voice was the loudest.

"Just to make love; it's really a terrific little person."

"So you just hopped in the sack with that disgusting thing, is that right? Didn't even give a thought to decent morals or contamination or your responsibility to us, or the mission, or anything? Just jumped right into the hay with that pukeable pervert?"

"It seemed like a good idea at the time," Enoch said.

"Well, it was a *lousy* idea, whaddaya think about *that,* Mirren? And there'll be repercussions, you can bet on that, too; repercussions! Investigations! Responsibility must be placed!" Bert was shouting again. Dr. Arpin was trying to calm him.

At that moment, Enoch heard an alarm go off somewhere. It came through the speakers in the ceiling quite clearly, and in a moment the speakers were cut off. But in that moment the sound filled the interrogation cell, its ululations signaling dire emergency. Enoch sat in silence, in darkness, naked, humming, waiting for the voices to return. He hoped he'd be allowed to get back to his Cissaldan pretty soon.

But they never came back. Not ever.

The alarm had rung because the disgusting thing had vanished. The alien morphologists who had been monitoring it through the one-way glass of the control booth fronting on the examination stage that formed the escape-proof study chamber had been turned away only a few seconds, accepting mugs of steaming stimulant-laced coffee from a Tech 3. When they turned back, the examination stage was empty. The disgusting thing was gone.

People began running around in ever-decreasing circles. Some of them disappeared into holes in the walls and made like they weren't there.

Three hours later they found the disgusting thing.

It was making love with Dr. Marilyn Hornback in a broom closet.

TimeSep Central, deep underground, was the primary locus of visitation, because it had taken the Cissaldan a little while to acclimate itself. But even as Bert, Dr. Inez Arpin, the studious type whose name does not matter, and all the others who came under the classification of chrono-experts were trying to unscramble their brains at the bizarre progression of events in TimeSep Central, matters were already out of their hands.

Cissaldans began appearing everywhere.

As though summoned by some silent song of space and time (which, in fact, was the case), disgusting things began popping into existence all over Earth. Like kernels of corn suddenly erupting into blossoms of popcorn, one moment there would be nothing—or a great deal of what passed for nothing—and the next moment a Cissaldan was there. Invariably right beside a human being. And in the next moment the invariable human being would get this *good* idea that it might be nice to, uh, er, that is, well, sorta *do it* with this creature.

Saffron-robed monks entering the mountain fastness of the Dalai Lama found that venerable fount of cosmic wisdom busily *shtupping* a disgusting thing. A beatific smile creased his wizened countenance.

An international conference of Violently Inclined Filmmakers at the Bel-Air Hotel in Beverly Hills was interrupted when it was noticed that Roman Polanski was under a table making violent love to a thing no one wanted to look at. Sam Peckinpah rushed over to abuse it. That went on, till Peckinpah's disgusting thing materialized and the director fell upon it, moaning.

In the middle of their telecasts, Carmelita Pope, Dinah Shore and Merv Griffin looked away from the cyclopean red eye of the live cameras, spotted disgusting things, disrobed themselves and went to it, thereby upping their ratings considerably.

His Glorious Majesty, the Right Honorable President, General Idi Amin Dada, while selecting material for his new cowboy suit (crushed velvet had his temporary nod as being in just the right vein of quiet good taste), witnessed a materialization right beside his adenoid-shaped swimming pool and fell on his back. The disgusting thing hopped on. No one paid any attention.

Truman Capote, popping Quaaludes like M&M's, rolled himself into a puffy little ball as his Cissaldan mounted him. The level of dope in his system, however, was so high that the disgusting thing went mad and strained itself straight up the urethra and hid itself against his prostate. Capote's voice instantly dropped three octaves.

Maidservants to Queen Elizabeth, knocking frantically on the door to her bedchamber, were greeted with silence. Guards instantly forced the door. They turned their heads away from the disgusting sight that greeted them. There was nothing regal, nothing imperial, nothing even remotely majestic about what was taking place there on the floor.

When Salvador Dali entered his Cissaldan, his waxed mustaches drooped alarmingly, like molten pocket watches.

Anita Bryant, locked in her bassinet-pink bathroom with her favorite vibrator, found herself suddenly assaulted by a disgusting thing. She fought it off and a second appeared. Then a third. Then a platoon. In moments the sounds of her outraged shrieks could be heard throughout that time zone, degenerating quickly into a bubbling, citraholic gurgle. It was the big bang theory actualized.

Cissaldans appeared to fourteen hundred assembly line workers in the automobile plant at Toyota City, just outside Yokohama. While the horny-handed sons and daughters of toil were busily getting it on, hundreds of half-assembled car bodies crashed and thundered into an untidy pile forty feet high.

Masters and Johnson had it off with the same one.

Billy Graham was discovered by his wife and members of his congregation having congress with a disgusting thing in a dust bin. He was "knowing" it, however, in the Biblical sense, murmuring, *"I* found it!"

Three fugitive *Reichsmarschalls,* posing as Bolivian sugar

cane workers while they plotted the renascence of the Third Reich, were confronted by suddenly materialized Cissaldans in a field near Cochabamba. Though the disgusting things looked disgustingly kosher, the unrepentant Nazis hurled themselves onto the creatures, visualizing pork-fat sandwiches.

William Shatner, because of his deep and profound experience with Third World Aliens, attempted to communicate with the disgusting thing that popped into existence in his dressing room. He began delivering a captainlike lecture on coexistence and the Cissaldan—bored—vanished, to find a more suitable mate. A few minutes later, a less discerning Cissaldan appeared and Shatner, now overcome with this *good* idea, fell on it, dislodging his hairpiece.

Evel Knievel took a running jump at a disgusting thing, overshot, hit the wall, and semiconscious, dragged himself back to the waiting aperture.

There in that other time/universe, the terrific little persons of Cissalda had spent an eternity making love to one another. But their capacity for passion was enormous, beyond calculation, intense and never-waning. It could be called *fornigalactic*. They had waited millennia for some other race to make itself known to them. But life springs into being only rarely, and their eons were spent in familiar sex with their own kind, and in loneliness. A loneliness monumental to conceive. When Enoch Mirren had come through the fabric of time and space to Earth$_2$, they had sent the most adept of their race to check him out. And the Cissaldan looked upon Enoch Mirren and found him to be *good*.

And so, like a reconnaissance ant sent out from the hill to scout the topography of a sugar cookie, that most talented of disgusting things sent back telepathic word to its kind: *We've got a live one here*.

Now, in mere moments, the flood of teleporting Cissaldans overflowed the Earth: one for every man, woman and child on the planet. Also leftovers for chickens and kangaroos with double vaginas.

The four top members of the Presidium of the Central Committee of the Supreme Soviet of the Communist Party (CPSU) of the Union of Soviet Socialist Republics—Brezhnev, Kosygin, Podgorny and Gromyko—deserted the four hefty ladies who had come as Peoples' Representatives to the National

Tractor Operators' Conference from the Ukraine, and began having wild—but socialistic—intercourse with the disgusting things that materialized on their conference table. The four hefty ladies did not care: four Cissaldans had popped into existence for *their* pleasure. It was better than being astride a tractor. Or Brezhnev, Kosygin, Podgorny and Gromyko.

All over the world Mort Sahl and Samuel Beckett and Fidel Castro and H.R. Haldeman and Ti-Grace Atkinson and Lord Snowdon and Jonas Salk and Jorge Luis Borges and Golda Meir and Earl Butz linked up with disgusting things and said no more. A stately and pleasant hush fell across the planet. Barbra Streisand hit the highest note of her career as she was penetrated. Philip Roth had guilt, but did it anyhow. Stevie Wonder fumbled, but got in finally. It was good.

All over the planet Earth it was quiet and it was *good*.

One week later, having established without room for discourse that Naugahyde was neither edible nor appetizing, Enoch Mirren decided he was being brutalized. He had not been fed, been spoken to, been permitted the use of lavatory facilities, or in even the smallest way been noticed since the moment he had heard the alarm go off and the speakers had been silenced. His interrogation cell smelled awful, he had lost considerable weight, he had a dreadful ringing in his ears from the silence and, to make matters terminal, the air was getting thin. "Okay, no more Mister Nice Guy," he said to the silence, and proceeded to effect his escape.

Clearly, easy egress from a 10'x10'x20' padded cell sunk half a mile down in the most top-secret installation in America was not possible. If there was a door to the cell, it was so cleverly concealed that hours of careful fingertip examination could not reveal it. There were speaker grilles in the ceiling of the cell, but that was a full twenty feet above him. He was tall, and thin—a lot thinner now—but even if he jumped, it was still a good ten feet out of reach.

He thought about his problem and wryly recalled a short story he had read in an adventure magazine many years before. It had been a cheap pulp magazine, filled with stories hastily written for scandalously penurious rates, and the craftsmanship had been employed accordingly. In the story that now came to Enoch's mind, the first installment of the serial had ended with the mightily thewed hero trapped at the bottom of a very deep pit floored with poison-tipped stakes as a horde of coral snakes slithered toward him, brackish water was pumped into the pit and was rising rapidly, his left arm was broken, he was without weapon, and a man-eating Sumatran black panther peered over the lip of the pit, watching him closely. Enoch remembered wondering—with supreme confidence in the writer's talents and ingenuity—how he would rescue his hero. The month-long wait till the next issue was on the newsstand was the longest month of Enoch's life. On the day of its release, he had pedaled down to the newsstand on his Schwinn and snagged the first copy of the adventure magazine from the bundle almost before the dealer had snipped the binding wire. He had dashed outside, thrown himself down on the curb and riffled through the magazine till he found the second installment of the cliffhanging serial. How would the writer, this master of suspense and derring-do, save the beleaguered hero?

Part two began:

"With one mighty leap, Vance Lionmane freed himself from the pit, overcoming the panther and rushing forward to save the lovely Ariadne from the aborigines."

Later, comma, after he had escaped from the interrogation cell, Enoch Mirren was to remember that moment, thinking again as he had when but a child: what a rotten lousy cheat that writer had been.

There were no Cissaldans left over. Everywhere Enoch went he found the terrific little persons shacked up with old men, young women, pre- and post-pubescent children, ducks, porpoises, wildebeests, dogs, arctic terns, llamas, young men, old women and, of course, chickens and kangaroos with double vaginas. But no love-mate for Enoch Mirren.

It became clear after several weeks of wandering, waiting for a materialization in his immediate vicinity, that the officials at TimeSep Central had dealt with him more severely than they could have known.

They had broken the rhythm. They had pulled him out of that disgusting thing, and now, because the Cissaldans were telepathically linked and were *all* privy to the knowledge, no

Cissaldan would have anything to do with him.

The disgusting things handled rejection very badly.

Enoch Mirren sat on a high cliff a few miles south of Carmel, California. The Peterbilt he had driven across the country in futile search of another human being who was not making love to a Cissaldan was parked on the shoulder of Route 1, the Pacific Coast Highway, above him. He sat on the cliff with his legs dangling over the Pacific Ocean. The guidebook beside him said the waters should be filled with seals at play, with sea otters wrapped in kelp while they floated on their backs cracking clams against their bellies, with whales migrating, because this was January and time for the great creatures to commence their journey. But it was cold, and the wind tore at him, and the sea was empty. Somewhere, elsewhere, no doubt, the seals and the cunning sea otters and the majestic whales were locked in passionate embrace with disgusting things from another time/universe.

Loneliness had driven him to thinking of those terrific little persons as disgusting things. Love and hate are merely obverse faces of the same devalued coin. Aristotle said that. Or Pythagoras. One of that crowd.

The first to know true love, he was the last to know total loneliness. He wasn't the last human on Earth, but a lot of good it did him. Everybody was busy, and he was alone. And long after they had all died of starvation, he would still be here . . . unless he decided some time in the ugly future to drive the Peterbilt off a cliff somewhere.

But not just yet. Not just now.

He pulled the notebook and pen from his parka pocket, and finished writing the story of what had happened. It was not a long story, and he had written it as an open letter, addressing it to whatever race or species inherited the Earth long after the Cissaldans had wearied of banging corpses and had returned to their own time/universe to wait for new lovers. He suspected that without a reconnaissance ant to lead them here, to establish a telepathic-teleportational link, they would not be able to get back here once they had left.

He only hoped it would not be the cockroaches who rose up through the evolutionary muck to take over the cute little

Earth, but he had a feeling that was to be the case. In all his travels across the land, the only creatures that could not get a Cissaldan to make love to them were the cockroaches. Apparently, even disgusting things had a nausea threshold. Unchecked, the cockroaches were already swarming across the world.

He finished the story, stuffed it in an empty Perrier Water bottle, capped it securely with a stopper and wax, and flung it by its neck as far out as he could into the ocean.

He watched it float in and out with the tide for a while, until a current caught it and took it away. Then he rose, wiped off his hands, and strode back up the slope to the 18-wheeler. He was smiling sadly. It had just occurred to him that his only consolation in bearing the knowledge that he had destroyed the human race was that for a little while, in the eyes of the best fuck in the universe, *he* had been the best fuck in the universe.

There wasn't a cockroach in the world who could claim the same.

Flop Sweat

INTRODUCTION

Writers take tours in other people's lives. Sometimes it's done casually, an evening stroll whistling down an innocent lane or around a familiar block. Innocent and familiar until the light is seen in the abandoned house, until the fabric of space and time is torn and the gaping hole opens onto The Other Place, until the lurker in the shadows emerges. "Flop Sweat" is one of those. I wrote it innocently enough; but something dark and unexpected happened here that I didn't plan on.

In December of 1977 I was contacted in Los Angeles by Carole Hemingway, host of the ABC radio affiliate KABC talk show bearing her name. I had done her program a number of times and had apparently been sufficiently weird for her vast audience to ask for return engagements. Several of these listeners remarked on my having written new stories in bookstore windows, and mentioned that I had even written a story over the radio for the Pacifica outlet here in L.A. She was intrigued and asked me if I would repeat the act on her show.

But with the enormous number of commercial interruptions endemic to the show's format, it was obvious to me that even with a two-hour time-slot I wouldn't be able to write anything coherent and still be able to carry on a conversation. So an alternate *modus operandi* was devised. And this was the method:

Carole would announce my forthcoming appearance for a number of days preceding, and as early as possible on the morning of the day I was to be her guest, she would call me and give me a specific thing she wanted me to use as the core of the story. I would take that basic situation or plot-element or *whatever* and write the story that day, completely that day, without any headstart or preliminary thinking...and have it finished to be read when we went on the air at 8:00 P.M.

Well, even under the most salutary conditions writing a story to order, with that pressing a deadline, from dead stop to completion, is a bit of a throw. But Carole made it that much more difficult by not calling till 1:00 in the afternoon; and when she did finally get through to me, her story springboard was—how shall I put this nicely—less than innervating.

Had she said, "An effluvium-covered brigantine without a living soul on board tacks into San Francisco harbor late in the winter of 1888. In the hold is an incredibly stout cage made of rare bubinga wood. The lock that seals the cage has affixed to it a strange, oddly disturbing runic seal. From within the cage come the sounds of something not-quite-human...in labor," yeah, had she said that, I'd have been home free.

Or had she said, "Start with a sixty-year-old Viennese violinist who has been having a love affair with a woman who comes to the seedy club where he has played for the past forty-five years since he was a young man, every year, but only once a year, on the anniversary of their first liaison. And he continues to age and wither...but she has stayed twenty years old," yeah, had she said that, I'd've whistled all the way to the studio that night.

Had she even said, "Disprove the existence of ghosts, or God, or Ronald Reagan," I'd have had something to sink my fangs into. "Tell me a story of the ancient spirit ghosts of the Mohawks, come again to bedevil those modern-day Amerind high-steel workers on Manhattan towers," okay, *that's* a story beginning. "Do me a story that explains why such a high percentage of big business crooks are practicing attorneys," not bad, a bit nebulous, but a workable basic concept; sure, I could have handled that.

But she said none of those. Nor anything else that might have made my life easier. What she said was:

"Write a story about a female talk show host."

I think I groaned.

A female talk show host wanted me to write a story about a female talk show host. If true love could ever possibly have blossomed between Carole Hemingway and me, it was brutally crippled in that moment. And it had been so many years since I'd done any radio interviewing myself, I wasn't sure I could write it with any degree of verisimilitude.

Nonetheless, undaunted, I accepted the challenge, sat down and started plotting. I had 6½ hours to devise and write a coherent story that wouldn't get me laughed off the air. In a few minutes I had the basic idea and started typing "Flop Sweat."

In the course of typing as fast as I could (I do about 120 words a minute on an Olympia office manual; never an electric, yucchhh; two fingers only), I found I needed some data I didn't have in my library. So I called her assistant at the station, Fred Harris, and asked him to describe the physical setup of the broadcast booth, how many and what kinds of telephone lines they had (it's a call-in show), and how many commercials per minute. And more. And more. That kind of stuff.

The dominant news story during that period, here in Los Angeles, was the mystery of the Hillside Strangler. I decided to use that as one of the basic elements in the piece, and I sat here writing the story with Ms. Hemingway's station blasting away so I'd get the proper cadence of talk-to-commercials that would make the story read realistically.

I wrote all day, and by 7:30 that night had completed the 4500 words...wasting myself in the process. But I then had to shower, get dressed (I'd been working in a bathrobe all day and I was, er, um, a bit fragrant), get in the car, and drive all the way across Los Angeles to KABC-AM.

The show went on the air at eight.

Fortunately, the top of the hour is given over to a five

minute news roundup that's fed from ABC New York. That was all the slack time I needed. In the car, speeding down the Santa Monica Freeway at 80 m.p.h., I heard Carole Hemingway on my radio, saying, "Harlan Ellison isn't here yet, but as you listeners know, he's a most unusual person, and I'm sure he'll rush into the control booth at any moment."

"I'm coming, godammit, I'm coming!" I screamed back at her, pounding the padded dashboard.

I hurtled into KABC-AM at 8:16 P.M., took a few minutes for salutations and the catching of breath...and proceeded—if one can judge from the subsequent phone calls to the program—to scare the shit out of thousands of radio listeners with the story you're about to read.

This story has not been revised. It comes to you precisely and exactly as it was written between the hours of 1:00 and 7:30 P.M. on December 21, 1977, the day it was performed over KABC TalkRadio.

Why does he tell me all this? Well, I tell it to you to prove that writers are not mythical creatures that live on crystal mountaintops. They are laborers working with inexplicable and invisible materials, but no more or less noble than a cabinetmaker who takes pride in his or her craft, who makes sure the rabbets are tight and smooth; no less approachable than a classy bricklayer who takes joy in the look of a line of bricks laid even and true; no more mysterious or honorable than a schoolteacher who can bring the Wars of the Roses to life for young people.

Flop Sweat

HER FIRST GUEST of the evening sat across the table from her, there in the tiny broadcast booth, staring at her with unreadable green eyes showing through the mask. She was dead certain he was crazy as a thousand battlefields; but he was, without a doubt, one of the best interviews she'd ever had on the program. She knew it without a doubt because her hands were soaking wet with perspiration and her upper lip above the glossed line of Ultima II was dewy with sweat.

When she had been in the theater, in the years before she had found that hosting a talk show was easier and steadier work, she had come to understand what the perspiration meant. In show biz they called it "flop sweat," the physical manifestation of nervousness just before going on stage. And during the seven years here at KDID the flop sweat had dampened her palms and upper lip every time she'd had a dynamite show. It was a certain barometer of something happening.

But to call this strange man, dressed all in black, wearing a cheap K-Mart domino mask, the kind children wear at Halloween, a "happening" was to fling oneself face-forward into understatement. Brother Michael Darkness was more than a happening; he was a force of nature, a powerful presence, a disturbing reality; even if he was obviously a certifiable nutcase, a card-carrying whacko, a psychotic in the top one-tenth

of the top percentile of emotional walking woundeds with
whom she shared airspace.

"Reverend Darkness," she said, "it's almost the top of the
hour and we have to break now for the network news,
but—"

"*Brother* Darkness," he said, cutting her off.

She was nonplused for a moment. His voice. It had the
deep, warm, musky timbre of secrets whispered in dark rooms.
When he spoke she thought of a stick of butter, squeezed
through a fist. "Yes, of course; I'm sorry. You've told me
several times you're not a minister. I'll try to remember,
Brother Darkness." He nodded politely. She could not read his
expression around the mask. He disturbed her fluid ease behind
the mike. That didn't happen very often. Seven years at this
gig had made her almost unflappable. "What I was about to
suggest, Brother Darkness, is that we break for the news and
you come back for the second hour of the show. My next guest
is Dr. Jacob Theiss, a very well-known psychiatrist who works
with the Los Angeles police; he'll be coming on to talk about
this epidemic of razorblade killings . . . and I think some of
what you've been saying about evil in our times might be very
interesting to have him comment on."

"I'd be pleased to stay, Miss Ketchum."

The way he said it made Theresa Ketchum almost regret she
had suggested it. He made his acceptance sound as if they had
entered into some kind of unholy alliance. But she signaled to
Jerry, the engineer in the control room, and he turned up the
network feed pot and the news rushed in with drums and trumpets and the voice of the sixty-thousand-dollar-a-year announcer from New York.

Now she was alone with Brother Darkness. The on-air studio
in which they sat was a claustrophial box, fifteen by ten, with
two windowed walls: one side looked into the control room;
the other looked into the waiting room where Millie sat taking
and screening phone calls from the general public. The studio
seemed somehow smaller than usual, and throat-cloggingly
filled with menace. And it had started out being such a *lovely*
day.

She took off her earphones and racked them. She stood up,
smoothing her skirt, and was suddenly aware of Brother Darkness looking at her not as a dispassionate "communicaster,"
but as an attractive woman, thirty-four years old, body tanned

and well toned from afternoons at the Beverly Hills Health Club, nose bobbed exquisitely by Dr. Parks, auburn hair coddled and cozened just so at Jon Peters's parlor in the Valley. She had a momentary flash of regret at not having worn something bulky and concealing. The blouse was too sheer, the skirt too tight, the whole image too provocative. But she had dressed for *after* the broadcast, for the party CBS was hosting that night at the Bonaventure to promote its new midseason sitcom. The party at which she would use the sensual good looks, the tanned and well-toned body, the exquisite nose and brushfire hair to play some ingratiating politics; to move herself out of a seven-year rut on local talk radio and into a network job. Dressing with care this afternoon, before coming in to the station, she had given no thought to the effect on her guests; only to how she would present herself at the party. Attention where it mattered.

But Brother Michael Darkness was staring at her the way men stared at her in the Polo Lounge or in the meat-rack pickup bar of the Rangoon Racquet Club. And she wished she were wearing a kaftan, a fur-lined parka, a severe three-piece tweed pantsuit.

"Would you like a cup of coffee?" She heard her voice coming thickly and distantly. Not at all the liquid honey tone she used as the trademark of an aural sex object when broadcasting.

"No thank you, Miss Ketchum. I'll just sit here, if that's all right."

She nodded. "Yes, of course. That'll be fine. I'll go get Dr. Theiss and be right back. We have five minutes before we're back on the air." And she escaped into the corridor quickly, finding herself leaning against the sea-green wall breathing very deeply.

Over the station speakers in the hall the newscaster was headlining the Los Angeles razorblade slayings, commenting on the discovery that morning of an eleventh young woman, nude and with throat sliced open, in the bushes near the Silverlake off-ramp of the Hollywood Freeway. She heard the voice, but paid no attention.

She stepped into the waiting room beside the studio. Jake Theiss was leaning against the wall sipping coffee from a paper cup. The telephone switchboard was lit from one end to the other, all ten lines strobing with urgency. Millie looked up from the log and rolled her eyes. "Jesus, Terri, you've got a live one tonight. They're crawling down the wires to talk to him."

She felt her heart racing. "Keep the best ones on hold; I'll try to get to them after I introduce Jake."

Then she turned to Jake Theiss, who smiled at her, and it was as if someone had returned her stolen security blanket. He had been on the show a dozen times before, and they had even gone out several evenings. His mere presence reassured her.

"Theresa," he said, stepping away from the wall and taking her hand, "you look a trifle whiplashed."

She hugged him and kissed his cheek. "My God, Jake, have you been *listening* to him?"

The psychiatrist nodded slowly. "I have indeed. But it's not so much *what* he says, as the *way* he says it. A little de Sade, a little Gilles de Rais, echoes of Proterius, a smidgeon of Cotton Mather and some direct quotes from the *Evangelium Nicodemi*, if memory serves well. All made contemporary by the addition of Jung, Freud, Adler and Werner Erhard's look-out-for-number-one. Nothing particularly spectacular about it; most modern demonologists plunder the same bag. But your Brother Michael in there has a sense of the dramatic, and a voice to match, and a nasty way of bringing in current events that . . . well . . . I can't say I'm looking forward to sharing a microphone with him."

She drew a deep breath. "Jake, *stop it!* This flake does a good enough job scaring the hell out of me on his own. I mean, it's like *Exorcist* time in there. When he starts talking about the return of the devils I swear to God I can *feel* the slimy things in that booth. And I never thought a kid's Halloween mask could chill me, but each time he looks at me with those green eyes I feel every part of my body trying to run away and leave my head behind."

Millie handed her a Kleenex from the box. "Your lip," she said. Theresa took the tissue and blotted herself.

"Okay, don't worry about it," Jake said, setting down the empty coffee cup. "I'll come on like the voice of rationality."

She smiled wanly, feeling like a fool. This was hardly professional behavior.

They walked back into the on-air studio just as the news was ending. Theresa moved to the console and flipped the toggle switch on the intercom. "Jerry, let's do the Southern

California Buick Dealers, Pacific Telephone and Roto-Rooter. Is there a live tag on the Roto-Rooter commercial?"

The tinny voice of Jerry from the other side of the control room glass filled the booth. "Yeah. Ten seconds."

He ran up the cartridges and for a moment, before she turned down the sound in the booth, the Buick announcer's voice filled the air. When she turned back to her guests, Jake Theiss had already seated himself at the empty third mike, to the right of her swivel chair. She drew a deep breath and sat down. "Jake, this is Brother Michael Darkness; Brother Darkness, Dr. Jacob Theiss." She watched them shake hands. She studied Jake's face closely, but if he reacted to the touch of Brother Michael's hand, as she had reacted the first time he had touched her, the *only* time he had touched her, earlier that evening, the psychiatrist concealed the fact. Jake did not shiver. He smiled at Brother Michael and said, "I've been listening to the interview. Pretty strong medicine for a lay audience just around dinnertime, wouldn't you say?"

Brother Michael's face was impassive. "If you think I'm a fraud, Dr. Theiss, why not just come out with it. Mendacity is unappealing in someone who professes to being a man of science. Even such an alleged science as the study of the mind."

Theresa's heart beat faster. It was as though she had just received two separate and powerful electrical shocks, so close together they seemed one: outrage and fear at the antagonism of the man in black, which might lead in a moment to a thrown punch; and delight at the instant animus between Jake and the Brother, guaranteeing a controversial second hour for the show. She hated herself for feeling pleasure, but it was always this way when something terrible but promotable happened on the show.

"I didn't know you also read minds, Brother Darkness," Jake said, swallowing the affront. "If I wanted to call you a fraud, I'd certainly wait till we were on the air."

Brother Michael's tone softened. He knew he wasn't going to get a fight. Not now, at any rate. "I'm pleased to know you recognize the apocryphal texts. Too few practitioners of what you call 'the healing arts' familiarize themselves with the black documents of antiquity."

Theresa was lost.

"I beg your pardon, what do you mean?" Jake said.

"I mean: you were correct in recognizing my quote from the *Evangelium Nicodemi*."

A chill spread its web across Theresa's back. Jake had said that in the waiting room. How could Brother Michael have heard it? She reached over and flapped the toggle for Millie. "Did we leave the intercom feed open?" Millie shook her head no. Theresa stared at her through the glass. The chill spread deeper and farther. She looked at Jake with confusion.

He caught the look. "A condemned document dating from the third century. It describes Christ's descent into hell and a session of Satan's sanhedrin, his court."

The Roto-Rooter jingle was just ending and Theresa held up a hand for silence as she riffled through the sheaf of tags for commercials, and simultaneously punched the square red button that gave her a live microphone.

"So say goodbye forever to clogged drains caused by those tree roots that've grown into pipes. Get to the *root* of your problem by calling your Roto-Rooter service representative..." She conversationalized the written tag, reading it with warmth and friendly understatement, but all the while keeping her eye on her guests.

"Well, we're back with Brother Michael Darkness, the head of the Euchite Sect, a group we're told has no affiliation with any orthodox or recognized religious denomination; a man who says he represents those who believe in the return of the dark forces that once ruled the Earth. And we're being joined now by Dr. Jacob Theiss, M.D., Ph.D., a member of the governing board of the American Psychiatric Association, he's on the staff at the UCLA Medical Center, and the winner of many prestigious awards in the field of human behavior. Dr. Theiss, have you been listening to the interview so far?"

"Yes, Theresa. And I'm most intrigued by Brother Darkness and what he's been saying. But I think you're mistaken when you say that the Euchites are an unrecognized sect.

"Brother Darkness, correct me if I'm wrong, but weren't the Euchites an early Christian sect who believed that each man had a congenital devil that could be expelled only by constant prayer? They were supposed to have repudiated the sacraments and moral law, to have worshiped Lucifer as the oldest son of the Creator, isn't that right? About twelfth century, if I remember correctly."

Brother Michael leaned forward till his face almost touched the microphone. "Very good, Dr. Theiss. I'm pleased and surprised at your erudition. Quite correct, on every point."

"And you're reviving this sect here in Los Angeles, in the middle of the Age of Plastic?"

"When better? The time is right."

"What do you mean by that?" Theresa said.

"Just look around," Brother Michael said softly. "Everywhere a belief in the irrational and the obscure takes greater hold daily. Films tell us we are being watched by aliens from other worlds or that demons infest the night; there is a frenzied rush to believe in astrology, in demonology and assassination conspiracies, in superstition and magic; we seek messiahs on all sides; Atlantis, the Bermuda Triangle, lost worlds at the center of the Earth, spirits speaking from the grave; Eastern mysticism . . . they dominate our every waking moment and plunge through our dreams at night. Do you think this is accidental? No, I'm sure you don't. You may be confused and frightened by it all, but in some secret part of your mind and your soul you understand that it is the first clarion call of the ancient devils, come again to rule us. As is only right and proper."

And they were off. Theresa barely had time to get in the live commercials required by the log and the FCC. She had to run them in clusters, knowing her listeners were pounding furiously on the busy telephone lines. Jake and the Brother went at it fiercely, with Jake trying to hold a line of logic and sanity against the ferocious dynamics of Brother Darkness's statements.

The first of the calls came in at twenty after the hour.

"Okay, let's take a break from this for a moment," Theresa said. "Wheeew! You two make my head spin. Let's hear what our listeners have to say. Dr. Theiss, Brother Darkness, if you'll use those headsets you'll be able to hear the caller. Okay. Hello, this is Theresa Ketchum and you're on KDID talk radio. Who's this?"

The voice that came across the line was strangely unisexual, neither male nor female, identifiable neither as young nor old. It seemed to be coming from a great distance, though it was clear and precise. "This is someone all of Los Angeles wants to know," the voice said. "I'm responsible for the razorblade cleansings. You call them slayings, but I assure you, they're cleansings."

Through the glass, Millie's face filled with horror.

She grabbed for the private line and dialed. Theresa saw her frantic movement and knew at once she was dialing the police emergency number, 9–1–1. Thank God Millie was on tonight, and not Charlie, who was so slow on the uptake that he often patched through rambling dingbats.

"Come on, whoever you are," Theresa said, stalling for time so the police could trace back across the phone company's machinery to the line on which this self-proclaimed killer was speaking, "we know there are enough cuckoos out there who like to confess to crimes to fill The Forum. Why should we believe you're the razorblade killer?"

"It isn't necessary that you believe. But here's a bit of information the police have been holding back: when I perform my cleansing operations, I always cut a pentacle into the sole of the left foot of my sacrifices."

He went on speaking, but Theresa saw Jake signaling her frantically. She hit the green button killing the live mike, and Jake gasped, "It's him! Or her! I can't tell which! But that's even been kept out of the coroner's reports."

"How do you know?"

"For God's sake, Terri, I'm *working* with the LAPD on this! It's the killer, I tell you!"

She punched the mike to life. "Why are you calling us?"

The voice went on carefully, very steadily, "I just wanted to say it would serve you to listen to what Brother Darkness is saying. He's right, you know."

The most violent reaction came from Brother Michael Darkness. He grabbed the boom on the mike and pulled the instrument to him. "Whoever you are . . . you've got to stop this . . . it's awful . . . it's not right . . . you're a sick person . . ."

But the line went dead. The dial tone came over the open mike.

They sat there in silence, knowing that all over Los Angeles pandemonium was gripping the thousands of listeners to this program; knowing that if the station management was listening they were already calling in on the private lines to find out why the four-and-a-half second time-delay intercept hadn't been used; knowing that the police were on their way to the station;

knowing that out there somewhere a lunatic was being primed to kill again. Surely that was what this portended. Another slaughter.

She didn't know what to say. For the first time in seven years she was too terrified and too stunned to let her sense of theatrics override her shock. But Jake had already jumped in.

"Brother Michael, do you know that person?"

"I swear to you, I have never heard that voice. I don't want you to think that my beliefs or the sect I represent have anything to do with murder."

"But that person, male or female I can't tell which, that person says your doctrine is correct. That speaker was an adherent of what you profess. *Now* do you see what your insane, your profane doctrine leads to? Chaos! Lunacy! It makes it all right for madmen to kill innocent people!"

And Millie was waving frantically from the other side of the glass, signaling Theresa to pick up line three.

She punched up line three and started to say, "You're on KDID talk radio..." but the voice from the night came once again. "Don't try to trace me; you'll have no luck. I just want you to know that it all begins and ends tonight."

Theresa heard herself gasp, and then she barely managed to say, "What do you mean?"

And the voice said, "It's all coming together tonight. Have you looked out at the moon? It's full tonight. And everything you people believe, all the mad things, all the terrible things, all the things Brother Darkness calls 'the irrational' come together. Belief in the dark things, the ancient fears, the crazy things you all believe in your souls *really* move the universe... all of it has become strong enough for the end of my cleansing labors... and the beginning of the Apocalypse."

And the mike went dead again.

Theresa cut in Millie's intercom. "Where did that come from?"

Millie was crying. "That was line three, from Orange County. But the first one was an L.A. line. It can't be!"

Jake's face was white with fear. "Oh, my God," he said, very quietly, the words trembling with terror.

Brother Michael was babbling, saying over and over, "I had nothing to do with it, nothing... I don't know him... I swear I didn't mean any harm..."

And as the hour wore to a close, there were two more calls. One on a line from Long Beach, the other on a line originating in Glendale. It was impossible for anyone to get from one of those far areas to another in the space of minutes; yet it was the same voice, and it happened.

And when the police came they took Brother Michael away. And Jake went with them, to help coordinate the mobilization of every available cop in the city. And when the hour ended Theresa was left sitting in the booth, shaking with terror.

Party tonight? No, not possible. No party tonight. Perhaps no party *any* night. That voice, the calm in the words, the certainty. Tonight: the Apocalypse. And one word from the razorblade killer's last message: Armageddon. The final battle between good and evil, the last battle between the forces of the Creator and the dark demons who had been banished before man walked the Earth.

"Terri, I'm going home now. Will you be okay?"

It was Millie's voice from the other side of the glass. The control room was empty. Jerry had gone. Theresa looked up dazedly, nodded once, and tried to rise. She found she had lost the strength to leave this terrible little box, at least for the moment. "Go ahead, Millie; I'll see you tomorrow." She let her hand lie on the console after releasing the toggle. Millie left.

She knew there were other people in the building. In other studios, KDID was carrying on; even in the face of what had gone out over the air tonight. She found that she was too frightened to leave, to go out through the corridors, past the security desk, into the parking lot with its high wire fence, to get into her car all alone, and to drive across town to her apartment. No. She would stay here. Safe in the booth. Locked away from whatever might happen tonight.

There was a faint light in the empty control room.

She looked through the glass, strained forward to see what it was, moving toward her. A faint purple light, soft and blurred, like a fading bruise on battered flesh. And now another light, in the glass of the waiting room on the other side of the studio. She stared from one to another, watching them moving slowly toward the glass partitions. Now another light in the control room. And another. Two more in the waiting room.

There was a rumbling beneath her feet. The studio trembled with the reverberation of an impact in the earth. Through the sound-proofed walls came the dull roar of explosions. Trem-blors rippled the floor, the vinyl tiles buckled around her feet.

The faint lights moved closer. Figures coming toward the glass. Stopping to stare in at her. Figures in long black gar-ments, with drawn cowls that covered their faces. And strange, sickly purple light, the faintest, most terrible glow, shining out from beneath the cowls. They stared in at her. She could see no eyes: but they were staring in at her.

They raised their arms slightly, slowly, and the sleeves of their black robes fell back revealing their hands. Theresa found that she could not breathe, that her chest was convulsing with the pain of her wildly beating heart.

Their fingers did not end in flesh. Metal. Sharp, cold metal; thin and final. This was the answer to how phone calls from the same person could come from distant sources.

There was the sound of movement just outside the door of the studio. The walls shook with the echoes of the cataclysm outside. The roaring was louder now.

And in the moment before the door opened she had the final, petrifying thought that she had been part of it all, had spread the doctrine of irrationality and superstition every night for seven years, had given a platform to every demented True Believer whose wild fantasies might build her audience.

And now her worshipers had come to sacrifice their very own prophet. She felt cold and dead already, could feel the chill slice of the thin, metal fingertips. Her palms were soaked with sweat in expectation of the final performance.

The door opened and they filed in to fill the studio. They stood staring at her as she felt her life clog up in her throat and arteries. They raised their arms and the sleeves fell back from pale flesh and metal fingertips. She waited for the first touch.

And they sank to their knees, lifting their arms in suppli-cation. She began to tremble with the rictus of a scream shaking her like a fever. Now she knew the worst, now she understood:

She was not to die. She had broadcast the word for them, every night for seven years, and she was not to die. She would be their dark priestess. Like the others who had done their spadework, like the others who had spread the word, she was to be kept alive, perhaps forever.

Dark priestess in a world of desolation, ruled by devils, cleansed of humanity. She would not die!

More ruinous than death: to rule forever in Hell. Lovelessly alive; worshiped by eaters of the darkness. To live on, coated always with a cold sweat, through a final performance that had no curtain, no exit lines.

Her scream could have shattered glass, but it didn't; it merely resonated against the metal fingertips of her subjects, her masters.

From the burning world beyond the studio came the wind whisper of the plague of locusts.

Would You Do It
for a Penny?

(Written in collaboration with Haskell Barkin)

INTRODUCTION

Writers take tours in other people's lives.

And every once in a while the observed becomes an integral part of the life of the observer. Make no mistake, and when the reviews are written and the idle chatter is passed—never permit the deletion: I did not write this story alone. It was a true collaboration between me and one of the most exemplary human beings I have ever known, Haskell Barkin.

We wrote this as a lark, a number of years ago, and it was published in *Playboy*. In that way, Huck—as we call him—helped me realize a secret desire. I had always wanted to see my work in *Playboy* but had been unsuccessful in getting them to consider the stories seriously enough. Not only because *Playboy* is arguably the highest-paying magazine market in the world, but because as times have changed and fiction has waned in importance for that journal, to be replaced by topical nonfiction, the pages allocated for fiction have diminished. They are always hot to publish Cheever or Updike or Le Carré (and with justification because they are excellent), but because those fiction pages are held so dear they are highly selective in whom they permit to occupy that space. Unless one has had a popular success, from which instant name-identification provides an added value for their table of contents, it is strictly the quality of the material that buys a writer the chance at that forum.

Despite my having sent *Playboy* virtually everything of what I considered first rank for many years, including stories that later won awards and became widely anthologized, I could never get the nod. On one occasion they rejected a story titled "Pretty Maggie Money-eyes" on the grounds that the female character was stronger than the male character. As I say, even at *Playboy* times have changed. But for many years I was on the outside looking in. And it galled me. On a low energy level, to be sure, but a burr under my saddle nonetheless.

Then one Sunday Huck stopped by with an idea for a story. He told it to me and suggested we write it together, because he'd never written short stories. "Horse puckey," I said, eschewing harsh language. "Write it yourself, kiddo. It's a terrific idea and you've got the stuff aplenty to write it properly. Never take two people to do a job one can do as well." (This, from a man who has written an entire book of collaborations. Do I contradict myself? Very well, then I contradict myself. I am large, I contain multitudes. And while I'm about it, thanks Walt.)

You see, Huck has one of the great antic senses of humor in the civilized world. If anyone ever asked me to define *droll*, I'd schlep them over to Huck's house and point at him. He *is* droll. So I was hardly being humble when I urged him to write the story himself. I was being logical: one hires an expert in matters vitreous when one requires an intricate job of glassblowing . . . not a window-washer.

The story-idea was a funny one.

And though I like to think many of my stories have an ample dollop of humor in them, droll is one of the many things I *ain't*.

So Huck went off and a while later he came back with a story of maybe half a dozen pages. I read them, and the skeleton was there, but it hadn't really been fleshed out. So I said, "Well, maybe we can make this a little better. Leave it with me, if you like, and I'll run it through the typewriter again."

Huck opined that would be peachykeen, and I shoved the story into a pending file till I had a little free time.

Ten thousand years later (to hear Barkin tell it), I got around to unshipping the manuscript, reread it, and did a final draft. I gave it to Huck to read, and he sat there laughing not at all. That's his way. Droll, yes; effusive, forget it. When he got finished I thought he'd tell me it was ka-ka. Instead, he smiled and said, "It's terrific; very funny." Go figure it.

So we sent it out to the late A.C. Spectorsky of *Playboy*, with a recommendation kindly added by Ted Sturgeon, who was high in favor at *Playboy* at the time. And a few weeks later they bought it. My first sale to *Playboy*, a secret dream actualized through the direct involvement in my life of Huck Barkin.

Why is he telling us all this?

I tell you all this because writers take tours in other people's lives and the dearest treasure one finds, second in importance only to wisdom and insight, is friendship. I write of friendship frequently. Oh, most of the time you may not recognize it, because I have it dressed up in outrageous garb, but that's one of the most important things in life, as I see it, and I try to examine it as closely as love or courage or the mortal dreads . . . real friendship. Elsewhere in these pages you'll find a very long tale about friendship called "All the Lies That Are My Life," and though *this* story isn't *about* friendship, it came into being *because* of friendship.

Huck has been my truest friend for a lot of years; going on twenty. The affection I've had lavished on me by Huck and his wife Carol and their daughter Tracy has carried me through many thorny times. He is one of the few people ever to call me out because of my bad behavior and do it in such a wise and loving way that I stopped doing what I'd been doing and changed my manner. Tracy has been a constant amazement to me, growing from a clever child into a remarkable young woman, and all the while providing a handy reminder that not all modern kids turn out to be me-generation nitwits or Texas-Tower snipers. Carol, as architect and self-fulfilling prophecy of female determinism in these most parlous times, has filled my home with light and beauty and loyalty.

It helps. God knows it helps. When a writer spends decades taking nasty sojourns through the brutalized lives of the kinds of people that make interesting fiction, being able to balance it off against a happily married, sensibly oriented, constantly growing, decent and honest family unit helps, God knows it helps.

And how do I repay these limitless kindnesses? In ways I do not think Amy Vanderbilt would have approved: first, I blame the faint cavalier tone of adolescent sexism in this story—however innocent and moronically slaphappy it may be—on Huck. It was *his* fault, Gloria! Second, I used Haskell Barkin's name for an utterly amoral, vacuous and psychopathic character in another story I wrote a long time ago. It is the perfect name for a big blond beach-bum kinda guy. Go sue me. Art sometimes demands rapacious behavior. (Or as Faulkner once put it: "If a writer has to rob his mother he will not hesitate; the *Ode on a Grecian Urn* is worth any number of old ladies.")

Would You Do It
for a Penny?

(Written in collaboration with Haskell Barkin)

ARLO, GREAT WHITE HUNTER, at midnight, poked a bored finger (attached to a bored hand attached to a bored arm attached to a bored Arlo) toward Fred MacMurray and Madeleine Carroll. It could not be said there was viciousness or even vindictiveness in the movement. But as von Clausewitz said in vol. II of *Vom Kriege*, any positive action, even if ultimately incorrect, is better than indecision, and no action at all. Fred and Madeleine were feigning animosity for one another as Arlo poked the *off* button.

They faded, it was still midnight, and Arlo was horny. So he decided to go shopping.

As a follow-up decision, he decided—since he was going to be in a supermarket anyway—to check the kitchen cabinets, to see what staples were vanishing.

Then he put on his stretch Levis and a Swiss velour; went out to his dusty eight-year-old Austin-Healey; headed for the statistically luckiest 24-hour supermarket, The Hollywood Ranch Market; went to Vine Street.

Arlo, Great White Hunter, at midnight plus ten.

He trundled the cart with the left rear wheel that did not revolve up and down the aisles for a while (with great difficulty), noting Signs Of The Times and The Advancement Of Man As Seen In His Artifacts:

There was now a boysenberry-flavored yogurt.

Civilization's greatest achievement—Saran Wrap—now came in a roll-package with knobs on the end so you could wind it back up if you rolled out a tot too much.

One-to-one eggs were selling well.

Sesame seed party crackers had fallen off a point or two, but barbecue snax were on the rise. (Good, good!)

He accumulated a carton of corn flakes with very pukey dehydrated peach slices in the box, a can of pink applesauce that resembled tree moss from fairyland, and a package of kosher hot dogs. But as for the main hunt, there was very little to stir the blood or put color in the cheeks. (Women with machines in their hair—and particularly those wearing snoods with cilia waving—would be restricted to the bathrooms of the world, never even the living room—much less a public supermarket—when Arlo was elected God.)

Just as he turned right at dog food, somewhat abaft of canary seed, he caught sight of a pair of floral-patterned hip-huggers with bell-bottoms, the outline of the lower rolled edge of the underpants barely discernible in relief. A trifle skinny perhaps, this silver blonde with the loose and lacy matching top cut in an octagon far down the spine, but still the pelvic girdle looked highly functional.

Arlo stalked her past detergents, floor waxes and aerosol bombs (staying upwind so the beast would not catch his spoor), trying to decide whether his opening gambit need necessarily be the standard collision of carts, the chancier request for advice about spring vegetables or a go-to-hell inquiry as to whether or not he had seen her on a daytime soap. The latter worked well enough in the Hollywood Ranch at this hour, but it smacked of "the Industry," and when coming on with ac-tresses, it was *always* terra incognita.

Before he could reconcile the tactic, she was joined at the juncture of doughnuts and fruit juices by a man in an open-weave T-shirt (brawny, shaved early in the day). They began discussing what to have for tomorrow's dinner as Arlo scurried past them. A foul oath escaped Arlo's clenched gonads.

It was neither May, nor fair, at the Mayfair Market on Fountain and La Brea. A vast wasteland of dozing clerks and Muzak. An empty repository for rows and rows of color-coded commodities. A stalking-ground without prey. A *shandah*. A pure pain in the ass. He wasted half an hour buying a can of Pledge and three tins of sardines in wine sauce. But as ye cruise, so shall ye be cruised: he was accosted briefly and toothily by an aging homosexual with liver spots, who asked him how you tell a fresh cantaloupe.

As a last resort, before bed and a Seconal, Arlo did not turn north up his street, but continued ahead to a usually arid desert, the Ralph's on Hollywood past Western. And there, as if the big greengrocer in the sky, he who smiles favorably on all such hegiras, had finally come back into the office and noticed Arlo's button lit on the board, and sent her to him—there she stood, limned by the fluorescents of dalliance, lush in the simplicity of her skintight yellow ochre capris, seen through a glass starkly, wrestling with a grocery cart in the immense front window of Ralph's. Arlo had almost gone shooting past the supermart—it was possible to clock the entire action in the store with a fast pass-down in the parking lot—but now, keeping one eye on the trembling roundnesses produced by her attempted disentanglement of the cart from its insertion into the long line of insertions (oh, lord, insertions!), he did a full three-hundred-sixty-degree turn and plowed to a stop, half on the concrete walk that edged the storefront.

Arlo sprinted into the store, twelve seconds tardy. She had wrenched the cart free from its paramour, next in the line, and she was wheeling it down the nearest aisle, a side-to-side hip-slung movement that was all sinuousness and the music of silks on silks. Arlo was transported. Oh, thank you thank you, Great Greengrocer In The Sky!

Arlo pursued, a cart before him like Quixote's lance and shield. A breakneck lurch that slowed and modified into his strolling pace as he neared her behind, as he neared behind her, as behind her . . .

Fearing she might turn at any moment, Arlo obfuscated: he wrenched camouflage from the shelves and flipped it into the cart, heedless of form or content to the act: a box of Tampax, a tin of litchi nuts, a jar of maraschino cherries, a pack of frozen prawns, dietetic grapefruit slices.

Now he swung alongside her, two vehicles steaming down the freeway aisles of life, destined to cross at a king's X of inevitability. Arlo perused prices, hefted weights, compared viscosities, his thoughts meanwhile cascading, plunging, avalanching down corridors of cunning. Tactics of encounter. This was no frippery, this statuesque color-coded commodity, fair traded and in highest demand by a legion of slavering consumers. No miniscule ploy for simpoleons—a fresh varient was required. How do I meet thee? Let me count the ways. Know your enemy. Loose hips sink kips. Wait, hark! See her now comparing bottled salad dressings, a bare minimal ten feet from you. What beauty, what form, what a goddam eternal verity, fade to black and ecstasy!

Now she moves on . . . having selected nothing. No clue, no hint, a major battle, this. Wait—there goes the vinegar into the cart, and now, joy of joys, the olive oil! An old-fashioned girl, no prepared dressings for her!

(I'm Pennsylvania Dutch Amish, Miss, and I, too, long for the simple delights of the pure life, wanna go to bed with—no, forget it, that wasn't right.)

Arlo's lust bayed at the fluorescent moon.

Now she's at pet foods. Dog or cat? Let it be a dog, dear Lord, let it be a dog. Parakeet seed? Well, Arlo would try anything once, no scene was too freaky, really: when you're in love, *anything* is correct.

Suddenly, she was looking at him. Not in his general direction, but directly at him. Staring, with an unfocused intensity. Arlo panicked. It wasn't supposed to work like this. Which way could he run? He was hemmed in by specials on one-calorie cola and potato chips. She was starting toward him.

"Excuse me, but don't I know you?"

Of all the phrases, words, sentences, polemics, diatribes, inducements, blandishments, lead-ins, rhetoric in Arlo's thesaurus of hustle, nowhere was there an answer to her ridiculously trite—disarming—question. Arlo clutched. His throat froze. He stared at her, a mastodon in ice, seven million centuries frozen solid, staring out of that giant popsicle at Amundsen and his party.

"Mmm. I'm sorry. I guess not."

She wheeled away, Arlo forgotten.

"Wait!"

"No, I was wrong. You look different up close. I'm not wearing my contacts."

Frantic was an industrious troll, deep inside Arlo's vitals, hauling out hanks of viscera and flinging them, underhand, like a dog scratching dirt, through a painful hole bored in the small of Arlo's back.

He followed her, hurriedly, aplomb blown. "Wait a second!" Baked bean pyramids and he collided, cans went clattering, he surged on heedless. "I want to take advantage of you. I mean, I was trying to uh, er, um, decide whether to ask your advice about something, except I'm a little shy about speaking to strangers. But now that you've broken the ice, I wonder if I could ask you how to tell a fresh cantaloupe..."

She stopped dead, whirled, hands flat in readiness for a kung fu chop. "You're about as shy as a mako shark, and you *don't* want my advice. Of all the things you might possibly want, my advice is *not* among them." She performed a stately *verónica* and tooled the cart away from him.

"You're evil!" he cried after her. "You torment men for kicks!"

In the parking lot, his brains having turned to cottage cheese, Arlo screamed senselessly at the cosmos. And the gas gauge he had neglected getting repaired. The Healey refused to start. It hacked a tubercular gasp and the electric fuel pump chittered like ground squirrels. Gasless. Arlo was pounding his head against the Derrington steering wheel when she came out of the supermarket with her groceries.

The nearest open gas station was two miles away, the corner of Franklin and Vine. And the only other car on the lot was hers. Arlo lurched out of the Healey and pursued her. His head ached terribly.

"Hey!"

"One step closer, Sunny Jim, and I give you an *ipponseoinage* over my right hip you'll never forget." She dumped the bag of groceries into the rear seat of the Dart and turned back quickly as if Arlo were a Vietcong cutthroat. He put his hands atop his head.

"I do not prowoke!"

"Vanish, masher."

"I'm outta gas. Honest."

"Now you are plumbing depths of ludicrousness unknown to Western Man."

"All I want is you should drive me down to the gas station corner of Franklin and Vine. I'll sit in the back seat. I'll sit on my hands. You can tie me up. I'm outta gas, it's late, I gotta headache."

"I don't believe you. You stink."

"Look. You don't trust me all that distance, two miles in the car alone with you, I'll go inside, buy a $2.98 garden hose, and cut off a piece I can use to siphon off a coupla liters of gas. With your permission."

"I'm convinced, get in."

He didn't move. "It's a trick. You'll hit me."

"I believe you. I believe you. Anybody who would volunteer to take a mouthful of gas without being at gunpoint must be telling the truth. Get in."

He sat on his hands all the way there, and back.

Though he was deathly afraid of her, Arlo pressed his meager advantage. With the fumey can of gas burbling into his tank, he stopped her before she could drive away.

"Maybe, uh, you should follow me back to the gas station to fill it up. I might have damaged the manifold housing coupler or something, trying to start it. It might conk out."

"There is no such thing in that beast as a manifold housing coupler."

"See, I'm driving a lemon. I *need* you to follow me."

"How the hell did I inherit you?"

"In Korea, if you save someone's life, you become responsible for them forever. Nice custom, don't you think?"

She grimaced. "Franz Kafka is up there, writing my life."

Arlo looked out from under thick eyelashes. It was his Jackie-Cooper-As-The-Kid look. "I've come to depend on you. You're so self-possessed."

Half an hour later they were on common civility terms, sharing the best chili dogs in Los Angeles, at Boris's Stand, corner of La Brea and Melrose, all beef, plenty hot, lotsa onions, two bits, you couldn't do better.

And half an hour later—inexplicably—they were on the verge of what Arlo called "a warm, humid experience," having driven out to Los Angeles International Airport, to a road bisecting a landing approach, where the jets landed directly over their heads.

"Can you tell me what we are doing here at 2:48 A.M. in the morning?" she asked Arlo. He said nothing. She rolled down the window. "Can *any*body tell me what I'm doing here at this dumb hour with a very possibly axe murderer and rapist?" she screamed into the night. There was no answer.

Helluva sense of whimsy, Arlo mused, edging closer.

"Tell me about yourself," Arlo gambited.

"This theatrical pose I wear is merely a snare and a delusion. I am, in reality, Anastasia, true Czarina of all the Russias, and I'm wearing a plastic nose. My father was Lamont Cranston, and he met an untimely end via the worst case of Dutch Elm Blight ever diagnosed at Johns Hopkins. He contracted it from Lupe Velez during a mad, passionate night deep in the heart of Mt. Etna, where my father was conducting guided tours. I am engaged to a Doberman Pinscher."

Helluva sense of whimsy, Arlo mused, edging closer.

"Stop edging closer," she suggested violently.

"Look!" Arlo said, "Here comes one."

The Boeing 707 came out of the night like Sinbad's roc, screaming shrilly, and Anastasia screamed shriller.

The great silvery bulk of it, totally obscuring the sky, sailed out of the blackness mere feet above them, all vastness and terror, like a flat stone two blocks long, skimmed over water, and shred their silences past them. The 707 touched down almost as soon as it passed over them, and an instant later was a half mile down the runway.

Anastasia had pulled closer to Arlo. She was now wrapped in his arms.

"Scary, isn't it?" Arlo smiled.

"I wet myself," she said. She did not seem delighted with Arlo.

He leaned across slightly and kissed her. "Easy," she said, inserting an elbow into the conversation. "And that's an order, not a description."

Progress! thought Arlo. "We'd better be getting back."

He started the car and made a U-turn.

"That was a helluva whimsical thing you said, when the plane passed over," Arlo chuckled.

"Which?"

"About what you did when the plane—"

"It was a statement of fact."

At Arlo's apartment, after she had hung things up to dry, he offered her an omelet. "I can make seven different varieties, all delicious."

She aimed a finger at him. "You're lucky I share an apartment with a light sleeper, because underwear or no underwear, I wouldn't have let you con me into coming up here."

"Spanish, Viennese, Ranch-style, Albanian—"

"You have an indomitable will. Nothing seems to get to you. Brick walls and your head have much in common."

"Corsican, Paraguayan—"

"Look: I'm very hungry, mostly because you had the bad taste to remind me, and I'd like nothing better than a good omelet; but when I say *nothing* better, I mean exactly that. You are still a casual pick-up, even though for some nutty reason we have managed to travel along this far together and my bikini briefs are drying over your shower curtain. Does my message penetrate?"

Arlo grinned infectiously. "Like a call from the spirit world. My father taught me. He was a master chef in New York hotels most of his life, except for a couple of years when he was captaining the kitchen of a luxury liner. Spanish, Corsican, Tibetan, German-Bavarian—"

She sat down on the arm of an overstuffed Morris chair, courtesy of the landlord. She pulled his blue bathrobe closer around her. A flash of leg reminded him there was nothing between them but the robe. "You know, Arlo, I have to tell you, concisely, I think you are the bummest trip I have ever been on. Not only are you funny looking, but there is a perceptible animal cunning in your face, and very frankly, but *nothing* could get me to go to bed with you, so forget the whole idea right now. How the hell do you make an Albanian omelet?"

Any second now, she'll notice them, Arlo gloated.

He moved in and kissed her. It was an act of humor on his part, an act of politeness on hers. "Now that we have that out of the way," he smiled, "one Albanian omelet coming up."

He vanished into the utility kitchen, tiny for the white stucco unit (furniture courtesy of landlord and Thrift Shops; what might have been termed Early Impecunity) but more than sufficient for his needs. He proceeded to make a Spanish omelet, which was, in actuality, the *only* kind he could make, and that the result of endless hours following the recipe in *Fanny Farmer's Boston Cookbook*. Escoffier had no trepidation about living in the same universe with Arlo. But this he *had* learned (Arlo, not Escoffier): one cannot make an omelet without breaking eggs. Arlo had broken dozens.

He threw in a palmful of paprika and brown sugar and oregano.

"You collect coins," she called from the other room.

Beachhead secured! he rejoiced.

"My father did," he answered, without turning from the stove. He had no need to go in the other room to see what she was doing. He could picture it perfectly. The picture was always the same, because it always happened just this way. She was standing before the flat, glass-covered case about the size of an opened newspaper. It stood on its own black wrought iron pedestal, a Herman Miller design that had been bolted to the underside of the case. The little Tensor lamp was turned in such a way that the beam fell directly on the arrangement of coins lying on their black velvet pad in the case.

"They're very handsome," she called.

"Yes, they were Dad's pride and joy," he said, not turning from the stove.

"They must be valuable," she said.

He turned from the stove, smiling a secret smile. Then he turned back to the stove, and scraped the ruined omelet into the sink disposal, started over again with gritted teeth, and knew he shouldn't have turned from the stove.

When he brought out their plates, and set them on the coffee table, she was still leaning over the case, mesmerized, hands behind her back, not wanting to put fingerprints on the carefully polished glass. Arlo smiled his own Spanish omelet of a secret smile.

She looked at the omelet uneasily as he went back to get the quart of milk from the refrigerator. She was back at the coin case when he returned with it. "Your omelet'll get cold," and she came over to the sofa, sat down and addressed herself to the egg without realizing Arlo was looking at the exposed left thigh.

"You keep them out where anyone could steal them?"

Arlo shrugged and ate a bite of omelet. It was awful. She wasn't saying anything about hers, however. "I seldom have people over," he explained. And mused that while he had just lied outrageously, the usual modus operandi had not been like this evening's. Underwear. He'd have to examine the ramifications of that ploy, at his leisure.

"It took Dad over thirty years to find all those. Myself, I could never understand the kick he got out of it. They never meant much to me—until he died . . ."

He choked up. She paused with a forkful on her way to mouth. The appraisal she gave him was the crucial one: if he could pass the sincerity test, the rest was downhill.

"But when he died . . . ?" she prompted him.

Arlo plunged on. "It was all he left me. All those years he worked so damned hard, and he had so little to show for it. Just those coins. He left them to me, and well, it may have seemed a dumb way to spend time, collecting coins, when I was younger and he was around. But when he was gone, they became very important. It was like keeping a little bit of him with me. He was a good guy—never really understood me, but I suppose that's typical with the parents of our generation."

Lofty. Very lofty, and as far away from sex talk as he could get without going into withdrawal. "They must be quite valuable," she said again.

He nodded, munching. "As a matter of fact, they are. Twice I got real flat and decided to sell them, but when it got right down to the old nitty-gritty, I couldn't do it. Once I took a job selling shoes and the other time I hocked my tape recorder. I didn't realize how important they'd become to me till then. They were worth about fifteen hundred when he died, but by now I could probably trade the collection in on a Maserati if I wanted to."

She seemed appalled. "That's a terrible idea."

He chuckled. "I was only kidding. I wouldn't do it. They meant so much to Dad, I guess it's rubbed off. They're important to me now. That nickel in the upper left hand corner is worth about two hundred and fifty bucks alone. How's the omelet?"

"Good." She smiled at him. He had depth now. Substance. A past. A present, lying there on black velvet.

When they finished eating she took the plates to the sink and washed them, and used a Brillo pad on the gooey skillet. Arlo watched quick flashes of her through the doorway, as she moved back and forth from the sink. He sank down in the sofa and felt secure. When she was finished and had dried her hands on the little dish towel, he called in to her, "There's a bottle of hand lotion under the sink."

He heard her open the cabinet. A few minutes later she reentered the living room, dry-washing her hands. "I gather you often have ladies wash your dishes; that bottle of lotion is almost empty."

"Not too often."

"It's a kindness only a man with female companions would appreciate."

"I appreciate all sorts of things; like your *doing* the dishes. That was very nice. You looked at home in there." He extended his hands. She took them.

"The least a girl can do is pay for her supper." He drew her down beside him on the sofa, but she scrunched away. "Whoops. Let me rephrase that."

Arlo scrunched closer, tried for a kiss, aimed for her lips, landed on her cheek.

"I thought we had all that settled?" she reminded him.

He ran an all-seeing finger across her high cheekbone. "If you were scrawny like a Keane painting, you could be a model with a face like that."

"I'm part Indian. My grandfather on my mother's side. I could even—" she slapped his hand away from there, "—speak a little Sioux when I was a kid." She slapped his hand a second time. "Please, Arlo." She stood up suddenly. "I'd better check, make sure my things are dry by now."

"Stay. I'll be good. Word of honor."

"I know about your honor. Tarnished."

"I've never spoken to an Indian before. An *Amer*indian, as a matter of cold fact. Talk some Sioux to me."

She took a step toward the bathroom, he grabbed her hand and she let him. "I don't remember any."

"It's just like English, isn't it?" Nonsense syllables. He was gibbering, and they both knew what was happening. "I mean, you leave out a few of the small words and put 'um' at the end of the others? Me wantum you?"

She laughed. He stood up and tried to hold her, but she did a fast two-step.

"I have the feeling," she said, imbedding a restraining finger in his chest (the fingernail was long, painted, and hurt like hell), "that I'm being turned into a tease. And I'm not. Maybe I'm not as bright as I ought to be, but . . . oh hell, I refuse to defend myself." Her voice softened. "Thanks for the omelet. I've got to get dressed. If my roommate wakes up and I'm not back she'll call the safe and loft squad, or whoever it is they call when a girl's been broken and entered."

They looked at each other for a long moment, over a distance that she increased geometrically as the micro-instants elapsed.

When she had attained a distance of several light-years, there in the dim living room, she turned away and went to the bathroom.

Consider now: all that firm girlstuff, busily hooking bra under breasts, pulling it around so the cups are in front, pulling it up, stuffing and handling gingerly; stepping into, putting on, pulling over, adjusting to, smoothing out, hooking on, slipping into. While over there, beyond lath and plaster, Arlo, Great White Hunter, coming to a rapid boil. Knowing now was the penultimate moment. And in some ways the best moment of all, for now was all anticipation without even the slightest disappointment. Now she was perfect, unflawed, and the best since Helen of Troy (and what's *she* doing now?).

She came out of the bathroom, gathered everything she needed, and as he made to rise, put out a palm against the air between them. He sank back. She smiled with genuine affection, nodded slightly as if to say it could never be, oh my Heathcliff, and went to the door.

No exit lines.

She turned the knob and pulled the door inward.

Quietly now, Arlo: "Do me one small favor before you go?" She turned and looked at him, wide open now that safety was a mere threshold away. He got up and went to the bookshelf near the kitchen. He took down a large Royal Doulton toby jug of Dick Turpin the Highwayman, and shook a key out of it.

Anastasia didn't move from the doorway. She merely watched as he moved smoothly across the room to the coin case, inserted the key in the lock, turned it, opened the glass top and removed something. He closed the case, relocked it, returned the key to the toby jug, and came to her, there in the doorway.

"Everybody grows up sometime," he said. "I'm going to have to sell this collection some day, probably some day soon. My Healey's about ready for Medicare. So what I'd like you to do for me—"

He hesitated, beat beat beat, then offered his hand to her, opening the fist. The penny lay there against his palm, and she stopped breathing.

He was humble about it. Truly humble. "I remember Dad coming home with this one. He was like a kid with a new toy. A guest on shipboard had given it to him in exchange for some well-made *pêche flambée*. Turned out to be rare."

"I can't!" she said absolutely.

He went on swiftly. "Oh, it's not as expensive as—say, a 1909 'S' mint Indian Head, or some of the English pennies—but it's pretty rare. Something about they pulled it off the counters soon after it was minted. I want you to have it. Please."

"I can't!"

"Please." He put the penny in her hand. She held it as though it was stuck together of dust and spiderwebs, just looking at it down there, blazing and glowing in her palm. "It was my Dad's, then it was mine, and now it's yours. You can't refuse a gift someone gives you like that."

"But why? Why me?"

"Because," he shrugged as a little boy might shrug, "you're nice people. Make it into a pin or something."

He closed her fingers around it. "Now, good night. I'll be talking to you."

He walked away from her and switched on the television set. It was a test pattern. He sat down and watched it for a moment, and then he heard the door close. When he turned at the sound, he was all awareness at that instant, she was still in the room, leaning against the door, fist closed over the wonder that lay therein, watching him.

Arlo woke just after one o'clock the next day. The scent of her perfume still occupied the other side of the bed. He stretched, kicked the sheet off his naked legs, and said to the familiar ceiling, "My, that was nice."

He showered and put the coffee on.

Then, as he finished dressing, he opened the little drawer beneath his cufflink box—the drawer you might not realize was there unless you were specifically looking for a little drawer right there in that particular cufflink box—and in anticipation of the coming evening, removed one of the three remaining old pennies (the last of fourteen he had bought in the batch) and carried it into the living room. As he unlocked the coin case, he made a mental note to stop down at the coin shop and pick up another batch of old pennies. He was running low.

He relocked the case, and was returning the key to the toby jug, when the phone rang.

He picked it up and said, "Hi," and got venom poured right into his ear.

"You bastard! You lying, low, thieving, seducing sonofabitch! You miserable con artist! You plague-bearer, you Typhoid Mary; you Communist fag ratfink bastard!"

"Hi."

"You low scum dog, you. You crud. Of all the low, rotten, ugly, really outright evil demeaning stinky things a creep fascist right-wing louse could pull, *that* was the most vile, nauseating, despicable, hideous—"

"Hi, Anastasia. What's new?"

"What's new, you shit? I'll *tell* you what's new! Among other things, that coin of your dear old Daddy's is new. New enough to be worth exactly one lousy cent. Not a rare! Not a valuable! Not a nothing, *that's* what's new!"

Horror coursed through Arlo's strangled words. "Wh—what?" He coughed, choked, swallowed hard. "What're you talking about? Whaddaya mean? Tell me...*tell me,* dammit!"

Her voice was less steamy. There was an edge of doubt now. "I took it down today, there's a numismatist in the office building where I work—"

Affront *lived* in his shock. "You *what?!?* You had my *father's* penny appraised? You did that? What kind of a person—"

"Listen, don't try to make me the heavy, Arlo! It wasn't valuable at all. It was just a miserable old penny like a million others, and you got me into bed with it, that's what! You lied to me!"

Softly, he crept in between her rebuilding attack. "I don't believe it."

"Well, it's true."

"No."

"Yes, yes, and yes! Worth a penny. Period."

"Oh my God," he husked. "Dad never knew. He always thought...how cruel...how awfully cruel...that man who gave it to him on shipboard...I can't believe it...oh Jeezus..."

There was silence at the other end.

"Oh, God..." he murmured. Then, after a while, gently, "I'm sorry, I didn't know...listen, I don't think I want to talk any more...excuse me..."

She stopped him. "Arlo?"

Silence.

"Arlo?" Very gently from her.

Silence again, then, almost a whisper: "Yeah...?"

"I'm sorry. I didn't mean to—"

"Forget it."

"No, really. It was a rotten thing for me to do. I'd—I'd like to—"

"It isn't necessary."

"No, really, I mean it. I'd like to . . . are you busy tonight . . . could I come over and maybe—"

Arlo held the phone with one hand, unlocked the case with the other. As he removed the penny, making a mental note to perhaps put off that trip to the coin shop for a week or so, he said with absolute sincerity into the mouthpiece, "I guess so. Yeah, okay. Why don't you stop off at a deli and pick up some corned beef and pickles and we can . . ."

The Man Who Was
Heavily into Revenge

INTRODUCTION

This trip is mapped through a dark passage in my recent past. It deals with a mortal dread we all share: the madness that betides us when we have been fucked over once too often by the petty thugs and conscienceless pillagers who infest the world—from venal politicians who manipulate our lives for personal gain, down to the building contractors who promise decent craftsmanship and leave you with leaking roofs. At some point you go blind with rage. *Why me?* you wail! I don't cheat people, I do my job honestly and with care...how can creeps like this be permitted to flourish?

Well, I offer you the words of the Polish poet Edward Yashinsky, who said, "Fear not your enemies, for they can only kill you; fear not your friends, for they can only betray you. Fear only the indifferent, who permit the killers and betrayers to walk safely on the earth."

When I was a kid there was a popular novel titled *Leave Her to Heaven.* Though the book has long since passed out of my memory, the title has stuck. I don't believe there is such a thing as "divine retribution." The universe is neither malign nor benign. It's *just there,* and it's too busy keeping itself together to balance the scales when some feep has jerked you around. I am a strong adherent of the philosophy that one must seek retribution oneself.

And if the courts of the land cannot deliver up these people to justice then don't form a lynch party, because that forces you to become what you have beheld, as vile as those who did you dirt. Instead, unleash primal forces against them. Force entry and take a trip through their lives in ways they will find most troublesome.

Write a story and let the power of the massmind git'm!

The Man Who Was
Heavily into Revenge

WILLIAM WEISEL pronounced his name why-*zell*, but many of the unfortunates for whom he had done remodeling and construction pronounced it *weasel*.

He had designed and built a new guest bathroom for Fred Tolliver, a man in his early sixties who had retired from the active life of a studio musician with the foolish belief that his fifteen-thousand-dollar-per-year annuity would sustain him in comfort. Weisel had snubbed the original specs on the job, had substituted inferior materials for those required by the codes, had used cheap Japanese pipe instead of galvanized or stressed plastic, had eschewed lath and plaster for wallboard that left lumpy seams, had skirted union wages by ferrying in green card workers from Tijuana every morning by dawn light, had—in short—done a spectacularly crummy job on Fred Tolliver's guest bathroom. That was the first mistake.

And for all of this ghastly workmanship, Weisel had overcharged Fred Tolliver by nine thousand dollars. That was the second mistake.

Fred Tolliver called William Weisel. His tone was soft and almost apologetic. Fred Tolliver was a gentle man, not given to fits of pique or demonstrations of anger. He politely asked Weisel to return and set matters to rights. William Weisel laughed at Fred Tolliver and told him that he had lived up to the letter of the original contract, that he would do nothing. That was the third mistake.

Putatively, what Weisel said was true. Building inspectors had been greased and the job had been signed off: legal according to the building codes. Legally, William Weisel was in the clear; no suit could be brought. Ethically it was a different matter. But even threats of revocation of license could not touch him.

Nonetheless, Fred Tolliver had a rotten guest bathroom, filled with leaks and seamed walls that were already cracking and bubbles in the vinyl flooring from what was certainly a break in the hot water line and pipes that clanked when the faucets were turned on, if they could *be* turned on.

Fred Tolliver asked for repairs more than once.

After a while, William Weisel's wife, Belle, who often acted as his secretary, to save a few bucks when they didn't want to hire a Kelly Girl, would not put through the calls.

Fred Tolliver told her, softly and politely, "Please convey to Mr. Weisel—" and he pronounced it why-*zell,* "—my feelings of annoyance. Please advise him that I won't stand for it. This is an awful thing he's done to me. It's not fair, it's not right."

She was chewing gum. She examined her nails. She had heard this all before: married to Weisel for eleven years: all of this, many times. "Lissen, Mistuh Tollivuh, whaddaya want *me* to do about it. *I* can't do nothing about it, y'know. I only work here. I c'n tell 'im, that's *all* I c'n do, is tell 'im you called again."

"But you're his wife! You can see how he's robbed me!"

"Lissen, Mistuh Tollivuh, I don't haveta lissen to this!"

It was the cavalier tone, the utterly uncaring tone: impertinent, rude, dismissing him as if he were a crank, a weirdo, as if he weren't asking only for what was due him. It was like a goad to an already maddened bull.

"This isn't fair!"

"I'll tell 'im, I'll tell 'im. Jeezus, I'm hanging up now."

"I'll get even! I will! There has to be justice—"

She dropped the receiver into its rest heavily, cracking her gum with annoyance, looking ceilingward like one massively put upon. She didn't even bother to convey the message to her husband.

And that was the biggest mistake of all.

The electrons dance. The emotions sing. Four billion, resonating like insects. The hive mind of the masses. The emotional gestalt. The charge builds and builds, surging down the line seeking a focus. The weakest link through which to discharge itself. Why this focus and not that? Chance, proximity, the tiniest fracture for leakage. You, I, him, her. Everyman, Anyman; the crap shoot selection is whatever man or woman born of man and woman whose rage at *that* moment is *that* potent.

Everyman: Fred Tolliver. Unknowing confluence.

He pulled up at the pump that dispensed supreme, and let the Rolls idle for a moment before shutting it off. When the attendant leaned in at the window, Weisel smiled around his pipe and said, "Morning, Gene. Fill it up with extra."

"Sorry, Mr. Weisel," Gene said, looking a little sad, "but I can't sell you any gas."

"Why the hell not? You out?"

"No, sir; just got our tanks topped off last night. Still can't sell you any."

"Why the hell not?!"

"Fred Tolliver doesn't want me to."

Weisel stared for a long moment. He couldn't have heard correctly. He'd been gassing up at this station for eleven years. He didn't even know they *knew* that creep Tolliver. "Don't be an asshole, Gene. Fill the damned tank!"

"I'm sorry, sir. No gas for you."

"What the hell is Tolliver to you? A relative or something?"

"No, sir. I never met him. Wouldn't know him if he drove in right now."

"Then what . . . what the hell . . . I—I—"

But nothing he could say would get Gene to pump one liter of gas into the Rolls.

Nor would the attendants at the next *six* stations down the avenue. When the Rolls ran out, a mile from his office, Weisel *almost* had time to pull to the curb. Not quite. He ran dry in the middle of Ventura Boulevard and tried to turn toward the curb, but though traffic had been light around him just a moment before, somehow it was now packing itself bumper-to-bumper. He turned his head wildly this way and that, dumbfounded at how many cars had suddenly pulled onto the boulevard around him. He could not get out of the crunch. It wouldn't have mattered. Improbably, for this non-business area, for the first time in his memory, there were *no* empty parking spaces at the curb.

Cursing foully, he put it in neutral, rolled down the window so he could hold the steering wheel from outside, and got out of the silent Rolls. He slammed the door, cursing Fred Tolliver's every breath, and stepped away from the car. He heard the hideous rending of irreplaceable fabric. His five hundred dollar cashmere suit jacket had been caught in the jamb.

A large piece of lovely fabric, soft as a doe's eye, wondrously ecru-closer-to-beige-than-fawn-colored, tailor-made for him in Paris, his most favorite jacket hung like slaughtered meat from the door. He whimpered; an involuntary sob of pain.

Then: "What the hell is going *on!*" he snarled, loud enough for pedestrians to hear. It was not a question, it was an imprecation. There was no answer; none was required; but there was the sound of thunder far off across the San Fernando Valley. Los Angeles was in the grip of a two-year drought, but there was a menacing buildup of soot-gray clouds over the San Bernardinos.

He reached in through the window, tried to turn the wheel toward the curb, but with the engine off the power steering prevented easy movement. But he strained and strained . . . and something went snap! in his groin. Incredible pain shot down both legs and he bent double, clutching himself. Flashbulbs went off behind his eyes. He stumbled around in small circles, holding himself awkwardly. Many groans. Much anguish. He leaned against the Rolls, and the pain began to subside; but he had broken something down there. After a few minutes he was able to stand semierect. His shirt was drenched with sweat. His deodorant was wearing off. Cars were swerving around the Rolls, honking incessantly, drivers swearing at him. He had to get the Rolls out of the middle of the street.

Still clutching his crotch with one hand, jacket hanging from him in tatters, beginning to smell very bad, William Weisel put his shoulder to the car, grabbed the steering wheel and strained once again; the wheel went around slowly. He readjusted himself, excruciating pain pulsing through his pelvis, put his shoulder against the window post and tried to push the behemoth. He thought of compacts and tiny sports cars. The Rolls moved a fraction of an inch, then slid back.

Sweat trickled into his eyes, making them sting. He huffed and lunged and applied as much pressure as the pain would permit. The car would not move.

He gave up. He needed help. *Help!*

Standing in the street behind the car, clutching his groin, jacket flapping around him, smelling like something ready for disposal, he signaled wildly for assistance with his free hand. But no one would stop. Thunder rolled around the Valley, and Weisel saw what looked like a pitchfork of lightning off across the flats where Van Nuys, Panorama City and North Hollywood lay gasping for water.

Cars thundered down on him and swerved at the very last moment, like matadors performing a complicated *verónica*. Several cars seemed to speed up, in fact, as they approached him, and he had the crazy impression the drivers were hunched over the wheels, lips skinned back from clenched teeth, like rabid wild things intent on killing him. Several nearly sideswiped him. He barely managed to hobble out of the way. One Datsun came so close that its side-view mirror ripped a nasty, raw gash down the entire right side of the Rolls. He cursed and gesticulated and pleaded. No one would stop. In fact, one fat woman leaned out of her window as her husband zoomed past, and she yelled something nasty. He caught only the word "Tolliver!"

Finally, he just left it there, with the hood up like the mouth of a hungry bird.

He walked the mile to his office, thinking he would call the Automobile Club to come and tow it to a station where it could be filled. He didn't have the time or the patience to walk to a gas station, get a can of fuel, and return to fill the tank. During the mile-long walk he even had time to wonder if he would be *able* to buy a can of gasoline.

Tolliver! God *damn* that old man!

There was no one in the office.

It took him a while to discover that fact, because he couldn't get an elevator in his building. He stood in front of one after another of the doors, waiting for a cage to come down, but they all seemed determined to stop at the second floor. Only when other passengers waited did an elevator arrive, and then he was always in front of the wrong one. He would dash to the open door, just as the others entered, but before he could get his hand into the opening to stop the retarder bar from slamming against the frame, the door would seem to slide faster, as if it possessed a malevolent intelligence. It went on that way for ten minutes, till it became obvious to him that something was terribly, hideously, inexplicably wrong.

So he took the stairs.

(On the stairs he somehow slipped and skinned his right knee as one of the steps caught his heel and tore it off his right shoe.)

Limping like a cripple, the tatters of his jacket flapping around him, clutching his groin, blood seeping through his pants to stain, he reached the eleventh floor and tried to open the door. It was, of course, for the first time in the thirty-five-year history of the building, locked.

He waited fifteen minutes and the door suddenly opened as a secretary, carrying some papers up one flight to the Xerox center, came boiling through. He barely managed to catch the door on its pneumatic closer. He stumbled frantically onto the eleventh floor and, like a man emerging gratefully from a vast desert to find an oasis, he fled down the corridor to the offices of the Weisel Construction Corporation.

There was no one in the office.

It was not locked. Was, in fact, wholly unattended and wide open to thieves, if such had chosen that office for plundering. The receptionist was not there, the estimators were not there, not even Belle, his wife, who served as secretary when he didn't want to hire a Kelly Girl, was there.

However, she had left him a note:

I'm leaving you. By the time you read this I will have already been to the bank and emptied the joint account. Don't try to find me. Goodbye.

Weisel sat down. He had the beginnings of what he was certain was a migraine, though he had never had a migraine in his life. He didn't know whether, in the vernacular of the United States Army, to shit or go blind.

He was not a stupid man. He had been given more than

sufficient evidence that something malevolent and purely anti-Weisel was floating across the land. It was out to get him...had, in fact, *already* gotten him...had, in fact, made a well-ordered and extremely comfortable life turn into a nasty, untidy, noisome pile of doggie-doo.

And it was named *Tolliver*.

Fred Tolliver...! How the hell...? Who does he know that could...? How did he...?

None of the questions reached a conclusion. He could not even formulate them. Clearly, this was insanity. No one he knew, not Gene at the gas station, not the people in the cars, not Belle, not his staff, not the *car door* or the building's *elevators* even knew who Tolliver was! Well, Belle knew, but what the hell did she have to do with *him?*

Okay, so it *wasn't* going so good with Belle. So they *hadn't* really reconciled that innocent little thing he'd had with the lab technician at Mt. Sinai. So what? That was no reason for her to ditch a good thing. *Damn that Tolliver!*

He slammed his hand onto the desk, missed slightly, caught the edge and drove a thick splinter of wood into the fat of his palm, at the same time scattering the small stack of telegrams across his lap and the floor.

Wincing with pain, he sucked at the splinter till it came out. He used one of the telegram envelopes to blot the blood from his hand.

Telegrams?

He opened the first one. The Bank of America, Beverly Hills branch 213, was pleased to advise him they were calling due his loans. All five of them. He opened the second one. His broker, Shearson Hayden Stone Inc., was overjoyed to let him know that all sixteen of the stocks in which he had speculated heavily, on margin, of course, had virtually plummeted off the big board and he had to come up with seventy-seven thousand dollars by noon today or his portfolio was wiped out. It was a quarter to eleven by the wall clock. (Or had it, inexplicably, stopped?) He opened the third one. He had failed his est class and Werner Erhard himself had sent the telegram, adding in what Weisel took to be an unnecessarily gloating tone, that Weisel had "no human potential worth expanding." He opened the fourth one. His Wassermann had come back from Mt. Sinai. It was positive. He opened the fifth one. The Internal Revenue Service was ecstatic at being able to let him know they were planning to audit his returns for the past five years, and were seeking a loophole in the tax laws that permitted them to go back further, possibly to the start of the Bronze Age.

There were others, five or six more. He didn't bother opening them. He didn't want to learn who had died, or that the state of Israel had discovered Weisel was, in actuality, Bruno "The Butcher" Krutzmeier, a former prison guard at Mauthausen, personally responsible for the deaths of three thousand Gypsies, Trade Unionists, Jews, Bolsheviks and Weimar democrats, or that the U.S. Coast and Geodetic Survey Department was gleefully taking this opportunity to advise him that the precise spot over which he sat was expected to collapse into the magma at the center of the Earth and by the way we've canceled your life insurance.

He let them lie.

The clock on the wall had, to be sure, stopped dead.

In fact, the electricity had been turned off.

The phone did not ring. He picked it up. Of course. It——like its friend the clock—was stone dead.

Tolliver! Tolliver! How was he *doing* all this?

Such things simply *do not* happen in an ordered universe of draglines and scoop-shovels and reinforced concrete.

He sat and thought dark, murderous thoughts about that old sonofabitch, Fred Tolliver.

A 747 boomed sonically overhead and the big heavy-plate window of his eleventh floor office cracked, splintered, and fell in around his feet.

Unknowing confluence of resonating emotions, Fred Tolliver sat in his house, head in hands, miserable beyond belief, aware only of pain and anger. His cello lay on its back on the floor beside him. He had tried playing a little today, but all he could think of was that terrible man Weisel, and the terrible bathroom that was filling with water, and the terrible stomach pains his feelings of hatred were giving him.

Electrons resonate. So do emotions.

Speak of "damned places" and one speaks of locations where powerful emotional forces have been penned up. One cannot doubt, if one has ever been inside a prison where the massed feelings of hatred, deprivation, claustrophobia and brutalization have seeped into the very stones. One can feel it. Emotions resonate: at a political rally, a football game, an encounter group, a rock concert, a lynching.

There are four billion people in the world. A world that has grown so complex and uncaring with systems and brutalization of individuals because of the inertia produced by those systems' perpetuation of self, that merely to live is to be assaulted daily by circumstances. Electrons dance. The emotions sing. Four billion, resonating like insects. The charge is built up; the surface tension is reached; the limit of elasticity is passed; the charge seeks release; the focus is sought: the weakest link, the fault line, the most tremblingly frangible element, AnyTolliver, EveryTolliver.

Like the discharge of a lightning bolt, the greater the charge on the Tolliver, the greater its tendency to escape. The force of the four billion driving the electrons in their mad dance away from the region of highest excess toward the region of greatest deficiency. Pain as electromotive force. Frustration as electric potential. The electrons jump the insulating gap of love and friendship and kindness and humane behavior and the power is unleashed.

Like the discharge of the lightning bolt, the power seeks and finds its focus, leaps the gap, and the bolt of energy is unleashed.

Does the lightning rod know it is draining off the dangerous electrical charge? Is there sentience in a Leyden jar? Does not the voltaic pile continue to sleep while current is drawn off? Does the focus know it has unleashed the anger and frustration of the four billion?

Fred Tolliver sat in misery, the cello forgotten, the pain of having been cheated, of being impotent against the injustice, eating at his stomach. His silent scream: at that moment the most dominant in the entire universe. Chance. It could have been anyone; or perhaps, as Chesterton said, "Coincidences are a spiritual sort of puns."

His phone rang. He did not move to pick up the receiver. It rang again. He did not move. His stomach burned and roiled. There was a scorched-earth desperation in him. Nine *thousand* dollars overcharge. Thirty-seven hundred dollars by the original contract. Twelve thousand seven hundred dollars. He had had to take a second mortgage on the house. Five more months than the estimated two Weisel had said it would take to complete the job. Seven months of filth and plaster dust and inept workmen tramping through his little house with mud and dirt and dropping cigarette butts on his floor.

I'm sixty-two years old, he thought, frantically. *My God, I'm an old man. A moment ago I was just middle-aged, and now I'm an old man . . . I never felt old before. It's good Betsy never lived to see me like this; she would cry. But this thing with the bathroom is a* terrible *thing, an awful thing, it's made me an old man, poor, in financial straits; and I don't know how to save myself. He's ruined my life . . . he's killed me . . . I'll never be able to get even, to put away a little . . . if the thing with the knees gets any worse, there could be big doctor bills, specialists maybe . . . the Blue Cross would never cover it . . . what am I going to do, please God help me . . . what am I going to do?*

He was an old man, retired and very tired, who had thought he could make it through. He had figured it out so he could just barely slide through. But the pains in the back of his knees had begun three years before, and though they had not flared up in sixteen months, he remembered how he would simply fall down, suddenly, ludicrously, fall down: the legs prickling with pins and needles as though he had sat cross-legged for a long time. He was afraid to think about the pains too much. They might come back if he thought about them too much.

But he didn't really believe that thinking about things could make them happen. Thinking didn't make things change in the real world. Fred Tolliver did not know about the dance of the emotions, the resonance of the electrons. He did not know about a sixty-two-year-old lightning rod that leaked off the terror and frustration of four billion people, all crying out silently just as Fred Tolliver cried out. For help that never came.

The phone continued to ring. He did not think about the pains he had felt in the back of his knees, as recently as sixteen months ago. He did not think about it, because he did not want it to return. It was only a low-level throbbing now, and he wanted it to stay that way. He didn't want to feel pins and needles. He *wanted* his money back. He *wanted* the sound of gurgling under the floor of the guest bathroom to stop. *He wanted William Weisel to make good.*

He answered the phone. It rang once too often for him to ignore it.

"Hello?"

"Mr. Tolliver? Is that you?"

"Yes, this is Fred Tolliver. Who's calling?"

"Evelyn Hand. I haven't heard from you about my violin, and I'm going to need it late next week . . ."

He had forgotten. In all the anguish with Weisel, he had forgotten Evelyn Hand, and her damaged violin. And she had paid him already.

"Oh, my gosh, Miss Hand, I'm awfully sorry! I've just had the most awful business going on these last months, a man built me a guest bathroom, and he overcharged me nine thousand dollars, and it's all broken and . . ."

He stopped. This was unbecoming. He coughed with embarrassment, giving himself a moment to gather his composure. "I'm just as terribly sorry and ashamed as I can be, Miss Hand. I haven't had a chance to get to the repairs. But I know you need it a week from today . . ."

"A week from *yesterday*, Mr. Tolliver. Thursday, not Friday."

"Oh. Yes, of course. Thursday." She was a nice woman, really. Very slim, delicate fingers and a gentle, warm voice. He had thought perhaps they might go to the Smorgasbord for a meal, and they might get to know each other. He wanted companionship. It was so necessary; now, particularly, it was so necessary. But the memory of Betsy was always there, singing softly within him; and he had said nothing to Evelyn Hand.

"Are you there, Mr. Tolliver?"

"Uh, yes. Yes, of course. Please forgive me. I'm so wrought up these days. I'll get to it right away. Please don't you worry about it."

"Well, I *am* rather concerned." She hesitated, as though reluctant to speak. She drew a deep breath and plunged on: "I did pay you in advance for the repairs, because you said you needed the money for bills, and . . ."

He didn't take offense. He understood perfectly. She had said something that otherwise she would have considered *déplacé*, but she was distraught and wanted to make the point as firmly as she could without being overly offensive.

"I'll get to it today, Miss Hand; I promise."

It would take time. It was a good instrument, a fine, old Gagliano. He knew he could finish the repairs in time if he kept at it without distraction.

Her tone softened. "Thank you, Mr. Tolliver. I'm sorry to have bothered you, but . . . you understand."

"Of course. Don't give it a thought. I'll call as soon as it's ready. I'll give it special attention, I promise."

"You're very kind."

They said their goodbyes and he stopped himself from suggesting dinner when the violin was ready. There was always time for that later, when appropriate. When the business with the bathroom was settled.

And that brought him back to the state of helpless fury and pain. That terrible man, Weisel!

Unknowing confluence of four billion resonating emotions, Fred Tolliver sat with head in hands; as the electrons danced.

Eight days later, in a filthy alley behind a boarded-up supermarket that had begun as a sumptuous gilt-and-brocade movie house in 1924, William Weisel sat in filth, trying to eat the butt of a stale loaf of pumpernickel he had stolen from a garbage can. He weighed ninety-seven pounds, had not shaved in seven days, his clothes were stained and torn rags, his shoes had been stolen while he slept, four days earlier, in the doorway outside the Midnight Mission, his eyes were rheumy and he had developed a terrible, wracking cough. The angry crimson weal on his left forearm where the bolt of lightning had just grazed him seemed to be infected. He gagged on the bread, realizing he had missed one of the maggots, and threw the granitelike butt across the alley.

He was incapable of crying. He had cried himself out. He knew, at last, that there was no way to save himself. On the third day, he had tried to get to Tolliver, to beg him to stop; to tell him he would repair the bathroom; to tell him he would build him a new house, a mansion, a palace, *anything!* Just stop this terror! *Please!*

But *he* had been stopped. He could not *get* to Tolliver. The first time he had set his mind to seeing the old man, he had been arrested by a California Highway Patrol officer who had him on his hot sheet for having left the Rolls in the middle of Ventura Boulevard. Weisel had managed to escape on foot, somehow, miraculously.

The second time he had been attacked by a pit bull while

skulking through back yards. He had lost his left pant leg below the knee.

The third time he had actually gotten as far as the street on which Tolliver's house sat, but a seven-car pileup had almost crushed him beneath tons of thundering metal, and he had fled, fearing an aircraft carrier might drop from the sky to bury him.

He knew now that he could not even make amends, that it was inertial, and that he was doomed.

He lay back, waiting for the finish. But it was not to be that easy. The song of the four billion is an unending symphony of incredible complexity. As he lay there, a derelict stumbled into the alley, saw him, and pulled the straight razor from his jacket pocket. He was almost upon him when William Weisel opened his eyes. He saw the rusty blade coming for his throat, had a moment of absolute mind-numbing horror wash over him, spasmed into shock, and did not hear the sound of the cop's service revolver as the derelict—who had serviced over a dozen other such bums as Weisel in this same manner—was blown in half.

He woke in the drunk tank, looked around, saw the company to which he had been condemned, knew that if he lived it would be through years of horror, and began tearing off strips of rags from what remained of his clothing.

When the attendant came to turn the men out into the exercise area, he found William Weisel hanging from the bars of the door, eyes bulging, tongue protruding like a charred leaf from his mouth. What he could not reconcile was that no one in the cell had even shouted, nor raised a hand to stop Weisel. That, and the look of voiceless anguish on the dead man's face, as though he had glimpsed, just at the instant of death, a view of an *eternity* of voiceless anguish.

The focus could direct the beam, but it could not heal itself. At the very moment that Weisel died, Fred Tolliver—still unaware of what he had done—sat in his home, realizing finally that the contractor had done him in. He could never repay the note, would perhaps have to get work again in some studio, and probably would be unable to do it with sufficient regularity to save the house. His twilight years would be spent in some dingy apartment. The modest final hope of his life had been denied him: he would not be able to just simply get by in peace. It was a terrible lonely thing to contemplate.

The phone rang.

He picked it up wearily. "Yes?"

There was a moment of silence, then the voice of Miss Evelyn Hand came across the line, icily. "Mr. Tolliver, this is Evelyn Hand. I waited all day yesterday. I was unable to participate in the recital. Please have my violin waiting for me, repaired or not."

He was too stunned, too depressed, even to be polite. "Okay."

"I want you to know you have caused me great pain, Mr. Tolliver. You are a very unreliable and evil man. I want you to know I'm going to take steps to rectify this matter. You have taken money from me under false pretenses, you have ruined a great opportunity I had, and you have caused me unnecessary anguish. You will have to pay for your irresponsibility; there must be justice. I will make certain you pay for what you've done!"

"Yes. Yes, of course," he said, dimly, faintly.

He hung up the receiver and sat there.

The emotions sang, the electrons danced, the focus shifted, and the symphony of frustration went on.

Fred Tolliver's cello lay unattended at his feet. He would never get through, just barely slide through. He felt the excruciating pain of pins and needles in his legs.

"No snowflake in an avalanche ever feels responsible."

S. J. LEC

Shoppe Keeper

INTRODUCTION

I was riding down Beverly Glen with Arthur Byron Cover. I said to Arthur, "You know, one of the things that always bothered me about those fantasies in which some dude comes across a magic shop that sells real magic, or three wishes, or genuine love potions, or whatever, is they never told you what kind of life was lived by the proprietor. I mean, where did he get his stock? In what sort of coin could you pay someone for things that valuable? When the dude leaves the shop it always vanishes; where does it go? What happened to the poor schmuck who ran the joint? Huh, answer me that?"

Arthur looked at me seriously and said, "You know, you're a very weird person."

That is how this story came to be written.

To satisfy my curiosity.

And you can stick it in your ear, Cover.

Shoppe Keeper

> *I often wonder what the Vintners buy*
> *One half so precious as the goods*
> *They sell.*
>
> *Stanza LXXXV,*
> *The Rubáyyat of Omar Khyyám*

A PALE, SHORT, young man wearing filthy blue jeans and goat-roper boots worn away at the heels came shuffling down Jamshyd Avenue. As he passed the narrow arcade alleyway, the rusty creaking of a sign hung on chains caught his attention. He stared at the sign with eyes that were just the slightest bit crossed and glazed. The sign proclaimed *Shoppe of Wonders* and beneath those words in curlicued but extremely readable Islamic calligraphy: *Your Heart's Desire.*

Only five feet, two inches tall, the young man paused at the mouth of the alley, stared at the swinging sign for a moment, ran a hand with dirty nails through his long hair, then turned in.

The shoppe was tiny, with leaded-paned windows, dusty and fly-specked. He could not see inside, but there was a dim and golden light shining through the murkiness of the glass. The door handle was a brass lizard with a forked tongue. The young man put his hand on the brass and it was warm. He opened the door, which opened easily, and he went inside.

The shoppe seemed to stretch on before him indefinitely. It defied dimensional description, like an Escher etching. Such a narrow shop could not possibly be so wide, and so deep, and so high. The frontage of the shoppe on the alley had seemed only twenty feet across, but here inside it was easily ten times as wide. The cathedral ceiling hung far away above him in dismal shadows, beamed and sloping, smelling faintly of mildew and sandalwood and tallow. The light that he had seen straining through the obscured glass of the windows was a mere glow, trembling through the murky interior from a distance so far in the rear of the shoppe that it was no more than a suggestion of light.

The shoppe was jammed with goods; filled with goods; odd goods.

Hobbyhorses with peculiarly mad expressions in their eyes, and with foam-flecked lips. Rows and rows of amphorae, tightly stoppered and each marked with indecipherable inscriptions, written with felt-tip pens. Cases of amulets and tokens, some Egyptian-looking, some contemporary and clearly the products of communes. Puppets hung on long wires from the rafters above, a community of brittle, brightly painted figures, all with broken necks. Shelves filled with anemones. A stack of abacuses. A wall of clocks, from all periods, some with nine or fifty-six divisions of time. Bookcases filled with grimoires, daybooks, hornbooks, arcane thesauri, enchiridia, illuminated manuscripts, diaries, palimpsests, incunabula, claviculae, parerga, ana and epilegomena. Incan icons. Glass phials within which emboli floated, turning slowly in a tideless tide. In one corner an enormous freestanding antique mirror with chased brass fittings; another land, dark and distressing, could be seen in the mirror. Showcases containing plastic doggie vomit and ice cubes with cockroaches in them. Whoopee cushions. Meteorites. Thousands of boxes, all sizes, stacked one atop another. Golden balls of all sizes. A butcher's-paper roller screwed to one wall, holding a large roll of gold-foil. Bugles. In one showcase a complete set of English vintage automobile cigarette packet cards, 50 to the set, with one hundred thirty-six duplicates of card #26, the 1925 Vauxhall. Orrises, embroideries of gold and silver lace, tossed willy-nilly over a rattan chair. Bolts of paduasoy. On a Duncan Phyfe table lay a folio of ottava rimas. A shelf containing tins of tennis balls. Oil lamps of the sort Aladdin rubbed to produce his genie.

Dangling from a hook on the wall, an uncountable number of fishhooks, with unnameable things still snagged thereon. Hanging over an arched doorway in the side wall, a gonfalon upon which was emblazoned a booted foot crushing a five-headed serpent, one of whose heads was arched back around with the fangs imbedded in the heel of the foot. Stoppered extra-thick glass bottles of vitriol: blue, green and white. Tubes of bismuth. Clothing racks of hair shirts, habergeons, hauberks and herringbone suits. Potted fleabane. Dolls with quarter-melon slices bitten out of their heads. Several dozen small cases containing dancing mice, dyed in rainbow hues. A glass-fronted cabinet originally intended to hold dental equipment, jammed full of severed paws, monkey, civet, fox, lynx, bear, and others, several with the claws extended, one that looked as though it had been lopped off a *yeti*. Philters labeled "love potion." Hexahedrons. Tomes on epigraphy (all with unreadable titles, of course). Kourbashes coiled on hooks on the wall. Beakers bearing the label "phlogiston." A complete run of *Amazing Stories* dated from April 1926 to December 2009. More grimoires (some in paperback editions). A plethora of keys, of all kinds, sizes, shapes and intricacies. Calling horns, some as simple as a *shofar,* others as cuculiform as a cornucopia. Scruples in breather-jars. Umbilically joined oxymora. Silver seashells that, when placed next to the ear, as the short young man did, reproduced not the sound of the sea, but the sound of the wind between the stars. Shrink-wrapped packages of miniature hydra heads. A thirty-foot-high glass-fronted cabinet that seemed to contain model toy soldiers, until the young man looked closer and saw that the models were not metal at all, but seemed to be miniaturized human beings, frozen and solidified in the moment of combat: the Battle of the Ardennes; Balaklava; Visigoths against Huns; Rough Riders against Villa; Luftwaffe and Wolf Legions at Stalingrad; the Battle of the Little Big Horn; Midway; Chosen Reservoir; the one hundred Spartans at the Hot Gates against Xerxes' millions; the French Foreign Legion at Dien Bien Phu; Spartacus and his gladiator army versus the Roman Imperial Legions . . . each soldier perfect, down to the expression of utter horror as he was whisked off the battlefield, shrunk, and concretized. Polish for the True Lamp. A fragment of Christ's molar in the wafer. Stigmata kits. Packets of dried Granny's Claw. Eyes of newts. Toes of frogs. Spiderweb poultices. Transmigration threads on huge spools bearing the Seal of Solomon on each. Cryogenically frozen pixies, nixies, niads and dryads. Pickled kraken tentacles. Fire-breathing salamanders in asbestos cages. Disintegrator pistols. Saintly relics—fingers, tibiae, fibulae, eyeballs. And everywhere the young man looked, in every nook and crevice, there was rubbish, junk, litter, rags, odds and ends, trash, offscourings, tares, waste, rubble, debris and dregs.

He was deep in a corner, examining what seemed to be 9-mm artillery shells made of sterling silver, when a voice from behind him said, "Those are intended for use in slaying were-dinosaurs. Only been one call for them; chap who swore his vicar changed into a killer stegosaurus at the full of the moon. Unlikely, but you never know. Try to keep up a full stock, y'know."

The young man turned around, looking for the speaker, but saw only a life-sized, ecclesiastically dressed figure leaning rather precariously against a wall. "Not me," the voice said. "That's St. Thomas Aquinas."

The young man looked amazed.

"Let you have him cheap," the voice went on. "Not much call for Aquinas these days. Not since his Proofs were disproved. Have to fix those knee joints; he keeps leaning like a kangaroo with a broken tail."

The young man with the filthy, caked hair and the ever so slightly crosseyed look was suddenly frightened. He could not see the person speaking. It sounded—at first—as if it were an old man, with an English accent. But the second time the mysterious voice spoke it was a much younger man, with the accent diminished. He came out of the corner and stood in the open area just inside the door. He looked behind him, through one of the dusty windows. Just outside in the arcade alley there was heavy fog. A roiling gray soup that seemed to be lit from moment to moment by flashes of lightning. His fear grew. He had read about places like this, in fantasy stories. It was *certainly* one of *those* shops.

"Over here, young feller," said the voice, now that of a seventy-year-old New England shopkeeper. "Over here, under the beaded lamp."

And a beaded lamp in the rear of the shoppe clicked on. There was an old man sitting in a rocking chair under the lamp. The young man could just make him out. It was that far away.

He turned and tried the doorknob. It wouldn't turn. He

pulled at the door, but it wouldn't budge. From outside the shoppe came the sounds of great beasts prowling, of thundering machines, of death and horror. He turned and stared down the length of the shoppe at the old man, who rocked slowly and waited. From outside came a thunderous explosion. Magnesium-flare brilliance illuminated the entire shoppe for an instant, revealing merchandise that made the young man's blood run cold; in the moment of chill white light the face of the old man seemed to run and bubble and change: first it was the face of a beautiful woman, then the face of a Congolese Songe mask, then the face of a robot without nose or mouth, then the face of an ancient god—perhaps Cernunnos of the Gauls. Then the moment of cold light was gone, and it was an old man once more, nothing but an old man once again.

"Don't mind the screams and shouts out there, son," the old man said. "Just an idea of the management to discourage walkouts. Keeps people browsing till the storm's over."

The young man didn't want to, but he suddenly found himself walking. Toward the rear of the shoppe. Toward the old man in the rocking chair. He tried to make his feet stop moving, but they placed themselves one in front of the other and he kept walking. But no matter how long he walked, the young man realized he was drawing no closer to the figure in the rocker.

He walked and walked, down among the fossilized remains of jabberwocks and eohippuses and broken reel-to-reel tape recorders, until his ankles began to blaze with pain from the walking. As if he had been striding uphill on a thirty degree slope. He found he was able to stop walking; he sat down on a three-legged stool to rest.

The old man said, "That's a nice item, that one. Belonged to William Rufus, the Incarnate King; had a nasty dustup with The Lady of the Lake, he did; something silly about a macaronic song, I believe. Or maybe it was who had the louder climax. Can't recall. Something like that. Let it go cheap if you're interested. Sitting on it's guaranteed to cure constipation instantly."

The grubby young man leaped off the stool.

The old man was chuckling in a very friendly key. "Aw, hell, kid, come on over; I'll stop playing around with you."

The young man started walking. He was able to approach the old man. In a few moments he was standing beside him.

"Now. What can I do for you?"

The young man stared at him with faintly glazed eyes lit by a peculiar light. Just stared. He didn't know what to say; he was actually, for the first time in his life, frightened down to the marrow. Even when he had been strapped in the orphanages, or beaten in the reformatories, or ganged in jail, he had never really known fear; it wasn't in him to understand that kind of fear. But here, in this strange matrix of imponderables, with the brutal bellowing of shuffling autochthones filling the air just beyond the fogged windows, he was paralyzed with fear. He could not speak, did not know what he could ask for, did not know what he could have.

But knew he could have *anything,* just for the asking, just for the buying. That was what this shoppe was here for.

The old man seemed to understand his problem. He stood up and patted the young man on the shoulder. "Well, truth in advertising, young feller. We're just what the sign says, a shoppe of wonders; your heart's desire is here, somewhere. Just have to figure out what it is. You only get one chance, you know. Purchases limited one to a customer."

He seemed about to say something more, but caught himself as his mouth opened. He looked at the young man a good deal more closely, and lines of worry appeared in his forehead. When he spoke again, there was an appreciable coolness in his manner. More businesslike, infinitely less friendly and playful. A bit more menacing.

"All sorts of items," he said. "Complete set of books listed in the *Index Librorum Prohibitorum,* including Bergson's 'L'Evolution Créatrice.' Cloak of invisibility. Just got in a fresh supply of black cobra blood from the Dinka; best black cobra blood on the market, you know; southern Sudanese; just smear some on the houseposts of your enemies. One hundred per cent guaranteed to produce incredible anguish and death. Love philters. Antigravitation discs. Dildos. Pills you can drop in your gas tank, just add water and it makes pure octane. Just name it, we've got it."

For the first time the young man spoke. "When I leave here, will this shop vanish the way they do in the stories?"

"I'm afraid so, yes."

"Why do they always do that?"

The old man sighed. "You know, you're the first one who ever asked me that."

But he didn't answer the question.

He walked toward a case filled with small objects. "Hey, come on over here. Maybe we have something in here to suit your fancy."

The young man scratched at his chest where his shirt lay open minus a button. He scratched at a bug bite. It was an angry red welt. He walked to the showcase and looked in. Eyes of newts. Toes of frogs. Other things.

They stood silently on opposite sides of the case for a few minutes. Finally in a strong young voice, the old man said, "Okay, bud, what's your heart's desire?"

The young man did not look up. "Power," he said.

"What kind of power?"

"I want people to do what I want them to do."

"That's easy enough." The old man reached into the case and brought out a black velvet pad on which lay a group of stones. They seemed to glisten and scintillate as though encrusted with dendrites. "Powerstones," the old man said. "To make others do your bidding. Two bucks a shot."

The young man looked up. "Why so cheap?"

The old man shrugged. He gave a little laugh that was no laugh at all. "Cheapest things in the universe. Two dollars each is a good price."

The young man reached for an octagonal-shaped stone. The old man stopped him with a word. "No!" The young man pulled back his hand. The old man picked up another one, diamond-shaped. "Here. This one."

"What was wrong with the other one?"

"Wouldn't have served your need. Take my word for it, this's the one you want. Two dollars. A steal at twice the price."

The young man took it from him. It was warm to the touch. He closed his fist around it. The heat grew in his palm. He opened his hand and stared down at the glowing rock. "How do I use it?"

"Just carry it with you. Heat it in your hand from time to time. It'll do the rest."

The young man fished around in his jeans pocket, brought up two moist and wrinkled dollar bills. He gave them to the old man. The old man took the bills, walked back to the area where the rocking chair sat under the beaded lamp, and reached into an open drawer. He brought out a ledger and a quill pen.

"I'll just enter the transaction," he said. He brought the

ledger over to the showcase, laid it down, opened it, and wrote a few words on the first empty line. He looked up from the ledger; the young man didn't like the look at all. "I'll need a tear," the old man said.

"A tear?"

"Yes, a tear."

"Not blood?"

"Beg pardon?"

"Sign these things in blood; isn't that supposed to be the way of it?"

"Just a tear, thank you."

"And how do I do that?"

"No problem."

The young man suddenly felt his eyes well up with tears. One rolled down his face, hung from his chin for a moment and then dropped onto the glass of the showcase. "Very good," the old man said, and dipped the quill in the tear. He wrote a few more words.

He closed the ledger slowly, and looked at the young man. "That's it," he said. "Anything else?" In fact, it was a dismissal. The young man paused a moment, as if trying to brazen out the instant; but the old man quite clearly did not want him in the shoppe any longer. He turned toward the door. It was clear afternoon out there.

"You wrote down my name, didn't you?"

"Goodbye," said the old man. "Come again."

"How did you know my name? I didn't say my name."

"Goodbye."

The young man got a nasty look on his face and seemed about to say something. He clutched the powerstone in his hand and waited for it to work. But he knew it wouldn't work on the shoppe keeper. He had once bought a revolver from a pawnbroker, and the hockshop owner had sold him the bullets in a sealed cartridge carton, with a band around it. Shopkeepers always took precautions so the merchandise wouldn't be turned against *them*.

The young man walked toward the front door. He had only taken three steps before he was there. But it had been such a long walk to reach the old man.

He put his hand on the knob—a crescent moon—and opened the door. He turned to look back at the old man, but the old man was gone. The light of the beaded lamp no longer shone. It was all darkness back there, with a swirling vortex of white mist where he had last seen the old man standing.

"I've read stories about this kind of place," he said defiantly, to nothingness. There was no answer from the misty vortex. "Nobody ever wrote one about who runs a place like this. Why you sell stuff like this so cheap? What's in it for you? Why do you keep coming and going like that? Who do you work for? *What's in it for you?*"

There was a final whisper of dismissal: *Goodbye.*

He stepped through the door, closed it behind him, and started away. He took three steps, as he had inside the shoppe, and turned around, thinking better of his purchase.

Where it had been, there was a blank wall between two boarded-up entranceways. As promised, the Shoppe of Wonders, in which the filthy young man with the unsavory manner had purchased his heart's desire, had vanished.

He stabilized his atoms and assumed his normal form. He was not an old man, nor was he a swirling vortex of white mist, nor was he a beautiful woman or a robot or Cernunnos of the Gauls. He was, himself, a young man, perhaps no older than the young man to whom he had sold the powerstone. The thin disc that had been slid between the atoms of the femur of his left leg had one thousand and eleven growth rings on it. He was a young man, only one thousand and eleven years old.

The shoppe solidified around him. Its outer walls were gone. He was back at Rubble Point. The world outside was ashes and darkness. The stasis field held the shoppe inviolate, but though he was safe from the Infinite Dark Mass that pressed against its walls, its potency could still be felt: pressing against the field, incredible devouring power exerting unceasing pressure. Outside the shoppe it was all sky, no land surface, no horizon. Sky, empty space, devoid of life, black, terrible and cold. Ashes and darkness.

He ran his hands wearily through his thick hair, and thought of Ahna.

The time he had spent with the shoppe just off Jamshyd Avenue could be quantified as thirty-five "minutes." Subjectively. But he had been gone only a tick in the objectified chronology of Rubble Point.

What he had done suddenly flooded in on him. He was—

all at once—as terrified as a child who had broken his mother's best china figurine. He *knew* what he had done was wrong! More than simply wrong. It had been personally destructive. But there were times when he could not help himself. It had now put Ahna in jeopardy, as well as himself, but he could not fully regret it; he knew he would do it again if the moment were to be repeated. Despite the job he had to do, despite the purpose that drove him obsessively, there were times when he could not help himself. He was, after all, an artist.

He stood there among the items of stock he had been given to sell, and he thought about his Art. In the face of what he had done, and what it meant for Ahna, he felt vain and foolish. Headstrong. Destructive. He turned and turned, looking for an answer to his actions, but everything in the shoppe spoke reproach. He remembered one special manifestation of his art that he had thought personified what he had to say:

In the Glass Square, having reassembled himself in the shape of a silver tetrahedron radiating light in waves of chromatic brilliance, sending the light through random phases of color in bursts and washes without once repeating the sequence. No one had paid any attention. But he had stayed there for a very long time, and finally, when it was a totality, and he was done, and the time for that particular piece of art to be disassembled, and he reformed himself, one of the Supervisors had solidified in front of him and had asked, "What was the name of that?" And he had said, "Integrity," and the Supervisor had looked at him without speaking. Then he had vanished. The gentle murmuring of the colors could still be heard faintly, dissipating.

He thought about that despicable young man with the powerstone. He was so anti-Art, so anti-life . . .

No! He would not think about it. They might not know; they couldn't be everywhere; they couldn't know everything; they had too much to supervise, too much to worry about; they would not discover what he had done. That was over, done, finished. He didn't want to think about it; it made him cold and dead inside to think about it. He wanted to think of Ahna, to think of the time when she would be with him again. He wanted to *see* Ahna. To reaffirm his purpose, to sublimate his need to create. To force the artist to sleep, so the man could do what he had to do.

He gathered muons to himself, concentrating them in the fingertips of his right hand, and made a sign in the empty air of the shoppe. The air ran and bubbled like lava and a communication frame was created. He looked into it and said, "This is Lhayne. I would like a pass to go to the vaults."

The blip of light in the upper left quadrant of the communication frame pulsed, "Aren't you on service at this time, friend Lhayne?"

Lhayne admitted he was. "I've just returned from my duty period." He knew the discrepancy would be noted. The blip pulsed, "There seems to be an imbalance. Your pass is, of course, granted; however, this break in your schedule will count against your quota." Lhayne said he understood that would certainly have to be the case. He was getting a trifle annoyed. He was, after all, a human being, and this was, after all, only a logging device to which he was speaking. He wanted to get to Ahna as quickly as possible, had to *see* her, actually *see* her, as quickly as possible. The blip pulsed, "This will be logged."

"Then log it!" Lhayne said, angrily.

Without rancor, the lower right quadrant of the frame strobed validation of the pass. Lhayne made another sign in the air and the communication frame wavered and scintillated and vanished.

Lhayne stood a moment, still trembling with fear; then he disassembled his atoms and save for a momentary watery quality to the air in the shoppe, he was gone and the shoppe was empty. Empty: with the silent, voracious pressure of the Infinite Dark Mass steadily pressing against it.

He could not entirely divorce himself from his sense of duty, no matter *what* had happened, *what* he had done back there during work-time, no matter how much he hungered to see Ahna. And so he paused in transit and re-formed in the Supply section.

Beyond the frame in that place he could see men and women working with photons, quarks and muons to create the supplies the shoppe used as stock. The glass beads and trinkets.

The communication frame greeted him politely and had the temerity to inquire why he wasn't out on work-time.

"I need restock," he said, "do you want to take my order or lecture me on attendance?"

"What do you need?" the blip pulsed.

"Stock is low on Omicrons, healing ointments and hula

hoops. I'll need seven-league boots in sizes 10 to 13 triple A. Three succubi, a gross of the Beethoven cubes, about a dozen pair of the eyeglasses that see through solid matter, and have you gotten those universal college entrance exam answers back in stock yet?"

The blip pulsed, "No, I'm sorry, friend Lhayne, not yet. But we do have the original Shakespeare first folios and a large supply of original copies of Cotton Mather's 'Wonders of the Invisible World.'"

He placed his order and vanished; he reformed in the Glass Square. All around him Rubble Point flickered with light. The world. What was left of the world. Maintained flickeringly against the Infinite Dark Mass all around, beyond the perimeter. It took enormous energy to maintain the bubble of Rubble Point against the pressure from outside. It flickered, but it continued to exist.

And beyond this silver bubble, ashes and darkness.

Here at Rubble Point, at the end of time and the imminent end of space, where entropy was programming the heat-death of the universe, only ten thousand humans remained to mark the place where life and intelligence and dreams of empire had lived.

In the Centers that ringed the Glass Square the on-duty Supervisors manipulated energy to keep the barriers solid against the Infinite Dark Mass.

And he had jeopardized all this with a moment's self-indulgence. What power had that loathesome young man in the shoppe already possessed to make friend Lhayne throw *all this*—and Ahna—into jeopardy?

He shivered, knowing it was not yet finished, not by any possible wish or hope.

And he suddenly had the chill feeling that this might be the last time he saw Ahna. He hurried to the vaults.

Ahna was there, behind glass. The erg-gauge was not even one-fourth filled. He stared at it for the longest time, trying to wish it full . . . the red line pressed against the very top of the counter . . . but it was nonmanipulable: it remained less than one-fourth filled.

He looked in at Ahna, sleeping. He could not detect the rise and fall of her chest. But she was only sleeping.

She had been sleeping for three hundred years.

He stared in at her, waiting for her to realize he was here, to open her eyes and smile with a wondrous mouth too large to be called correct for her slim face. But she only slept and though he tried to bring back the exact sound of her voice, he only heard words, a conversation between himself and himself in the empty places of his memory.

"How long will your new piece take?"

"I think a week."

"I'll miss you."

"Come and see me."

"Not this time, please, Lhayne."

"I won't be in pain."

"Yes, but you *look* as if you're in pain. I can't bear it."

"I have to create, Ahna."

"You know I understand. But it hurts me to see you."

"They have to see. They need to remember what it was like to be just human beings, not gods. 'Fire and Sleep' will be my best work. They won't be able to reject it, or ignore it."

"But you burn."

Sleeping. Here at Rubble Point the last thousand of the ten thousand humans who had survived the ages slept in their vaults, waiting for those who loved them to buy their release from induced catalepsy. Here at Rubble Point the surviving ten thousand had taken their stand against the moment when the last planet fell into the last sun, and the last sun was swallowed by the Infinite Dark Mass. Here at Rubble Point, where everything came to an end until the universe could be reborn and begin again its stately pavan toward nothingness, the ten thousand had rescued a piece of the space-time substance and made it a world of survival. They had taken the energy of entropy itself, the heat that flows during the thermodynamic process, the heat entropy provides as criteria for spontaneous chemical changes and thus chemical equilibrium, the energy that still exists but is lost for the purpose of doing work . . . the entropic heat generated in quantifiable time, a piece of a second, a chunk of a minute, a slice of an hour . . . and they had used it to maintain their bit of a world, Rubble Point, against the voracious appetite of the Mad Conqueror, Entropy, eating everything till it swallowed *itself,* leaving nothing but the Infinite Dark Mass that would inevitably explode from its own engorgement of time and space.

They had used what they could steal from the past to maintain their world. But each one of the nine thousand who lived

and survived in the world of Rubble Point used a carefull
calculated amount of antientropic energy, gauged in ergs,
course. And there was x amount allocated simply to mainta
Rubble Point's existence against the pull of the Infinite Da
Mass. Those who had been unfortunate enough to be plac
in the vaults, to be wakened only when there was sufficie
anti-entropic energy available for their maintenance could
no other than wait.

Wait: for energy to be brought forward to the end of tin
from all of the past that still lived in the megaflow. Wait: f
those who had a stake in their revival to earn their freedor
Wait: for loved ones to journey into the dangerous past to ste
minutes, hours, days. Wait: for the anti-entropic heat-energ
to be generated by pivotal events that the nine thousand creat
in the past, events programmed by those who danced the
dance here at Rubble Point, at the end of time.

Ahna slept, waiting.

And her erg counter was less than one-fourth filled.

He stood before the vault, staring in at her sleeping feature
A sleep more than merely sleep; endless if he could not tra
worthless trinkets for vital energy. The powerstone, for i
stance. A trinket. A child's plaything here at Rubble Point. B
to a young man whose present was codified as March 2
1967 . . . a heart's desire.

The ten thousand bartered at the very best rate of interes
Caveat emptor. They traded toys for time. Time against tl
onrush of nothingness; time as heat-energy; time as a weapo
the only weapon that could halt the Mad Conqueror, Entrop
What was it the young man had said? *What's in it for you?*

Everything.

Survival. Existence. Life. Being. Everything.

Purchasable only in The Shoppe of Wonders.

"She'll be a long time coming out," said a voice beside hir
Lhayne heard the voice, but was too overcome with the sig
of Ahna, too mortified by what he had done, too sunk in h
own thoughts of the past, the present, the hopelessness of
future without her to comprehend what had been said.

He looked the wrong way. Then he looked to his left ai
saw the old woman. She had obviously chosen to remain a
old woman, had not bothered reassembling herself into
younger body. "I beg your pardon," he said.

"I see her counter's way down," the old woman said, moving closer to the erg counter and scrutinizing it very carefully. "My son's in the next vault. I come here every chance I get. I know he can't hear me but I come and stand and talk to him; I tell him it won't be much longer."

Lhayne looked around at the next vault. The erg counter was only a hair below full. How long had this old woman been working to buy her son's freedom? She looked five thousand years old.

"All he needs is one little boost and I can get him out," she said. There was a tone beneath the tone in her voice. "You know, such a little boost wouldn't make much difference to you, and your lady. She has such a long way to go. . . ."

He knew what she wanted. They hung around the vaults night and day. Beggars of time.

"Leave me alone," he said, turning back to Ahna's lovely sleeping face.

"You wouldn't keep a mother from her only son, would you? I can see what a good person you are, how much you love your lady. . . ."

"Get away from me, you thug!" he screamed.

The old woman snarled something obscene and her atoms began to shift. She re-formed. She was younger than Lhayne, and wickedly beautiful, with a hunger in her face that he knew could only be assuaged by the man in the vault.

"You'd better let me take that boost," she said, the hunger in her face distorting her beautiful features. "Or I'll make you sorry you ever lived!"

It was idle malevolence, utterly without possibility of being implemented. They were immortal, replenishable, inviolate against assault. But she had clearly gone mad, and the sight of the naked lunacy terrified Lhayne. He had seen other examples of this imprisoned madness. They were *all* going crazy, out here where time and space came to an end and the pressure from outside could be felt as filth on the skin. He wondered if what he had done with that foul little young man in the shoppe was *his* most recent manifestation of insanity.

He started to edge away from her. *Goodbye, Ahna.*

This beggar of time had blighted his moment with Ahna. He hated her. But could do nothing to get even with her.

And why should he bother? Her misery was far greater than

any he could impose. *Goodbye, Ahna. Goodbye*.

He ran away from the screaming beggar, with her voice echoing foulnesses down the crystal corridors.

When he returned to the shoppe, one of the Supervisors was waiting for him.

"I've been looking through your ledger," the Supervisor said. Lhayne had no idea which one this was; it might have been Dorell or Keys or even Kathrhn with her atoms rearranged to form a blank mask without features. "Your last trip produced some variations in the megaflow that could not be ignored. Why did you do it? You certainly couldn't have thought you'd get away with it?"

"I read his mind. He was a filthy little scum."

"Nonetheless!"

"Don't yell at me."

"This isn't a game, friend Lhayne. This is survival."

"It's always survival. But not necessarily Art."

"Oh yes. I'd forgotten. You're still calling yourself an artist, aren't you?"

"That's what I am. It's the correct word."

The Supervisor snickered. There were no features to the mask, so it was impossible to tell how much of a sneer accompanied the sound. "Correct? Perhaps operable is what you mean. An Artist who is himself the Art. Standing in a public place and letting rain wash over you, and calling it 'Rebirth.' Crawling through broken glass till your body is torn and calling it 'The Eternal Apollonian-Dionysian Conflict.' I suppose that's Art."

"I don't tell you how to supervise."

"Art criticism is as old as Art."

"I rearrange the universe. That is the nature of my Art."

"No, friend Lhayne. We *all* rearrange the universe. What's left of it. The ten thousand of us, here at the end of time. That is the nature of survival."

"My *personal* universe, then. I rearrange that."

The Supervisor picked up the ledger. "But you may *not* rearrange it for the rest of us. We are all precariously balanced; we each pay our way; there is no room for self-indulgence."

"No room for freedom, you mean."

"There is no freedom in oblivion." The Supervisor shoved the ledger toward Lhayne. *"These* gave us our freedom."

The ledger was filled, page after page. Deals. Sales. Time bought with toys. The ability to mold a bear out of clay, the artistic eye, and the basis of god-worship . . . sold to a nameless australopithecene in South Africa. The "way of seeing" that turned a pointed stick used for scratching in the earth into the first spear . . . sold to a bright-eyed Neanderthaler in Pleistocene Prussia. The ultimate weapon, gunpowder, sold to a mandarin warlord in Choukoutien village. Godsight, sold to Joan of Arc. The concept of the assembly-line, sold to Henry Ford. Page after page, line after filled line, each one signed with a smeared name or illiterate mark of identification. Signed as if the quill had been dipped in some watery, vital fluid more binding than blood, some fluid that might serve as an energy conductor. Michelangelo, Anaxagoras, Socrates, Pasteur, Méliès, Freud, Jefferson, Roger Williams, Confucius. Names, thousands of names that meant nothing against the pull of the Infinite Dark Mass save as moments of rearranged time that bought survival.

Lhayne stared numbly at the ledger and knew he had been wrong. The madness he had seen in the beggar of time in the corridor of the vaults had possessed him, might soon possess them all. And then what point was there to survival?

He wanted to say *I'm sorry,* but the artist in him would not let the words emerge. It was stronger than the frail human being that contained the artistic spirit. It knew there was only one thing that stood between humanity and the engorgement of the Infinite Dark Mass. And it was not merely the frantic need to survive. There was survival . . . and there was something finer, greater beyond survival. What was existence without Art? Empty as the Infinite Dark Mass that gnawed at the perimeters of Rubble Point.

"Your trips are ended," the Supervisor said.

It was said without feeling, but a tone crept through from behind the mask.

"I'll find another way of buying her freedom. She deserves to live."

"No doubt."

"I'll find another way."

"I think not, friend Lhayne. Your own account will be overdrawn because of this." He pointed to the last entry . . . the young man who had bought the powerstone for two dollars and a measure of the past. "I'm afraid there's a vault waiting for you."

Lhayne wanted to beg him, *Put me in the vault beside her; there's one about to be emptied right beside Ahna.* But the Supervisor was already making a sign in the air. Lhayne's body began to bubble and scintillate. Then it was gone.

The shoppe was silent.

Pressure from outside came through the walls. Cancerous darkness lapped at the stasis field.

The Supervisor sighed. It was never easy. But neither was survival.

The grubby young man had taken only one more step when he heard the voice behind him. "Hey! You!"

He turned. The shoppe that had been gone a moment before, was back again. Appear, disappear, appear again . . .

He stopped. The young woman with the long blonde hair was standing in the open doorway, motioning to him urgently. "Hey, come on back. He sold you the wrong stone."

He hesitated. The powerstone was warm in his hand. Unnaturally warm. It was beginning to be uncomfortable.

He turned and walked back. She was extraordinarily beautiful. She held out the octagonal stone he had wanted to select before the old man made him buy the diamond-shaped one. "Better take this one," she said, smiling up at him with affection. Then a shadow came over her face, her eyes seemed to darken as though she saw something disturbing, and then the smile was strong again. "This is the one you want."

"Where's the old man?" he asked.

"He was just minding the place for me; just a replacement. He's always making some kind of stupid mistake. We want our customers to be satisfied; better take this one."

He handed her the diamond-shaped stone, now almost unbearably hot. He took the octagonal stone. It was cool and seemed to radiate power. Yes, this was the right one.

"I still want to know," he said, "what do you get out of this? Who are you, how do you make a living in a place like this?"

"Just serving the community and the commonweal, that's the only reward we get. A force for good in your time." Her smile was fixed, implacable, eternally sincere. *Caveat emptor*.

She held the diamond-shaped stone that would have killed him the first time he tried to use it, and she stared at him with her alabaster smile, and she knew what forces had been set in motion by his ownership of the stone that would make people do what he wanted them to do. And she thought of the thousand in their vaults, now one thousand and one. She thought of friend Lhayne and his Ahna who would remain in their vaults perhaps until the universe was reborn, because there was no one who had the spare time to buy them *their* time. And she wanted the young man to go away and begin fulfilling the destiny that would produce antientropic energy by hastening the onrush of the Infinite Dark Mass.

"Is there anything else?" she asked.

"He wrote down my name."

"Yes. That's just company policy. So we have a record."

"Who sees that record?"

"No one, Mr. Manson. That's just for our files."

"He wrote Charles. That's not right. It's Charlie. Can you change it?"

"We won't have to. It's all right."

He started to walk away. "It's Charlie; don't forget."

There was Art, and there was survival, and sometimes they were mutually exclusive.

The voice came from a swirling matrix of white mist that twisted inside the shoppe. *We won't forget.* And the door slammed. And the shoppe was gone. And the grubby young man turned once more onto Jamshyd Avenue; and was, in a moment, a part of the crowd, and a part of the Infinite Dark Mass.

*With a grateful nod to the writings
of Michael Moorcock.*

All the Lies
That Are My Life

INTRODUCTION

Art, someone said, is meant to clarify and elucidate complex experience.

This story is intended as clarification and elucidation. The topic under discussion is friendship. As I warned earlier in these pages, this is the long one that forms the core of the collection. It is 22,300 words in length, and it has taken me about twelve years to write it. No, I don't mean I've spent the last twelve years working on this piece to the exclusion of all others... I mean it's been perking and getting itself born for that long. I knew bits and pieces of it a long time ago; but other parts I simply wasn't old enough or self-aware enough to understand.

I'm not saying I'm any smarter now than when I first went at this idea. What I *am* saying is that some stories refuse to let you at them until they're sure you know what the hell you're doing.

(Later on in this book there's a story I wrote before it was ready to be written. I've included it because it's a recent work and I want it in print; but before this book makes the transition from copyedited manuscript to galleys I'll try to thrash the bejeezus out of that story in hopes I've learned enough in the last two years to make it come right. If not, you'll read a crippled thing. I don't have to tell you which one it is: you'll know.)

This is my most recent writing. It tries to deal with just what we mean when we say of someone else, "He's my friend."

One time I was arrested and canned for being an "outside agitator" in Valdosta, Georgia. I was not alone; there were quite a few other "outside agitators" who also got swept up by the Laws. But I suppose it was my assertion that I could not possibly be an "outside agitator" because I was a member of the human race, a citizen of the world, just another link in the chain, that prevented me from paying the fine like the others, and being carted to the state line for instant dispersal. They decided to hold me for a few days, just to teach me a lesson.

And sitting there in the Valdosta slam, I complained to the innkeeper that I hadn't eaten all day and I'd like something plain and downhome. After he stopped laughing he advised me that brunch had long since been served and that I'd have to wait till that night for the sumptuous county-provided meal.

In the next cell was an old man who'd been hauled in for pissing on some woman's garden. He never told me why he'd taken it upon himself to nourish the flora in that way.

He dug around in his pockets and came up with a half-eaten Power House candy bar. He offered it to me, and I took it. There was no reason why he should have done that, but he did it, and I thanked him. Several times I thanked him.

For a few minutes there in Valdosta, Georgia, that old man was my friend.

Another time, just recently, a man who had been a close friend for eight years, who had assured me that when and if I needed his assistance he would be there, who had always talked a very courageous talk, who came to my home and who shared meals with me, who acted (in all ways that required no demonstration of risk) as if he were my friend...betrayed me in a court of law, while under oath, renouncing what he had said in sworn deposition...and all to the end of trying to cripple a lawsuit it took me four years of my life to get before a judge and jury.

The pain of listening to him dissemble, there in that

courtroom, was infinitely greater than the pain inflicted on me by the original injustice, by the days, weeks and months I have lost trying to get justice, by the vast sums of money I have expended trying to counter powerful opponents. During the time he testified I felt the pain of watching a friend die. Despite his perfidy, I won...and won *big*.

I can only suppose he did it out of self-interest, out of lack of courage, out of fear. Nonetheless, I now realize he could never have been my friend.

So what *is* friendship?

My answers to that question are no more formidable than my answers to the questions what is love or what is art?

It redefines itself each time the question is confronted. But this I do think is true: there is an element of risk in friendship. It is a quality that defines itself in terms of love and loyalty as the readiness to inconvenience oneself at risk of something valuable. And that seldom means money. It means the skin goes on the line.

I think that's right.

But maybe not.

In this story a writer delivers his own obituary. Some of that last will and testament is mine. Some is not. The narrator and the protagonist are partially me and partially a close friend of mine, a man I've called friend for over twenty-five years. The two of us are purposely intermingled, and large chunks of pure invention have been added to both. This is fiction, not personal memoir. Try not to read too much one-for-one into the bits and pieces of this work.

Writers take tours in other people's lives, and readers must be canny enough to understand that some writers like to play a mean little game of misdirection when it looks as if they're inviting entry into the private back rooms of the writer himself.

All the Lies
That Are My Life

THEY BURIED Jimmy Crowstairs today.

My closest, oldest, best friend: the world-famous fantasist, Kercher Oliver James Crowstairs.

They put him down the rectangular hole this morning, and I was one of the dozen people *inside* the black, plush velvet, upholstered ropes. Also in there among the select few was an ex-President of the United States, for whom I had not voted; also two actresses, one of whom, though age thirty, keeps being cast as late teens beachbait, despite her excellence as a serious thesp, mostly on the basis of her chubby cheeks and a pair of breasts—if you'll pardon the pragmatism—only slightly smaller than Bosnia and Herzegovina; the other one I didn't know, but she made a good impression on me when, as we were walking up the hill to the grave from the limos, she graciously waved off a small knot of ghouls seeking her autograph; Jimmy's publisher, whose chief claims to fame are his rejection of Jerzy Kosinski's first novel on the basis that it was morbid and depressing, and his ongoing participation as a panelist on a television game show now into its seventh year of syndication; Jimmy's sister, eight years his senior, whom he had not spoken to for over twenty years and to whom he referred as SylviaTheCunt, all one word; a great bear of an English novelist, a French film director who wore clothes so elegantly it made everyone else feel like breadline standbys, a plasma physicist from Princeton who's up for the Nobel this year because of his major breakthrough in magnetic containment fusion; and two married couples Jimmy considered close friends, mostly because they proved to him, as living examples, that it is possible for Man and Woman to cleave together under the same roof, bound by The Paper (as he constantly referred to it), without emotionally disemboweling each other. How many is that? Counting me, that's thirteen. Well, okay, thirteen, not twelve. Even so, it was a select cadre of mourners.

Set apart by black, plush velvet, upholstered ropes from the vast throng of his fans and idle groupies of the great, the near-great, the celebrated and the hemidemisemicelebrated.

History tells us that when Victor Hugo died on May 22nd, 1885, over two million Parisians followed the pauper's hearse he had specified from the Arc de Triomphe to the Panthéon, where he was buried.

Jimmy's entourage wasn't quite that large; but for a contemporary author, in a nation where illiteracy has gone beyond mere totemization, well into deification . . . it was eminently satisfactory. Maybe two or three thousand. Not bad at all for a guy they steadfastly called a "sci-fi writer."

You'll notice *I* never use that hideous neologism.

Jimmy spent the last twenty-five years of his life trying to get that ugly categorization off his books and out of the biographies they wrote about him. He wrote fantasy, if specific pigeonholes are needed; but he insisted on being called simply a *writer*. He didn't even like being referred to as an "author." He once told me the difference, as he saw it, between an *author* and a *writer*. "An *author* [he said] is what you put on your passport, because in Europe they think a *writer* is a newspaperman. An *author* is somebody who gets his name on the spine of leatherbound volumes that are never read; a *writer* is someone who gets hemorrhoids from sitting on his ass all his life . . . *writing*."

Either way, whatever they *called* him, he managed by sheer dint of hard work and careful manipulation of his public image to become three things, almost always mutually contradictory: a staggeringly wealthy bestselling novelist, a serious artist who was seriously regarded by all the "serious" critics, and a legend in his own time. A household name like Salk or Babe Ruth or Hemingway—or Nixon or Jack the Ripper or Hitler.

And this morning they lowered him into darkness, and wonderful words were read over him by Rabbi Ashkenazi, Monsignor McCalla, Dr. Ehlen, Carl Sagan and me. Mine were the best.

Naturally: I knew him best. And as Jimmy so often told interviewers, with that abundance of humble largesse that so endeared him to *People* magazine, *The Paris Review* and *The National Enquirer*, "Larry Bedloe is a good solid writer; he's got a nice little talent working there."

That popped up in my thoughts as I stood there watching them crank down the gunmetal-blue anodized aluminum casket. Right across from me, on the other side of the black, plush velvet, upholstered ropes, was a chubby little woman in basic black and pearls. Her face was all puffy from crying. She was clutching the Literary Guild boxed set of his *Radimore* trilogy. Chances of her getting it autographed were very slim.

Kerch, as everyone but his ex-wife Leslie and I called him, was already on his way to stardom when I met him. We were both just turning twenty—I scampered ahead only six months older—which meant that for half of each year he could refer to me as "old man" and I could admonish him to speak with respect to his elders—and we had both been science fiction fans.

Every ingroup coterie had its mystiques, its craziness. Masons have secret handshakes; jazz musicians run a special patois incomprehensible to squares; only in the motion picture industry can you get a laugh when you tell the one about the Polish starlet . . . who fucked the *writer;* antiquarian bookdealers share arcane rituals of buy&sell that bind them in terms of verso, recto, foxing, gutters and true firsts.

The deranged traditions of science fiction "fandom" are overwhelmingly attractive, particularly to those few boys and girls who are the outcasts of their high school classes because of wonky thought processes, a flair for the bizarre, and physical appearance that denies them the treasures of sorority membership or a position on the football team. For the pimply, the short, the weird and intelligent . . . for those to whom sex is frightening and to whom come odd dreams in the middle of study hall, the camaraderie of fandom is a gleaming, beckoning Erewhon; an extended family of other wimps, twinks, flakes and oddballs.

We had never met, though we'd corresponded heavily for several years. The nexus of our incipient friendship was the maelstrom of fannish publishing—"fanzines." Mimeographed amateur magazines of comment about the writers and the works in the genre, and a smattering of dreary fan fiction. His fanzine was titled, with becoming modesty, *The World's Greatest SF Fanzine Including Venus;* mine was called *Visitations.*

But it was at the tenth annual World Science Fiction Convention (neologized as ChiCon II), in Chicago, 1952, that we actually met.

I was walking through the lobby of the Hotel Morrison. Being short on funds, I had arranged to stay in a two-room suite with half a dozen other fans from different parts of the country; and I was looking for the one in whose name the rooms were registered, so I could get the key and dump my suitcase.

The lobby was jammed with a horde of fans checking in, renewing acquaintances, screaming across through the potted plants for directions, rolling in dollies with cartons of used books for the huckster room, making arrangements for cheeseburger dinners that night. And in the midst of that cyclical flow of sweaty aficionados who had driven or flown or hitchhiked or crawled in from Minneapolis and Kansas City and Cleveland, Jake Repnich tracked me down.

I felt a hand grab the back of my shirt as I tried to elbow through a knot of kids divvying up suitcases for the trek to the elevators (thereby saving the bellboy's tip), and I reeled backward as the tension was applied. Then someone clubbed me a shot in the kidney.

I pitched forward, but couldn't fall down because the back of my shirt was still wrapped in a fist. So my feet went out from under me and I dropped to my knees. I tried to look around behind me; I was in such exquisite pain that my head wouldn't turn on my neck. Everything seemed to be slipping off the edge. But I could tell from the expressions on the faces of the crowd that something awful was about to happen, and that I was on the visitation end of that unnamed awfulness.

A foot was planted between my shoulder blades and the fist let go of my shirt, and I was booted forward onto my suitcase, which slid a few feet, carrying me as on a raft.

I fell off, rolled over, and tried to sit up.

Conquest, Slaughter, Famine and Death were staring down at me.

The courageous and loving extended family had moved back to clear a circle in which I could be conveniently stomped to pudding. Erewhon had been invaded.

The nastiest-looking of the Four Horsemen—whom I instantly recognized as Death—leaned forward, providing me with a dandy view of his terminal acne, and (in the pulp magazine vernacular of the period) lipped thinly, "I'm Jake Repnich, you little sonofabitch. You wanna tweak my nose?"

It all became hideously clear what was happening. Six months earlier, among the batches of fanzines I traded for *Visitations* by mail, I'd received an ineptly hektographed crudzine called *Uranium-236*. It was "edited," if one takes semiliteracy, quadruple amputee syntax and sophomoric screeds against any writer with aspirations of writing literature above the level of shootouts in space as editing, by one Jake Repnich. It came out of Secaucus, New Jersey. Need more be said?

As the voice of reason, I had cast caution to the Four Horsemen (without knowing it), and had responded to a particularly stupid article in which Repnich had said H. P. Lovecraft was a better writer than Poe, with the published remarks that good old Jake had about as much literary savvy as a storm drain, and that someone ought to tweak his nose. The point being that merely slapping his pinkies wasn't due and proper for the intellectual crimes of a pimplebrain like good old Jake, a.k.a. Death.

Now Jake and three of his buddies, who no doubt spent their off-hours chewing broken glass and flogging cripples, had come all the way to Chicago from Secaucus, New Jersey, to more than tweak the nose of Larry Bedloe.

The smell of the Jersey swamps was still on them.

And I hadn't, at that point, lived enough of a life to have it flash before my eyes.

With three stories out to market, without even having had my shot at immortality, with the National Book Award and Martha Foley's *Best of the Year* and intimate conversations with Styron and Mailer and Hemingway and Steinbeck just within my grasp, I was about to become a problem for the carpet cleaners of the Hotel Morrison. *Quelle ironie!*

At which moment Jake Repnich's nose spouted blood and he went pinwheeling past me to land in a hideous heap against the check-in counter.

A foot and a half behind the spot he had just occupied stood a wild-eyed, babbling apparition, part vampire bat, part slavering derangement, part avenging Fury. The attaché case he had used to break Death's nose was dangling from one of his little pixie fists. The other fist was balled and seemed to be waiting for a target of opportunity.

Feet planted far apart, this pint-sized Zorro, no less than Destiny's Tot, stared at the three remaining teddy boys with eyes that could have triggered an A-bomb. "You want trouble, you pustulent slugs? You want a hassle, huh? You want to come in here where law-abiding science fiction fans are trying to share good times, and start a fracas? Huh, that what you want? Well, we're ready! Right, *everybody?*"

He directed the challenge at the extended family, cowering in confusion and naked cowardice around the lobby.

From here and there in the crowd came timorous responses of "Yeah, you tell 'em," and "We're with you, all the way!"

In that instant I understood the dangerous power of Willie Stark, Elmer Gantry, Jean Paul Marat and Aimee Semple McPherson.

Gorgo the Small then instructed Conquest, Slaughter and Famine to gather up the weeping, bleeding carcass of their leader and, with the crowd backing him all the way, in some unfathomable power-pull, he moved the guerrilla band through the lobby, down the steps, across the landing, down some other steps, through the revolving doors, and out onto the street. The potential assassins were held there for a few minutes, I suppose to get explicit directions from the Goliath-slayer how to find their way back to the sewers that emptied out onto the Jersey flats—with detailed warnings of what would happen to them should they try to return to the ChiCon—and then the throng returned.

I was still on the floor.

Peter Pan reached down, pulled me to my feet and said, with a wide, infectious grin, "Hi, you're Larry Bedloe, right? I'm Kerch Crowstairs, we're sharing the room upstairs. I just sold my first novel, Crowell's publishing it in the spring, it's called *Death Dance on Sirius 7*. You're going to love it, I promise you."

Say hello to Kercher O. J. Crowstairs.

It started raining as the funeral party filed away from Jimmy's grave. I looked up into the slanting gray downpour.

My parents were Wesleyan Methodists. Straight out of the Book of Discipline: no movies, no books except the Bible and the Book of Hymns, no eating in restaurants that hold a liquor license, church four times a week, tithes, and praying out loud in unison till it all melds into a droning chant. Some of the clearest thinking of the early 1700s. God is love and no intermediary is needed to intercede for his children. Not to mention that I confess Jesus Christ as my Savior and Lord and pledge my allegiance to His Kingdom.

From this background I fled Pittsburgh and my family with the cynicism that served as Maginot Line against the rape of my sanity, yet unable to shake the inculcated, subcutaneous certainty that God Is Watching. God, the art director; God, the set designer; God, the stage manager.

Who always makes it rain at the most dramatic moments in the burial ceremonies. Just once, I thought, why doesn't the Holy Director go against form, against type-casting, against cliche. A hail of frogs, perhaps. Or a celestial chorus, and marching band decked out like a New Orleans jazz funeral, with selections ranging from *Muskrat Ramble* to *Jesus Doesn't Want Me for a Sunbeam*.

I stood there as everyone else filed away, directed by the attendants. Since I was still inside the black, plush velvet, upholstered ropes they let me remain for a moment.

Almost thirty years. I knew you through most of my life, Jimmy. Friends. I don't even know what that means. I'm sure you must have done things for me on the basis of friendship, but I'll be damned if I can remember a single one of them. I remember another time of rain, a night in New York, years ago, when we had dinner together and you left me standing in the wet outside the restaurant, I remember that. You hustled down the sidewalk to your car and popped into the Porsche and drove off uptown, never even thinking to offer me a ride back to my hotel. It took me the better part of an hour to get a cab; I remember that.

But friends. Never occurred to me to question that word as the operative definition of our liaison. But what the hell did that ever *mean*, functionally speaking? You knew almost everything about me, and I knew quite a lot about you, but then so do *all* your readers, what with the confessional nature of most of what you wrote.

I was one of your readers. Every word published that I could lay hands on.

Which is more than we can say for the reverse, eh, Kerch?

You read "The Hourglass" ten years ago, chum; and made a point of mentioning how good it was every time we got together. I wrote that short story *ten years ago,* Jimmy! Ten fucking *years* ago! Nine books since. But by the mute testimony of your failure to mention even one of them, old friend now gone, you told me that it had all been downhill. Ten years ago, Jimmy. That was *it,* right? The one high spot and then nothing but mouth-to-mouth resuscitation, right? Too controlled, that's what you used to tell me on the nights when we'd sit across from each other at the kitchen table, after your staff had gone to bed, when we'd sit and drink instant and reminisce. Too controlled, too cautious. There wasn't enough wildness in what I put on the paper. Right? Right.

You had enough wildness for both of us, Jimmy.

Jesus, I'm lonely without you. Christ, I'm glad you're gone.

I'd stamped muddy spots around my feet. The tops of my shoes were covered. And I looked across the grave, through the rain that was coming down cold and nasty, and Jimmy's ex-wife Leslie was staring at me. She'd cried so much her nose had swollen and closed both eyes to slits. She held her head to the side like a little girl who's seen her dolly run over by a speeding car. I couldn't hear the short, sharp thistles of her sobs, but those Audrey Hepburn shoulders went up and down, each intake of breath painful.

You had enough wildness for both of us, Jimmy.

I walked around the grave and stepped over the black, plush velvet, upholstered rope and scuffed through the pedicured grass to her. She could barely see me, but she knew who it was. We knew how each of us moved, even in the darkness.

I took her in my arms and she buried her face in the hollow of my shoulder. Her dress was soaked through and she was cold, heaving with sobs but not shivering. The weather report had said nothing about rain.

Every few years I was privileged to hold her like this. Usually she was crying. We fitted together, in this way, like ancient stones.

"Come on, love," I said, over her head, into the rain. "It's all done now. We've got to go put a lid on it."

She spoke words I couldn't understand, sending them into the fabric of my jacket. Then more words, two of which were

Jimmy's name and my name. And I turned her slightly, and started to walk her away from the grave site.

"I can't go over there, Larry. Do I have to go over there?"

I said yes, she had to go over there, it was her due, it was the payoff for all the good times *and* all the bad times. I said I'd be there with her, and it would be quick, and then we could both go out somewhere and have a couple of dozen extremely potent drinks, and pretend the past was smoother and kinder than flawless recall permitted us to *mis*remember it.

And the last of the limousines was waiting, and we let the chauffeur hold the door for us, and we got in and went off to Jimmy's baronial mansion to hear the reading of the will.

And Kerch, left behind in the rain, went with us.

Jimmy had been having simultaneous affairs with four women, any one of whom would have been sufficiently daunting to scare even Vlad the Impaler into impotence. One was an Olympic gymnast, no more than twenty years old, what is usually referred to as coltish, natural blonde naturally, and much given to scenes in restaurants where the maître d' objected to her carrying a coatimundi on her shoulder. Her name was Muriel. One was an authority on machine intelligence, in her early thirties, with what used to be referred to as "bee-stung" lips, a mass of heavy, thick black, lustrous hair the shade of thoughts for which one can be jailed without bail, and an intellect that made virtually everything she said incomprehensible to all but five or six of the finest minds on the planet. Her name was Andrea. One was a Cuban actress who had fled Batista's tyranny mere hours before an order for her arrest on grounds of moral turpitude was issued, whose exiled status in America had been guaranteed by the extension of said warrant whose grounds of moral turpitude had been upheld by Castro; not yet thirty, in appearance no more than twenty-five, she claimed to be Chicana, Puerto Rican, Venezuelan or Castilian, depending on what the casting director was seeking, with a pair of legs usually referred to as "terminating just under her chin," with a voice and range that could have shamed Yma Sumac, and a temper that frequently manifested itself in a splendid right cross. Her name was Edith. One was a consumer advocate for CBS television, a former runner-up to Miss North Carolina in the Miss America contest, thirty years old, rather puckishly committed to a variation on the original Ann-Margret coiffure which, given all proper due, admirably suited her auburn hair, opinionated, contentious beyond belief, and directly responsible for a Xerox price rollback that had cost the firm nearly a quarter of a million dollars. Her name was Mary Louise.

I had been seeing Leslie for three years.

Not until six years after they'd married did Jimmy bother to ask if I'd been troubled by the heat-death of the universe. Simply never occurred to him to worry about it. Not that he was bone-stick-stone insensitive; no indeed: it was that he moved too fast for consideration of the emotional debacles at any given point along the scenic route.

They were living in Connecticut, near Crown Point, in a stately manse brought over from Thomas Hardy country, somewhere near Dorset, brick-by-brick, in the early 1900s by a Dutch robber baron who'd made his boodle in association with Elisha Otis on the development of the gearless traction elevator. It was one of those fumed oak, parquet-floored, wine-cellared beauties all writers dream about owning; just the right setting when one receives the word that one has been awarded a Nobel, or a Pulitzer, or an American Book Award, or a high six-figure purchase offer from Paramount. Two, and almost three, of those came to Jimmy in his stately manse. I was writing a lot of book reviews for *The Village Voice* and Kirkus.

He called late in the afternoon; the last spear of light permitted entrance by the surrounding buildings, had almost vanished from the airshaft, and I sat in gloomy relaxation trying to decipher the Mayan Codex that Doubleday charmingly called a royalty statement.

"What're you up to?" he said, without identifying himself.

"I'm locked in nonorgasmic congress with Doubleday's bookkeepers. It's the first time I've ever been fucked by a mindless octopus."

"How about dinner?"

"When, tonight?"

"Yeah. I'm in the city. You free?"

"According to my royalty statements that's exactly what I am."

"The new book isn't doing well?"

"How could it? They must have taken the entire printing, loaded it on barges, floated it out the Narrows and deep-sixed it. Weighted down, no doubt, by the excess profits from their latest bestselling cookbook."

"You don't sound like the man to cheer me up tonight."

"Sure I am. You can spend my last exuberant evening with me before I establish residency in the nearest leper colony."

"That would be the Carrville Leprosarium. In Louisiana. And they don't call it leprosy any more. Hansen's Disease."

"Why aren't I grateful for that information?"

"I could stop off at Abercrombie & Fitch on my way over, and pick up a nice big bell for you. Or maybe a cassette of Frankie Laine singing 'Unclean, Unclean.' Do wonders for getting you a seat on the subway during rush hour."

Badinage. Brightalk. Never a discouraging word, and the deer and the antelope play. The ritual incantations of those who had resonated to Salinger. I still had my red baseball cap in the bottom of a carton of old clothes, at the back of the bedroom closet. Nostalgia somehow cannot survive the smell of mothballs.

"I'm here; come on over whenever you're free."

"About an hour. We'll go have a steak. I'm paying."

I smiled. Naturally, you're paying. With a five thousand copy printrun of Laurence Bedloe's most recent astonishment, *The Salamander Enchantment,* rapidly being carried by salutary sea-currents toward the Bermuda Triangle, naturally you're paying for steaks. Now if you're up for Twinkies and Hawaiian Punch, I'm paying.

"See you when you get here."

"Take care."

"So long."

I listened to the dial tone for about two minutes. Then I sat in the growing darkness, thinking about Arctic tundra. Somehow it didn't make the Carrville Leprosarium seem more attractive.

After a while the doorbell buzzed and I put on some lights and let him in. He had the look of a man who had broken some vows.

"I need a drink," he said. He fell into the rocker with the leather seat, toed off his loafers, and sank down onto his spine, eyes closed. "By the unspeakable name of the slavering hordes of Yog-Sothoth, though Allah be the wiser...I do fiercely need a drink."

"Can be done, chum. Give it a speakable name and I'll put it in your paw in moments."

He rubbed his closed eyes ferociously. From inside his hands he mumbled, "Any damn thing. Largeish, if you will."

I went into the kitchen and opened the cupboard and gave the cognac a pass. This looked like heavy weather drinking. I poured Wild Turkey into a big water glass without benefit of jigger, tossed in a single ice cube, raised the level with a little tap water, and carried the Bomber's Moon back into the living room.

Jimmy was sitting on the floor, in the darkness near the window. I couldn't see him that well, but I could hear him sobbing. I think I grabbed for the doorjamb to steady myself. In the fifteen years we'd been friends, I'd never seen him cry. I'd never known him to cry. I'd never heard anyone mention that they'd seen him cry. It had never occurred to me that he might one day, in my presence, cry. I didn't even know if he was *able* to cry.

He didn't know I was there, staring at him.

Very quietly, I carried the glass over to him, put it down beside his crossed legs, and I went back across the room and sat just outside a pool of lamplight, my face in darkness. I had no idea what to do, didn't want to say something wrong, definitely didn't want whatever I finally said to be banality or homey homily; so I waited. Eventually, it seemed to me, he'd stop, take a drink, and we'd talk.

Eventually he stopped, noticed the glass, reached for it slowly and drank long and deep; and then he looked around for me.

"Here's a new one for you," he said.

I spoke softly. "Not so new; I do it all the time."

A marvelous waiting silence resumed.

Quite a while later he said, "I never asked you: were you pissed off at me for marrying Leslie?"

I thought about the right answer. Not necessarily the kindest answer, or the most polite answer, or the truthful answer, just the right one. "I think we were about done with each other."

"That's no answer."

"It's an answer. You want others, I can make up others.

But that's definitely *an* answer."

More silence. He finished the drink, I went in and threw a lot of cubes in a mixing bowl, brought the bowl and the bottle, and set them down in front of him. He worked at it slowly. Neither of us would end up alcoholics: we weren't passionate enough about the juice. Oh hi there, I'm recruiting for Richard the Lion-Hearted; we're putting together a *wonderful* follow-up to last year's big hit, The Children's Crusade. This year it's The Wino's March on Mecca, from the people who brought you the Black Death. You'll just love it—all the Sterno and Grand Marnier you can osmose. Whaddaya say?

Listen, I'll talk to you later. You go save Mecca, I'll have a go at writing the Great American Novel, and we'll meet right next to the big lions on the steps of the New York Public Library two years from now. You can't miss me, I'll be the one *without* the Holy Grail.

"You know, I've always felt like your kid brother," he said.

"It's only six months, Jimmy."

"Always felt faintly ridiculous around you. Loudmouthed, gauche, coming on too strong even when I was purposely speaking so softly I knew people had to strain to hear me."

"It's only six months, Jimmy."

"You know I'm a better writer than you, don't you? Not just sales . . . *better*. There's heat in my stuff; it works, it pulls the plow. *Better*."

"For Christ's sake, Larry, there's nothing but cold dead air blowing through your books. They ought to hand out woolly mittens with every copy of your stuff."

I thought about Arctic tundra. "Six months, Jimmy; just six months."

He started crying again. "For Christ's sake, Larry, *help* me! You've got it all together, you've got the answers, you've *always* had the answers. I don't know whether I'm coming or going, I'm falling apart. I feel like I'm being emptied out, like a hot water bottle; it's all running away from me. I'm going to kill somebody, I swear to God I'm going to run through the streets killing strangers."

"How about some gin rummy, tenth of a cent a point?"

He got up, went into the bathroom and washed his face.

When he came back he sat down in the rocker, looking bushed. "You ready to talk about it now?" I asked.

He stretched his hands out on the arms of the rocker until

the fingertips were just at the edge. Just at the edge. "This open marriage with Leslie is killing me. I can't stand it."

It was the first I'd heard of it. When he married her I stopped thinking about anything in that area. I never knew what went on with them in that way. I felt my stomach getting cold. That's the way I respond to photographs of Dachau.

"So get out of it," I said.

"Don't be an asshole."

"It's only six months, Jimmy."

He started yelling. "Give me a break, will you? I've got nobody else in the world to talk to. You're my best friend, maybe the only friend I can really trust. I'm *talking* to you, I'm asking for help!"

What I *wanted* to say was: come off it, Jimmy! You've got exactly and precisely what you always wanted. You're rich, you're well-liked, you're urbane and charming; you've got a beautiful, intelligent wife, a big classy home steeped in authentic antiquity; everywhere you go they know you, your face is on the tube and they don't hold you for the last fifteen minutes of the Carson Show; you go where you want, do what you want, you're a workaholic under the weight of the Puritan Work Ethic, so you get off on slaving night and day . . .

You're who you made you, Jimmy; so come off it.

Wanted to say that. But didn't. Sat there and said, "Go ahead, tell me what's happening." Remember when you were a kid, how awful it was when you bit down on the tinfoil?

And he went on for about two hours, telling me everything about his life, and Leslie's life, and my life, and about how dear I was to him because I was his role-model. All of this went in and flowed out again, and I must confess there were even three or four things that disgusted me.

And then we went out to O. Henry's Steak House and had magisterial chunks of some King of the Beasts, and I put ketchup on mine and Kercher Oliver James Crowstairs, the best-selling and critically acclaimed author winced and said, "That's disgusting, Larry."

And I said: "Chalk it up to improper toilet training."

Jimmy's baronial mansion was not the one in which he'd lived with Leslie. That had been Connecticut. This was Los Angeles. The Crown Point mansion had been brought over

stone-by-stone from Dorset. This one looked as if it had been
brought over ticky-by-tacky from the back lot at Twentieth.

But it had a "library." Yes, indeed, it had a library that held
the 37,000 books Jimmy had owned at the moment of his death.
He read a book a day, summer or winter, bright or cloudy,
naked or clothed.

And we gathered there, in the high-arched library, for the
reading of the will, the last will and testament of Jimmy, beloved Kerch, American literary treasure.

It was not what I expected. But then, Jimmy never did the
expected. There was an evening we spent together at a reception
for the Brazilian ambassador to the United States, at the Spanish
legation in Washington, during which Jimmy had a meaningful
relationship with a gigantic silver Cellini tureen filled with
applesauce . . .

It was not what I expected.

The room had been set up with deep, comfortable chairs all
facing an enormous beam-television screen. The projector was
hooked up with a Sony Betamax unit. An impish-looking man
of middle height, wearing what was clearly a very expensive
three-piece suit that had not been properly tailored to the slump
of his shoulders, stood before the screen holding a document
that was very likely the last hurrah of my friend Jimmy Crowstairs.

Despite the serious manner of the imp in the three-piece
suit, intended I suppose to give the occasion the proper por-
tentous ambiance, it was impossible to get away from a festive
feeling in that room. Jimmy had been an inveterate collector—
of everything. The library was floor-to-ceiling with books,
almost all hardcovers, arranged alphabetically by author, from
Aeschylus, Aldiss and Algren at the left of the topmost shelf
of the first bookcase to the left side of the entranceway . . . to
Zamyatin, Zelazny and Zola at the bottom of the last bookcase
all the way around the enormous room at the right side of the
entrance. But there were also glass cases spotted across the
room, containing pewter figurines, Makundi sculpture from
Mozambique, lacquered boxes from Russia, T'ang dynasty
glazes, gold scarabs encrusted with lapis lazuli from Egypt's
Middle Kingdom, scrimshaw from whaling villages in New
England, Amerindian pottery, German kinetic sculptures flick-
ering and strobing, ceramic statues from the Austrian courts,
fantasy bronzes by Enzenbacher, Spacher and Rumph; and

lucite easels with paintings: Kanemitsu, Stamitz, Pebworth, David Hockney, the Dillons, Wunderlich, Bash, Wyeth, Rothko, Kley, Campanile and Willardson. And in the dead center of the room was a nine foot tall model of the Abominable Snowman that Steve Kirk had designed for the Matterhorn at Disneyland.

No matter how hard the imp in the three-piece suit worked at it, he could not possibly overcome the lunatic frivolity of that *yeti*.

The five chairs were arranged in a semicircle. At the extreme left, already seated, Jimmy's sister SylviaTheCunt stared straight ahead, folding and refolding the telegram that had commanded her appearance here. The next chair was empty. And the next chair. In the fourth chair sat Jimmy's friend Bran Winslow, himself a writer, and probably the gentlest human being I'd ever met. He had not been at the burial ceremony. In the last chair, at the extreme right, sat Missy, which was short for Mississippi, who was—and for the past fifteen years had been—Jimmy's assistant, good right hand, troubleshooter, basic office staff and Person Friday. She let no one call her a "girl," even if the word Friday followed it.

Obviously the two empty chairs were for Leslie and me.

We moved toward the chairs and started to sit down, but the imp stopped us, saying, "Mrs. Crowstairs, would you take the third seat please; Mr. Bedloe, Kerch wanted you to sit in the second seat." We rearranged ourselves. It made good sense: I separated Leslie and SylviaTheCunt, who looked on each other with the enthusiasm one might evince at the prospect of root canal surgery.

The imp waited till we were settled, then he said, "My name is Kenneth L. Gross; I was the attorney for Kercher Oliver James Crowstairs and remain legal counsel for both his estate and The Kerch Corporation in which Mr. Crowstairs was the principal party of record."

He showed us the document we had all come to hear.

"This document is Mr. Crowstairs's last will and testament, as you might have supposed. However, it will not be read here today."

Why had I suspected Jimmy wasn't finished with us yet?

He waited a moment for the effect, then went on. "Mr. Crowstairs, as you all know, was a rather remarkable man, with a flair for the original. One day, several years ago, we were discussing the preparation of this document, and I mentioned, almost as a joke, that he ought to videotape the reading of his will. Kerch . . . Mr. Crowstairs immediately fastened on the idea and instructed me to look into the legal ramifications of such a videotaping.

"At first there were questions of validity, but Mr. Crowstairs financed the appropriate research, and in a decision handed down just eight months ago by the Supreme Court of the State of California, such a procedure was adjudged permissible, contingent on a written document being prepared as it has been historically.

"Many of the smaller grants in this document will be handed directly through my office, but the principal beneficiaries are gathered here, per Mr. Crowstairs's instructions; and you will now hear your bequests directly from the deceased. This extended element of the basic instrument was videotaped four months ago . . . before any of us had any idea . . . we never thought . . ."

He faltered to silence. I liked him a lot. He had cared about Jimmy.

Then he went behind us and turned on the television set from the projection module, cut in the Betamax, light appeared on the enormous screen, color-bands of leader ran through, and suddenly we were looking at this room, with Jimmy, the attorney, Missy, a tall, thin black woman I didn't recognize, and Bran Winslow, sitting at Jimmy's desk. It was obvious that Missy, the black woman and Bran Winslow were the witnesses to the execution of the will, and I now understood how two people as close to Jimmy as Missy and Bran had been, who had been there only a few months before when this document had been merely an act of preparing for the long, far inevitable future, had chosen not to attend the burial service.

They all sat up there, larger than life, on the screen, and I thought with the faintest flutter of trepidation, *What a field day the archivists will have with* this *little chunk of literary gossip.*

Roll 'em, C.B. It's magic time, I thought. *Break a leg, Jimmy.*

He once took me along with him on what he called a "dangerous mission of research."

Because of the confessional nature of much of what
wrote—Jimmy had believed Hemingway when Poppa s.
"a writer should never write what he doesn't know"—K
was forever putting himself in crazy situations where raw
terial for books had to be obtained first-hand, usually at
of one's life or sanity; or at very least at risk of one's c
plexion.

He had scaled mountains, raced sports cars, worked i
steel foundry, traveled cross-county on a Vincent Bl
Shadow with Hell's Angels, marched with Chavez in
Coachella Valley, spent time in Southern jails for civil ri
activities, chummed it up with a Mafia *capo*, managed to
a trio of radical feminist lesbians into a four-way sexual liais
covered a South American revolution, hired himself out
firm specializing in industrial espionage, and God knows v
all else.

He had no secrets when he wrote. He talked about
feelings when his mother had lingered in her endless midn
coma and he signed the order to kick out the plug on her l
support system; he revealed the most intimate secrets of
love life, with Leslie and others; he told stories on himself
men with more humility and a greater sense of shame wo
have buried in the vaults of their family secrets. Probably
cause of that open conversation that went on between Jim
and his millions of readers, his popularity grew and grew
was possible to trust a man who told *everything*, a man v
could not be morally or literarily blackmailed. It made it s
reasonable that he would go to the burning core of whate
he wrote, because he was not afraid of sunlight striking
tomb of the vampire.

And once he took me with him.

I was living in Chicago at the time, doing editorial w
on a men's magazine. He called and asked if I was free
night, and if I was free would I like to accompany him c
"dangerous mission of research."

Evenings spent in Jimmy's company were many things,
they were seldom dull or uneventful. I said I was stoked
an adventure.

He picked me up in a Hertz rental at the office, and al
would say was that we were going deep into the South :
of the city, the section commonly known as Back of the Ya
Oh yes, he said one more thing: he was going to see a wo

who had given him a case of the crabs.

I think I responded with the remark, "Frankly, I'm underwhelmed."

But when we got there—*there* being a rundown tenement in a scuzzy section—I found an apartment half-filled with card-carrying criminals. They had the appearance of righteous gypsies, some kind of hyperthyroid Romany rejects. Eleven of them, looking like road company understudies for "The Wolf Man," starring Madame Maria Ouspenskaya.

Four flights up, in what would have been called a railroad flat, had we been in New York and not Chicago, they sat around the kitchen staring at Jimmy and me with dark, hooded eyes. I felt like a cobra at a mongoose rally.

An extremely attractive young woman had opened the apartment door after Jimmy had knocked in a special cadence: two shorts close together, pause, then three more shorts.

"'Open, Sesame' isn't required, eh? How convenient," I said. He gave me one of his looks.

And the door was opened by this extremely attractive young woman, who threw her arms around him and kissed him full on the mouth. I stared beyond them, into the kitchen, and was greeted by the massed nastiness contained in ten pairs of dark, hooded eyes.

He held her away from him and murmured something too quietly for the gypsies to hear. What he said, Jimmy always the romantic, was: "What're you pushing this time . . . cancer?"

She grinned and gave him a playful punch in the stomach—playful enough to straighten him out with a whooze of pain. Then she led him into the apartment. I followed, not happily.

Let me cut through all the subsequent hours of weird happenings. The background was this:

Jimmy had been out on the lecture circuit the year before. In Kansas City the usual gaggle of esurient sycophants who cannot differentiate between the Artist and the Art rushed the podium for autographs and cheap thrills such as the pressing of flesh. In the crowd had been an extremely attractive young woman who, when her turn came to thrust a book and a pen under Jimmy's nose, had thrust neither. She had moved in quickly and thrust *herself*. Reaching for him, she had put her mouth to his ear and whispered, "Why don't we go back up to your hotel room and see if you can make me groan."

Needless to say . . .

About a week later, Jimmy back home, a phone call on his private line. It was the extremely attractive young woman whom Jimmy had made groan. Her name, she told him, was not Mia, as she had told him. She was not, strictly speaking, a bank teller, as she had told him. She was, in fact, a member of a rather large family that specialized in robbing banks. When they were between jobs, she worked as a bank teller. "Who better?" Jimmy had replied to that one. She was on the dodge, spent most of her time underground with different aliases and different pseudo-lives, and she had had a wonderful time with Jimmy whose books, during those long hours underground, had brought her endless pleasure.

When Jimmy inquired why she was revealing all this to him, she shamefacedly admitted—though he couldn't see her face—that she had probably given him a cataclysmic dose of the crabs.

Without even bothering to check, Jimmy perceived that he had, at last, an understanding of why he had been scratching furiously for the preceding week. As it was his first exposure to *Phthirus pubis,* he dropped instantly into panic. "I would rather," he said later, "have ten thousand years of tertiary syphilis than ten seconds of the crabs." He had an urgent Candygram from his autonomic nervous system, directing him in the most stridently hysterical tones, to rush off and set fire to his crotch.

She had gone on—unaware that Jimmy was no longer within ratiocination range—to say she hadn't known about it herself, that she was sorry as hell, and that she thought it was a crummy thing to do to someone who had given her so many hours of pleasure, both in print and in bed. And *that,* she told him, was why she was calling him to tell him . . . and spilling the beans about herself. (Which wasn't that big a deal, apparently, because she wasn't in Kansas City any more; and *he* couldn't very well find her, or the family, if the FBI, the Federal Reserve System, the Organized Crime Task force, Brink's and the Pinkertons couldn't find them.)

Ever the polite chap, Jimmy had thanked her decently for taking the time to call on such a piddling matter when she obviously had bigger problems to worry about. Then he hung up the phone, hyperventilated, and sent Missy to the pharmacy to buy copious quantities of A-200 Pyrinate Liquid, Cuprex, Kwell cream *and* Kwell lotion—and a thermite bomb just to be prepared in the event a scorched-earth policy proved necessary.

Now a year later, the Mia-*manqué* had summoned Jimmy from California to Chicago to act as intermediary in the family's surrender to the Laws (as she called them, reminiscent of the colorful patois of Bonnie & Clyde).

And this once he had taken me with him.

Pseudo-Mia took him by the hand and started to lead him down the hallway toward the rear of the apartment. "Hey!" I said. The sound made by a ferret caught in a clampjaw trap.

Jimmy turned, still being led by the hand, walked backward and said, "Make yourself at home. Strike up new acquaintances. Establish meaningful relationships. I'll be back."

And Not-Mia opened a door to what I presumed was a bedroom off the hall—thereby illuminating her family's liberal, one might even say cavalier, attitude toward her sexual egalitarianism—and she disappeared inside; followed by Jimmy's disappearing hand, arm, body, and face, leaving behind only the smile of the Cheshire Cat.

I turned to stare at ten pairs of dark, hooded eyes that were staring at me.

A man in his thirties got up, stood aside, and indicated the empty chair at the kitchen table. I sat down, not happily.

At almost the instant I realized there was a wonderful, dark brown smell of something baking in the apartment, the old woman—an old *old* woman, shapeless and infinitely corrugated with wrinkles—sitting directly across from me reached behind her, wearing a potholder mitt, opened the door of the oven, pulled out a metal bread pan, and slapped it down on the table between us.

"Langos," she said. She pronounced it *lahng*-osh.

It smelled sensational. Some kind of deep-fried bread dough she'd apparently been keeping warm in the oven. I looked at it. The guy who had given me his seat took a bowl full of garlic cloves off the sink and put it down in front of me.

"Bread," he said. "Rub it with the garlic."

I reached in, took a piece of *langos*, burned my fingertips, squeaked, provoked ten smiles, added an eleventh, my own, and rubbed the hot surface with a clove of garlic. It tasted sensational.

Then the old, old woman began rattling off at me. She spoke uninterruptedly for about a minute. In Hungarian. I smiled. I nodded. She stopped and looked at me, waiting for a response. I thought of Arctic tundra.

A man in his fifties, sitting to my left, said, "She asks if you know if Laurie will marry Vic Lamont and if Cookie will go crazy and will Simon Jessup kill Orin Hillyer?"

I stopped chewing. I smiled. I nodded. I looked from one to another of them, hoping someone would take pity on a man lost in the desert.

The old, old woman, hearing what the man in his fifties had said, added a few more words. I looked at the interpreter. He spoke resignedly: "And will Adam Drake fall in love with Nicole?"

I hoped, with profound desperation, that Mia was neither greedy nor afflicted with the *djam karet* attendant on ownership of a hooded clitoris.

"I'm sorry," I said slowly, "but I don't know what she's talking about." I smiled. I nodded.

There was an appreciable drop in temperature around the table. The man in his fifties said something short to the old, old woman. She snorted that special snort translatable in *any* language as, "Who asked for you, who sent for you; who sent for you, who asked for you?"

And so, every instant anguish, I sat there for the better part of an hour. In Indonesia they have a name for it: *djam karet* . . . the hour that stretches.

Eventually, open covenants having apparently been openly entered into, Other-Than-Mia and Jimmy emerged from the bedroom. It looked like a draw.

I got up at a signal from Jimmy, who drew me aside. I started to whisper my consternation, but he pressed my bicep for silence. Maybe-Mia took my seat, and began speaking in a low, intense voice. In Hungarian. Or Urdu. Or tongues, maybe. What do I know about glossolalia?

She was about fifteen seconds into the recitation when they *all* started replying. Eleven gypsies, all going at it like the Russians were invading Evanston. A hailstorm of babble.

Jimmy leaned in and said, "You know the FBI's list of Ten Most Wanted?"

I nodded. Not happily.

"They just made it to number one."

"Terrific. I'll meet you in the car; say my goodbyes for me."

"Shut up and listen.

"It's a hype. It's a publicity dodge. The Feds never put *anyone* on that list till a week or two before they're going to make an arrest. That way, they spread it around about all these dangerous felons at large, and a week or so later the Bureau makes a pinch, making it look as if they're right on top of things. People they *can't* find never even get *on* the list."

"You're telling me Jimmy Stewart's going to break in here any minute with a Thompson submachine gun, is that it?"

"I'm telling you they want to give themselves up; but they're afraid they'll get wiped out if they just wait for the Feds to find them."

"Why don't they run? God knows they're in practice."

"Shut up and listen.

"They want me to be the go-between. To get the press and some responsible local officials in here before they pull the plug."

"Listen, Jimmy . . . they pull the plug and you're liable to lose the baby with the bathwater. I'm referring to *me*, baby, in case you had any doubts . . ."

"Take it easy. I did a docudrama about a Chicago psychiatrist for CBS last year . . ."

I hadn't heard the word *docudrama* before. I was looking at him with confusion. He understood my problem and said, "Fictionalized documentary. Semi-real. Touches truth in at least ten places. Anyhow . . ."

The babble was growing louder. The old, old woman was now silent, watching and listening. The thirty-year-old guy and the fifty-year-old guy were obviously on opposite sides of the question—whatever the question *was*—and I could see the crowd was about evenly divided. The older guy was with Mia, whatever she was proposing, and I had the certain feeling that if the thirty-year-old guy's point of view prevailed, that this baby might go down the drain *before* Jimmy Stewart made one of his rare personal appearances.

"Are you *listening* to me?" Kerch demanded, squeezing my arm.

"No," I whispered, "I'm listening to *them*. Somehow I get the feeling what they're saying has more to do with my living to a dignified old age."

"Just shut up and listen, for Christ's sake!

"Marvin Ziporyn is his name . . . the psychiatrist. He's the top shrink for the state. Works with the Cook County authorities. Concert violinist, big social mover, wrote a couple of books; he's got access to Kup and the Mayor and everybody else."

I was staring openly now. Hell, anybody could get to the Mayor; but access to Irv Kupcinet, the columnist; well, that was the Big Time.

"So?"

"So I call Marvin, tell him what I'm into, get him to contact Kup, who'll love it a lot. They pull in a few of the local squires and top cossacks . . . and Mia and the crowd remand themselves into proper custody."

"Before Jimmy Stewart breaks in . . ."

"Right, right."

"I'll meet you at the car. Thank the old lady for the bread." I started toward the door. The thirty-year-old guy erupted from his seat and if there was anything else in that lousy kitchen but the gigantic .45 in his hairy paw, I didn't see it. There is a quality about blue-steel gunmetal that gathers all light in a room; like a black diamond.

He was pointing it at me.

I grinned stupidly, placed both palms against the air and tittered like the village idiot. He seemed somewhat mollified and the barrel of the automatic lowered to the vicinity of my crotch. For a moment there it had been like staring into the mouth of the Holland Tunnel, only bigger.

"Damn it, Larry, stop acting like a schmuck. Let Mia handle it."

"Her name isn't Mia."

"Whatever her name is; let her handle it."

So I stood there with him, leaning against the wall, for the better part of an hour while the Sanhedrin decided my fate.

Sometime during that hour I asked him, "Who's Vic Lamont?"

He said, "Who?"

I said, "Vic Lamont."

He said, "Never heard of him."

I said, "Will Laurie marry him?"

He said, "What the fuck are you talking about?"

I said, "Will Laurie marry Vic Lamont; will Cookie go crazy; will Simon Somebody-or-other kill Orin Hillyer; will Adam Something-or-other fall in love with Nicole?"

He stared at me.

"The old lady seemed miffed I didn't know the answers," I whispered.

He thought about it a minute. Then he said, *"The Edge of Night.* It's a soap opera."

I said, "Why me?"

He said. "Because you're with me, and Mia told them I'm a famous television writer, and that means *you're* a famous television writer, and that means you know what happens to all those characters in the soap operas, because they're not characters, they're real people, and I suppose when you're on the lam the only consistency in your life is the surrogate life of people in soap operas. What'd you tell her?"

"I didn't tell her anything. I didn't have the faintest idea what she was talking about."

He said, "How'd she take it?"

I said, "Not terrific."

He nodded, thought about it a minute, then called Mia over. He took her aside, whispered at her for a little while, then sent her back to the table. She bent down over the old, old woman, whispered in her ear for a while longer, and when she straightened up the old, old woman was grinning wide as a death's-head. Her mouth was a classic argument for compulsory remedial orthodontia.

Whatsername sat down and smiled, waiting.

Then the old, old woman said something sharp and hard. In Hungarian. Everybody shut up and stared at her. Then she said something else, not quite as sharp and hard, and the thirty-year-old guy packing the Holland Tunnel bowed his thorny head, nodded in supplication, and murmured words of acquiescence.

The fifty-year-old spoke rapidly to the Ghost of Mia Past, every once in a while pointing at Jimmy or me, or Jimmy *and* me. Once, damned sure, he was making a threat; and once, damned certain, he was giving warning. She nodded, said okay okay okay every few sentences, added a thought here and there and, finally, it all seemed settled.

She got up, came over to us, and said, "All set. Do your stuff, Kerch."

He gave her a little kiss and started toward the old black two-handed pedestal telephone on the kitchen counter. I asked the Memory of Mia, "What's all set?"

She patted me on the cheek and answered, "They're not going to cut you into small pieces and leave you in garbage cans all over the South Side." Then she went away, to join my best friend, Kercher Oliver James Crowstairs, who had brought me along into the jaws of death on a "dangerous mission of research."

It was not till a week later, after the gypsy bank robbers had given themselves up with attendant headlines and photos of Jimmy leading them out of the tenement into the waiting arms of Irv Kupcinet, the Mayor of Chicago and the bureau Chief of the Midwest Regional FBI office (not to mention several thousand cops and G-Men armed for the apocalypse), that Kerch bothered to tell me that what had saved our lives was Mia's imparting to her dear old Granny the information that I was a close family friend of everyone on *The Edge of Night* and that when (or if) Granny ever got sprung from the federal slam, I would introduce her to Laurie, Vic Lamont, Simon Jessup, Orin Hillyer, Cookie, Nicole and Adam Drake, *whoever* the hell they were!

"My name is Kercher O. J. Crowstairs," said the Kercher O. J. Crowstairs three times life-size on the screen before us. The camera pulled back into a medium shot and Jimmy up there whipped open the wallet lying on the desk. He pulled out a sheaf of cards and held the first one up to the camera, which obligingly zoomed in for a closeup. Jimmy's voice, off-camera, said, "And this is my driver's license, issued by the state of California. You'll notice it has a rather unflattering photograph of me right here in the lower left-hand corner, which will identify me as the one and only K. O. J. Crowstairs, your friendly neighborhood testator."

The camera had slowly pulled back to include the attorney, Kenneth L. Gross. He was making a small moue at Jimmy's levity. The moue became a stricture as Jimmy held up one card after another:

"And this is my BankAmericard/Visa card; and this is my Master Charge card; and this is my Diners Club card, but I don't use it much; and this is my Carte Blanche; and this one will rent me a Hertz, and this one an Avis, and this one will get me a tacky room in any Holiday Inn across the face of the Earth; and this one is for Neiman-Marcus, and this one is for good old Bloomingdale's, and . . ."

He must have caught the strangled moan from Gross, because he stopped. He dropped the rest of the thick pack of cards, and looked into the camera.

"Look: we're doing this videotape so no one, and that means *no one* will be able to raise the question of my competency after I've croaked. By competency they mean was I of sound mind and body, and under no duress, such as being held captive by the Symbionese Liberation Army. But if I played it absolutely straight, and didn't laugh at all this somber bullshit, then anyone who's known me more than ten minutes would suspect I *was* out of my skull.

"Nonetheless . . ." and he said this hurriedly, because Gross was making the kind of strangling noises that, had he uttered them in a good restaurant, would have brought the maître d' running to administer the Heimlich Maneuver, "nonetheless, moving right along to the serious stuff, folks, here's my friend and advisor, the world-famous corporate attorney, Mr. Kenneth L. Gross, who'd like to say a few words. Let's give him a big funeral day welcome . . . *Kenny Gross!*"

The attorney was the color of old toothpaste as he read from a prepared form. "Mr. Crowstairs, you have now established your identity for those who may be seeing this recording at a later date. You have retained this office in connection with estate planning and more specifically to prepare your will. The document I now show you (handing will to client), is the final draft of that will. Would you please take a moment to review it?"

The screen now went to split-frame, the right side being a copy of the will. Jimmy took the document Gross handed him and scanned it. "But this is a laundry list, Kenny." The attorney damned near fainted. Jimmy laughed and hurriedly corrected himself. "I'm *kidding,* I'm just kidding; this is my will; honest to God, I swear it is!"

Gross was breathing hard. I felt for the poor devil. "Is this the document that you have, hopefully, previously read?"

"Yes, it is. But you don't mean *hopefully,* Kenny. You mean *I hope,* or *it is to be hoped,* or *one hopes.* You see, when you use the word 'hopefully,' you're reporting a subjective state of mind; that is, *full of hope.* Your error is in attributing *your* hope to the object, in this case the will . . . or is the object *me?* I'm never really sure of parts of speech. In any case, if you were to reverse the word, you'd see how wrong it's being used: *hopelessly* I've read it. See what I mean? Good grammar, Kenny; always good grammar. Your mother and I have chided you about this on numerous occasions..."

Gross exploded. *"Mister* Crowstairs! If you will, sir! This is a serious undertaking! Now *is this,* or is this *not* the document previously read by yourself?"

"It is, it is! Nag, nag, nag."

Gross gave it up. He bulled forward. Not happily. "Are you executing this document or prepared to execute this document... no, wait... I'm out of sequence! Damn it, Kerch!"

Jimmy grinned infectiously. He was never happier than when he was stirring up the soup. He laid a placating hand on Gross's. "Take it easy, Kenny. Don't fumfuh."

Gross swallowed; as they say, he looked daggers at his client, pulled a weathered pipe with a large Oom Paul bowl and a bent stem from his vest pocket, puffed it alight with a kitchen match taken from his *other* vest pocket, harrumphed once, and began again.

"All right, then: In my presence, and in the presence of these witnesses, and cognizant of the fact that these proceedings are being videotaped, does this document reflect your exclusive and entire wishes with regard to the disposition of your property?"

Testator responded in the affirmative: "I respond in the affirmative."

The attorney now turned to the three witnesses. "Each of you has known Mr. Crowstairs for many years. You have been asked to participate in these proceedings for the purpose of further identification. Will you now, each in turn, declare who you are, your relationship to Mr. Crowstairs, and verify that this is, in fact, Mr. Kercher Oliver James Crowstairs."

Camera came into closeup on the first witness as the split-screen went to solo image.

"My name is Brandon Winslow. I have been a close personal friend, house guest and sometime-collaborator of Kercher Crowstairs for almost fourteen years; and I hereby declare that the man over there with all the credit cards is, in fact and as he's stated, the Crowstairs he says he is."

Well, well, I thought, *oh my ears and whiskers.*

"Sometime-collaborator." Now there's one phrase I never thought I'd hear in connection with Jimmy. So Bran had been paying off the loans and the live-in companionship with something more valuable than coin of the realm. He had worked on some of the books. That went a long way toward explaining how Jimmy could turn out his novel *and* a short story collection every year as regular as the swallows visiting Capistrano, plus finding the time for all the introductions, newspaper columns, background pieces for *TV Guide;* the lectures, the television talk show appearances, the writing workshops; *and* the women. He had another laborer in the vineyard. A bond slave.

I cast back through the long list of Crowstairs publications trying to figure out which ones had been co-written—*entirely ghost-written?!?!*—no, it was unthinkable—but then, *collaboration* had been unthinkable till Bran had let the black cat cross the path—and I came up with two immediately.

Bakelite Radio Fantasies and *Fearsome Noises*. They were gentler, more thoughtful than was Jimmy's wont. There was greater lyricism in them, closer in tone to Bran's own solo novel—his *only* novel—*Knowledge of Two Kinds*. They were a couple of my favorite Crowstairs creations.

And my heart contracted in my chest as I realized that in some way Bran Winslow had sold himself to Jimmy, had denied his own career, to add a few more chapters to the myth of Kercher Crowstairs. I didn't want to know what Jimmy had had on Bran, that could make him, seemingly willingly, put aside his own work, to become a secret shadow of the public Kerch.

To me, it was unthinkable. The more I thought about it, the more often the word *unthinkable* burned in the darkness. Unthinkable: Jimmy was many kinds of a man, but blackmailer wasn't one of them. Unthinkable: Brandon Winslow was as fiercely committed to his art as was I, as was Jimmy . . .

Unthinkable!

No one has that kind of charisma. I simply wouldn't go for it. There had to be something deeper, something more potent. It was unthinkable that a writer of Bran Winslow's sincerity and dedication would simply give over his life to Jimmy; it was unthinkable that Jimmy's fever could be passed on to another writer—possibly a *better* writer, a more important writer, an intrinsically more valuable, a *worthier* writer—to cause him to deny the song of his own Muse. But now that I'd thought it, as unthinkable as it had seemed . . .

Kercher Crowstairs refused to acknowledge the night.

He had a quote from Thomas Carlyle taped to the molding of the bookcase right over his typewriter:

> *Produce! Produce! Were it but the pitifullest infinitesimal fraction of a Product, produce it, in God's name! 'Tis the utmost thou hast in thee: out with it, then. Up, up! Whatsoever thy hand findeth to do, do it with thy whole might. Work while it is called Today; for the night cometh, wherein no man can work.*

He refused to cower against the fear of scaled or furry or fanged creatures moving toward him in the night.

He was a sharpened stick.

He was in motion, no sitting target.

He did not play poker, yet he never sat with his back to the door.

But such a level of energy *has* to dissipate itself before it can consume another writer. It has to! Sheer force of will, massed totality of personality, unleashed waves of charismatic power...no one has that. No one! Unthinkable goddam you Kerch Jimmy!

What the fuck did you have on Bran Winslow to turn him into your Uncle Tom? Your Stepin Fetchit? Your coolie laborer? Second sax in your brass section? Make-work creative typist?

Oh, Jesus, Jimmy, this is most hateful; and I don't even know what was behind it.

Poor Bran.

Damn! Stop that! Stop thinking that way. There was a reason, a solid, good reason. There had to be. No writer can do that to another writer who knows how good he is, who has the books in him crying out to be released. No one. No damn you, *no one!*

My head was swimming. I felt sick to my stomach.

"Can you hold the tape," I heard myself saying; and then as the film vanished and white screen appeared, I bolted out of my chair and rushed for the toilet.

That dyspeptic old fart Nelson Algren got three out of four. He wrote: "Never play cards with a man named *Doc*. Never eat in a place called *Mom's*. Never sleep with a woman whose troubles are worse than your own."

Close. Very close.

But he missed a fourth:

"Never let anyone catch you down on your knees puking into a toilet bowl."

Especially not a woman whose troubles are worse than your own.

I should have locked the door. But the bile was pushing as if it were spring-loaded; I barely had time to get into the can before I felt it coming like the Sunshine Express. Down on my knees, loving the toilet bowl, and then the river of fire.

Leslie was in there, right behind me, trying to hold my forehead, *for Christ's consumptive sake,* with me hurling and heaving like a boa constrictor that's swallowed a Peterbilt. I shoved at her, ineffectually, as she continued to play Lady Bountiful to my bounty.

I flailed my free arm behind me, trying to get her to *back off.* I think in that moment I realized just how insensitive she is. There'd always been hints... such as her revelation at a group dinner many years before that she had, as a child, thrown a hamster into a window fan... and then, of course, she'd stayed married to Jimmy; that had to indicate more than a *soupçon* of the obdurate.

But the level of insensitivity it takes to force someone in the most degrading condition known to humanity to think that he's being *watched* while he glops up his guts, no matter if it's misguidedly interpreted as "concern" or "out of love," is a bestial level whereon one finds only flagstones or spent shell casings. *Back off!*

After a while I got up, filled the sink with cold water, put my face into it completely, and lay there for quite a length of time, allowing the spittle and other nastiness to float away on the tide. My eyes were burning. I could not, thank God, see my face in the water.

I emptied the bowl, washed thoroughly, gargled as best I could with icy water, and reached for a towel. Leslie was standing there with one in her outstretched hand.

I took it. "Thank you very much."

"How do you feel?"

"Dandy. Just dandy."

"That was awful."

I looked a surprised look. "Oh, really? It usually brings down the house. The awestruck expressions of the crowd are usually upon me." *Back* the fuck *off!*

"My God," she said, "you know you're even starting to *talk* like him?"

Have you never perceived that before, my love? Have you never caught on that my interior monologues are *never* in my own voice, never the way *I* write or speak? They are pure Jimmy. That quick-silver turn of the phrase, all that heat and color; not the plodding, methodical, reasonably reasoned wise uncle with good, solid thinking of Laurence Bedloe, but rather the bold, sure spring of the tiger, and I believe in you. Never caught that, eh? How sad, how sorry: if I were to write up the relationship between the Recently Departed and Larry Bedloe it would be in the assumed voice of Kerch Jimmy. You didn't pick up on that? You're simply not paying attention.

"The hamster isn't the *most* awful I've ever heard," I said, "although it *is* in the top tenth of a percentile of the most awful."

"What are you *talking* about? Are you okay?"

"The *most* awful, I guess, was something Missy told me. She said that when she was a kid Down South they used to take baby ducks and chicks, and they'd bury them up to their no-necks in the dirt, and then they'd run the lawn mower over them. Now *that* is yucchh."

Her face was all pulled out of shape. "I'm calling the doctor."

There was a set of silver-backed military brushes on the counter. I picked them up and started brushing back my wet hair. I looked at her in the mirror and said, "Very good idea. You call the doctor. Make it a voodoo doctor, if you can get Inboard to clear a line to Haiti. Get a specialist in resurrection. Tell him we're not sure Jimmy is completely all the way dead . . . that he seems to be clinging ferociously to life . . . *your* life, *my* life, *Bran's* life . . ."

She started to cry. I put the brushes down and turned to her; but I didn't take her in my arms, usually *pro forma*. I just stared at her. She had the heels of her hands in her eyes and she was starting to get into it.

"Come on, Leslie! Pack it in, darlin'!"

She fell against me, put her arms around me.

"Then," I said, "he pushed her away." And I pushed her away.

She looked at me. She said, "What?"

"He stared back at her," I said, "and said simply, 'We don't walk backward, do we? You're his wife; you'll *always* be his wife, even if you remarry, even if you're canonized; he owns you. You say no, but five years from now you'll make a deal with Simon & Schuster and have poor Bran out there ghostwrite your memoirs—*I Was Kercher's Koncubine.*' And he shook his head sadly," I said, "and he walked to the door and walked out." And then I walked past her to the door and walked out.

Not so hard ghostwriting in the voice of a ghost.

They all looked at me as I reentered the library. I patted the Abominable Snowman on the belly and resumed my appointed seat, ready to let Jimmy have another go at me. Bamboo shoots under the fingernails would have been a happier prospect.

They were still looking at me as Leslie came in. "Something I ate, perhaps. An undigested bit of beef, a blot of mustard, a fragment of underdone potato. More of gravy than of grave. Do let's continue with the show." All but Leslie continued to stare at me, touched by astonishment. Ah, of what good are literary allusions in the Land of Functional Illiterates, close to the borders of the Kingdom of the Blind?

But we continued.

The videotape began playing again, and once again we were in this library, weeks ago, only a moment after Bran had identified Jimmy as Jimmy and caused me to lose a perfectly lovely breakfast from DuPar's Farmhouse. The tall, thin black woman I didn't recognize now spoke, as the camera came in on her.

"My name is Eusona Parker, and I have been Mr. Crowstairs's housekeeper for eighteen, going on nineteen years; and that's him sitting right there; and don't *no*body try to say he's not in his sound mind and body 'cause I have *known* him all these years and he's just as sharp and clean and neat as a pin as he's *ever* been. Is that what I'm supposed to say?"

No wonder I didn't recognize her. Eusona Parker had lost about eighty pounds.

Every Wednesday. That was Eusona's day. I'd only seen her half a dozen times through the years, when I was in Los Angeles and visiting Jimmy. But if anyone knew his state of health, it was Ms. Parker. She had been more of a true mother to Jimmy than his own natural mother. What I remembered best about her was the "hearing aid."

She had a memory that should have been on display in the Smithsonian. It might be three or four years between our seeing each other; but when I'd come out of the blue guest room searching for coffee early on a Wednesday morning during one of my visits, there would be Eusona, dusting Jimmy's vast, endless hoard of *tchotchkes;* and she'd look up and grin as if I'd been there uninterruptedly for years, and she'd say, "Good morning, Larry, sleep good?" And I'd scream at her, "Hello, Eusona, how are you?" And she'd answer, "Doin' just fine, Larry; water's still hot." And I'd scream, "Thanks, Eusona."

The reason I screamed was that she wore a hearing aid. One of those little button things shoved into her ear, the cord trailing down to disappear into the capacious pocket of her wraparound apron where the shape of the battery pack bulged.

And we went on that way, amiably, until one time she stopped me in the back corridor leading to the greenhouse, took me by the hand like a small boy who's been caught eating worms in the schoolyard, and she said, "Mr. Bedloe, why do you always scream at me?"

She never called Jimmy "Mr. Crowstairs" unless he was behaving badly or living with a woman who left globs of mascara on the mirror in the bathroom, and she never called me anything but Larry unless I had left my bed unmade. Ms. Parker made it clear she was a *housekeeper,* not a maid; and if I slept in it, I ought to make it when I got out of it. "Mr. Bedloe" was her way of politely saying *pay close attention now, asshole*.

"Why, uh, I'm sorry, Eusona," I said, terribly embarrassed as one can only be embarrassed when one has been caught staring at the empty place between eyes and mouth where a leper's nose has fallen off. "I was speaking loudly because I wanted you to hear me."

"Well, I'm not hard of hearin', dear."

That *dear* of hers: butter would not have melted in her mouth. I've never understood what that meant, it never made sense to me, butter not melting. Whatever it meant, it's what that *dear* was all about. The *dear* you use when you say, "No, dear, the round hole is for the *round* peg."

"You're not?"

"No, Mr. Bedloe, dear, I'm not hard of hearing."

Mr. Bedloe *and* dear.

"But you wear a hearing aid."

"Mistuh Bedloe, this is not a hearing aid." And she pulled the earphone of the transistor radio in her apron, out of her ear and, faintly, like fairy trumpets, I heard the tinny sound of Steve Garvey batting the brains out of the Cardinals' relief pitcher, bottom of the seventh, two out, a man on third.

All that went through my head as Kenneth L. Gross said, "Yes, Miss Parker, that's all you have to do, is identify Mr. Crowstairs."

"That's him. I said it."

"Thank you, Miss Parker."

"Neat as a pin, everything right in place; always been like that, eighteen going on nineteen years."

"Thank you, Miss Parker."

"You're welcome, dear."

Then Missy identified him; then Jimmy as testator stated the date and stated that the will being made on that date took precedence over all other wills previously made by him, including any that might be found written in cuneiform on stone tablets by gas station attendants roaming in the Nevada deserts.

Then the roundelay went like this:

Kenny: Are you executing this document or prepared to execute this document with a complete satisfaction on your part that it says what you wish it to say, and that you understand it in its entirety?

Jimmy: Affirmative. And it should be noted for the record that the last person to marry a duck lived four hundred years ago.

Kenny: Choke. Are you prepared to execute this document and accordingly state for the record, in my presence and in the presence of witnesses, that in so doing you are not acting under duress, undue influence, or under the influence of any drug or other substance that may impair your mental capacity?

Jimmy: I had a Coca-Cola about half an hour ago, does that count?

Kenny: No sir, it does not. Please!

Jimmy: Are you sure, Kenny? I mean, if you take a piece of raw meat and you put it in a glass of Coke and leave it overnight it comes out looking like something from a James Bond movie. You know, all those little piranha bubbles in there, they could chew the shit out of your brain cells.

Kenny: *It doesn't count, damn it!*

Jimmy: Then how about all the stuff I put up my nose just before we started filming?

Kenny: *Aaaargh!*

Jimmy: Okay, okay, take it easy. I'm just clowning. I don't use dope, you know that. Everybody knows it. I couldn't possibly write the crap I write if I was ripped. Having my nostrils Tefloned was just for a lark, you know that.

The attorney laid his head down on his arms and pounded the tabletop with his fist. It was pathetic what Jimmy was doing to this poor soul. We all looked around in the semidark but Kenneth L. Gross was back there in the shadows, no doubt chewing through the bit of his pipe.

On the screen Jimmy was being upbraided by his three witnesses. They whipped him into a semblance of probity and urged Kenny Gross to resume the proceedings.

The attorney said, "Therefore, in my presence and in the presence of the witnesses, God help us, is it your wish that you now execute the document and that we sign the document as witnesses thereto?"

Client responded in the affirmative.

"I will then ask, Mr. Crowstairs, that you now initial each and every page in the lower right-hand corner . . ."

"I'm left-handed."

"Then do it in the lower *left*-hand corner but for God's sake initial the damned thing already!" He was shouting; it seemed to quell Jimmy. He started initialing. Gross went on weakly, "Up to but not including the signature page. For your information and for the record, this is being done so that no pages can be substituted in the future into this document."

He was standing now, over Jimmy's right shoulder, behind him, turning the pages to verify each one was properly initialed (and possibly to insure that Jimmy didn't sign *Herman Melville* or *Frederick VIII, Duke of Schleswig-Holstein-Sonderburg-Augustenburg*).

It went on that way without hindrance. Jimmy had clearly grown bored with the activity and even bored with the japery that had made the proceedings minimally tolerable. Jimmy reached the signature page and filled in the location of execution of the will, then the date, and then he signed it. Then each of the witnesses signed location, date and name. The latter two added their place of residence. The will was returned to Gross, who asked if Jimmy wanted the will kept in the attorney's vault and a conformed copy provided to Jimmy, or if the client wanted to keep the original with a conformed copy in Gross's possession. Jimmy waved a hand negligently. "You keep it; send me a copy."

Gross said he would do so and, painfully aware that the juice was running out of the presentation, said, "For the record, the witnesses need not be present during any videotaping portion which is about to occur and the only people who will be present will be myself, Mr. Crowstairs, and the two camera persons."

Yo-ho-ho. Here we go. Up there on the screen Missy, Bran and Eusona Parker rose, walked out of camera range and damned certainly out of the room, and Gross turned to Jimmy and said, "Mr. Crowstairs, if you wish, you may say some words to your beneficiaries or for that matter, to anyone who may have been excluded by you under your last will which we have just executed."

He placed what was obviously a seating diagram of this room as Jimmy had planned it to be arranged on the desk in front of Jimmy, got up, and backed out of camera range. Now all we had on the screen was Jimmy sitting behind his desk, hands folded demurely, staring out at us, looking right to left as if he really could see us, back there four months ago when he had known for certain that he would live forever.

He looked first at SylviaTheCunt, then at me, then at Leslie, then at Bran who was seeing and hearing this for the first time—which may have been why he hadn't attended the burial ceremonies—and finally, at my right but Jimmy's extreme left, Missy. She hadn't spoken all day.

But I'd make book she knew what was coming.

Jimmy stared at us, and we stared back at him. He kept us waiting. I don't know what the others wanted—vindication, protestations of love, vast wealth, security for their twilight years, remorse, the slam bang of gin and vermouth, a trip to the moon on gossamer wings—but all *I* wanted was to be turned loose. Tempest-tossed, righteous card-carrying wretched refuse, I merely yearned to breathe free. To sever the bond with Jimmy. I heard a sound. I'll tell you what that sound sounded like:

On July 28, 1945, a foggy Saturday on the East Coast, Army Air Forces Lt. Colonel William Franklin Smith, Jr. took off from Bedford, Massachusetts in a B-25 light bomber for La Guardia Field in New York. A few minutes after 10:00 A.M. Lt. Col. Smith crashed his two-engine bomber into the north side of the Empire State Building at the level of the 78th and 79th floors.

On the 75th floor of the Empire State Building an office worker who had come in to do some extra work over the weekend heard a sound. A terrifying, ominous, hurtling-to-ward-him sound. He looked out the window to see, emerging from the fog, ten tons of screaming airplane rushing toward him at 225 m.p.h.

I sat staring, waiting for Jimmy to speak to us from beyond the grave. I heard a sound, rushing toward me out of the fog at 225 m.p.h.

This is how Jimmy died.

The story was in all the papers.

It was pried loose, finally, from one of the three *culeros* they pulled out of the other wreck. All three of them lived; one of them lost his left leg; one of them has no teeth. But that was Jimmy, not the crash.

Appropriately enough it was Halloween. That's Bradbury's favorite holiday; and it's mine, and it was Jimmy's. It was last week.

Jimmy had spent the evening at a party thrown by one of the two married couples who had been inside the black, plush velvet, upholstered ropes at the burial ceremonies. Huck and Carol Barkin. She's an architect, he's a writer. They were very close to Jimmy.

Around midnight Jimmy had left. He'd only had a couple of glasses of wine, perfectly sober and, in fact, had been drinking Perrier since ten o'clock. That figures in the story.

He took a cold quart bottle of Perrier with him when he left, swigging it straight from the mouth to his mouth in the car. Then he realized he was almost out of gas, probably couldn't make it back to the Valley and the ancestral manse, went looking for an open station on a holiday, near midnight, in Los Angeles where odd-even allocation is taken seriously.

He found a serve-yourself that was open, but they wouldn't let him fill up because it was an odd-numbered day and he had license plates that ended in an even number. So he pulled off to one side and waited for the clock to run past midnight when it would be the next day and he could get pumped up.

I wasn't there, no one was there in his head, but I know what he was like, and from the story the *culeros* told, it had to have happened like this. And even if it didn't let's see how well we can get inside the characters, let's see how fluidly we can carry the action, let's see if we can plumb the intricate motivations. This is called sensitive, creative writing; full of heat, Jimmy; pulling the plow, Jimmy; getting the powerhouse up to peak efficiency.

What we need is a good opening, a tough literary hook.

Kerch Crowstairs slumped behind the wheel of the Rolls Corniche, listening to the second movement, the *Allegro appassionato,* of Brahms's Concerto in B-flat major. In the chopped and channeled Chevy beside him the raucous clatter of the Eagles banged uneasy counterpoint . . .

No, too esoteric. Not Hammett enough.

How about this:

He was distracted. Thinking about the past, the future, indefinite times and opportunities passing too fast for analysis. Under him the Rolls hummed softly, waiting for the light to change. Beside him three Chicanos in a decked Chevy raced their motor. Drag for pink slips, mister?

No, too diffuse. Not enough oomph.

I can't do it, Jimmy. I can't *write* like you! I can talk and think in your voice, because I can *hear* you . . . I've always had phonographic recall. But I can't put it down in your bloodthirsty Visigoth way.

What happened was . . .

He filled the tank. He drove back out onto the street. He was listening to the classical music on KFAC-FM. He was smoking his pipe. He was sitting at the light, waiting for it to change, simply enjoying the cool night air and the pleasant music and the smoke rising from the pipe. The empty Perrier bottle lay on the passenger seat. A car pulled up beside him in the left lane. Someone spoke in the night. He was caught up in the gentle feel of the music washing over him, the sense of ease and leisure. He was relaxed. For once, he wasn't on, he wasn't angry, he wasn't hyper. He was feeling good; and he paid no attention to the voice. But it spoke again, louder, coarser, directed at him. He looked across. Two young men, late teens, maybe early twenties, in the front seat. Another one in the back seat, looked asleep. The kid closest to him yelled again. "Hey! *Cabrón!* What're you smokin' in the pipe?" The light changed. He took off. At the next light they raced up, gunned the motor, closer to his lane now. "Hey, man, *de dónde?* I ast you what the fuck you smokin' in the pipe?" He stared ahead. He didn't want any hassles. God, don't these lights change? "Hey, *mamador,* you gonna answer me or I'm gonna come over there an' whip your ass?" He looked at them. If Rich Garza or Pano Del Rio were here, they'd have just the right words to back these clowns off. But he was alone. "I'm smoking Essence of Asshole," he said. "I'm smokin' your mama." And the light changed, and he hit it. They ran up his tailpipe to the next light. Jesus, how many lights are there before the freeway? As he screeched to a halt the one on the passenger side jumped out and came across to grab him. He dumped it into reverse, backed up three feet, threw open the door and knocked the silly sonofabitch flat on his ass. Then he took off through the just-changing light. Behind him the passenger was climbing back aboard as the driver decked it. They caught him at the next light and he thought about going straight through: the freeway was one street up. But now the adrenalin was pumping. He stopped at the light and grabbed the empty Perrier bottle. When the passenger got to his window he swung the bottle in his left hand with a flat, scythelike movement and busted out the guy's teeth, emptied his mouth and sent him careening backward into the Chevy. *Then* he went through the light, turned sharp left, ran down the side street to the freeway entrance, hit the ramp doing sixty and was on the San Diego before the driver could load his buddy back into the trashwagon. *¡Huo de la chingada!*

They caught him just beyond the interchange of the San Diego and Santa Monica freeways. He was in the fast lane, the number one next to the divider. He was doing seventy-five. The Chevy came up on the right and the berserk latino swung it over hard; lock to lock, maybe not—but *hard*. The Rolls took it just behind the door, slewed into the cyclone fence, scraped along throwing sparks back in a fan, then shot ahead as Jimmy floored the Corniche. *¡Puto pendejo!*

Doing ninety, he cut out of the number one lane, slanted across the second, third and fourth lanes, and ran away. The Chevy caught up on the grade leading through the saddle of the hills to the Valley. The *culeros* rear-ended him. Hard; once twice three times. Jimmy braked, speeded up, cut in and out, but the Chevy was hot, it ran him down like a bulldogger. *¡Vatos locos!*

Two miles before the Mulholland offramp the *cholos* said aw, fuck it, and decided to boom him. They came up in the number three, doing ninety-five, went ahead by two car-lengths and slant-drove across his bow. Jimmy stood on the brake but it didn't count. They impacted at eighty-five, the Corniche went in hard on the right front, ricocheted, spun out and went over the side. The Rolls hit the berm, dropped and began to somersault. The Chevy was horizontal across the three and four lanes, caught a centerpunch from a long-distance moving van, lifted, went tail-over onto its roof, sliding across the shoulder, followed Jimmy over the side two hundred yards beyond him and came to rest against a low hillside.

Behind the latinos the Rolls Corniche took one last roll, hit the crumbling hillside and went off like a can of beer shaken in a centrifuge. It blew apart scattering hot metal and parts of Jimmy all over the Santa Monica Mountains.

Say goodbye to Kercher O.J. Crowstairs.

"I'm not feeling too giddy about all this, now that we're alone," Jimmy said from the screen. "You five are the most I've got left. Everybody else has been taken care of; okay, they're okay; I took good care of them, in the ancillary sections of the will. But you five are the big scores, and I wanted you to hear it straight from me."

He stopped, wiped his mouth. *Jimmy nervous?* Come on, give me a break here.

"Missy, you're first," he said, looking all the way to his left, directly where Mississippi was slouched in her seat, long legs crossed straight out in front of her. "You get The Kerch Corporation and all its holdings."

SylviaTheCunt gasped, off to my left. The smell of cardiac arrest was there in the library.

Jimmy went on. "You keep it running. There's the land up at Lake Isabella, we own it free and clear now, and it'll be built up pretty big within the next five years, they're putting in that Kern County International Airport. Keep adding to the art, find a place to show it, something nice and stately like the Norton Simon Museum...you know...something toney and really chi-chi. Set your own salary, keep on as much of the staff as you need, hire more, fire some, do what the hell you want with it. It was just a dodge to keep the tax fuckers off my carcass, anyhow. You make it into something terrific, kiddo. I love you, babe. You watched out for me real good."

Missy was crying. Toughest woman I ever met, but she— even she—lost it when Jimmy went to work at the top of his form. In Iran there's a word—*zirangī*—it means cleverness, or wiliness. The Machiavellian quality. It's much admired by the Shiites. Jimmy would have been a smash in Islam.

"And for the record," Jimmy added, "let it be known that never once in all the years you and I worked together, did we once so much as fondle each other's genitalia. The bantlings will need their gossip, m'love; and they'll fasten first on she who was my amanuensis. Let the slushfaces herewith take note: you and I worked together for fifteen years plus however many more wash under the bridge from the date of this taping before I bite the big one, mostly on the basis of your being the best goddamned pool-shooter I ever met. I would have fired your tidy ass a million times, kiddo, if it hadn't been that you shot the most unbelievable three-bank cushions into the hip pockets."

Missy was dry now. And smiling gently.

Then he turned to Brandon Winslow sitting right beside her.

"Bran, my friend . . . I've done you right, and I've done you wrong. But you never once treated me like a hotshot, and for that I cannot thank you enough. Other people were in awe, or they wanted to drink my blood, or they came sharpshooting. But you were my friend and my colleague, and you started out as something like my student but went beyond what I could show you. And you maintained, chum. You make the Hall of Fame for hanging in there. So this house is yours. The house and the grounds and everything in it. Live here, and change it any way you want to make your nest the way I made it *my* nest. I built the west wing full of separate apartments for other writers who need a place to flop. I never could afford to buy San Simeon from the state of California; I always thought the old Hearst castle would be a dynamite place for a no-obligation writers' colony where kids who had the real stuff could come and work without worrying about rent or getting fed. So lay in half a dozen real outlaws, Bran. And the only rule ought to be that they can stay and be happy as long as they *write*. If they turn into leaners, if you catch them sitting around all day watching *The Price is Right* boot their asses into the street. But if they're producing, they can live here forever. Alone is okay, but loneliness can kill a good writer . . . you know that. Give them a community of sharp, witty minds . . . and three squares a day. You'll be the only landlord who writes books that chew on the hearts of the literary establishment.

"Do it for me and for you, Bran."

SylviaTheCunt was making sounds like the *Titanic* going down.

Then Jimmy looked straight ahead. At Leslie.

He didn't say anything. He just stared.

Leslie took it for about thirty seconds. Then she got up and walked to the side of the room where she stood with her arms folded, watching the screen, still curious, but—once having freed herself of Jimmy's power—unwilling to let him manipulate her beyond a certain point of tolerable terror.

Now Jimmy was staring at an empty seat.

She's insensitive, or maybe desensitized; but she's tough. Which also explains how she could have stayed married to him as long as she did. High-fashion barbed wire wrapped in Spandex.

"Leslie, you did okay in the settlement. But I suppose you rate more than a standard 'I'm sorry,' which doesn't count for shit . . ."

"You can say that again," Leslie murmured from the side of the room.

" . . . so the Corporation is depositing a million in the Bermuda account for you; I've signed over ownership of the magazine to your name; Kenny will transfer the chalet at Villarvolard to you . . . so you can keep that ski bum of yours on the string a little longer; and Missy'll find a letter in the safe that transfers a substantial block of non-voting stock in The Kerch Corporation to you. Stay out of the business, take the dividends, and try to remember me fondly."

"Right," Leslie said from the side of the room.

Now he looked all the way to his right, directly at SylviaTheCunt, who *had* to know what was coming. There was still a lot in the till, and from what Jimmy had said of her in years past I knew she'd be bolted to that chair till the final farthing had been accounted for; but, for a wonder, she *had* to know what was on the way.

"To my beloved sister, Sylvia . . .

"And that's the first time in over twenty years I've said your name without adding the sobriquet. Seems truncated, but these are formal proceedings and I want to do it without flaw so after

I've finished talking to you—which you'll sit through right to the last syllable on just the off-chance that I might act like a brother even though we both know I despise you with a pure, blue flame of loathing, and you might be able to cadge a few bucks—where was I? Fouled in my own syntax. Oh, yeah, I was saying you'll sit through all this maleficent defoedation—Kenny, if she needs help with that, stop the tape and get her the definitions—you'll find them in something called *Mrs. Byrne's Dictionary*, in the reference shelf to the left of my typewriter in the office—shit, I lost myself again. Oh, yeah, I remember. You'll sit through it because you cling to greedy hope like a leech on floating garbage. You figure I can't be that big a prick after all these years, and so you'll wait for the last rotten word I'm going to speak to you, sister dearest. And I'm doing this without flaw so that you won't even have a scintilla of hope that you can contest this will. It's solid, Sylvia; ironclad, rockribbed, diamond-encrusted solid.

"And the bottom line is that you get zip.

"Not a cent.

"Not a penny.

"Not a farthing.

"Not a grubnik. (Which is worth 13¢ American.)

"Not even a Blue Chip Stamp.

"Nothing is what you get. Nada, nyet, nihil, nil, nihilum! Nothing, because if I have any dislike of women as a species it comes from you. Nothing because if I haven't been able, my whole life, entirely to trust a woman, it's because of what you ran on me when I was a kid.

"Sylvia, I don't think I've ever had a chance to tell you how deeply and thoroughly I loathe you. No, that isn't even correctly put. I loathed you for *most* of my life, but about twelve years ago I just sort of dropped you out of the universe. You ceased to exist. You were never there.

"I know you can't doubt that, because you were on the other end of the phone that time when—"

SylviaTheCunt screamed.

"Stop it! *Stop him right now!*"

Kenny Gross moved in from the shadowy rear of the library and cut off the Betamax. The screen went white. So did SylviaTheCunt. She was on her feet, the veins standing out in her forehead; a dumpy, big-bosomed woman in middle years. Jimmy always said she was one of those pathetic creatures that had been assembled by The Great Engineer in the Sky without a love mechanism in her. It didn't take a writer to see that. She had the look of old stone walls that had never even been considered for monuments or pyramids or standing circles.

"This is criminal!" she shouted. She clutched her purse to her stomach and kept hitting it with her fist. She wanted to strike out at something more offensive, but that was under dirt now. "I'll fight this! I will!"

Missy came around her chair. She towered over Sylvia-TheCunt and looked down at her, eyes blazing. It may not have been Jimmy reborn, but the spirit had floated out of the grave, off the silent screen, and had entered the body of his most stalwart defender. "You won't do *shit*, dolly. You *knew* what he had for you. You've always known. He hasn't *spoken* to you for twenty years till now. You'll fight? It is to laugh, dolly! He left the Corporation to me and I'll put ten fucking *thousand* attorneys on it. We'll block you and tie you up and make you look like the scumbag you are. Wanna fight, dolly? I'm waiting!"

It drained her. Bran came around and took her by the shoulders and took her back to her seat. Missy slumped down, murmuring, "That bitch . . . she hated him . . . she never thought he'd make it . . ." Bran whispered soft things close to her ear and she quieted down.

"For the record I'd suggest you watch the rest of the videotape, no matter how distasteful," Kenny Gross said to SylviaTheCunt. "In the event you *do* contemplate any legal action. Or if you prefer, you can wait in the living room and when the tape is finished I can run this section for you alone."

She stared at him with animosity. She looked around the room at the rest of us, her eyes like slag-heaps. Then she went back and resumed her seat.

Jimmy was really putting us through it. It reminded me of the piece he had written after his mother's funeral, where SylviaTheCunt had stood up right in the middle of the eulogy he had written and was reading, and had started screaming that Jimmy was defiling her mother's funeral. It had shattered Jimmy. He could almost have forgiven her anything she'd done to him as a kid, as a young man, as an adult: but not that. She was doing it again.

It was posthumous revenge, but it didn't ennoble Jimmy in the least. And it was hell for the rest of us.

The attorney started the tape again, and for the next twenty minutes Jimmy rang every charge he could on the woman. How she had brutalized him as a child, with specific deeds that he had remembered with that quirky selective memory of his. Affronts and mean tricks that were almost ludicrous but which, if you remembered how susceptible you were as a little kid, were monstrously cruel. How she had fucked over her own kids, Jimmy's nephew and niece. How she had beaten down her husband, whom Jimmy had liked even though he wouldn't stand up to her. How she had become a deplorable human being—racist, bigoted, coarse, provincial and, for Jimmy the most inexcusable of all, bone-stick-stone stupid.

For twenty minutes we all averted our eyes as Jimmy got into it like a 'lude-stoked jazz musician trying to blow Bud Powell back from the Great Beyond. It was a bravura ugly performance, many riffs, a lot of high shrieking runs and a lot of low animal growls. None of us could look. There are beasts that go right in and suck the marrow, clean the bones to a glistening white.

But SylviaTheCunt looked.

With hard, mean eyes; straight up at the screen; locked in eternal combat with the creature for whom she had seldom felt anything but the most destructive kind of sibling rivalry.

Jimmy once told me how he had gotten SylviaTheCunt to stop pulling his hair. He said one time when she grabbed a fistful of his straight, brown hair he had gritted his teeth and started turning his body in her grasp. Around and around until the hair pulled so tight the pain went all the way to the soles of his feet. It was so horrible, so excruciating, that *she* had been appalled at how painful it must have been . . . and she let him loose. And whenever she would try it again, he would inflict that pain on himself. Until she was so horrified by it that she stopped. "That's how I developed a very high threshold for pain," he had said.

I remember when he got done telling me that . . . I was gritting *my* teeth.

But finally, thank God finally, Jimmy had had all of it even *he* could handle. He had turned and turned till the pain was insupportable, even for him. Even my best friend, Jimmy, with that seemingly limitless capacity for revenge, for not just getting *even*, but for getting a bit more of the vigorish in shylock interest, even *he* had had all he could stomach. And not a moment too soon.

"You can stop it now," SylviaTheCunt said. And she stood up. The screen went white again, lights came on in the library where evening had descended, and Jimmy's sister looked around at all of us.

"You haven't heard the last of me," she said softly, and then she left. *You haven't heard the last of me*.

But I had the sure feeling that we had; we had heard the last of her. Jimmy had called in all the debts from his childhood.

We sat down again, the lights went off, the Betamax went on, and Jimmy turned his head slightly to the left, looking straight at me in my chair. He had saved me for last and he said, "Larry, buddy? You out there?"

We were driving from Chicago to New Orleans in an attempt to make Mardi Gras, which we would miss by a full day, arriving on Ash Wednesday, because in the next five miles we would spin out across the snow-covered highway, escape being piledriven by an oncoming truck by inches, plunge off the side of the road, and bury the Corvette headfirst to its rear wheels in snowbanks fifteen feet deep. But we were still five miles away from missing Mardi Gras when he said the thing I remember most clearly from all the years that we knew each other.

He was driving. He said, "You know the one thing about me that I'm terrified anyone will ever find out. The one lie that makes all of my life a lie."

"I do?"

"Yep. You know it, but you don't know you know it."

"That makes no sense. If I knew it, then I'd know it."

"You know more about me than anyone else, and you have the data; but you don't know how much I fear it, how frightened I am that it might come out."

"I'll never tell."

"You might. Get pissed off at me sometime in the future; I might screw you; you might let it slip without knowing it."

"Never. I'll never tell a living soul; honest to God, you can trust me, Rocco: I'll take the filthy secret to my grave."

"No, I'll take it to *my* grave. But you might still tell it."

"If you're dead there'd be no way you could protect against that, is there?"

He thought about that for a while. This was before he married Leslie. We were good and close friends, whatever that meant. But he thought about it, seriously thought about this terrible thing I knew that he was ashamed of, the one thing in a life like his so filled with things any normal human being might find the cause of sleepless nights, that didn't bother him in the slightest way. He thought about the knowledge I possessed, this Damoclean sword I held over his life and his career and his work in which he revealed *everything*. Everything except the one bit of knowledge that made all of his life a lie.

And he said, "I'll have to figure out a way to keep you quiet after I'm dead."

"Good luck," I said, laughing lightly; and then we hit the icy patch and started to spin out.

He looked straight at me, having saved me for last.

"Larry, I herewith make you the executor of my literary estate. You have control of every novel, short story, essay, article, review, anthology and introduction I ever wrote. All those millions of words are in your care, buddy. You're the one they'll have to come to if they want to reprint even one of my commas."

I sat stunned. If he had done me the way he'd done SylviaTheCunt, taken this last chance to purge all the swamp animosity of a lifetime . . . or if he had done me the way he'd done Leslie, tried to clear his conscience of real or fancied harm he'd visited on her . . . if he'd done me as he'd done Missy and Bran, paid off for loyalty and friendship and domination of their lives . . . I wouldn't have been surprised.

But, oh you malicious wonderful sonofabitch! You did the one thing I cannot bear: *you tied me to you forever*.

Malicious? Probably not. It was just Jimmy insuring his memory. Going for posterity, and dragging me along with him, kicking and screaming every micromillimeter of the way. What a mind, what a fucking sweetly conniving mind. I couldn't even condemn him; hate him, yes, revile him, yes, rail at what he was doing, yes—*against which I had no defense*—but he was merely demonstrating as a perfect paradigm for his whole breakneck plunge of a life . . . the ugliness of simply being human.

I sat stunned. And the voice of the turtle was heard in the library: "Would you mind cutting it for a minute?"

Turtle, the voice was mine; stunned, I sat in the darkness.

The sound of very old, rinkytink music played distantly in the empty concert hall of my head.

Jimmy had set me up to be either his servant or his Griswold. Poe. Jimmy got the idea from Poe.

He saw himself as Edgar Allan, cut off in his prime from the benefits of posterity's accolades; he saw me as the Reverend Rufus W. Griswold, but a Griswold who was walled up himself, not free to blacken Poe's name, a Griswold never free of the sound of the tell-tale heart, Jimmy's heart, still beating, his will indomitable, his presence felt until the last moment of my own Griswold-trapped life.

We had talked of this. Poe was one of Jimmy's idols. He was more than an amusing storyteller to me. But Jimmy even had a puppet made of Edgar Allan, had it hanging in the living room as an ever-present reminder of what heights fantasy could reach.

And we had discussed what Griswold had done to Poe.

He had buried him for a hundred years.

What a poor judge of human nature Poe had been. What an ass. But let the critic Daniel Hoffman (Doubleday, 1972) tell it:

> *Most of all, [Poe's] own Imp of the Perverse so arranged the history of his career that his literary executor was his most invidious enemy, the Reverend Rufus W. Griswold. This man, an ex-minister, a busybody of letters, an incessant anthologist and publicizer, a failed poetaster fattening on the writings of others as does a moth eating Gobelin tapestries, went to extraordinary pains, after Poe's death, to present the deceased writer in a manner designed to make his name a household word for the dissolute, immoral, recklessly debauched. Griswold falsified the facts of Poe's life, and he revised the texts of Poe's letters, always with this calumnious end in view. . . .*
>
> *The scoundrel's punishment is this: he is now known everywhere, if known at all, as the maligner of a helpless genius; whereas had he done his job honestly, he'd have won his proper modest niche among the footnotes by which the nearly forgotten are saved from total oblivion.*

How better to keep me quiet? What insanity! I didn't even know *which* of the many seamy facts of Jimmy's life was the

one that so paralyzed him with fear of its disclosure! I would
have talked about him; I wanted to be *free* of him. I simp
wanted to be able to say, when asked, "Yeah, Kerch Crowsta
and I were close friends for over a quarter of a century; he
be missed; his like will never come again"; the usual bullsh
That's *all* I wanted.

But the crazy paranoid sonofabitch couldn't even credit
with decent motivations *after* he was gone. My God, does fe
have a life of its own, to keep feeding on the living after t
carrier of the plague has gone down the hole?

"Okay, you can start it again," I said.

Kenny Gross ran it back and hit the *play* button. Jimmy w
in the middle of what he'd been saying when my heart h
begun to slam at me. "—if they want to reprint even one
my commas."

He looked so damned innocent up there.

Just chatting with his best friend; just asking his best chu
buddy to take care of his memory.

"Larry, you know I'm not afraid of dying. Not that, a
nothing else. Not spiders, snakes, being burned, being cripple
heights, closed-in places, ridicule, rejection...none of the
ever got to me. Very high pain threshold, remember? But it
tomorrow that gets me, Larry. The day *after* you see this tap
Will they still read me? Will I be on the bookshelves, th
Modern Library, matched sets in good bindings? *That's* wh
I'm afraid of, Larry. Posterity. I want a chance to go on aft
I'm gone. Fifty years from now I want them to come back
my stuff, the way they did to Poe's, and Dickens's, an
Conrad's. I don't want to wind up like Clark Ashton Smith
Cabell or the other Smith, Thorne Smith. I don't want bits an
pieces of my unfinished stories written by the literary vampire
You've got to promise me, Larry: nobody will ever touch or
of the fragments in my file. I probably won't know when I'
going to buy the farm, probably won't have time to get int
the file with a blowtorch and crisp all the false starts and hal
attempts. I've got them locked up, everything that's not fi
ished, all in one file drawer in the office. Missy has the onl
other key. Get all that stuff out of there and burn it for me
buddy.

"Pride isn't part of it...honest to God it isn't! You re
member when we talked about Poe how I said he had the rig

idea, that it was the *work,* it was Art, that held the high road, not religion, or good deeds or friendship or patriotism? None of those. The stories, the books. That's all you can put a bet on. That continues. And I couldn't bear to think of some half-assed science fiction hack dredging up a line or two I started and didn't know how to finish, and writing a whole fucking book off it, the way they've done to poor old Robert E. Howard, or 'Doc' Smith. They even did it to Poe and Jack London and . . . oh Christ, Larry, you *know* what I'm saying. Promise me!"

He waited. He watched that camera and he waited, four months ago. I murmured, "I promise, Jimmy."

"You take care of me when I'm gone, Larry. You're the only one I can trust to do it. Keep me alive, Larry."

And if there was more to that vile videotaped document I don't remember it. After a while I was sitting there and the lights were on, and everybody else had left the room.

He did it. The clever sonofabitch did it. He figured a way to keep me tied to him. He knew I'd do the job.

I'd make sure there were regular retrospectives of his germinal stories; I'd write the best kind of interesting essays and articles about how significant Kercher O.J. Crowstairs had been in the parade of contemporary American letters; I'd set up seminars at the Modern Language Association conclaves; I'd edit anthologies of his work, putting the stories into fresh and insightful contexts; I'd keep him alive through his seriously considered work.

And in the bargain I'd sublimate my own talent. I'd spend a part of every day living with Jimmy. I'd hear his voice and finally start writing the way he did. And if I ever ever ever figured out what it was I knew about him that made all of his life a lie, I'd keep it to myself till the cancer killed me, too.

And at last I know the nature of our friendship.

Say goodbye to Laurence Kercher O.J. Bedloe.

Django

INTRODUCTION

I wrote this story on the 8th and 9th day of November, 1977, sitting in the front window of the Avenue Victor Hugo Bookstore in Boston.

Bill Desmond effected a sound hookup that permitted me to play the wonderful music of the French-Algerian guitar genius, Django Reinhardt, while I worked.

Writing in the window was a promotional gimmick to bring people into the bookstore because the owners of the shop were footing my hotel bill while I was in Boston lecturing.

As I wrote that story, I had the strangest feeling I was being watched from a far distance by someone no longer with us. Understand: I am a pragmatist. I do not believe in reincarnation or messages from Beyond or ghosts or even the Nameless Ones who lie sleeping in Ultimate Darkness. But I had a prickly feeling all that time in the window.

And it unnerved me as I am seldom unnerved when writing. As if someone were over my shoulder, watching anxiously to make sure I did it right.

Consequently, I had the feeling I'd written the story all wrong; that I didn't really know what I was writing; that I didn't understand my own subtext.

When the story was finished I offered it to the editors

of *Galileo* magazine who, not coincidentally, also own the Avenue Victor Hugo Bookstore. They had wanted a story from me for some time, and I'd promised them the fruits of my labors in their windows. I offered the story with trepidation.

While I am occasionally rejected by magazines, even these days, it happens infrequently enough to scare the hell out of me when it seems possible. I suppose one is never inured to the fear of that kind of rejection.

But they liked it, they bought it, they published it, and the story drew sufficient praise to dull my worries. Not enough praise to flense the fear completely, but sufficient to permit my continued arrogance.

When you're all alone out there, on the end of the typewriter, with each new story a new appraisal by the world of whether you can still get it up or not, arrogance and self-esteem and deep breathing are all you have.

It often looks like egomania. I assure you it's the bold coverup of the absolutely terrified.

It was not until the story was selected—in a blind judging by Poul Anderson, himself an excellent writer, who did not know who had written what—as the winner of the annual *Galileo* short story contest, from all the stories the magazine had published that year, that my fears were laid to rest.

Success, no matter how complete, no matter how persistent and ongoing, cannot totally shield us from the mortal dreads.

I wish it were otherwise, gentle readers, but the simple truth is that I am in the box with you.

And there is *always* someone over your shoulder...watching.

Django

He stood in the Portobello Road and screamed up at the closed windows. "Anatole! Anatole, hey! Come to the window! Open up, hey, Anatole! The war's started!"

London, on that Sunday morning, was filled with the sound of air raid sirens. Unearthly wailing. Foreshadowed sounds. He stood there and screamed louder. Finally, a window on the third floor squeaked up in its tracks and Anatole's white hair and white face were thrust out into the morning chill.

He stared down at Michel, trying to focus him with sleep-bleary eyes. He worked his mouth to get the mugginess thinned. "Are you insane? It's very early! Everyone is asleep!"

Then he actually heard the sirens. He had *been* hearing them for some time, but had not codified the cacophony. Now he *heard* it. "What is that?"

Michel shouted. "War. It's the war; come down; I'm leaving!"

"Leaving? Leaving where, you fool?"

"I'm going. Back to France. The war!"

"Don't be a fool, Michel. We have a concert tonight."

"Piss on the concert. I'm leaving! Come down now. I didn't know war had been declared, but I'm off now!"

"What do you expect *me* to do about it? Do you think I can go off and stop it like Chamberlain? I'm a violinist, not a political person!"

"If you don't come down straightaway, I'm off without you!"

"We have contracts! The tour! We will be sued, you fool! Stay in England, play your guitar! You're no young boy, you're no soldier...they have enough young boys to play soldier...you're a musician...come back...Michel! *Michel!* Come back, you idiot!"

But he ran down the road and fought in the underground with the *maquis,* and he lost the ring finger and the little finger of his fretting hand, his left hand, and he never saw Anatole, the combo's violinist, ever again. He became a jazz legend.

His name was Michel Hervé and he died honorably.

Silver droplets fell on the black river. Spattering and then shattering as moonlight carried the molten silver downstream. He sat by the edge of the river, contemplating onyx. He held his guitar tightly, as he had held the manila rappelling sling during that last suspension traversal before the others fell to their death. He thought about them, Bernot and Claudeville and little Gaston, lying dead at the bottom of the crevasse, and he clutched the guitar more tightly. He wanted to play something for them, but he had lost his sentimentality at least a year before, in the face of withering fire from a water-cooled machine gun; and playing a new composition for broken corpses was beyond him now.

He sensed movement at the edge of the river, almost directly across from him where silt had built up the shore and a crossing was possible. He sat very still, hoping the shadows cast by the trees still cloaked him from the eye of the moon. It was an animal. Something sleek and quick. It dipped its head and thrust its muzzle into the black water. And drank.

Something oily and thick extruded itself from the water and wrapped itself around the animal's neck. There was a moment of slithering, tightening; then the cracking of a twig. The tentacle withdrew below the onyx surface of unrippled water, dragging the dead animal by its neck. A courteous plash of water, and the bank of the river was silent again.

He edged back.

Now he was afraid to play in the darkness. Calling up that killer from the river was a terrifying possibility. And so he sat quietly, holding the guitar tightly; and finally, he slept.

Beside him, the canister of radioactive isotopes cooked, holding death, promising nirvana.

There were wolves in the hollow, and they were eating. Whatever was being eaten was screaming, still alive and very much in pain. He detoured around the rim of the bowl, dragging the canister behind him through the golden sand at the end of a twenty-five-foot length of climbing rope. He had been traveling exclusively by night, burrowing into the sand during the day, hiding from roaming skirmisher packs of Nazi *stürmerkommandos*, the canister leaking its death in a pit fifty yards away.

On the rim, someone had erected a cairn of stones, pried out of the desert from God only knew where. He had not seen a rock or stone for days. The cairn seemed to be an altar of some sort. He decided to pause there, and have something to eat. He fancied strawberries, but all he had left was the heel of the rye bread and some carrots. He settled slowly to the ground, leaned back against the cairn of dark stones, and took the bread from his jacket pocket.

He ate with eyes closed, pretending to rest. Perhaps there would be a sun tomorrow. For many days now he had been hoping for a sun, any kind of sun. It might tell him where he was. He had the carrots lined up like pens in his inside jacket pocket, with the bushy leaves bunched against his armpit. He withdrew one and took a bite. If there was a sun tomorrow, he would see what color it was, and that might at least tell him if he was still in the world. But what if the sun came up green or blue?

He lay back against the altar with eyes closed and thought about little Gaston. His smile, the dimple that appeared in his chin when he smiled. Lying dead at the bottom of the crevasse now, unsmiling. They shouldn't have used manila. Would hemp have been any better? Probably not. But climbing had been the only way to escape.

He had trouble putting it all in sequence. Every time he tried, the music would run through his head and he would make up a new tune. He wanted to play a few of them, but there was always the chance that the Nazis were on his trail, following the sound of the music in his head.

It was still bothersome to him that *they* had managed to pull themselves through when Claudeville and Bernot and little Gaston had fallen and died. It wasn't right, it wasn't fair. He wanted desperately to play them a going-away song.

He shifted around and unslung the guitar. He laid it on his lap and touched the strings. He wasn't sure he could even play with two fingers missing, but the healing had somehow been speeded up by the passage through to this place, and he had been thinking for many days about how he could lay his hand on the neck to do what he wanted to do. It would be a different sound, but it might be a fine sound. He wanted to try, and to try this first time as a going-away song for them.

Knowing he was taking a terrible chance, he raised the guitar and fitted himself to it. Then he began to play, very softly. It wasn't one of the new tunes from his head, it was one little Gaston had enjoyed. "Rosetta."

It worked. The fingers that were left accommodated themselves and the song jumped up and out.

He sat there on the golden sand, a carpet of black beneath him, without moon, and the bright snowfall of too many stars above, with his back to the dark altar, and he played. And the shapes that had waited in the darkness came to listen.

One was a creature without eyes that sank its filaments into the sand and absorbed the sound by vibration. Another rolled into a ball and pulsed with soft pastel colors through its scales. Another looked like a flower but had feet and pods where hands should have been. There was a tall, thin one that hummed softly; and a snakelike creature with a woman's face; and a paper-thin flying wing that swooped in to pick up the sound of "Rosetta" and then sailed away into darkness, only to return again and again as though refilling itself.

After a long while, Michel Hervé realized he was not alone. Because his eyes had been closed, and because he had been living with the music, he had been in their company and had not known. He stopped playing.

The flower began to wilt, the ball of pastel scales went gray, the flying wing sailed away and did not return, the creatures grew silent and hummed no more. He understood, and began strumming softly. They perked up. He smiled.

"Do any of you speak?" he asked.

There was no answer, but they listened.

"We had to climb to escape the *Boches*," he said, talking to them, not to himself, and letting the music of one of the new tunes flow along as background. "I'll have to tell Bernot's daughter how he died, if I ever get back. I could hear him asking for absolution as he fell. He was much older than Gaston, and I didn't know him as much, but I think that long after I've forgotten certain things about Gaston, I'll be able to smell Bernot's pipe tobacco."

The flying wing sailed back overhead, dipped, caught a downdraft, swooped and filled itself with sound, and rose on its forked tail. It went straight up and was lost among the spilled milk of the stars.

"The rope was frayed. I think it must have rubbed against some rocks. We didn't see. We could have gotten away, I'm sure of that. Hemp. Perhaps we would have done better had we used hemp instead of manila. Some day they'll make better ropes."

A gentle purple light began to seep out of the dark stones of the altar. Michel felt warmth at his back. He looked over his shoulder and the glow was growing, enveloping him. It was like a tepid bath. It cut off the chill of the night, but not the darkness. The darkness remained and the silent creatures remained, but the *maquisards* were dead and could not return.

"They fell. And I fell with them. But something very peculiar happened. There was a place in the air, and I fell through it, and the others went down, but I didn't. You may think it odd that I don't question what happened. My mother was a gypsy. I don't question such things. Or the music. Magic shouldn't be questioned. If this is magic. I don't know. But, listen, all of you, listen for a moment longer, then I'll play you many songs, "Avalon" and "Nuages" and even a lovely song I know, "Stardust," that you will enjoy. What I need to know is the way back. I don't question, you understand, but I want to get back, to tell some people what happened to little Gaston and Claudeville; and I really must tell Bernot's daughter that he died for her and for France. Can you understand what I'm asking? Do any of you speak?"

But there was only silence.

So he played the songs for them, because they would have spoken if they could. He knew that. And they enjoyed the music. He was a wonderful musician.

And the *stürmerkommandos* did not come.

The purple glow settled around Michel Hervé and the silent

creatures watched him, and suddenly he stopped playing. They watched him for a time, but he did not seem inclined to play more, and they went away silently, one by one.

He dragged the canister wearily. If he had known why he was compelled to burden himself so, it might have been easier. But he had no idea. The canister had been there in the golden sand when he had drifted down through the air from the space where the peculiar passage had occurred. He had understood, without questioning, that this was a thing he had to keep with him. He even knew it was leaking death, but he had attached the rope and had assumed the burden.

And when he came to the second altar, much larger but exactly identical to the tiny one of dark stones where he had rested, he knew he should bury the canister there.

So he did, and he lay down a good distance from the leaking metal container, and he waited for someone to come and tell him what he should do. He perceived that he had no control over what was happening to him, that where he was and what it meant would probably never be revealed to him, but that he must be patient.

All through the night that stretched on without end, he waited; sometimes sleeping, sometimes letting the music have its life. And in the night the dark stones of the great altar let loose the purple glow, and he was bathed in the radiance. When he awoke, there was day all around him, and the purple glow was faintly discernible, but there was still no sun, not of any color.

But Claudeville and Bernot and little Gaston were there. They sat around him, cross-legged on the golden sand, and they waited for him to awaken. For just an instant he was happy to see them, but then he understood that they were dead, and he sat up with pain in his face.

"Now I must make the choice, is that it?" he said.

They watched him. They did not plead nor did they try by their deaths to shame him. They merely sat quietly, as the animals had sat. They presented him with the other side of the question by their presence.

"If the music, then you cannot go home, eh, Gaston, little friend? Claudeville? Bernot, I'll never smell your pipe tobacco again? Is that it? If I want to make the music?"

The glow from the altar surrounded them, because the time for making the decision was at hand.

"And what of this metal thing with the death in it? Does that come with me and my music, or does it stay here where no one will ever suffer from it?"

Spectacular runs of notes cascaded through his mind.

He began to breathe very heavily. He felt himself about to cry. He didn't want to cry; he knew what that would make him decide.

"I *have no* choice," he said. "It is the music. It was always the music. Forgive me. You understand, perhaps you won't understand, but you died for something you loved, and I would do the same. But to live for it is even better."

And he made the choice, and was returned, and the dead remained dead, and the canister came soon after, but not soon enough for the *stürmerkommandos* to use it.

And he made great music for a while, for just the little while that he bought in that peculiar place of silent animals and dark stone altars. And it was *great* music, because he became a jazz legend, even with two dead fingers, and buying those few years was the only brave thing he could do.

His name was Michel Hervé and when he died, he died honorably.

> *This story is dedicated to the memory of Django Reinhardt, the greatest jazz guitarist who ever lived; and to the music that he left us.*

Count the Clock
that Tells the Time

INTRODUCTION

For those whose reading taste runs to *People Magazine* and *TV Guide,* whose idea of "conversation" is the self-aggrandizement and flotsam-jetsam chitchat of *The Merv Griffin Show,* who cannot wait to buy books that reveal Elvis Presley was a dope addict and that Errol Flynn was a Nazi spy (Jesus, do you believe *that* lunacy? Robin Hood was a Nazi spy! Gimme a break, Lord!)—for all such open receivers of meretricious, mischievous gossip who happened to wander in here, I offer the current information that my fourth marriage broke up several years ago and I am once again loose on the streets of the world.

Why does he tell us this?

I tell you this because the story you're about to read was begun on the shores of Loch Tummel in Scotland on October 12, 1975, during a stay at the Queen's View Inn while in company with Lori, whom I later married. (For historians of trivia, I asked Lori to marry me on Saturday, May 8, 1976; we were married on Saturday, June 5, 1976; she left me for Smilin' Jack on Saturday, November 20, 1976; and the divorce was effected on Wednesday, March 16, 1977.)

I was in love. Apparently Lori was in love. We were in love with each other. And I began what I intended as a love story. Things began falling apart, though, even before we were married; and I wrote only three pages of the story that Sunday night at the Queen's View. The day before we'd taken the train to Edinburgh, we'd wasted most of the day sleeping in at the Portobello Hotel in London. I'd awakened several times during that lazy morning and afternoon that I'd intended to spend revisiting for the third time the Tate Gallery, and I was struck by how much valuable time is wasted in even the most adventurous and event-filled life. Thought about that, lying there staring out through the French doors at the Stanley Gardens, and went back to sleep. Woke later, more time gone, and thought about it again as a fly buzzed through our room. And slept again.

Just so are stories born. Apocryphally, on that day were sown the seeds of the dissolution of love and marriage— even then, before we were wed, it was falling apart.

And the next evening, in Scotland, where I'd longed to live for as far back as I could remember, sitting there before a roaring fireplace in the Queen's View Inn, I was overcome with the painful knowledge that I was alien to that place, that love somehow would not endure, that I could never come to make my home in Scotland, and I began the story.

I did not finish that story until September of 1978.

It was concluded in four days of sporadic writing while sitting in a plastic tent on the mezzanine of the Hyatt Regency Hotel in Phoenix, Arizona. I was engaged in two mutually contradictory activities at that time. I was the Guest of Honor at the 36th annual World Science Fiction Convention (the IguanaCon) and I was protesting Arizona's failure to ratify the Equal Rights Amendment. Quite a lot has been written about all that, and it hasn't much to do with the writing of this story, so I'll skip over it, leaving to those whose curiosity has been piqued, all the reams of copy about my subversive, fandom-destroying activities in the name of equal rights.

To the point: because I felt that too often Guests of Honor are inaccessible to the mass of attendees at such World Conventions, I arranged for the IguanaCon committee to erect a work-space in full and open view of the entire membership of the Convention. I promised to write a new story, to be taped to the wall for progressive reading as I worked, that would keep me available to the attendees but would also provide a minimal loss of writing time during that long weekend of Guest-of-Honoring.

I concluded "Count the Clock that Tells the Time" on Sunday, September 3, 1978, just a few hours before I won my seventh Hugo award for "Jeffty is Five," the story that opens this book.

I finished the story, I won another Hugo, I fulfilled my moral and ethical obligations...and I was once again alone. How time flies when you're enjoying yourself...

Count the Clock
that Tells the Time

When I do count the clock that tells the time,
And see the brave day sunk in hideous night;
When I behold the violet past prime,
And sable curls all silver'd o'er with white;
When lofty trees I see barren of leaves
Which erst from heat did canopy the herd,
And summer's green all girdled up in sheaves
Borne on the bier with white and bristly beard,
Then of thy beauty do I question make,
That thou among the wastes of time must go . . .

WILLIAM SHAKESPEARE,
the XIIth Sonnet

WAKING IN THE COOL and cloudy absolute dead middle of a
Saturday afternoon, one day, Ian Ross felt lost and vaguely
frightened. Lying there in his bed, he was disoriented; and it
took him a moment to remember when it was and where he
was. Where he was: in the bed where he had awakened every
day of his thirty-five-year-old life. When it was: the Saturday
he had resolved to spend *doing* something. But as he lay there
he realized he had come to life in the early hours just after
dawn, it had looked as though it would rain, the sky seen
through the high French windows, and he had turned over and

gone back to sleep. Now the clock-radio on the bedside table told him it was the absolute dead middle of the afternoon; and the world outside his windows was cool and cloudy.

"Where does the time go?" he said.

He was alone, as always: there was no one to hear him or to answer. So he continued lying there, wasting time, feeling vaguely frightened. As though something important were passing him by.

A fly buzzed him, circled, buzzed him again. It had been annoying him for some time. He tried to ignore the intruder and stared off across Loch Tummel to the amazing flesh tones of the October trees, preparing themselves for winter's disingenuous attentions and the utter absence of tourism. The silver birches were already a blazing gold, the larches and ash trees still blending off from green to rust; in a few weeks the Norway spruces and the other conifers would darken until they seemed mere shadows against the slate sky.

Perthshire was most beautiful at this time of year. He had taken the time to learn to pronounce the names—Schiehallion, Killiecrankie, Pitlochry, Aberfeldy—and had come here to sit. The dream. The one he had always held: silent, close to him, unspoken, in his idle thoughts. The dream of going to Scotland. For what reason he could not say. But this was the place that had always called, and he had come.

For the first time in his life, Ian Ross had *done* something. Thirty-seven years old, rooted to a tiny apartment in Chicago, virtually friendless, working five days a week at a drafting table in a firm of industrial designers, watching television till sign-off, tidying the two-and-a-half rooms till every picture hung from the walls in perfect true with the junctures of walls and ceiling, entering each checkbook notation in the little ledger with a fine point ink pen, unable to remember what had happened last Thursday that made it different from last Wednesday, seeing himself reflected in the window of the cafeteria slowly eating the $2.95 Christmas Dinner Special, a solitary man, somehow never marking the change of the seasons save to understand only by his skin that it was warmer or colder, never tasting joy because he could never remember having been told what it was, reading books about *things* and *subject matter*, topics not people, because he knew so few people and *knew* none of them, drawing straight lines, feeling deserted but never knowing where to put his hands to relieve that feeling, a transient man, passing down the same streets every day and perceiving only dimly that there were streets *beyond* those streets, drinking water, and apple juice, and water, replying when he was addressed directly, looking around sometimes when he was addressed to see if it was, in fact, himself to whom the speaker was speaking, buying gray socks and white undershorts, staring out the windows of his apartment at the Chicago snow, staring for hours at the invisible sky, feeling the demon wind off Lake Michigan rattling the window glass in its frame and thinking this year he would re-putty and this year failing to re-putty, combing his hair as he always had, cooking his own meals, alone with the memories of his mother and father who had died within a year of each other and both from cancer, never having been able to speak more than a few awkward sentences to any woman but his mother . . . Ian Ross had lived his life like the dust that lay in a film across the unseen top of the tall wardrobe cabinet in his bedroom: colorless, unnoticed, inarticulate, neither giving nor taking.

Until one day he had said, "Where does the time go?" And in the months following those words he had come to realize he had not, in any remotely valuable manner, *lived* his life. He had wasted it. Months after the first words came, unbidden and tremulous, he admitted to himself that he had wasted his life.

He resolved to actualize at least the one dream. To go to Scotland. Perhaps to live. To rent or even buy a crofter's cottage on the edge of a moor, or overlooking one of the lochs he had dreamed about. He had all the insurance money still put by, he hadn't touched a cent of it. And there, in that far, chill place in the north he would live . . . walking the hills with a dog by his side, smoking a pipe that trailed a fragrant pennant of blue-white smoke, hands thrust deep into the pockets of a fleece-lined jacket. He would *live* there. That was the dream.

So he had taken the vacations he had never taken, all of them at one time, saved up from eleven years at the drafting table, and he flew to London. Not directly to Edinburgh, because he wanted to come upon the dream very slowly, creep up on it so it wouldn't vanish like a woodland elf hiding its kettle of gold.

And from King's Cross Station he had taken the 21.30 sleeper to Edinburgh, and he had walked the Royal Mile and gazed in wonder at Edinburgh Castle high on the bluff overlooking that bountiful city, and finally he had rented a car and had driven north out the Queensferry Road, across the bridge that spanned the Firth of Forth, on up the A-90 till he reached Pitlochry. Then a left, a random left, but not so random that he did not know it would come out overlooking the Queen's View, said to be the most beautiful view in the world, certainly in Scotland, and he had driven the twisting, narrow road till he was deep in the hills of Perth.

And there he had pulled off the road, gotten out of the car, leaving the door open, and walked away down the October hills to sit, finally and at last, staring at the loch, green and blue and silent as the mirror of his memory.

Where only the buzzing fly reminded him of the past.

He had been thirty-five when he said, "Where does the time go?" And he was thirty-seven as he sat on the hill.

And it was there that the dream died.

He stared at the hills, at the valley that ran off to left and right, at the sparkling water of the loch, and knew he had wasted his time again. He had resolved to *do* something; but he had done nothing. Again.

There was no place for him here.

He was out of phase with all around him. He was an alien object. A beer can thrown into the grass. A broken wall untended and falling back into the earth from which it had been wrenched stone by stone.

He felt lonely, starved, incapable of clenching his hands or clearing his throat. A ruin from another world, set down in foreign soil, drinking air that was not his to drink. There were no tears, no pains in his body, no deep and trembling sighs. In a moment, with a fly buzzing, the dream died for him. He had not been saved; had, in fact, come in an instant to understand that he had been a child to think it could ever change. What do you want to be when you grow up? Nothing. As I have always been nothing.

The sky began to bleach out.

The achingly beautiful golds and oranges and yellows began to drift toward sepia. The blue of the loch slid softly toward chalkiness, like an ineptly prepared painting left too long in direct sunlight. The sounds of birds and forest creatures and insects faded, the gain turned down slowly. The sun gradually cooled for Ian Ross. The sky began to bleach out toward a gray-white newsprint colorlessness. The fly was gone. It was cold now; very cold now.

Shadows began to superimpose themselves over the dusty mezzotint of the bloodless day:

A city of towers and minarets, as seen through shallow, disturbed water; a mountain range of glaciers with snow untracked and endless as an ocean; an ocean, with massive, serpent-necked creatures gliding through the jade deeps; a parade of ragged children bearing crosses hewn from tree branches; a great walled fortress in the middle of a parched wasteland, the yellow earth split like strokes of lightning all around the structure; a motorway with hundreds of cars speeding past so quickly they seemed to be stroboscopic lines of colored light; a battlefield with men in flowing robes and riding great-chested stallions, the sunlight dancing off curved swords and helmets; a tornado careening through a small town of slatback stores and houses, lifting entire buildings from their foundations and flinging them into the sky; a river of lava bursting through a fissure in the ground and boiling toward a shadowy indication of an amusement park, with throngs of holiday tourists moving in clots from one attraction to another.

Ian Ross sat, frozen, on the hillside. The world was dying around him. No . . . it was vanishing, fading out, dematerializing. As if all the sand had run out of the hourglass around him: as if he were the only permanent, fixed and immutable object in a metamorphosing universe suddenly cut loose from its time-anchor.

The world faded out around Ian Ross, the shadows boiled and seethed and slithered past him, caught in a cyclonic wind tunnel and swept away past him, leaving him in darkness.

He sat now, still, quiet, too isolated to be frightened.

He thought perhaps clouds had covered the sun.

There was no sun.

He thought perhaps it had been an eclipse, that his deep concentration of his hopeless state had kept him from noticing.

There was no sun.

No sky. The ground beneath him was gone. He sat, merely sat, but on nothing, surrounded by nothing, seeing and feeling nothing save a vague chill. It was cold now, very cold now.

After a long time he decided to stand and *did* stand: there was nothing beneath or above him. He stood in darkness.

He could remember everything that had ever happened to him in his life. Every moment of it, with absolute clarity. It was something he had never experienced before. His memory had been no better or worse than anyone else's, but he had forgotten all the details, many years in which nothing had happened, during which he had wasted time—almost as a mute witness at the dull rendition of his life.

But now, as he walked through the limbo that was all he had been left of the world, he recalled everything perfectly. The look of terror on his mother's face when he had sliced through the tendons of his left hand with the lid from the tin can of pink lemonade: he had been four years old. The feel of his new Thom McAn shoes that had always been too tight, from the moment they had been bought, but which he had been forced to wear to school every day, even though they rubbed him raw at the back of his heels: he had been seven years old. The Four Freshmen standing and singing for the graduation dance. He had been alone. He had bought one ticket to support the school event. He had been sixteen. The taste of egg roll at Choy's, the first time. He had been twenty-four. The woman he had met at the library, in the section where they kept the book on animals. She had used a white lace handkerchief to dry her temples. It had smelled of perfume. He had been thirty. He remembered all the sharp edges of every moment from his past. It was remarkable. In this nowhere.

And he walked through gray spaces, with the shadows of other times and other places swirling past. The sound of rushing wind, as thought the emptiness through which he moved was being constantly filled and emptied, endlessly, without measure or substance.

Had he known what emotions to call on for release, he would have done so. But he was numb in his skin. Not merely chilled, as this empty place was chilled, but somehow inured to feeling from the edge of his perceptions to the center of his soul. Sharp, clear, drawn back from the absolute past, he remembered a day when he had been eleven, when his mother had suggested that for his birthday they make a small party, to which he would invite a few friends. And so (he remembered with diamond-bright perfection) he had invited six boys and girls. They had never come. He sat alone in the house that Saturday, all his comic books laid out in case the cake and party favors and pin-the-tail-on-the-donkey did not hold their attention sufficiently. Never came. It grew dark. He sat alone, with his mother occasionally walking through the living room to make some consoling remark. But he was alone, and he knew there was only one reason for it: they had all forgotten. It was simply that he was a waste of time for those actually living their lives. Invisible, by token of being unimportant. A thing unnoticed: on a street, who notices the mailbox, the fire hydrant, the crosswalk lines? He was an invisible, useless thing.

He had never permitted another party to be thrown for him.

He remembered that Saturday now. And found the emotion, twenty-six years late, to react to this terrible vanishment of the world. He began to tremble uncontrollably, and he sat down where there was nothing to sit down on, and he rubbed his hands together, feeling the tremors in his knuckles and the ends of his fingers. Then he felt the constriction in his throat, he turned his head this way and that, looking for a nameless exit from self-pity and loneliness; and then he cried. Lightly, softly, because he had no experience at it.

A crippled old woman came out of the gray mist of nowhere and stood watching him. His eyes were closed, or he would have seen her coming.

After a while, he snuffled, opened his eyes, and saw her standing in front of him. He stared at her. She was standing. At a level somewhat below him, as though the invisible ground of this nonexistent place was on a lower plane that that on which he sat.

"That won't help much," she said. She wasn't surly, but neither was there much succor in her tone.

He looked at her, and immediately stopped crying.

"Probably just got sucked in here," she said. It was not quite a question, though it had something of query in it. She knew, and was going carefully.

He continued to look at her, hoping she could tell him what had happened to him. And to her? She was here, too.

"Could be worse," she said, crossing her arms and shifting her weight off her twisted left leg. "I could've been a Saracen or a ribbon clerk or even one of those hairy prehumans." He didn't respond. He didn't know what she was talking about.

She smiled wryly, remembering. "First person I met was some kind of a retard, a little boy about fifteen or so. Must have spent what there'd been of his life in some padded cell or a hospital bed, something like that. He just sat there and stared at me, drooled a little, couldn't tell me a thing. I was scared out of my mind, ran around like a chicken with its head cut off. Wasn't till a long time after that before I met someone spoke English."

He tried to speak and found his throat was dry. His voice came out in a croak. He swallowed and wet his lips. "Are there many other, uh, other people . . . we're not all alone . . . ?"

"Lots of others. Hundreds, thousands, God only knows; maybe whole countries full of people here. No animals, though. They don't waste it the way we do."

"Waste it? What?"

"Time, son. Precious, lovely time. That's all there is, just time. Sweet, flowing time. Animals don't know about time."

As she spoke, a slipping shadow of some wild scene whirled past and through them. It was a great city in flames. It seemed more substantial than the vagrant wisps of countryside or sea-scenes that had been ribboning past them as they spoke. The wooden buildings and city towers seemed almost solid enough to crush anything in their path. Flames leaped toward the gray, dead skin sky; enormous tongues of crackling flame that ate the city's gut and chewed the phantom image, leaving ash. (But even the dead ashes had more life than the grayness through which the vision swirled.)

Ian Ross ducked, frightened. Then it was gone.

"Don't worry about it, son," the old woman said. "Looked a lot like London during the big fire. First the plague, then the fire. I've seen its like before. Can't hurt you. None of it can hurt you."

He tried to stand, found himself still weak. "But what *is* it?"

She shrugged. "No one's ever been able to tell me for sure. Bet there's some around in here who can, though. One day I'll run into one of them. If I find out and we ever meet again I'll be sure to let you know. Bound to happen." But her face grew infinitely sad and there was desolation in her expression. "Maybe. Maybe we'll meet again. Never happens, but it might. Never saw that retarded boy again. But it might happen."

She started to walk away, hobbling awkwardly. Ian got to

his feet with difficulty, but as quickly as he could. "Hey, wait! Where are you going? Please, lady, don't leave me here all alone. I'm scared to be here by myself."

She stopped and turned, tilting oddly on her bad leg. "Got to keep moving. Keep going, you know? If you stay in one place you don't get anywhere; there's a way out . . . you've just got to keep moving till you find it." She started again, saying, over her shoulder, "I guess I won't be seeing you again; I don't think it's likely."

He ran after her and grabbed her arm. She seemed very startled. As if no one had ever touched her in this place during all the time she had been here.

"Listen, you've got to tell me some things, whatever you know. I'm awfully scared, don't you understand? You have to have some understanding."

She looked at him carefully. "All right, as much as I can, then you'll let me go?"

He nodded.

"I don't know what happened to me . . . or to you. Did it all fade away and just disappear, and everything that was left was this, just this gray nothing?"

He nodded.

She sighed. "How old are you, son?"

"I'm thirty-seven. My name is Ian—"

She waved his name away with an impatient gesture. "That doesn't matter. I can see you don't know any better than I do. So I don't have the time to waste on you. You'll learn that, too. Just keep walking, just keep looking for a way out."

He made fists. "That doesn't tell me *anything!* What was that burning city, what are these shadows that go past all the time?" As if to mark his question a vagrant filmy phantom caravan of cassowarylike animals drifted through them.

She shrugged and sighed. "I think it's history. I'm not sure . . . I'm guessing, you understand. But I *think* it's all the bits and pieces of the past, going through on its way somewhere."

He waited. She shrugged again, and her silence indicated— with a kind of helpless appeal to be let go—that she could tell him nothing further.

He nodded resignedly. "All right. Thank you."

She turned with her bad leg trembling: she had stood with

her weight on it for too long. And she started to walk off into the gray limbo. When she was almost out of sight, he found himself able to speak again, and he said . . . too softly to reach her . . . "Goodbye, lady. Thank you."

He wondered how old she was. How long she had been here. If he would one time far from now be like her. If it was all over and if he would wander in shadows forever.

He wondered if people died here.

Before he met Catherine, a long time before he met her, he met the lunatic who told him where he was, what had happened to him, and why it had happened.

They saw each other standing on opposite sides of a particularly vivid phantom of the Battle of Waterloo. The battle raged past them, and through the clash and slaughter of Napoleon's and Wellington's forces they waved to each other.

When the sliding vision had rushed by, leaving emptiness between them, the lunatic rushed forward, clapping his hands as if preparing himself for a long, arduous, but pleasurable chore. He was of indeterminate age, but clearly past his middle years. His hair was long and wild, he wore a pair of rimless antique spectacles, and his suit was turn-of-the-eighteenth-century. "Well, well, well," he called, across the narrowing space between them, "so good to see you, sir!"

Ian Ross was startled. In the timeless time he had wandered through this limbo, he had encountered coolies and Berbers and Thracian traders and silent Goths . . . an endless stream of hurrying humanity that would neither speak nor stop. This man was something different. Immediately, Ian knew he was insane. But he wanted to *talk!*

The older man reached Ian and extended his hand. "Cowper, sir. Justinian Cowper. Alchemist, metaphysician, consultant to the forces of time and space, ah yes, *time!* Do I perceive in you, sir, one only recently come to our little Valhalla, one in need of illumination? Certainly! Definitely, I can see that is the case."

Ian began to say something, almost anything, in response, but the wildly gesticulating old man pressed on without drawing a breath. "This most recent manifestation, the one we were both privileged to witness was, I'm certain you're aware, the pivotal moment at Waterloo in which the Little Corporal had his fat chewed good and proper. Fascinating piece of recent history, wouldn't you say?"

Recent history? Ian started to ask him how long he had been in this gray place, but the old man barely paused before a fresh torrent of words spilled out.

"Stunningly reminiscent of that marvelous scene in Stendhal's *Charterhouse of Parma* in which Fabrizio, young, innocent, fresh to that environ, found himself walking across a large meadow on which men were running in all directions, noise, shouts, confusion . . . and he knew not what was happening, and not till several chapters later do we learn—ah, marvelous!—that it was, in fact, the Battle of Waterloo through which he moved, totally unaware of history in the shaping all around him. He was there, while *not* there. Precisely *our* situation, wouldn't you say?"

He had run out of breath. He stopped, and Ian plunged into the gap. "That's what I'd like to know, Mr. Cowper: what's happened to me? I've lost *everything*, but I can *remember* everything, too. I know I should be going crazy or frightened, and I *am* scared, but not out of my mind with it . . . I seem to *accept* this, whatever it is. I—I don't know how to take it, but I know I'm not feeling it yet. And I've been here a long time!"

The old man slipped his arm around Ian's back and began walking with him, two gentlemen strolling in confidence on a summer afternoon by the edge of a cool park. "Quite correct, sir, quite correct. Dissociative behavior; mark of the man unable to accept his destiny. Accept it, sir, I urge you; and fascination follows. Perhaps even obsession, but we must run that risk, mustn't we?"

Ian wrenched away from him, turned to face him. "Look, mister, I don't want to hear all that craziness! I want to know where I am and how I get out of here. And if you can't tell me, then leave me alone!"

"Nothing easier, my good man. Explanation is the least of it. Observation of phenomena, ah, *that's* the key. You can follow? Well, then: we are victims of the law of conservation of time. Precisely and exactly linked to the law of the conservation of matter; matter, which can neither be created nor destroyed. Time exists without end. But there is an ineluctable entropic balance, absolutely necessary to maintain order in the universe. Keeps events discrete, you see. As matter approaches universal distribution, there is a counterbalancing, how shall I put it, a counterbalancing 'leaching out' of time. Unused time is not wasted in places where nothing happens. *It goes somewhere*. It goes here, to be precise. In measurable units (which I've decided, after considerable thought, to call 'chronons')."

He paused, perhaps hoping Ian would compliment him on his choice of nomenclature. Ian put a hand to his forehead; his brain was swimming. "That's insane. It doesn't make sense."

"Makes perfectly *good* sense, I assure you. I was a top savant in my time; what I've told you is the only theory that fits the facts. Time unused is not wasted; it is leached out, drained through the normal space-time continuum and recycled. All this history you see shooting past us is that part of the time-flow that was wasted. Entropic balance, I assure you."

"But what am *I* doing here?"

"You force me to hurt your feelings, sir."

"What am I doing here?!"

"You wasted your life. Wasted time. All around you, throughout your life, unused chronons were being leached out, drawn away from the contiguous universe, until their pull on you was irresistible. Then you went on through, pulled loose like a piece of wood in a rushing torrent, a bit of chaff whirled away on the wind. Like Fabrizio, you were never really *there*. You wandered through, never seeing, never participating, and so there was nothing to moor you solidly in your own time."

"But how long will I stay here?"

The old man looked sad and spoke kindly for the first time: "Forever. You never used your time, so you have nothing to rely on as anchorage in normal space."

"But everyone here thinks there's a way out. I know it! They keep walking, trying to find an exit."

"Fools. There is no way back."

"But you don't seem to be the sort of person who wasted his life. Some of the others I've seen, yes, I can see that; but *you?*"

The old man's eyes grew misty. He spoke with difficulty. "Yes, I belong here..."

Then he turned and, like one in a dream, lost, wandered away. Lunatic, observing phenomena. And then gone in the grayness of time-gorged limbo. Part of a glacial period slid past Ian Ross and he resumed his walk without destination.

And after a long, long time that was timeless but filled with an abundance of time, he met Catherine.

He saw her as a spot of darkness against the gray limbo. She was quite a distance away, and he walked on for a while, watching the dark blotch against gray, and then decided to change direction. It didn't matter. Nothing mattered: he was alone with his memories, replaying again and again.

The sinking of the Titanic wafted through him.

She did not move, even though he was approaching on a direct line.

When he was quite close he could see that she was sitting cross-legged on nothingness; she was asleep. Her head was propped in one hand, the bracing arm supported by her knee. Asleep.

He came right up to her and stood there simply watching. He smiled. She was like a bird, he thought, with her head tucked under her wing. Not really, but that was how he saw her. Though her cupped hand covered half her face he could make out a sweet face, very pale skin, a mole on her throat; her hair was brown, cut quite short. Her eyes were closed: he decided they would be blue.

The Greek senate, the age of Pericles, men in a crowd—property owners—screaming at Lycurgus' exhortations in behalf of socialism. The shadow of it sailed past not very far away.

Ian stood staring, and after a while he sat down opposite her. He leaned back on his arms and watched. He hummed an old tune the name of which he did not know.

Finally, she opened her brown eyes and stared at him.

At first momentary terror, shock, chagrin, curiosity. Then she took umbrage. "How long have *you* been there?"

"My name is Ian Ross," he said.

"I don't care what your name is!" she said angrily. "I asked you how long you've been sitting there watching me?"

"I don't know. A while."

"I don't like being watched; you're being very rude."

He got to his feet without answering, and began walking away. Oh well.

She ran after him. "Hey, wait!"

He kept walking. He didn't have to be bothered like that. She caught up with him and ran around to stand in front of him. "I suppose you just think you can walk off like that!"

"Yes, I can. I'm sorry I bothered you. Please get out of my way if you don't want me around."

"I didn't say that."

"You said I was being rude. I am *never* rude; I'm a very well-mannered person and you were just being insulting."

He walked around her. She ran after him.

"All right, okay, maybe I was a little out of sorts. I *was* asleep, after all."

He stopped. She stood in front of him. Now it was her move. "My name is Catherine Molnar. How do you do?"

"Not too well, that's how."

"Have you been here long?"

"Longer than I wanted to be here, *that's* for sure."

"Can you explain what's happened to me?"

He thought about it. Walking *with* someone would be a nice change. "Let me ask you something," Ian Ross said, beginning to stroll off toward the phantom image of the hanging gardens of Babylon wafting past them, "did you waste a lot of time, sitting around, not doing much, maybe watching television a lot?"

They were lying down side-by-side because they were tired. Nothing more than that. The Battle of the Ardennes, First World War, was all around them. Not a sound. Just movement. Mist, fog, turretless tanks, shattered trees all around them. Some corpses left lying in the middle of no man's land. They had been together for a space of time . . . it was three hours, it was six weeks, it was a month of Sundays, it was a year to remember, it was the best of times, it was the worst of times: who could measure it, there were no signposts, no town criers, no grandfather clocks, no change of seasons, who could measure it?

They had begun to talk freely. He told her again that his name was Ian Ross and she said Catherine, Catherine Molnar again. She confirmed his guess that her life had been empty. "Plain," she said. "I was plain. I *am* plain. No, don't bother to say you think I have nice cheekbones or a trim figure; it won't change a thing. If you want plain, I've got it."

He didn't say she had nice cheekbones or a trim figure. But he didn't think she was plain.

The Battle of the Ardennes was swirling away now.

She suggested they make love.

Ian Ross got to his feet quickly and walked away.

She watched him for a while, keeping him in sight. Then she got up, dusted off her hands though there was nothing on them, an act of memory, and followed him. Quite a long time later, after trailing him but not trying to catch up to him, she ran to match his pace and finally, gasping for breath, reached him. "I'm sorry," she said.

"Nothing to be sorry about."

"I offended you."

"No, you didn't. I just felt like walking."

"Stop it, Ian. I did, I offended you."

He stopped and spun on her. "Do you think I'm a virgin? I'm not a virgin."

His vehemence pulled her back from the edge of boldness. "No, of course you're not. I never thought such a thing." Then she said, "Well . . . I am."

"Sorry," he said, because he didn't know the right thing to say, if there *was* a right thing.

"Not your fault," she said. Which *was* the right thing to say.

From nothing *to* nothing. Thirty-four years old, the properly desperate age for unmarried, unmotherhooded, unloved. Catherine Molnar, Janesville, Wisconsin. Straightening the trinkets in her jewelry box, ironing her clothes, removing and refolding the sweaters in her drawers, hanging the slacks with the slacks, skirts with the skirts, blouses with the blouses, coats with the coats, all in order in the closet, reading every word in *Time* and *Reader's Digest,* learning seven new words every day, never using seven new words every day, mopping the floors in the three-room apartment, putting aside one full evening to pay the bills and spelling out Wisconsin completely, never the WI abbreviation on the return envelopes, listening to talk radio, calling for the correct time to set the clocks, spooning out the droppings from the kitty box, repasting photos in the album of scenes with round-faced people, pinching back the buds on the coleus, calling Aunt Beatrice every Tuesday at seven o'clock, talking brightly to the waitress in the orange and blue uniform at the chicken pie shoppe, repainting fingernails carefully so the moon on each nail is showing, heating morning water for herself alone for the cup of herbal tea, setting the table with a cloth napkin and a placemat, doing dishes, going to the office and straightening the bills of lading precisely. Thirty-four. *From* nothing *to* nothing.

They lay side-by-side but they were not tired. There was more to it than that.

"I hate men who can't think past the pillow," she said, touching his hair.

"What's that?"

"Oh, it's just something I practiced, to say after the first time I slept with a man. I always felt there should be something original to say, instead of all the things I read in novels."

"I think it's a very clever phrase." Even now, he found it hard to touch her. He lay with hands at his sides.

She changed the subject. "I was never able to get very far playing the piano. I have absolutely *no* give between the thumb and first finger. And that's essential, you know. You have to have a long reach, a good spread I think they call it, to play Chopin. A tenth: that's two notes over an octave. A *full* octave, a *perfect* octave, those are just technical terms. Octave is good enough. I don't have that."

"I like piano playing," he said, realizing how silly and dull he must sound, and frightened (very suddenly) that she would find him so, that she would leave him. Then he remembered where they were and he smiled. Where could she go? Where could *he* go?

"I always hated the fellows at parties who could play the piano . . . all the girls clustered around those people. Except these days it's not so much piano, not too many people have pianos in their homes any more. The kids grow up and go away and nobody takes lessons and the kids don't buy pianos. They get those electric guitars."

"Acoustical guitars."

"Yes, those. I don't think it would be much better for fellows like me who don't play, even if it's acoustical guitars."

They got up and walked again.

Once they discussed how they had wasted their lives, how they had sat there with hands folded as time filled space around them, swept through, was drained off, and their own "chron-ons" (he had told her about the lunatic; she said it sounded like Benjamin Franklin; he said the man hadn't looked like Ben-jamin Franklin, but maybe, it might have been) had been leached of all potency.

Once they discussed the guillotine executions in the Paris of the Revolution, because it was keeping pace with them. Once they chased the Devonian and almost caught it. Once they were privileged to enjoy themselves in the center of an Arctic snowstorm that held around them for a measure of mea-sureless time. Once they saw nothing for an eternity but were truly chilled—unlike the Arctic snowstorm that had had no effect on them—by the winds that blew past them. And once he turned to her and said, "I love you, Catherine."

But when she looked at him with a gentle smile, he noticed for the first time that her eyes seemed to be getting gray and pale.

Then, not too soon after, she said she loved him, too.

But she could see mist through the flesh of his hands when he reached out to touch her face.

They walked with their arms around each other, having found each other. They said many times, and agreed it was so, that they were in love, and being together was the most im-portant thing in that endless world of gray spaces, even if they never found their way back.

And they began to *use* their time together, setting small goals for each "day" upon awakening. We will walk *that* far; we will play word games in which *you* have to begin the name of a female movie star from the last letter of a male movie star's name that *I* have to begin off the last letter of a female movie star; we will exchange shirt and blouse and see how it feels for a while; we will sing every camp song we can re-member. They began to *enjoy* their time together. They began to live.

And sometimes his voice faded out and she could see him moving his lips but there was no sound.

And sometimes when the mist cleared she was invisible from the ankles down and her body moved as through thick soup.

And as they used their time, they became alien in that place where wasted time had gone to rest.

And they began to fade. As the world had leached out for Ian Ross in Scotland, and for Catherine Molnar in Wisconsin, *they* began to vanish from limbo. Matter could neither be created nor destroyed, but it could be disassembled and sent where it was needed for entropic balance.

He saw her pale skin become transparent.

She saw his hands as clear as glass.

And they thought: *too late. It comes too late.*

Invisible motes of their selves were drawn off and were sent away from that gray place. Were sent where needed to maintain balance. One and one and one, separated on the wind and blown to the farthest corners of the tapestry that was time and space. And could never be recalled. And could never be rejoined.

So they touched, there in that vast limbo of wasted time, for the last time, and shadows existed for an instant, and then were gone; he first, leaving her behind for the merest instant of terrible loneliness and loss, and then she, without shadow, pulled apart and scattered, followed. Separation without hope of return.

Great events hushed in mist swirled past. Ptolemy crowned king of Egypt, the Battle of the Teutoburger Forest, Jesus crucified, the founding of Constantinople, the Vandals plundering Rome, the massacre of the Omayyad family, the court of the Fujiwaras in Japan, Jerusalem falling to Saladin . . . and on and on . . . great events . . . empty time . . . and the timeless population trudged past endlessly . . . endlessly . . . unaware that finally, at last, hopelessly and too late . . . two of their nameless order had found the way out.

In the Fourth Year of the War

INTRODUCTION

When I was a very little boy in Painesville, Ohio, a woman who lived up the street had my dog, Puddles, picked up by the dogcatcher and gassed while I was away at summer camp. I've never forgotten her. I think I hate her as much today, forty years after the fact, as I did the day I came back from camp and my father took me in his arms and explained that Puddles was dead. That old woman is no doubt long gone, but the hate lives on.

Each of us moves through life shadowed by childhood memories. We never forget. We are bent and shaped and changed by those ancient fears and hatreds. They are the mortal dreads that in a million small ways block us off or drive us toward our destiny.

Is it impossible to realize that those memories are merely the dead, ineffectual past; that they need not chain us?

A fine writer named Meyer Levin once wrote, "Three evils plague the writer's world: suppression, plagiarism, and falsification."

The first two are obvious. They are monstrous and must be fought at whatever cost, wherever they surface.

The last is more insidious. It makes writers lie in their work. Not because they want to, but because the truth is so terribly clouded by insubstantial wraiths, personal traumas, the detritus of adolescent impressions. Who among us can deny that within each adult is caged a frightened child?

This is a horror story.

There are no ghosts or slimy monsters or antichrist omens. At least none that can physically reach out and muss the hair. The horrors are the ones we create for ourselves; and they are the ones we all share.

This is also a cautionary tale, intended to say *You are not alone.* We all carry the past with us like the chambered nautilus; and we all must find ways to exorcise it at peril of our destiny.

In the Fourth Year
of the War

> The King grew vain;
> Fought all his battles o'er again;
>   And thrice he routed all his foes,
>   And thrice he slew the slain.
>
>   JOHN DRYDEN, ·
>   *Alexander's Feast, 1697*

IN THE FOURTH YEAR of the war with the despicable personage that had come to live in my brain, the utterly vile tenant who called himself Jerry Olander, I was ordered to kill for the first time.

It came as no surprise. It had taken Jerry Olander four years, plus or minus a couple of months, to get sufficient control over my motor responses. He had been working toward just such a program of monstrous actions, and though I never knew till the moment he ordered the hit that the form of his evil was to be murder, that was one of the few possibilities. Even though I wasn't surprised, I was sickened, and refused. It didn't do me any good, of course. Jerry was strong enough after four years of constant warfare within my brain; I was just weak enough, weary enough, just enough filled with battle fatigue, to put up a losing argument.

The target was to be my mother's older brother, my Uncle Carl. Had Jerry Olander suggested the Pope, or the President of the United States, or some notorious public figure, I might have grasped a thin edge of rationality in the order. But Uncle Carl? A man in his late sixties, a retired jeweler whose wife had died of cancer fifteen years earlier, who lived quietly and inoffensively in a suburb of Chicago. Carl? Why should the unwanted roommate of my brain want to see old Uncle Carl dead?

"Don't *you* want to see him dead?" Jerry replied, when I put the question to him.

"Who, Carl?" I didn't mean to sound stupid; but I was nonplused; and sounded stupid.

Jerry laughed. I had come to know that miserable sound. In the dead of night, when I was hovering on the lip between wakefulness and whatever was strobing across the face of my bedside television set, and the abyss of thankful sleep, he would begin laughing. It was the sound I'm certain was made when the broken-handled claw hammer wrenched out the rusty spikes from Jesus's crucified wrists.

He laughed that rusty laugh and mimicked me. "Who, Carl? Yes, Carl. Old Uncle Carl, who killed your father's dreams. Don't begin to tell me, don't even *begin* to tell me that you've forgotten all that, chum."

"Don't call me chum."

"Well, then, using the short form: yes, Uncle Carl."

"You're crazy. I can't do it . . . *won't* do it!"

"Oh, you'll *do it,* all right. We have no problem on that score. As for my being crazy, I won't argue the point. One would have to be a bit crazy to share a mind with you."

"Carl never did anything to my father," I said.

"Think about it," Jerry said. I hated his smugness.

But I thought about it. And from the quicklime pit of forgotten memories something dead but still moving rose from corruption and dragged itself into my consciousness. A zombie recollection, a foulness from childhood, half-understood, miserable, something that intellectually I knew was a lie, yet a thing I believed true with that trapped child's refusal to abandon the terrors of the past.

Jerry laughed. "Yeah, that's it, chum. Remember now?"

"That isn't true. I know it isn't. I only thought that was the way it was . . . because I was a kid. I didn't know any better."

"Nobody's evil, right? No black and white. Just a shitload world of grays. Right? Then how come you still believe it?"

He was really gnawing at me now. I tried to send that shambling awfulness back to its quicklime grave, but it stalked through my mind, led forward by Jerry's voice. "Look at it, chum. Consider Uncle Carl and what he did to your old man."

The memory grew larger in my mind. I found myself unable to turn away from its rotted flesh and stinking breath, the dead eyes covered with a gray film. I found myself remembering my father . . .

He had managed Carl's jewelry store during the war, when Carl had gone off to the navy. My father had been too old, had had a heart condition; so he had worked in the store instead of serving. Carl had pulled strings and wound up on the West Coast, at one of the supply terminals. And my father had worked twelve, fifteen, eighteen hours a day building up the clientele. He had always wanted his own store, to be in business for himself, to go to Tucson or San Francisco, a warm and wonderful place away from the snow and the biting Lake Michigan winds. But my mother had insisted that family was more important than self-realization. "Stay with family," she had said. "Carl told you he'd make you a partner. The family always keeps its promises."

So my father had let his dreams fade, and had stayed on with the store.

When the war was over, and Carl came home, and my father finally summoned up the courage to call in the promise, Carl had thrown him out of the store.

I never knew why, really. I was a child. Children are never told the whys of family disasters. They just happen. You wouldn't understand, children are told; and then, in the next breath, they are told, You mustn't hate your Uncle Carl for this, he has his reasons.

But my father had to start all over again. At the age of fifty. He rented a small apartment on the second floor in a business district close to the Loop, and he opened a jewelry shop. It was two long flights up, one steep set of stairs, a landing, and a switchback flight half as long but just as steep. And the drive from Evanston, back and forth, each day. Working far into the evening to catch the late foot traffic; on the phone with customers, trying to hustle an extra sale, even at night when he was home and should have been relaxing. A grinding, terrible schedule without break or release, to keep my mother and myself fed and clothed, not to lose the house.

One year. He lasted one year, almost to the week of opening the new store. And on a Sunday morning, sitting in his big chair by the old Philco radio, he had a sudden smash of a coronary thrombosis and he died. In a moment, as I watched, he went pale and his eyes popped open so I could see how blue they were, and his mouth drooped at one side, and he died. He had no last words.

The zombie memory would not free me. I saw things I never could have imagined as a child. My father's blue eyes, with the realization in them that all the dreams had been stolen from him, that he had lived his life and it had come to nothing, that he was dead and had never made his mark, had been here and was gone, and no one would remember or care. I saw, I remembered, I cared.

My child's memories were of hatred, and revenge. Carl.

"My father did it to himself," I said, walking upstairs. "He allowed his dreams to die. If he'd really had the courage to break loose and go to the Coast he would have done it," I said entering my bedroom and going to the closet. "Carl had nothing to do with it. If it hadn't been Carl, it would have been someone else in whom my father placed his trust. I can't hate a man for not keeping a promise twenty-five years ago," I said, pulling down my overnight case. "This is crazy. You can't get me to do this." I began packing for the flight to Chicago. I heard the sound of spikes being twisted out of wormwood.

It took Carl a long time to answer the door. He had a serious arthritic condition, and it was late. Highland Park was silent and sleeping. I stood under the porch light and saw Carl's pale, tired eyes peering at me through the open-weave curtain behind the door's glass panes. He blinked many times, and finally seemed to recognize me. He opened the door.

"You didn't tell me you were coming," he said. I put my hand against the half-opened door and pushed it slowly inward. Carl moved back and I walked in. My overnight case was still lying on the back seat of the rental compact at the curb. "Why didn't you call me and tell me you were coming? How's your mother?"

"Mom died three years ago."

He blinked again. His liver-spotted forehead drew down and he thought about it. "Yes. I'd forgotten. Why didn't you call me up on the phone and tell me you were coming?"

He closed and locked the door behind me. I walked into the darkened living room, only faintly outlined by the hall light. He followed me. He was wearing something I had only seen in period movies, a long nightgown that reached to his thin calves, white with blue veins prominent. The fabric was rough cotton, and like his calves was veined with blue pinstriping. I turned around to look at him. In my head I said, "This is crazy. Look at him. He's an old man. He won't even remember. What's the point of this?"

And Jerry Olander said, "It doesn't matter if *he* doesn't remember. *You* remember. But if it makes you feel any better, tell him why you've come to kill him."

"What are you doing here in the dead of night, I wish you'd called me up on the phone and told me," Carl said.

I couldn't see his face. He was standing with the hall light behind him. It was a black circle without feature. I said to him, "Do you remember a night a long time ago, in the red brick house you had on Maple Street, when Lillian was alive?"

"I remember the house. It was a small house. We had much bigger houses. Maybe you called and I was asleep."

I moved toward him till he could see *my* face, lit along the sharp planes of cheeks and nose by the light over his shoulder. "I see it all now the way a little boy would see it, Uncle Carl. I'm looking out from under a dining room table, through the legs and cross-braces of chairs, watching you and my father on the screened back porch. You're arguing. It was the first time I ever heard my father swear or raise his voice. I remember it very clearly, even if it isn't true, because he was such a quiet person. You know that. He never raised his voice or got angry. He should have. He might not have died when he did, or died so miserably, if he'd raised his voice a few times."

"What are you talking about?" Carl said. He was beginning to realize he wanted to be annoyed at his nephew barging in on him at three o'clock in the morning while he was still half-asleep. "Do you want something to eat? What are you doing here in Chicago? Don't you live out there in California now?"

He hadn't seen me in years. We had no contact. And here I stood before him, dragging him back through the dead years to a night he didn't even remember. "Then you stood up and yelled at him, and he pushed back his chair till it fell over, and he yelled at you, and then you swung at him, and he hit you with a cushion off one of the chairs. And the next day he didn't go down at seven-thirty to open the store while you stayed in and slept late and had a nice breakfast with Lillian. Do you remember all that, Uncle Carl?"

"Lillian is dead. She's been gone a long time."

I walked to the sofa and looked down. Then I walked back to him and took him by the arm. He resisted for a moment, but he was very old, and I wasn't, and he came with me to the sofa, and I forced him to sit down. Then I took the pillow with the fringe, and I held it in one hand as I shoved him down, and held it over his face while he thrust himself up against it, until he stopped. It was over much more quickly than I'd thought. I'd always thought people struggle much harder to cling to life. But he was old, and his memories were gone.

And all the while I was begging Jerry Olander to stop. But he had spent four full years of wresting control from me, and in those four years of the war I had come to know he would win a battle or two. This was the first battle. And he had won.

"Very efficient," Jerry Olander said.

In the fourth year of the war with the homicidal maniac that had come to nest in my brain, a second hit was ordered. A woman I wasn't even certain was still alive. She had had my dog gassed, *put to sleep* as they tell it to children, one summer when I was away at camp. Her name was Mrs. Corley, and she had lived down at the end of our street in Evanston.

I argued with Jerry Olander. "Why did you pick me to live in?" I had asked that question surely more than a hundred and fifty thousand times in four years.

"No particular reason. You haven't got a wife, or many friends. You work at home most of the time—though I still can't see how you make any kind of a living with that mail order catalogue—and nobody's going to put you away too quickly because you talk to yourself."

"Who *are* you?" I screamed, because I couldn't get him out of me. He was like the eardrums refusing to pop when a plane lands. I couldn't break his hold on me, no matter how hard I swallowed or held my nose and blew.

"The name is Jerry Olander," he said, lightly, adding in an uncannily accurate imitation of Bogart, "and somebody's always gotta take the fall, shweetheart."

Then he made me go to the main branch of the public library, to look at all the telephone books. He didn't have control of my vocal cords, couldn't make my brain call the 312-555-1212 information operator in Chicago, to establish if Mrs. Corley still lived in Evanston. But he *could* make my legs carry me to my car, make my hands place themselves at 11:50 and 12:05 on the steering wheel, make my eyes run down the columns of names and phone numbers in the Evanston telephone directory in the library's stacks.

She lived in the same house, at the same address, in the same world I had shared with her as a child.

Jerry Olander made my body drive to the savings and loan where I had my small account, made my right hand ink in the withdrawal slip, made my mouth smile as the teller handed me my last five hundred dollars.

And Jerry Olander made me tape the basement window of Mrs. Corley's house before I broke it with a rock. Fighting him every step of the way, I was nonetheless made to walk silently through the basement to the steps, was made to climb them to the kitchen where I found old Mrs. Corley fixing herself a vegetarian dinner, and was made to tie and gag her.

But when I refused to go further, Jerry Olander's voice played Pied Piper to the living dead in the quicklime pit of memory, and another shambling, rotted thing dragged itself up onto the landscape of my mind, and I saw myself as a child, coming home from a ghastly month at some nameless summer camp. And, of course, the name was right there, unremembered for thirty years, just as fresh as if I had come home yesterday. Camp Bellefaire. On Lake Belle. I had hated it, had pleaded with my mother and father every Sunday when they had come to visit me—like seeing a Death Row resident during visitation hours—"Please take me home, Momma, Poppa, *please,* I don't like it here!" But they had never understood that there are some children for whom organized activities in which they can *never* distinguish themselves is a special sort of debasement.

And I had come home gladly, to see Charlie, my dog; to move around freely in my room with the Erector set and the comic books and my very own radio; to build Stukas and Lightnings and Grumman seaplanes, and smell TesTor's cement once again.

And Charlie was dead. "Do you remember that summer, Mrs. Corley?" I heard myself saying, and Jerry Olander wasn't making me say it. "Do you remember how you told the man at the pound that the dog was running loose for a week? Do you remember how you found Charlie's tags caught on your bush in the backyard, and didn't turn them in? I remember, Mrs. Corley, because you told Mrs. Abrams next door, and she told my Momma, and I overheard my Momma telling my Poppa. You knew who Charlie belonged to, Mrs. Corley; he'd lived here for ten years, so you *had* to know."

And then I pushed Mrs. Corley to her knees, and turned on all four jets of the gas range, and opened the oven and put her head inside while she struggled, and hit her once sharply behind the left ear, and laid her head down on the open door of the oven, left her kneeling there in prayer, final prayer, ultimate prayer... and went away.

"I liked the part about the dog tags best," Jerry Olander said, on the plane back to California.

In the fourth year of the war with that evil intelligence in my brain, I was ordered to kill, and *did* kill, seven people, including my Uncle Carl and old Mrs. Corley. And each one made me sick to think about it. I had no idea if Jerry Olander was merely the product of my own mind, a sick and twisted, deranged and malevolent phantom of a personality that had finally split, or if he was a disembodied spirit, an astral projection, a dybbuk or poltergeist or alien from the center of the Earth that had come to wreak murder on the race of humans, using me as his unwitting tool. I have seen enough motion pictures, read enough mystery stories, seen enough television programs in which a man's evil nature takes him over, to know that is the most rational answer.

There is no reason to believe me, but I *swear*, Jerry Olander never came from within me. He was from outside, a rejected thing. And he inhabited me without my consent. It had been war, and he had won battle after battle, and I knew if those killings were ever traced to me I would spend the rest of my life in a home for the criminally insane... but further than saying, as quietly and as miserably as I can... I was not Jerry Olander... what can I say to convince...

And finally, it came the time I had known would arrive, from the moment he ordered the death of my Uncle Carl.

Jerry Olander said to me, as the fourth year of the war drew to an end, "Now it's time to kill Nancy."

"No!" I screamed. "No. I won't do it. I'll kill myself first. You can't make me, there's no way you can make me, I'll fight you, you're not going to make me do *that!*"

Nancy was my ex-wife. She had left me, but there wasn't the faintest vestige of bad feeling in me about it. She had made her reasons for wanting a divorce plain to me, and they were good and sound reasons. We had been married when we were too young to know better, and through the years we had loved each other. But Nancy had learned she was more than a wife, that she had never been provided the opportunity to know herself, to expand herself, to fulfill the dreams she had had. And we had parted with love.

Now she lived in Pasadena, working with an orthopedic shoe company that had designed a special footgear for those who suffered with Hansen's Disease. Her life was full, she was responsible and settled, mature and wonderful. We talked from time to time, occasionally had dinner together.

I meant her no harm.

"There's no sense to this!" I said, pleading with Jerry Olander. "There's no sense to any of this. Please let me alone, let me kill myself if that'll give you some satisfaction! But don't try to make me do this!"

"It all makes sense," he said, getting nastily quiet. "Everything you do is colored by those memories. How many nights have you lain awake in pain from a toothache, rather than going to a dentist because the family sent you to Cousin Franklyn to save a few dollars on dental bills? How many of your teeth that might have been saved did he pull because he was no damned good, should have been a butcher instead of a dentist? You're afraid of dentists to this day because of Cousin Franklyn. And how many women who might have loved you have you walked away from, picked fights with, ignored, considered better or worse than you, not your 'type,' because of Peggy Mantle and the way she laughed at you when you were fifteen? How many times have you walked past a store where you needed to buy something, because you remembered the way old man Clareborne threw you out of his department store when you were a little boy? How much of what you think is free will is just a programmed reaction to things you've buried, memories you don't want to remember, pains and slights and affronts you suffered as a child? How many, chum? How goddam many? Oh, there's sense here!"

Jerry Olander had me walk across the room. To the telephone.

"But I'm all alone now. I have no one. No wife, no children, no mother, no father, not even too many people I can call friends. I'm all alone; won't you leave me Nancy!"

I began to dial a number.

The phone began to ring.

"You're not alone, chum," Jerry Olander said softly. "I'm right here with you. And I've got a long, long memory."

The receiver was picked up at the other end and a voice said, "Hello."

Zombie things from the quicklime pit began emerging, one after another of them; dozens of them, summoned by Jerry Olander's long, long memory. I wanted to shout, to make a terrible dying sound, to clarion a warning, and found I could not even do that. In the fourth year of our war, Jerry Olander had even gained control of my words, and I had lost, I had lost, I had lost!

"Hi, Nancy," I heard myself saying, "what are you doing for dinner tonight?"

> *Life is too short to occupy oneself with the slaying of the slain more than once.*
> · THOMAS HENRY HUXLEY, c. 1861

Alive and Well and on a Friendless Voyage

INTRODUCTION

In recent years—and you've probably heard me bitching about this elsewhere—writers of contemporary fantasy have come in for considerable attention from Academe. I've been spared more of that kind of literary disembowelment than, say, Bradbury or Heinlein or Le Guin, mostly because I tend to move too fast and too shiftily for any publish-or-perish professor to get a handle on me. (There are those who contend I'm unworthy of serious attention, and to them a tip of the hat. I have this paranoid belief that the more acceptable one becomes to the Establishment, the less dangerous and troublesome is one's work.)

Notwithstanding these baseless canards, there have been essays and monographs and even treatises published in learned journals about the rampant symbolism in my stories, my preoccupation with the Machine As God, the deeply religious anti-religiousness in *Deathbird Stories,* obvious uses of the Jungian archetypes, the crucifixion and resurrection symbology peppered through my stories, and the frequency of the use of the word "ka-ka."

I am always startled at the depths revealed in my stories by these erudite critics. I try not to argue with them. I just smile knowingly and respond, "You little devil, you. You found me out!"

The more profound they think they are, the more they require their students to read you; and that means the poor kids have to buy the books containing my stories. And that means a fat and happy life of work, free from the horrors of maybe having to write television scripts. So who am I to say nay, who am I to suggest they're stuffed topfull of wild blueberry muffins?

What is beginning to unman me is that this plague seems to be spreading to my readers. Now I conceive of all of you as the noblest, wittiest, most intelligent audience in the world. Otherwise you'd be off reading ka-ka like that proffered by Judith Krantz and Sidney Sheldon, to name only two of the creative typists masquerading as writers.

Well, sir. You can imagine my horror and surprise when I received a letter last February from a reader that went like this:*

Dear Mr. Ellison:

Last summer I found, by accident, your story "Croatoan" and was disturbed and excited by the resemblances to the sixth book of Vergil's *Aeneid.* There were too many to be accidental, but I still couldn't imagine you following Vergil intentionally, even to the meeting with the man with no hands. I was afraid I had stumbled on something out of the universal subconscious, and felt responsible for doing something about it.

Tonight I browsed through *Strange Wine* and noticed the references to Isak Dinesen and [Cyril Connolly's book of essays] *The Unquiet Grave.* I read the story again and wondered why the comparison of the child to a lemur hadn't tipped me off. I'm relieved to think you knew what you were doing.

Thanks for giving us, along with a good story, new ways to think about Vergil.

Sincerely yours,
James Griffin

What can I say? Humbly, I bow my head and dimple winsomely. Paw the dirt with my hoof, tug my forelock, suck my thumb and murmur aw, shucks. You're very per-

*Letter reprinted by permission of James Griffin, Philadelphia, Pa.

ceptive. That's exactly what I was doing. You little devil, you. You found me out!

There's just one small glitch in the smooth flow.

I've never read Vergil's *Aeneid.*

The story you are about to read is stuffed full of very conscious symbolism. Catch it now, friends; I don't do it that often; maybe three times in twenty-five years.

This story was written in direct response to the killing pain of my last wife taking off with another guy. The pain lasted at least twelve minutes, which is the actually recorded duration of genuine pain. Everything *over* twelve minutes is self-indulgence and pointless attempts to make the first twelve minutes seem more important. We are a vainglorious species, and if we were able to cop to the fact that even the most *sauvage* of what the French call *la grande passion* commands only twelve true minutes of intense pain before it begins to mellow, we would all dash to the cliffs and do a lemming. So we justify it by enhancing it, by making it seem more important, more consuming. We wander around for twenty years after the affair has broken up, beating our breasts and wailing at the sky.

No nobler than you, I wandered for several months after my last marriage broke up, beating my breast and wailing at the sky, not to mention my friends, who (with uncommon good sense) told me to shut up already. And one night, during a performance of *Jacques Brel Is Alive and Well in Paris,* a line from one of his wonderful songs struck right to the core of my lost love, and I wrote this story.

I wish to God I could remember what the line was.

Alive and Well and on a Friendless Voyage

"Quae nocent docent."

THEN, AND ONLY THEN, like some mysterious Prisoner in the Iron Mask hidden from everyone's sight, only then, when the gigantic vessel slipped out of normal continuity and entered the megaflow, only then did the man they called Moth emerge from his stateroom.

As the immense tambour shields rolled down into the body of the vessel, exposing the boiling white jelly that was the megaflow surging past beyond the great crystal ports, the door to his stateroom rolled up and he emerged, dressed entirely in white. Clown-white circles around his dark, haunted eyes. Everyone looked and stopped talking.

The lounge of the gigantic vessel was packed, with voyagers grouped by twos and threes and fours at the bubble tables with their thin stalk supports. Voyagers who had boarded at 4:00, at Now, at Here, at three dimensions—bound for 41:00, for the 85th of February, for Yet To Be, for There, for the last stop before the end of measurable space and time and thought. They looked at Moth and they stopped talking.

Their faces said: *Who is this person?*

And he walked down among them haltingly; he did not know them. This ship of strangers, and Moth.

He sat down at a table with one empty chair. A man and

a woman already sat there. The woman was slim, neither attractive nor unattractive, a mild-looking woman, difficult to discompose. The man looked kind, there were crinkle lines at the corners of his eyes. Moth sat down across from them, as the gigantic vessel hurtled through the megaflow, and the kind-looking man said, "It wasn't your fault."

Moth looked sad. "I can't believe that. I think it must have been my fault."

"No, no," the unperturbed woman said quickly, "it *wasn't!* There was nothing that could be done. Your son would have died nonetheless. You can't castigate yourself for believing in God. You *mustn't.*"

Moth leaned forward and put his face in his hands. His voice came faintly. "It was insane. Dead is dead. I should have known that . . . I *did* know it."

The kind-looking man reached across and touched Moth's hand. "The sickness was put on him by God, because of something you had done, you or your wife. It couldn't have been the child. He was too young to have known sin. But *you* knew you or your wife were filled with sin. And so your child fell ill. But if you could be as brave as the Bible said you must be, you could save him."

The calm woman gently pried Moth's hands away from his face and forced him to look into her eyes. She held his hands across the table and said, "Doctors could not save him . . . you *knew* that. God sets no store by science, only faith. Keeping them from the child was necessary. Hiding him in the basement was *important.*"

Moth whispered, "But he grew worse. He sickened. It was too cold down there, perhaps. I might have let the family do what they wanted, let a physician *see* him, at least."

"No," the kind man said imperatively. "No! Faith cannot be broken. You maintained. You were right. Even when he died."

"It was holy the way you sat vigil over him," the woman said. "Day after day. You said he would rise on the second or third day. And you had belief in God."

Moth began to cry silently. "He lay there. Three days, and he lay there. His color changed."

"Then a week," the kind man said. "Faith! You had faith! In a week he would rise."

"No," Moth said, "not in a week. Dead."

"Twenty-one days, a magic number. It would have been on the twenty-first day. But they came and the law made you give him up, and they arrested you, and all through the hearings you insisted on God's Will, and your good wife, she stood by you through the hatred and the anguish as outsiders reviled you."

"He never rose. They buried him in the earth," Moth said, drying his eyes. The clown-white had run down his cheeks.

"So you were forced to leave. To go outside. To get away to a place where God would hear you. It was the right way; you had no other choice. Either believe, or become one with the faithless people who filled your world. You need not have guilt," the kind man said. He touched Moth's sleeve.

"You'll find peace," the calm woman said.

"Thank you," Moth said, rising and leaving them.

The man and woman sank back in their chairs, and the lights that had been lit in their eyes as they spoke to Moth . . . dimmed and grew sullen. Moth moved through the lounge.

A young man with an intense expression and nervous hand movements sat alone. He stared out the port at the megaflow.

"May I sit down here?" Moth asked.

The young man looked at him, taking his eyes off the swirling, bubbling jelly of the megaflow reluctantly. But he did not reply. There was loathing in his expression. He turned back to the crystal port without answering Moth.

"Please. May I sit with you? I want to talk to you."

"I don't talk to cowards," the young man said. His jaw muscles spasmed with anger.

"I'm a coward, yes, I'll admit it," Moth said helplessly. "But, please, let me sit."

"Oh, for Christ's sake, *sit* already! But just shut your mouth; don't speak to me!" He turned once again to the port.

Moth sat down, folded his hands on the table, did not speak, stared steadily at the young man's profile.

After a few moments the young man turned his face. He looked at Moth. "You make me sick. I'd like to punch you in the face, you disgusting coward."

"Yes," said Moth miserably, "I wouldn't stop you. I'm a coward, as you say."

"Worse! Worse than just a coward. A hypocrite, a silly posturing fool! You spent your whole life playing the big man, the big stud, the cavalier. The tough, cynical mover and shaker.

But you weren't any smarter or tougher than any other simple-minded jerk who thought with his groin."

"I made mistakes," Moth said. "Just like everybody else. There's never enough experience. I thought I knew what I was doing. I fell in love with her."

"Oh, that's terrific," the young man said. The tone was frankly vicious. "Terrific. *You fell in love.* You moron! She was nineteen. You were over twice her age. Why did you let her whipsaw you into marriage? Come on, you idiot, why?"

"She said she loved me, thought I was better than other men, said if I didn't marry her she would go away and I'd never see her again. I was in love, I'd only been in love once before. No, that isn't right: I'd only *loved* once before. The thought of never seeing that face again filled me with fear. That was it: I was afraid I'd never see her again. I couldn't live with that."

"So you married her."

"Yes."

"But you couldn't sleep with her, couldn't make love to her. What did you expect from her? She was a child."

"She *talked* like a woman. She said all the right things an adult woman says. I didn't realize she was still confused, didn't know what she wanted."

"But you couldn't make love to her, isn't that so?"

"Yes, it's so. She was like a child, a daughter; my thoughts weren't straight; I didn't realize that was what was happening. All interest in sex just vanished; for her, for any woman. I thought—"

"What *she* thought. That you were impotent. That you were falling apart. She got more frightened every day. A lifetime to spend with a man who would never show her any passion."

"But there was love. I loved her. Without reserve. I showed it in a million ways, every hour of the day that we spent together."

"Gifts."

"Yes, gifts. Touches. Hugs and kisses and smiles."

"Purchases. You tried buying her."

"No, never that."

"Rented, then. It was the same."

The young man clenched and unclenched his hands. They seemed to have movement directed from somewhere outside him. The hands moved and seemed to want to strike Moth.

The man in clown-white could not have failed to notice, but he did not flinch, did not move away. He sat waiting for the next assault, willing victim.

"How did it feel when you found out she was sleeping with him?"

"It hurt terribly. Worse than anything I'd ever felt. There was a ball of pain in the bottom of my lungs, like something inside breathing, a second heart. I don't know; and every time it breathed, the pain was worse."

The young man sneered. "And what did you do about it, big man?"

"I wanted to kill him."

"Why him? He was only picking up on the available goodies. You leave something lying around unused, there'll always be someone who'll put it to use."

Moth sat forlornly, "It was the way she was doing it."

The young man laughed nastily. "You ass. There's *always* some stupid rationalization cuckolds like you fasten on to make it seem dramatic. If it hadn't been this way, it would have been another; and you'd have found some aspect of *that* in bad taste. Can't you understand it's all excuses?"

"But when I found out, and asked her to leave, she said she would go to stay with her family, to think it out. But she moved in with him."

The young man moved suddenly. He leaned across and grabbed Moth's shirt. He pulled him halfway across the table and his voice became a low snarl of hatred. *"Then* what did you do, hero? Huh, what happened then?"

Moth spoke softly, as if ashamed. "I loaded a gun and went down there to his apartment and kicked in the door. I put my shoe flat against the jamb right beside the lock and pulled back and slammed it as hard as I could. It popped the lock right out of the frame. I went straight through the living room of that awful little apartment and into the bedroom, and they were on the bed naked. It was just the way I'd been seeing it in my head, with him on top of her, except they'd heard the lock shatter and he was trying to get untangled from the sheets and I caught him with one foot on the floor."

The young man shook Moth. Not too hard, but hard enough to show how angry he was, how disgusted he was. Beyond them, the megaflow took on a scar-tissue appearance, inflamed, nastily pink with burned blue tinges. He continued shaking

Moth gently, as if jangling coins from a small bank.

"I rushed him and shoved the gun into his mouth. I heard him start to moan something and then his teeth broke when the muzzle of the gun went into his mouth. I pushed him flat on his back, down onto the bed, and I kneeled with my right leg on his chest, and I told her to get dressed, that I was taking her out of there."

The young man shoved him back. Moth sat silently.

"What a stupid, miserable, pitiful little mind you are. None of that is true, is it?"

Moth looked away. Softly, he said, "No. None of it."

"What *did* you do when you found out she was with him, after four months of marriage?"

"Nothing."

"You loaded the gun and did nothing."

"Yes."

"You couldn't even bring yourself to make the act real, could you?"

"No. I'm a coward. I wanted to kill him, and then kill myself."

"But not her."

"No. Never her. I loved her. I couldn't kill her, so I wanted to kill everything else in the world."

"Get away from me, you pathetic little shit. Just get up and walk away from me and don't talk to me any more. You ran away. You're running now. But you're not going to escape."

Moth said, "In time, I'll forget."

"You'll never completely forget it. Time will dull it, and maybe it'll be supportable. But you'll never forget."

"Perhaps not," Moth said, and stood up. He turned away, and as he turned away, the light that had blazed madly in the young man's eyes dimmed and went out. He turned back to the scar-tissue of the megaflow and stared at nothingness.

Moth walked through the lounge, breathing deeply.

He passed a beautiful woman with pale yellow hair and almost white eyebrows who was sitting in company with two nondescript men at a table for four. As Moth came abreast of her, she reached out and touched his arm. "I feel more sorrow for you than animosity," she said, in a gentle and deep voice. Her words were filled with rich tones.

Moth sat down in the empty chair. The two men seemed

not to see him, though they listened to the conversation between Moth and the beautiful woman.

"No one should ever be judged heartless because he tended to his own personal survival," she said. She held an unlit cigarette in a short holder. One of the men in attendance moved to light it, but she waved him away sharply. Her attention was solidly with Moth.

"I could have saved one of them," Moth responded. He pressed the back of his hand to his mouth, as though seeing again a terrible vision from the past. "The fire, the Home ballooning with flames from the windows, the sound of their screams. They were so old, so helpless."

The pale yellow hair shimmered as the beautiful woman shook her head. "You were only the caretaker of their lives; it wasn't written on stone that you had to *die* for them. You were conscientious, you were a good administrator; there was never the slightest impropriety in the Home. But what could you do? You were *afraid!* Everyone has a secret fear. For some it's growing old, for others it's snakes or spiders or being buried alive. Drowning, being laughed at in public, closed-in spaces, being rejected. *Every*one has something."

"I didn't know it was fire. I swear to God I didn't realize. But when I came down the hall that night and smelled the smoke, I was paralyzed. I stood there in the hall, just staring at the wire-screen door to the dormitory section. We *always* kept it locked at night. It wasn't a jail . . . it was for their own protection: they were so old, and some of them roamed at night. We couldn't keep watch all the time, it just wasn't feasible."

"I know, I know," the beautiful woman said, soothing him. "It was for their own protection. They had their television in the dorm, and bathroom facilities. It was lovely up there, just the same as the private rooms on the lower floors. But they *roamed*, they walked at night; they might fall down stairs or have an attack and there would be no one to help them, no call button for you or an orderly nearby. I understand why you kept the screen locked."

Moth spread his hands helplessly. He looked this way and that, as if seeking a white light that would release him from the pain of memory. "I smelled the smoke, and as I stood there, not knowing what to do, almost ready to rush forward and unlock the door and go inside, a blast of heat and flame came right through the screen! The heat was so intense I fell back. But even then . . . *even then* I would have done something, but the cat . . ."

The beautiful woman nodded. "It was the sight of the cat that terrified you, that made you suddenly realize it was fire that hid down there in your mind, waiting to possess you. I understand, anyone would understand!"

"I don't know how it got through the screen. It . . . it *strained itself* through, and it was on fire, burning, one of the old woman's cats. It was on fire. The smell of the fur, the crackling, it was burning like fat in a fire. It screamed, oh God the sound of the screaming, the tail all black and the parts of it bubbling . . ."

"Don't!" the beautiful woman said, feeling Moth's pain. "Don't torment yourself. You ran. I understand why you ran. There was nothing you could do."

"No one knew I had had the choice. I stood outside and watched, and once I saw a face at one of the windows. It was wrapped in flames, an old man, his long hair burning. It was ghastly, terrible, I couldn't bear it. I cried and screamed up at them, and the ones who had escaped, some of the orderlies tried to get back up there, and one of *them* was killed, when the ceiling fell in. But no one knew I had had a chance to save them, I *might* have saved them, perhaps only one of them, but I *could* have done something."

"No," the woman with the pale hair reassured him, "no. You would have been burned alive, too. And there had been the cat. No one ever need know."

"But *I* know!"

"You survived. That's what counts."

"The pain. The knowledge, the pain."

"It will pass."

"No. Never."

One of the two men moved again to light her cigarette. She put the cigarette and the holder on the table. Moth shook himself as if awakening from a nightmare, and stood up. He turned away from the woman and her silent companions. The light in her eyes faded.

Moth walked through the lounge.

The gigantic vessel plowed on through the roiling megaflow jelly, bound for the end of appreciable space, asymptotically struggling toward the verge of time, pulling itself forward inexorably to the precipice of measurable thought. The voyage included only three stops: embarkation, principal debarkation and over the edge. The voyagers sat dull and silent, occasionally sipping off drinks that had been ordered through the punch-button system on each chair. The only sounds in the lounge were the susurations as the panels in the tables opened to allow drinks to rise to the surface, the random sounds of fingernails or teeth on glass, and the ever-present hiss of the megaflow as it rampaged past the vessel. Voices could be heard in the boiling jelly, carried through the hull of the vessel, like voices of the dead, whispering for their final hearing, their day in the court of judgment. But no coherent thoughts came with those voices, no actual words, no messages from the beyond that could be of any use to the voyagers within.

Entombed outside time and space and thought, the voyagers sat silently within their trip ship, facing in any direction they chose. Direction did not matter. The vessel only traveled in one direction. And they, within, entombed.

Moth wandered through the lounge, sitting here for a few moments to tell a fat man of how he had taken a girl who worked for him as a secretary away from her husband and children, had set her up in an expensive apartment, and then, weary of her, had left her with the unbreakable lease and no funds, even without a job because it simply isn't good business to be having an affair with someone who works for you. Particularly not with a woman who is so suicide-prone. And he told the fat man how he had set up a trust fund for the children after it was over, after the girl who had worked for him as a secretary had become a self-fulfilling prophecy. Wandered through the lounge, sitting there for a long time confessing to an old woman with many rings how he had mercilessly used his age and illness to bind his sons and daughters to him till long past the time when they could find joyful lives for themselves, with no intention of *ever* signing over his wealth to them. Wandered through the lounge sitting over there for a time to reveal to a tall, thin chocolate-colored man how he had betrayed the other members of a group to which he had belonged, naming names and, from the dark interior of the back seat of a large automobile, pointing out the ones who had led the movement, and watching as they had been battered to their knees in the rain and the mud, and wincing as the thugs with the lead pipes had smashed in the back of each head, very professionally, very smoothly, only one solid downstroke for each man. Wandered through the lounge and talked to a pretty young girl about the devious mind games he had played with lovers, unnerving them and unsettling them and forcing them to spend all their time trying to dance and sing their dances and songs of life for his amusement, until their dances had degenerated into feeble tremblings and their songs had died away to rattles. Wandered through the lounge being penitent, remorseful, contrite. Sat and recanted, rued, confessed, humbled himself and wept occasionally.

And each person, as he walked away leaving them to their secret thoughts, flickered for a moment with life in the eyes, and then the lights died and they were once again alone.

He came to a table where a thin, plain-looking young woman sat alone, biting her thumbnail.

"I'd like to sit down and discuss something with you," he said. She shrugged as if she didn't care, and he sat.

"I've come to realize we're all alone," he said.

She did not reply. Merely stared at him.

"No matter how many people love us or care for us or want to ease our burden in this life," Moth said, "we are all, all of us, always alone. Something Aldous Huxley once said, I'm not sure I know it exactly. I've looked and looked and can't find the quote, but I remember part of it. He said: 'We are, each of us, an island universe in a sea of space.' I think that was it."

She looked at him without expression. Her face was thin and without remarkable features. No engaging smile, no intricate intriguing bone structure, no sudden dimple or angle that revealed her as even momentarily attractive. The look she gave him was the one she had perfected. Neutral.

"My life has always been sad music," Moth said, with enormous sincerity. "Like a long symphony played all in minors. Wind in trees and conversations heard through walls at night. No one looked at me, no one wanted to know. But I maintained; that's all there is. There's one day, and the end of it, and night, and sleep that comes slowly, and then another day. Until there are as many behind as there are ahead. No questions, no answers, alone. But I maintain. I don't let it bend me. And the song continues."

The unprepossessing young woman smiled faintly.

She reached across and touched his hand.

Moth's eyes sparkled for a moment.

Then the gigantic vessel began to slow.

They sat that way, her hand on his, until the tambour windows rolled up and they were encysted totally. And soon the gigantic vessel ceased its movement. They had arrived at the edge, at the point of debarkation.

Everyone rose to leave.

Moth stood and walked away from them. He walked back through the lounge and no one spoke to him, no one touched him. He came to the door to his stateroom and he turned.

"Excuse me," he said. They watched, silently.

"Is there anyone here who will change places with me, please? Anyone who will take my place for the rest of the voyage?" He looked out at them from his white makeup, and he waited a decent time.

No one answered, though the unremarkable young woman seemed to want to say something. But she didn't.

Moth smiled. "I thought not," he said softly.

Then he turned and the door to his stateroom rolled up and he went inside. The door rolled down and everyone left the gigantic vessel quietly.

After a moment the debarkation port irised shut, and the gigantic vessel began to move again. On into final darkness, from which there was no return.

All the Birds
Come Home to Roost

INTRODUCTION

In twenty-five years as a professional writer, I've had the kind of Olympian, enriching experience with an editor, mythologized by the career of Maxwell Perkins in relation to Wolfe, Fitzgerald, Hemingway, Ring Lardner and James Jones...only twice. What I mean to say is that I have worked hard at learning my craft; there is a continuity in the material; a stance that is my own, a voice I hope is singular: I know more about what I do than anyone else in the world.

Most of the editors with whom I've had liaisons have had salient points to make, valid suggestions for tightening up this or that, directions they thought I might take. But only twice have I been lifted beyond my abilities by the direct intervention of an editor.

This story is the most significant example, and speaks to a deep sense of loss in me.

"All the Birds Come Home to Roost" took many years to write. I had the idea back in the early seventies. It came to me because a number of women with whom I'd had relationships, which relationships had broken up and the women vanished from my world, suddenly began reappearing. Nothing mysterious about it: when I'd known them they were young and they'd gone off to begin careers, to get married, to discover themselves. Now, eight, nine, ten years later they were going through transition. Marriages dissolved, career changes, youthful escapades having palled on them, they were returning to the scenes of happier times. And they were getting back in touch with those they knew in those brighter days.

But with the mind of the fantasist I made the leap into a fictional construct: what if some guy found his life being run in reverse but only in terms of the women he'd known?

And that meant something ominous had to be at the end of the chain.

Since the story paralleled my own experiences in many ways, experiences shared by so many of us, I decided to take one of those tours through others' lives by taking one through mine. I used as the focus of the story the fact that the protagonist had had a disastrous first marriage that had haunted him across the years, that had blighted his subsequent relations with women.

Before I proceed, let me reiterate: *I do not write diary.* A writer cannibalizes his own life and memories, yes, that is true. All we have to work with is what we know and what we dream. But nothing is more boring than *kvetching* in fiction. Thinly disguised personal reminiscence is not fiction. Those who, in the past, have identified me with everything that goes down in my stories have assumed I am a murderer, a transvestite, a cannibal, a sexist, a feminist, a racist, an egalitarian, an elitist, a vegetarian, an esthete, a commoner, a psychopath, a pacifist, a pederast, a womanizer, a layabout and a workaholic. Despite the fact that I have never used drugs, there is a large segment of my readership that swears I'm a heavy doper.

Why is he telling us all this?

I'm telling you all this because the protagonist of the story before you speaks of his first wife as having been in an insane asylum for many years, and my first wife also went through many years of emotional disorder. But though I have drawn on my own experiences, I am not the Michael Kirxby of this story.

I tell you this to explain why the intervention of my editor at *Playboy*, Victoria Chen Haider, was so important to the story, and to me. I tell you this because her wisdom is so rare in editorial circles that it *must not* be forgotten.

After I'd written the story and sent it to Vicky Haider,

she called and said she was very high on it, wanted to use it in *Playboy,* and had only one reservation. I asked her what that might be.

She made reference to the section in the story where Kirxby is talking about how terrible his marriage had been, how it had damned near driven *him* crazy, and how he knew if he ever got into his ex-wife's clutches again it *would* end in his confinement to a madhouse. Vicky Haider said there was something missing at that point.

"*What* was so awful about the marriage?" she wanted to know.

My blood ran cold.

Vicky Haider knew nothing of my background, had no awareness of the terror that lurked back there in my past, the four deadly years with Charlotte.

She had no way of knowing that I was only now, twenty-some years later, able to speak of that monstrous period in my life. Oh, I wasn't paralyzed by it. Not that extreme. I had relegated all those awful memories to a dark cell at the farthest point at the rear of a dank, chill subterranean cavern in my mind. And from time to time I would descend the slippery stone stairs to that cavern, pass between the moist evil-smelling walls and shine a dim light into the cell. I could take quick, short glimpses in there when I had to; but it wasn't anything I wanted to spend a lot of time examining.

My conscience was clear about what happened to Charlotte, but no one escapes that kind of relationship without feeling some vestigial guilt, deserved or not.

I had mentioned the affair indirectly in one or another story through the years, but I'd never used it as a major element in my fiction. This time I'd been brave, I'd gone down the steps, through the cavern to the cell, and held the dim light up to the barred window for longer than ever before. It had shaken me, but I'd thought I was really courageous in doing it.

Now here was Vicky Haider asking me to go down there and *open the door* and stare for a long time at the horrible memories chained to the wall. Without any indication save her remarkable instincts as an editor, she had struck directly to the flaming core of the torment in the story. What she was asking me to do was more terrifying than suggestions of diving into a tank of hammerhead sharks. She wanted me to confront one of the most deeply hidden secrets of my life.

How could she have known?

She was an *editor,* in the noblest, most innovative sense of that word. She was not one of the parvenus who wind up behind desks and *call* themselves editors; she *was* an editor. She understood story, understood that it is only when a writer comes to grips with the darkest fears and mortal dreads in his caverns of memory that dangerous, meaningful fiction is produced.

I swallowed hard and told her I'd see what I could do.

Though it had taken years to get the story written, once I'd begun the actual writing it had gone swiftly, only a few full days of unceasing labor.

It took me two months to produce the ten paragraphs she needed, the mere two pages of additional copy that would encapsulate with one incident the four year hell through which Charlotte and I had toiled.

How do you sum it up? What *one* escapade foreshadows and memorializes all the cumulative ghastliness that ends in divorce and madness? Relationships aren't like that. They don't have clear-cut melodramatic parameters. They're amalgams of a million isolated, minuscule slights, affronts, cruelties and brutalities.

Two months. It took me two months, but I finally did it, and it left me sweating and cold. I sent her the pages and she said, "Yes, this is what was missing." Yes, it was. The soul of darkness.

This story is one of my best, I now think. It is certainly one of my most painful. And I owe it all to Victoria Chen Haider. I'm glad I got to tell her that.

On May 25, 1979, Vicky Haider died in the O'Hare Airport crash of an American Airlines DC-10. She was on her way to the American Booksellers Association convention here in Los Angeles. We had planned to meet for the first time.

I never talked to Vicky Haider face-to-face, and now she is gone; and as a writer who once tasted the wonder of working with an exceptional editor who knew more about what I was doing than even I knew, my sense of loss is beyond the telling.

When you're alone, as a writer is alone, locked in single combat with the imagination, allies are rare and special.

Those who understand are even rarer.

This story is as much Vicky Haider's as it is mine.

And all of us are the poorer because she will never again work her editorial magic.

All The Birds
Come Home to Roost

HE TURNED onto his left side in the bed, trying to avoid the wet spot. He propped his hand against his cheek, smiled grimly, and prepared himself to tell her the truth about why he had been married and divorced three times.

"Three times!" she had said, her eyes widening, that familiar line of perplexity appearing vertically between her brows. "Three times. Christ, in all the time we went together, I never knew that. Three, huh?"

Michael Kirxby tightened the grim smile slightly. "You never asked, so I never mentioned it," he said. "There's a lot of things I never bother to mention: I flunked French in high school and had to work and go to summer school so I could graduate a semester late; I once worked as a short-order cook in a diner in New Jersey near the Turnpike; I've had the clap maybe half a dozen times and the crabs twice..."

"Ichhh, don't talk about it!" She buried her naked face in the pillow. He reached out and ran his hand up under her thick, chestnut hair, ran it all the way up to the occipital ridge and massaged the cleft. She came up from where she had hidden.

That had been a few moments ago. Now he propped himself on his bent arm and proceeded to tell her the truth about it. He never lied; it simply wasn't worth the trouble. But it *was* a long story, and he'd told it a million times; and even though he had developed a storyteller's facility with the interminable history

227

of it, he had learned to sketch in whole sections with apocryphal sentences, had developed the use of artful time-lapse jumps. Still, it took a good fifteen minutes to do it right, to achieve the proper reaction and, quite frankly, he was bored with the recitation. But there were occasions when it served its purpose, and this was one of them, so he launched into it.

"I got married the first time when I was twenty, twenty-one, something like that. I'm lousy on dates. Anyhow, she was a sick girl, disturbed before I ever met her; family thing, hated her mother, loved her father—he was an ex-Marine, big, good-looking—secretly wanted to ball the old man but never could cop to it. He died of cancer of the brain but before he went, he began acting erratically, treating the mother like shit. Not that the mother didn't deserve it . . . she was a harridan, a real termagant. But it was really outrageous, he wasn't coming home nights, beating up the mother, that sort of thing. So my wife sided with the mother against him. When they found out his brain was being eaten up by the tumor, she flipped and went off the deep end. Made my life a furnace! After I divorced her, the mother had her committed. She's been in the asylum over seventeen years now. For me, it was close; too damned close. She very nearly took me with her to the madhouse. I got away just in time. A little longer, I wouldn't be here today."

He watched her face. Martha was listening closely now. Heartmeat information. This was the sort of thing they loved to hear; the fiber material, the formative chunks, something they could sink their neat, small teeth into. He sat up, reached over and clicked on the bed lamp. The light was on his right side as he stared toward the foot of the bed, apparently conjuring up the painful past; the light limned his profile. He had a Dick Tracy chin and deep-set brown eyes. He cut his own hair, did it badly, and it shagged over his ears as though he had just crawled out of bed. Fortunately, it was wavy and he *was* in bed: he knew the light and the profile were good. Particularly for the story.

"I was in crap shape after her. Almost went down the tube. She came within a finger of pulling me onto the shock table with her. She always, *always* had the hoodoo sign on me; I had very little defense against her. Really scares me when I think about it."

The naked Martha looked at him. "Mike . . . what was her name?"

He swallowed hard. Even now, years later, after it was ended he found himself unable to cleanse the memories of pain and fear. "Her name was Cindy."

"Well, uh, what did she do that was so awful?"

He thought about it for a second. This was a departure from the routine. He wasn't usually asked for further specifics. And running back through the memories he found most of them had blurred into one indistinguishable throb of misery. There were incidents he remembered, incidents so heavily freighted with anguish that he could feel his gorge becoming buoyant, but they were part of the whole terrible time with Cindy, and trying to pick them out so they would convey, in microcosm, the shrieking hell of their marriage, was like retelling something funny from the day before, to people who had not been there. Not funny. Oh, well, you'd have to be there.

What had she done that was so awful, apart from the constant attempts at suicide, the endless remarks intended to make him feel inadequate, the erratic behavior, the morning he had re-turned from ten weeks of basic training a day earlier than expected and found her in bed with some skinny guy from on the block, the times she took off and sold the furniture and cleaned out the savings account? What had she done beyond that? Oh, hell, Martha, nothing much.

He couldn't say that. He had to encapsulate the four years of their marriage. One moment that summed it up.

He said, "I was trying to pass my bar exams. I was really studying hard. It wasn't easy for me the way it was for a lot of people. And she used to mumble."

"She mumbled?"

"Yeah. She'd walk around, making remarks you just *knew* were crummy, but she'd do it under her breath, just at the threshold of audibility. And me trying to concentrate. She knew it made me crazy, but she always did it. So one time . . . I was really behind in the work and trying to catch up . . . and she started that, that . . ." He *remembered!* "That damned *mumbling*, in the living room and the bedroom and the bathroom . . . but she wouldn't come in the kitchen where I was studying. And it went on and on and on . . ."

He was trembling. Jesus, why had she asked for this, wasn't in the script.

" . . . and finally I just stood up and screamed, 'Wh hell are you mumbling? What the hell do you want fro

Can't you see I'm busting my ass studying? Can't you for Christ sake leave me alone for just five fucking minutes?'"

With almost phonographic recall he knew he was saying precisely, exactly what he had screamed all those years ago.

"And I ran into the bedroom, and she was in her bathrobe and slippers, and she started in on me, accusing me of this and that and every other damned thing, and I guess I finally went over the edge, and I punched her right in the face. As hard as I could. The way I'd hit some slob in the street. Hard, real hard. And then somehow I had her bedroom slipper in my hand and I was sitting on her chest on the bed, and beating her in the face with that goddam slipper . . . and . . . and . . . I woke up and *saw me hitting her,* and it was the first time I'd ever hit a woman, and I fell away from her, and I crawled across the floor and I was sitting there like a scared animal, my hands over my eyes . . . crying . . . scared to death . . ."

She stared at him silently. He was shaking terribly.

"Jesus," she said, softly.

And they stayed that way for a while, without speaking. He had answered her question. More than she wanted to know.

The mood was tainted now. He could feel himself split—one part of him here and now with the naked Martha, in this bedroom with the light low—another part he had thought long gone, in that other bedroom, hunkered down against the baseboard, hands over eyes, whimpering like a crippled dog, Cindy sprawled half on the floor, half on the bed, her face puffed and bloodied. He tried desperately to get control of himself.

After some long moments he was able to breathe regularly. She was still staring at him, her eyes wide. He said, almost with reverence, "Thank God for Marcie."

She waited and then said, "Who's Marcie?"

"Who *was* Marcie. Haven't seen her in something like fifteen years."

"Well, who *was* Marcie?"

"She was the one who picked up the pieces and focused my eyes. If it hadn't been for her, I'd have walked around on my knees for another year . . . or two . . . or ten . . ."

"What happened to her?"

"Who knows? You can take it from our recently severed ——n; I seem to have some difficulty hanging on to good ——n."

"——, Mike!"

"Hey, take it easy. You split for good and sound reasons. I think I'm doomed to be a bachelor . . . maybe a *recluse* for the rest of my life. But that's okay. I've tried it three times. I just don't have the facility. I'm good for a woman for short stretches, but over the long haul I think I'm just too high-pressure."

She smiled wanly, trying to ease what she took to be pain. He *wasn't* in pain, but she had never been able to tell the difference with him. Precisely that inability to penetrate his façade had been the seed of their dissolution. "It was okay with us."

"For a while."

"Yeah. For a while." She reached across him to the night-stand and picked up the heavy Orrefors highball glass with the remains of the Mendocino Gray Riesling. "It was so strange running into you at Allison's party. I'd heard you were seeing some model or actress . . . or something."

He shook his head. "Nope. You were my last and greatest love."

She made a wet, bratting sound. "Bullshit."

"Mmm. Yeah, it is a bit, ain't it."

And they stayed that way, silently, for a while. Once, he touched her naked thigh, feeling the nerve jump under his hand; and once, she reached across to lay her hand on his chest, to feel him breathing. But they didn't make love again. And after a space of time in which they thought they could hear the dust settling in the room, she said, "Well, I've got to get home to feed the cats."

"You want to stay the night?"

She thought about it a moment. "No thanks, Mike. Maybe another night when I come prepared. You know my thing about putting on the same clothes the next day." He knew. And smiled.

She crawled out of bed and began getting dressed. He watched her, ivory-lit by the single bed lamp. It never would have worked. But then, he'd known that almost from the first. It never worked well for an extended period. There was no Holy Grail. Yet the search went on, reflexively. It was like eating potato chips.

She came back to the bed, leaned over and kissed him. It was the merest touch of lips, and meant nothing. "Bye. Call me."

"No doubt about it," he said; but he wouldn't.

Then she left. He sat up in bed for a while, thinking that it was odd how people couldn't leave it alone. Like a scab, they had to pick at it. He'd dated her rather heavily for a month, and they had broken up for no particular reason save that it was finished. And tonight the party, and he was alone, and she was alone, and they had come together for an anticlimax.

A returning. To a place neither had known very well. A devalued neighborhood.

He knew he would never see Martha again.

The bubble of sadness bobbed on the surface for a moment, then burst; the sense of loss flavored the air a moment longer; then he turned off the light, rolled over onto the dried wet spot, and went to sleep.

He was hacking out the progression of interrogatories pursuant to the Blieler brief with one of the other attorneys in the office when his secretary stuck her head into the conference room and said he had a visitor. Rubbing his eyes, he realized they had been at it for three straight hours. He shoved back from the conference table, swept the papers into the folio, and said, "Let's knock off for lunch." The other attorney stretched, and musculature crackled. "Okay. Call it four o'clock. I've got to go over to the 9000 Building to pick up Barbarossi's deposition." He got up and left. Kirxby sighed, simply sitting there, all at once overcome by a nameless malaise. As though something dark and forbidding were slouching towards his personal Bethlehem.

Then he went into his office to meet his visitor.

She turned half-around in the big leather chair and smiled at him. "Jerri!" he said, all surprise and pleasure. His first reaction: surprised pleasure. "My God, it's been . . . how long . . . ?"

The smile lifted at one corner: her bemused smile.

"It's been six months. Seem longer?"

He grinned and shrugged. It had been his choice to break up the affair after two years. For Martha. Who had lasted a month.

"How time flies when you're enjoying yourself," she said. She crossed her legs. A summary judgment on his profligacy.

He walked around and sat down behind the desk. "Come on, Jerri, gimme some slack."

Another returning. First Martha, out of the blue; now Jerri. Emerging from the mauve, perhaps? "What brings you back into my web?" He tried to stare at her levelly, but she was on to that; it made him feel guilty.

"I suppose I could have cobbled up something spectacular along the lines of a multimillion-dollar lawsuit against one of my competitors," she said, "but the truth is just that I felt an urgent need to see you again."

He opened and closed the top drawer of his desk, to buy a few seconds. Then, carefully avoiding her gaze, he said, "What is this, Jerri? Christ, isn't there enough crap in the world without detouring to find a fresh supply?" He said it softly, because he had said I love you to her for two years, excluding the final seven months when he had said fuck off, never realizing they were the same phrase.

But he took her to lunch, and they made a date for dinner, and he took her back to his apartment and they were two or three drinks too impatient to get to the bed and made it on the living room carpet still half-clothed. He cherished silence when making love, even when only screwing, and she remembered and didn't make a sound. And it was as good or as bad as it had ever been between them for two years minus the last seven months. And when she awoke hours later, there on the living room carpet, with her skirt up around her hips, and Michael lying on his side with his head cradled on his arm, still sleeping, she breathed deeply and slitted her eyes and commanded the hangover to permit her the strength to rise; and she rose, and she covered him with a small lap-robe he had pilfered off an American Airlines flight to Boston; and she went away. Neither loving him nor hating him. Having merely satisfied the urgent compulsion in her to return to him once more, to see him once more, to have his body once more. And there was nothing more to it than that.

The next morning he rolled onto his back, lying there on the floor, kept his eyes closed, and knew he would never see her again. And there was no more to it than that.

Two days later he received a phone call from Anita. He had had two dates with Anita, more than two-and-a-half years earlier, during the week before he had met Jerri and had taken up with her. She said she had been thinking about him. She said she had been weeding out old phone numbers in her book and had come across his, and just wanted to call to see how he was. They made a date for that night and had sex and she left quickly. And he knew he would never see her again.

And the next day at lunch at the Oasis he saw Corinne sitting across the room. He had lived with Corinne for a year, just prior to meeting Anita, just prior to meeting Jerri. Corinne came across the room and kissed him on the back of the neck and said, "You've lost weight. You look good enough to eat." And they got together that night, and one thing and another, and he was, and she did, and then he did, and she stayed the night but left after coffee the next morning. And he knew he would never see her again.

But he began to have an unsettling feeling that something strange was happening to him.

Over the next month, in reverse order of having known them, every female with whom he had had a liaison magically reappeared in his life. Before Corinne, he had had a string of one-nighters and casual weekends with Hannah, Nancy, Robin and Cylvia; Elizabeth, Penny, Margie and Herta; Eileen, Gail, Holly and Kathleen. One by one, in unbroken string, they came back to him like waifs returning to the empty kettle for one last spoonful of gruel. Once, and then gone again, forever.

Leaving behind pinpoint lights of isolated memory. Each one of them an incomplete yet somehow total summation of the woman: Hannah and her need for certain words in the bed; the pressure of Nancy's legs over his shoulders; Robin and the wet towels; Cylvia who never came, perhaps could *not* come; Elizabeth so thin that her pelvis left him sore for days; having to send out for ribs for Penny, before and after; a spade-shaped mole on Margie's inner thigh; Herta falling asleep in a second after sex, as if she had been clubbed; the sound of Eileen's laugh, like the wind in Aspen; Gail's revulsion and animosity when he couldn't get an erection and tried to go down on her; Holly's endless retelling of the good times they had known; Kathleen still needing to delude herself that he was seducing her, even after all this time.

One sharp point of memory. One quick flare of light. Then gone forever and there was no more to it than that.

But by the end of that month, the suspicion had grown into a dread certainty; a certainty that led him inexorably to an inevitable end place that was too horrible to consider. Every time he followed the logical progression to its finale, his mind skittered away . . . that whimpering, crippled dog.

His fear grew. Each woman returned built the fear higher. Fear coalesced into terror and he fled the city, hoping by exiling himself to break the links.

But there he sat, by the fireplace at The Round Hearth, in Stowe, Vermont . . . and the next one in line, Sonja, whom he had not seen in years, Sonja came in off the slopes and saw him, and she went a good deal whiter than the wind chill factor outside accounted for.

They spent the night together and she buried her face in the pillow so her sounds would not carry. She lied to her husband about her absence and the next morning, before Kirxby came out of his room, they were gone.

But Sonja *had* come back. And that meant the next one before her had been Gretchen. He waited in fear, but she did not appear in Vermont, and he felt if he stayed there he was a sitting target and he called the office and told them he was going down to the Bahamas for a few days, that his partners should parcel out his caseload among them, for just a few more days, don't ask questions.

And Gretchen was working in a tourist shop specializing in wicker goods; and she looked at him as he came through the door, and she said, "Oh, my God, *Michael!* I've had you on my mind almost constantly for the past week. I was going to call you—"

And she gave a small sharp scream as he fainted, collapsing face-forward into a pyramid of woven wicker clothing hampers.

The apartment was dark. He sat there in silence, and refused to answer the phone. The gourmet delicatessen had been given specific instructions. The delivery boy with the food had to knock in a specific, certain cadence, or the apartment door would not be opened.

Kirxby had locked himself away. The terror was very real now. It was impossible to ignore what was happening to him. All the birds were coming home to roost.

Back across nineteen years, from his twentieth birthday to the present, in reverse order of having known them, every woman he had ever loved or fucked or had an encounter of substance with . . . was homing in on him. Martha the latest,

from which point the forward momentum of his relationships
had been arrested, like a pendulum swung as far as it would
go, and back again, back, back, swinging back past Jerri and
Anita, back to Corinne and Hannah, back, and Nancy, back,
and Robin and all of them, straight back to Gretchen, who was
just three women before . . .

He wouldn't think about it.

He *couldn't*. It was too frightening.

The special, specific, certain cadence of a knock on his
apartment door. In the darkness he found his way to the door
and removed the chain. He opened the door to take the box of
groceries, and saw the teenaged Puerto Rican boy sent by the
deli. And standing behind him was Kate. She was twelve years
older, a lot less the gamin, classy and self-possessed now, but
it was Kate nonetheless.

He began to cry.

He slumped against the open door and wept, hiding his face
in his hands partially because he was ashamed, but more because he was frightened.

She gave the boy a tip, took the box, and edged inside the
apartment, moving Kirxby with her, gently. She closed the
door, turned on a light, and helped him to the sofa.

When she came back from putting away the groceries, she
slipped out of her shoes and sat as far away from him as the
length of the sofa would permit. The light was behind her and
she could see his swollen, terrified face clearly. His eyes were
very bright. There was a trapped expression on his face. For
a long time she said nothing.

Finally, when his breathing became regular, she said,
"Michael, what the hell *is* it? Tell me."

But he could not speak of it. He was too frightened to name
it. As long as he kept it to himself, it was just barely possible
it was a figment of delusion, a ravening beast of the mind that
would vanish as soon as he was able to draw a deep breath.
He knew he was lying to himself. It was real. It was happening
to him, inexorably.

She kept at him, speaking softly, cajoling him, prising the
story from him. And so he told her. Of the reversal of his life.
Of the film running backward. Of the river flowing upstream.
Carrying him back and back and back into a dark land from
which there could never be escape.

"And I ran away. I went to St. Kitts. And I walked into a shop, some dumb shop, just some dumb kind of tourist goods shop . . ."

"And what was her name . . . Greta . . . ?"

"Gretchen."

". . . Gretchen. And Gretchen was there."

"Yes."

"Oh, my God, Michael. You're making yourself crazy. This is lunatic. You've got to stop it."

"*Stop it!?!* Jesus, I wish I *could* stop it. But I can't. Don't you see, you're *part* of it. It's unstoppable, it's crazy but it's hellish. I haven't slept in days. I'm afraid to go to sleep. God knows what might happen."

"You're building all this in your mind, Michael. It isn't real. Lack of sleep is making you paranoid."

"No . . . no . . . listen . . . here, listen to this . . . I remembered it from years ago . . . I read it . . . I found it when I went looking for it . . ." He lurched off the sofa, found the book on the wet bar and brought it back under the light. It was *The Plague* by Camus, in a Modern Library edition. He thumbed through the book and could not find the place. Then she took it from him and laid it on her palm and it fell open to the page, because he had read and reread the section. She read it aloud, where he had underlined it:

"'Had he been less tired, his senses more alert, that all-pervading odor of death might have made him sentimental. But when a man has had only four hours' sleep, he isn't sentimental. He sees things as they are; that is to say, he sees them in the garish light of justice—hideous, witless justice.'" She closed the book and stared at him. "You really believe this, don't you?"

"Don't I? Of course I do! I'd be what you think I am, crazy . . . *not* to believe it. Kate, listen to me. Look, here you are. It's twelve years. Twelve years and another life. But here you are, back with me again, just in sequence. You were my lover before I met Gretchen. I *knew* it would be you!"

"Michael, don't let this make you stop thinking. There's no way you could have known. Bill and I have been divorced for two years. I just moved back to the city last week. Of *course* I'd look you up. We had a very good thing together. If I hadn't met Bill we might *still* be together."

"Jesus, Kate, you're not *listening* to me. I'm trying to tell you this is some kind of terrible justice. I'm rolling back through time with the women I've known. There's you, and if there's you, then the next one before you was Marcie. And if I go back to her, then that means that after Marcie . . . after Marcie . . . *before* Marcie there was . . ."

He couldn't speak the name.

She said the name. His face went white again. It was the speaking of the unspeakable.

"Oh God, Kate, oh dear God, I'm screwed, I'm screwed . . ."

"Cindy can't get you, Mike. She's still in the Home, isn't she?"

He nodded, unable to answer.

Kate slid across and held him. He was shaking. "It's all right. It's going to be all right."

She tried to rock him, like a child in pain, but his terror was an electric current surging through him. "I'll take care of you," she said. "Till you're better. There won't be any Marcie, and there certainly won't be any Cindy."

"*No!*" he screamed, pulling away from her. "*No!*"

He stumbled toward the door. "I've got to get out of here. They can find me here. I've got to go somewhere out away from here, fast, fast, where they can't find me ever."

He yanked open the door and ran into the hall. The elevator was not there. It was never there when he needed it, needed it badly, needed it desperately.

He ran down the stairs and into the vestibule of the building. The doorman was standing looking out into the street, the glass doors tightly shut against the wind and the cold.

Michael Kirxby ran past him, head down, arms close to his body. He heard the man say something, but it was lost in the rush of wind and chill as he jammed through onto the sidewalk.

Terror enveloped him. He ran toward the corner and turned toward the darkness. If he could just get into the darkness, where he couldn't be found, then he was safe. Perhaps he would be safe.

He rounded the corner. A woman, head down against the wind, bumped into him. They rebounded and in the vague light of the street lamp looked into each other's faces.

"Hello," said Marcie.

Opium

INTRODUCTION

This one was written to be read on television.

I've done so on two occasions: first, on an NBC interview show called *At One With...*, with the estimable Keith Berwick as host; the second time I read it over the Canadian Broadcasting Company during the *90 Minutes Live* show, then-hosted by Peter Gzowski.

Bringing the spoken word to the tube-enslaved masses.

No, I'm not going to enter another crazed screed against television and its manifest horrors. Consult my last book for everything I care to say on that dreary topic.

Then why does he tell us all this?

I tell you all this because "Opium" was intended as a bit of guerrilla warfare. It is a story that says only one thing: we are entertaining ourselves into oblivion.

I can't stand it, we say. I work my ass off all day, and I just want to get away from it all, we say. I don't want any heavy stuff, I just want to be entertained, we say. And so we spend the major part of our nonworking hours escaping the Real World, the pragmatic universe, if you will. Whether it be fast sex, fundamentalist religion, cheap novels, empty-headed movies, booze, dope, sword'n'sorcery fantasy, endless television-watching, fast food or miniature golf, we run from dealings with the Real World like ants from Raid.

So I wrote this story to say that Entropy tries to maintain the status quo in order to keep the system working. And that permits of very little outlawry, very little berserk behavior. And from the desperados, whether they be Einstein or Elizabeth Cady Stanton, come the strength and the upheaval that moves the world forward toward light and reason.

And the "opium of the people" (as Marx called religion) has changed through the centuries. Now it's all the elements noted above that keep people distracted and dumb. And that includes the deification of sports. (Quoting from another great philosopher, Howard Cosell, who said: "Sports are the Toy Department of life...the primary means for sustaining delusion and illusion.")

This story, intended as fifth column warfare against the medium of television, to be read *on* television, says simply that if the Real World isn't interesting enough to command the attention of the lives it contains, then maybe the Real World will alter itself magically to keep us away from Taco Bell and *Laverne & Shirley*.

This moment of softness has been brought to you by Zee Toilet Tissue.

Opium

ANNE MARIE STEBNER placed the tip of the double-edged razor blade against her left wrist, just below the place in her palm where the life line turned toward the thumb on the Mount of Venus. At the precise spot where the life line ended, she slid the blade into the skin, and began drawing it deeply down the length of her arm toward the inside of her elbow. She had heard that if one *really* wanted to slash her wrists, she should open the arm lengthwise, not across the veins. It was too easy for them to hold it together and tape it up if one cut across. Up the arms was the way to do it, if one was serious about suicide.

File clerk in a large recording company, what blind dates would call "really plain, but does it like a rabbit," thirty-one years old without even the usual range of dull prospects, she had wakened several hours earlier to find the grad student she had met at the party last night already cleared out. He had not, thoughtfully, used her lipstick to write his name and phone number on the bathroom mirror. But he had left a pile of wet towels, corpselike, draped over the tub.

She was quite serious about the double-edged razor blade.

As she pulled the blade up her arm, encountering only minor resistance, she looked out the front window of her duplex. On the front lawn, at least five of the Seven Dwarfs were planting a beautiful bonsai tree.

She smiled at the way they worked so industriously, scooping out the dirt and placing it neatly on a tarpaulin, how Grumpy removed the wrappings around the roots, and how Dopey clapped his hands as the hole was dug. She knew she was hallucinating, possibly shock, probably from loss of blood, but she felt she would like to go out there to die, out where the sun was shining. It had not been shining when she'd crawled out of bed. In fact, it had been raining.

She walked to the door, leaving dark stains on the cheap carpet, and opened the door to the front yard. The razor blade lay on the coffee table. If necessary, she could do the other arm later. She didn't think it would be necessary.

As she approached them, they looked up at her.

"Good morning!" Doc said, giving her a big smile. "Do you like it? I think it's about a hundred years old."

"It's really lovely," Anne Marie said. "But why are you planting it here, on Sunday morning?"

Bashful came up to her, and took her by her right arm, the arm that was not bleeding. "Brightening up the real world for you, Miss Stebner," he said.

She was startled: she could feel his tiny hand in hers. She could smell the faint, not unpleasant odor of their work-sweat. She could hear the ratchety sound of their spades in the dirt. Was this the way it was when one was on the way out?

She was led by the dwarf to a place right beside the bonsai, which Sleepy and Grumpy had put in the hole. Dopey was packing in the earth around the bole. She reached out and touched the tree. It was real.

"Have a nice day," Doc said, and began gathering up the planting tools.

"You've wasted your time," she said. "I'm dying; can't you see that?"

One by one they came to her and hugged her, as she sat there, and then they went away. In a few moments, with the intricate hieroglyphics of the bonsai's branches before her eyes, she felt faint, lay back, and became unconscious.

She sat up in the hospital bed, her arm taped to the elbow, and listened to the young intern. The married couple who had just moved into the other side of the duplex had found her on the front lawn, as they emerged to go for Sunday brunch. She had not seen them yet, so she had not been able to ask how they had saved her; she had been *certain* it was impossible to save someone who had cut lengthwise rather than across. But they had saved her, and she sat up in the hospital bed, and the intern tried to be supportive.

"Everybody wants to get away from the world," he said. "Whether it's dope or booze or religion or television or quick sex or trashy novels, everybody wants to run away. We all want to be entertained all the time. And when it doesn't work, when none of it is enough, we try to kill ourselves to escape."

She didn't think he understood just how lonely she was.

"The real world is terrific," the young intern said. "I promise you, Anne Marie, it's wonderful. People are always complaining, 'Oh, I need to get away, I need to relax, I don't want to think about it.' If they turn on the tube and it's some program about current events they rush to change the channel to get some silly rerun of a sitcom. We spend ninety percent of our lives escaping. If you really, truly, completely deal with the real world . . . it's fascinating!"

She asked him to go away. She said she wanted to sleep, to get away from it all. So he left, but she didn't sleep. She started to turn on the television set high on the wall across from her bed, but a flicker of movement out of the corner of her eye claimed her attention. Out there in the sky, turning in tight maneuvers, a Sopwith Camel was having a dogfight with a large green and gray pterodactyl.

She knew it was really happening out there, because from the angle at which she lay she could see other windows in the wing of the hospital to her right, and there were people leaning out and pointing at the sky.

For a long time she watched the marvelous ballet of wood-and-fabric airplane and Cretaceous flying reptile.

She was waiting on the sidewalk outside the recording company for the married executive to pick her up for their date. He had called it their "illegal tryst" and she had not liked the way his face pulled up on one side when he smiled like that; but she had been empty of plans for that night, and it was something to do not to be alone. The married executive had promised her dinner and a movie. They were going to see a very popular space war movie that everyone said was the return of entertainment. It was something to do.

As she stood there at the curb, a 1941 Packard pulled up and a woman rolled down the window. It was a green Packard, highly polished, as though someone who loved it had waxed it endlessly. "Anne Marie," the woman called from the car.

She walked over. It was her mother.

Her father was driving. The scent of pipe tobacco came from inside the car. "We thought we might have a picnic, like the old times, just the three of us," her mother said. "Would you like to come along?"

She began to cry, even as she nodded and her mother reached back to unlock the rear door. She got inside and sat very quietly beside the picnic basket. The Packard thrummed to life, and pulled away.

Anne Marie Stebner's mother and father had been dead for eleven years. It was a *wonderful* picnic.

Sailing the catamaran through the reefs of sapphire rocks, she made for the island. The wind smelled of freshly mowed grass and carried with it the faint tinkling of wind chimes.

"If it gets too lonely out here," she said aloud, "perhaps I'll start a fast-food franchise. Something with Lebanese food, maybe."

As she spoke, a group of golden-tanned men and women emerged from behind a dune on the island, and waved at her, waved her in through the precious reefs.

"Or I can always rent a television set somewhere," she said, smiling broadly. Several of the golden people produced oddly shaped musical instruments and began playing Hoagy Carmichael's "Skylark." It had always been her favorite tune.

She tacked against the wind, and headed in to the island. Reality was fighting back. If the real world was too horrible for the lives it served, then the real world would alter itself. Anne Marie Stebner beached the catamaran and ran up the sand toward the golden island dwellers.

"Hi," she called to them. "I've always wanted to live in a place like this, I just didn't know where to go to find it. What's happening around here?"

So they told her. And she could not, in her wildest dreams, have believed anything could be that terrifically interesting. But it was. There in the real world.

The Other Eye of
Polyphemus

INTRODUCTION

I was dragged, kicking and screaming, on a tour through
the lives of two women, once upon a time.

It was one of the most awful experiences of all time.

Including the Spanish Inquisition, the murder of Garcia
Lorca, the genocide of the Brazilian indians, the crucifixion
of Spartacus' army of slaves, the sinking of the Titanic,
the fire-bombing of Dresden and the trial of the Scottsboro
Boys. This experience, I tell you, contained elements of
all of the above, plus a few personal nasties that make
me shudder when I think of them.

The experience does not, in any but one isolated reference, appear in this story. But it was that long night that
inspired the writing.

Further, deponent sayeth not.

Yuccchhhh.

The Other Eye of Polyphemus

THIS IS ABOUT Brubaker, who is a man, but who might as easily have been a woman; and it would have been the same, no difference: painful and endless.

She was in her early forties and crippled. Something with the left leg and the spine. She went sidewise, slowly, like a sailor leaving a ship after a long time at sea. Her face was unindexed as to the rejections she had known; one could search randomly and find a shadow here beneath the eyes that came from the supermarket manager named Charlie; a crease in the space beside her mouth, just at the left side, that had been carved from a two nights' association with Clara from the florist shop; a moistness here at the right temple each time she recalled the words spoken the morning after the night with the fellow who drove the dry cleaner's van, Barry or Benny. But there was no sure record. It was all there, everywhere in her face.

Brubaker had not wanted to sleep with her. He had not wanted to take her home or go to her home, but he had. Her apartment was small and faced out onto a narrow court that permitted sunlight only during the hour before and the hour following high noon. She had pictures from magazines taped to the walls. The bed was narrow.

When she touched him, he felt himself going away. Thinking of warm places where he had rested on afternoons many years before; afternoons when he had been alone and had thought that was not as successful a thing to be as he now understood it to be. He did not want to think of it in this way, but he thought of himself as a bricklayer doing a methodical job. Laying the bricks straight and true.

He made love to her in the narrow bed, and was not there. He was doing a job, and thought how unkind and how unworthy such thoughts seemed to be . . . even though she would not know he was away somewhere else. He had done this before, and kindness was something he did very well. She would feel treasured, and attended, and certainly that was the least he could do. Her limp, her sad and lined face. She would think he was in attendance, treasuring her. He had no needs of his own, so it was possible to give her all that without trembling.

They both came awake when an ambulance screamed cross-town just beneath her window, and she looked at him warmly and said, "I have to get up early in the morning, we're doing inventory at the office, the files are really in terrible shape." But her face held a footnote expression that might have been interpreted as *You can stay if you want, but I've been left in beds where the other side grows cool quickly, and I don't want to see your face in the morning with that look that tells me you're trying to work up an excuse to leave so you can rush home to take the kind of shower that washes the memory of me off you. So I'm giving you the chance to go now, because if you stay it means you'll call tomorrow sometime before noon and ask if I'd like to have dinner and see an early movie.*

So he kissed her several times, on the cheeks and once—gently—on the mouth, with lips closed; a treasuring kiss. And he left her apartment.

The breeze blew gently and coolly off the East River, and he decided to walk down past Henderson Place to sit in the park. To give himself time to come back from those far places. He felt partially dissolved, as if in sending himself out of that apartment he had indulged in some kind of minimal astral projection. And now that he was ready to receive himself again, there was a bit of his soul missing, left behind in her bed.

He had a tiny headache, the finest point of pain, just between and above his eyes, somewhere pierced behind the hard bone over the bridge of his nose. As he walked toward the park, he rubbed the angles of his nose between thumb and forefinger.

Carl Schurz Park was calm. Unlike vast sections of the city, it could be visited after dark without fear. The stillness, the calmness: marauders seldom lurked there.

He took a bench and sat staring off across the cave of water. The pain was persistent and he massaged the inner corners of his eyes with a gentle fingertip.

There had been a woman he had met at a cocktail party. From Maine. He hesitated to think of her in such simplified ways, but there was no denying her sweetness and virginity. Congregationalist, raised too well for life in this city, she had come here from Maine to work in publishing, and the men had not been good to her. Attracted by her well-scrubbed face and her light, gentle manner, they had stepped out with her two, three, once even four times. But she had been raised too well for life taken in late-night sessions, and they had drifted back to their meat racks and their loneliness mutually shared. One had even suggested she seduce a platonic friend of hers, a gentle young man coming to grips with his sexuality, and then she would be fit for a proper affair. She had asked him to leave. The following week he was seeing the wife of a production assistant at the publishing house in which they all labored, and the girl from Maine had signed up for tap dancing lessons.

She had met Brubaker at the cocktail party and they had talked, leaning out the thirty-first floor window to escape the smoke and the chatter.

It became clear to him that she had decided he was the one. Reality and upbringing waged their war in her, and she had decided to capitulate. He walked her home and she said, "Come in for a graham cracker. I have lots of them." He said, "What time is it?" His watch said 12:07. "I'll come up till twelve-fifteen." She smiled shyly and said, "I'm being aggressive. It's not easy for me." He said, "I don't want to come up for very long. We might get into trouble." He meant it. He liked her. But she was hurting. "It's not a kind of trouble you haven't been in before," she said. He smiled gently and said, "No, but it's a kind of trouble *you've* never been in."

But he could not refuse her. And he was good with her, as good as he could be, accepting the responsibility, hoping when she found the man she had been saving herself for, he would be very very loving. At least, he knew, he had put her out of reach of the kind of men who sought virgins. Neither the sort who would marry *only* a virgin, nor the predators who went on safari for such endangered species were human enough for her.

And when he left, the next morning, he had a headache. The same pinpoint of anguish that now pulsed between and above his eyes as he sat in the park. He had felt changed after leaving *her,* just as he did tonight. Was there a diminishing taking place?

Why did imperfect people seek him out and need him?

He knew himself to be no wiser, no nobler, no kinder than most people were capable of being, if given the chance. But he seemed to be a focal point for those who were in need of kindness, gentle words, soft touches. It had always been so for him. Yet he had no needs of his own.

Was it possible never to be touched, to give endlessly, no matter how much was asked, and never to name one's own desire? It was like living behind a pane of one-way glass; seeing out, while no one could see in. Polyphemus, the one-eyed, trapped in his cave, ready victim for all the storm-tossed Odysseus creatures who came to him unbidden. And like Polyphemus, denied half his sight, was he always to be a victim of the storm-tossed? Was there a limit to how much he could give? All he knew of need was what was demanded of him, blind in one eye to personal necessities.

The wind rose and shivered the tops of the trees.

It smelled very clean and fresh. As she had.

Out on the East River a dark shape slid smoothly across his line of sight and he thought of some lonely scow carrying the castoff remnants of life downtide to a nameless grave where blind fish and things with many legs sculled through the darkness, picking over the remains.

He rose from the bench and walked down through the park.

To his right, in the empty playground, the wind pushed the children's swings. They squealed and creaked. The dark shape out there, skimming along obscuring Roosevelt Island, was heading south downriver. He decided to pace it. He might have gone straight ahead till Schurz Park ended, then crossed the John Finley Walkway over the East River Drive traffic, but the dark shape out there fascinated him. As far as he could tell, he had no connection with it, in any way, of any kind. Utterly uninvolved with the shape. It meant nothing to him; and for that reason, chiefly, it was something to follow.

At 79th Street, the park's southern boundary behind him,

East End Avenue came to a dead end facing the side of the East End Hotel. To his left, where 79th Street's eastern extremity terminated against the edge of Manhattan Island, worlds-end, a low metal barrier blocked off the street from the Drive. He walked to the barrier. Out there the black shape had come to rest on the river.

Cars flashed past like accelerated particles, their lights blending one into another till chromatic bands of blue and red and silver and white formed a larger barrier beyond the low metal fence blocking his passage. Passage where? Across six lanes of thundering traffic and a median that provided no protection? Protection from what? He stepped off the curb and did not realize he had climbed over the metal fencing to do so. He stepped off into the seamless, light-banded traffic.

Like walking across water. He crossed the uptown-bound lanes, between the cars, walking between the raindrops, untouched. He reached the median and kept going. Through the downtown-bound bands of light to the far side.

He looked back at the traffic. It had never touched him; but that didn't seem strange, somehow. He knew it should, but between the now-blistering headache and his feeling of being partially disembodied, it was inconsequential.

He climbed the low metal barrier and stood on the narrow ledge of concrete. The East River lay below him. He sat down on the concrete ledge and let his legs dangle. The black shape was directly across from him, in the middle of the river. He lowered himself down the face of the concrete wall till his feet touched the black skin of the East River.

He had met a woman at a library sale two years before. The New York Public Library on 42nd Street and Fifth Avenue had been clearing out excess and damaged stock. They had set up the tables in tiny Bryant Park abutting the library on the 42nd Street side. He had reached for a copy of José Ortega y Gasset's *The Revolt of the Masses* in the 25th anniversary Norton edition, just as she had reached for it. They came up with the book together, and looked across the table at each other. He took her for coffee at the Swiss Chalet on East 48th.

They went to bed only once, though he continued to see her for several months while she tried to make up her mind whether she would return to her husband; he was in the restaurant linen supply business. For the most part, Brubaker sat and listened to her.

"The thing I most hate about Ed is that he's so damned self-sufficient," she said. "I always feel if I were to vanish, he'd forget me in a week and get himself another woman and keep right on the way he is."

Brubaker said, "People have confided in me, and they've been almost ashamed of saying it, though I don't know why they should be, that the pain of losing someone only lasts about a week. At least with any intensity. And then it's simply a dull ache for a while until someone else comes along."

"I feel so guilty seeing you and not, uh, you know."

"That's all right," he said, "I enjoy your company. And if I can be of any use, talking to me, so you get your thoughts straight, well, that's better than being a factor that keeps you and Ed apart."

"You're so kind. Jesus, if Ed were only a fraction as kind as you, we'd have no problems. But he's so *selfish!* Little things. He'll squeeze the toothpaste tube from the middle, especially a new one, and he knows how that absolutely *unhinges* me, and he'll spit the paste all over the fixtures so I have to go at them a hundred times a week—"

And he listened to her and listened to her and listened to her, but she was too nervous for sex, and that was all right; he really did like her and wanted to be of some help.

There were times when she cried in his arms, and said they should take an apartment together, and she'd do it in a minute if it weren't for the children and half the business being in her name. There were times when she raged around his apartment, slamming cabinet doors and talking back to the television, cursing Ed for some cruelty he had visited on her. There were times when she would sit curled up staring out the window of Brubaker's apartment, running the past through her mind like prayer beads of sorrow.

Finally, one last night, she came into his bed and made ferocious love to him, then told Brubaker she was going back to Ed. For all the right reasons, she said. And a part of Brubaker had gone away, never to return. He had experienced the headache.

Now he simply walked across the soaked-black water to the dark shape. Like walking through traffic. Untouched. The tiniest ripples circled out from beneath his feet, silvered and delicate for just a moment before vanishing to either side of him.

He walked out across the East River and stepped into the

dark shape. It was all mist and soft cottony fog. He stepped inside and the only light was that which he produced himself, through the tiniest pinpoint that had opened between and above his eyes. The darkness smoothed around him and he was well within the shifting shape now.

It was not his sort of gathering. Everyone seemed much too intense. And the odor of their need was more pervasive than anything he had ever known before.

They lounged around in the fog, dim in the darkness, illuminated only when Brubaker's light struck them, washed them for a moment with soft pink-white luminescence and then they became dim moving shapes in the fog. He moved among them, and once a hand touched his arm. He drew back. For the first time in his life he drew back.

He realized what he had done, and felt sorry about it.

He swept his light around through the darkness and caught the stare of a woman who had clearly been watching him. Had she been the person who had touched him? He looked at her and she smiled. It seemed a very familiar smile. The woman with the limp? The virgin? Ed's wife? One of the many other people he had known?

People moved in the darkness, rearranging themselves. He could not tell if they were carrying on conversations in the darkness, he could hear no voices, only the faint sound of fog whispering around the shadowed shapes. Were they coupling, was this some bizarre orgy? No, there was no frenetic energy being expended, no special writhing that one knew as sexual activity, even in darkness.

But they were all watching him now. He felt utterly alone among them. He was not one of them, they had not been waiting for him, their eyes did not shine.

She was still watching him, still smiling.

"Did you touch me?" he asked.

"No," she said. "No one touched you."

"I'm sure someone—"

"No one touched you." She watched him, the smile more than an answer, considerably less than a question. "No one here touched you. No one here wants anything from you."

A man spoke from behind him, saying something Brubaker could not make out. He turned away from the woman with the serious smile, trying to locate the man in the darkness. His light fell on a man lying in the fog, resting back on his elbows.

There was something familiar about him, but Brubaker could not place it; something from the past, like a specific word for a specific thing that just fitted perfectly and could be recalled if he thought of nothing else.

"Did you say something?"

The man looked at him with what seemed to be concern.

"I said: you deserve better."

"If you say so."

"No, if *you* say so. That's one of the three things you most need to understand."

"Three things?"

"You deserve better. Everyone deserves better."

Brubaker did not understand. He was here in a place that seemed without substance or attachment to real time, speaking plainly to people who were—he now realized—naked—and why had he not realized it before?—and he did not wonder about it; neither did he understand what they were saying to him.

"What are the other two things I need to know?" he asked the man.

But it was a woman in the darkness who answered. Yet another woman than the one with the smile. "No one should live in fear," she said, from the fog, and he skimmed his light around to find her. She had a harelip.

"Do you mean me? That I live in fear?"

"No one should live like that," she said. "It isn't necessary. It can be overcome. Courage is as easy to replicate as cowardice. You need only practice. Do it once, then twice, and the third time it's easier, and the fourth time a matter of course, and after that it's done without even consideration. Fear washes away and everything is possible."

He wanted to settle down among them. He felt one with them now. But they made no move to invite him in. He was something they did not want among them.

"Who are you all?"

"We thought you knew," said the woman with the smile. He recognized her voice. It came and went in rises and falls of tone, as though speaking over a bad telephone connection, incomplete, partial. He felt he might be missing parts of the conversation.

"No, I have no idea," he said.

"You'll be leaving now," she said. He shone the light on

her. Her eyes were milky with cataracts.

His light swept across them. They were all malformed in some way or other. Hairless, blind, atrophied, ruined. But he did not know who they were.

His light went out.

The dark shape seemed to be withdrawing from around him. The fog and mist swarmed and swirled away, and he was left standing in darkness on the East River. A vagrant whisper of one of their voices came to him as the dark shape moved off downriver: "You'd better hurry."

He felt water lapping at his ankles, and he hurried back toward the concrete breakwall. By the time he reached it, he was swimming. The wind had died away, but he shivered with the chill of the water that soaked his clothes.

He pulled himself up the face of the wall and lay on the ledge gasping for breath.

"May I help you?" he heard someone say.

A hand touched his shoulder. He looked up and saw a woman in a long beige duster coat. She was kneeling down, deeply concerned.

"I wasn't trying to kill myself," he heard himself say.

"I hadn't thought of that," she said. "I just thought you might need a hand up out of the water."

"Yes," he said, "I could use a hand."

She helped him up. The headache seemed to be leaving him. He heard someone speak, far out on the river, and he looked at her. "Did you hear that?"

"Yes," she said, "someone spoke. It must be one of those tricks of echo."

"I'm sure that's what it was," he said.

"Do you need something to warm you up?" she asked. "I live right over there in that building. Some coffee?"

"Yes," he said, allowing her to help him up the slope. "I need something to warm me up."

Whatever you need in life you must go and get, had been the words from out there on the river where the lost bits of himself were doomed to sail forever. Damaged, forlorn; but no longer bound to him. He seemed to be able to see more clearly now.

And he went with her, for a while, for a long while or a short while; but he went to get something to warm him; he went to get what he needed.

The Executioner of the
Malformed Children

INTRODUCTION

I have nothing to say about this story.

The Executioner of the Malformed Children

D–12 IN BIN 39.

M–1 in Bin 85.

00–87 in Bin 506.

We stand here tonight paying our last respects to him. One of those who committed their bodies at birth to our defense. One of those who had no hope for the future, no hope for real or lasting joy; one of those who said, with every breath he ever drew, "I'll stand between." Of what use are words from me? Words, mere words, mean nothing. He served. Again: he served. And died for it. So we meet to pay last respects, to conduct a funeral for someone who denied himself all his life that we might live. What is there to say in behalf of someone like Alan Pryor that hasn't been said of his like since the brave first died? What is there to say about an Alan Pryor that won't sound stupid and mawkish and ridiculously melodramatic? He knew what lay ahead of him and not once, at no point of decision when he might have freely chosen to live like everyone else, did he turn away and give up the task of being paladin to us all. There aren't enough thanks in the world for Alan Pryor. But still we meet here for this polite ceremony, and hope it will suffice. It won't, of course, but we still hope.

L–4 in Bin 55.

He was seven years old when it really began for him. When he was born the hospital ran the tests required by the government security agency, and his dossier fiche had been flagged potential sensitive. But his mother and father had been horrified at the suggestion he be sold to the training school, and refused to release him. So the government had politely thanked them for their time, apologized for having inconvenienced them in any smallest way, and put Alan's name in the *wait* file.

And when Alan reached age seven, things changed radically. His parents had come on hard times. What had been a promising career for Alan's father had somehow, inexplicably, gone sour at every little juncture where it might have led to better things. There was no reason for it; not even Alan's mother's frequent paranoid delusions that the government was behind it made any sense. Things just went sour. And they were constantly pressed.

And he was seven years old when he had the accident.

On the school playground, positioned as far left seeker in a sandlot game of kinneys-and-trespass, he had not seen the great birdlike shadow that had swiftly fallen over him, and even as his friends had screamed *look out, Al*, one of those senseless freak accidents had occurred. The pak on a jitney had failed, the craft had fallen out of the sky, and crushed the child beneath its rotors at impact.

What a jitney was doing that far off the regular transit routes, at that odd hour, was never explained. But the passengers—a man and his wife from Topeka, Kansas—had been killed instantly, and Alan had been rushed to the hospital.

Lying cocooned in spinex preservative, Alan had never regained consciousness. His body was broken and irreparable. His parents came and stared through the spinex, seeing the lusterless bruise their child had become.

"Mrs. Pryor . . . Mr. Pryor . . ."

They turned at the soft voice behind them.

"Doctor," Alan's mother pleaded, "save him . . . isn't there *some*thing you can do . . ." Then she looked back and added, very softly, "He's so small . . ."

The doctor was a large man. Had he been rigged out in heavy wool, with a lumberjack waldo attached to his right arm, he would have seemed quite right in a logging camp. He put one great, thick arm around the woman's shoulders and said (in the gentlest voice for such a huge man), "I'm sorry. I've done all I can."

Alan's father began to cry. Tight, dusty little sobs that failed to stir the air.

"There is one thing . . ."

Alan's father was beyond hearing him, but *she* turned—still under his touch—and looked into his face for an answer from faraway.

"The people from the training school. They registered a call for him. If he lives. If you'll grant permission."

She stood without speaking for a moment, then lay her hand on her husband's chest. His head came up and he stared at her. "Dennis, please." He had not heard, so she had to tell him. And when he heard, he started to shake his head, but she grabbed his coat and her voice was desperate. "Dennis, I'm going to do it . . . the only way. They can save him. They have the skill to do it. I will!"

So the collection men came and took Alan Pryor away in aircars with shutters that had been opaqued. They took him to the Island, where the paladins were trained, and they saved his life. They did things to his body the Pryors' doctor never knew could be done. They saved Alan Pryor's life, and they saved that bright yellow spark in his mind that was the mark of the sensitive.

Alan's parents never saw him again. But they had known it would turn out that way when they signed the release. It was better that he should live, even as a paladin, even if they never saw him again.

Alan's mother waited for their life to improve quickly after the school received their boy. But it never did.

A–32 in Bin 11.

T–28 in Bin 277.

Alan Pryor was a sensitive. He had a power we still do not understand. All we can do is thank God that we were given such kinds of powerful talents when we needed them. Surely they are the most lonely figures on our green Earth, and if they were not here to save us, the Earth would have been lost long ago. No nonsensitive has ever seen the face of the menace that continues to threaten us. Only paladins like Alan Pryor have seen it, and they have never told us what it is like. Yet it exists. No one who has ever seen a blasted area, or lost a loved one when that terrible wind blows, could doubt that these guardians of our world stand at the edge of horror every moment of their lives. The way Alan Pryor died should be proof enough. To those whose love of anarchy blinds them to such realities, to those who cry out for investigation

of the paladins and the Island, we offer the example of Alan Pryor,
and swear he shall not have died in vain.

T–65 in Bin 288.

"This is a shock focus room," the paladin said.

The children followed him with their eyes as he moved around the room, touching the eggshell white walls. It was a box. Empty of anything save four walls, ceiling and floor; eggshell white. No break, no stain, no aperture, no carpeting. The class had been brought in through one of the walls that had slid aside. And when they were inside, and seated on the floor, the wall had eased back, sealing them in. The paladin was very old. His skull was shaved clean and they could see where a metal plate had been laid to cover the right side. He had only one hand. He had served many years as a paladin and now—after all the battles—had been given a sinecure as teacher of the young.

There were eight of them, boys and girls, none older than ten, and they sat in a semicircle watching him, and listening. "This is where you'll spend most of your time. It's a training room." He seemed very tired. "In this room we will try to make you sensitive. Do you know what that means?"

None of them knew what it meant.

The old paladin closed his eyes for a moment and the skin of his upper lip pulled down as he concentrated.

The walls began to shimmer and heat came from somewhere. Then there was the feel of a breeze, a stirring of warmth, an uncomfortable rush of air from another place. The wind rose. It climbed in intensity, hot, stifling, a sirocco. The children tried to sit in their places but the wind roared toward them, onto them, through them, past them, and they were slammed into the walls of the empty room. It was a wind from nowhere.

And then, behind the wind came the sounds. Sounds of things that were not metal or plastic or glass but neither were they human. Sounds of rising notes, of chitinous surfaces sandpapering against one another, of water being heated to steam, of tympani echoing from a mountaintop. The sounds seemed to pour from a single spot in the room. From a place high up in the middle of the air, where now the children could see a strange orange spiderweb of light spreading like a starburst of filament-fine lines, crazing in the trembling air as a projectile crazes glass.

"This is how it begins. When you hear these sounds and you see that orange light, you know it's beginning. You will call it a spiracle; that is what we call it. And it means a hole is being made. Do you know what comes through that hole?"

The children could not answer. The wind had passed, but they lay in terror, tossed in a pile in a corner, and the sounds ratcheted and grated and scraped at their nerves, and they were frightened.

"This is what comes through the hole," the old paladin said, closing his eyes again, concentrating again.

The orange spiderweb grew larger, split down the air, became a ten-foot rip in nothingness, and beyond it, as though seen through trembling water . . . darkness.

Things moved in the darkness.

The children scrambled together, arms and legs struggling to get farther away, closer to the white wall, out of sight and out of line of that fissure in the air, that color of orangeness that seemed to continue beyond the spectrum their eyes could perceive, those sounds that clattered in their bones and made their teeth hurt. And the things began to come through from the darkness.

The first one was squat and thick and the color of potatoes. It had no face but it had a ring of slit-eyes that ran round its forehead; the top of its mealy form—what might have been a head, had it not been so unlike a head—ended with a million trembling cilia, each suet-white and wormlike. It did not have legs, but it was divided up the middle and its substance compressed the two stubs like dough as it shambled forward.

The second was glass-smooth but dark. Light seemed to touch it and vanish, to be gathered in and nullified. It was faceted and part of it appeared and disappeared like reflections in mirrors when the surfaces were turned. It was large and thin and tall, then it was tiny and endwise and razored; then it was gone, then it was back.

And behind them came a thing that moved like a chicken, arching itself forward then hauling itself up behind and under. It was covered with matted fur like a rat that has soaked itself in oil. The tips of the hairs gave off a faint green light.

And behind it came a thing that looked like cheesecloth, but it was made of flesh. It was oozing with dark blood, and there were mouths everywhere on it, and rings of teeth and the blood could be seen pumping and circulating through the tubes that joined the empty holes in its rotting cheesecloth form.

And behind it came four snapping things that tore chunks from one another as they gibbered toward the hole in the air. And then came a slab of wood with human hands growing all over its surface, and it scuttled along on the hands. There were others, seen only dimly in the darkness, and seen at all only because they gave off their own moist, green light.

The children screamed and some of them cried, and all of them tried to get away, to become small and hide in the corner, and the paladin was speaking to them and even through the terrible noises they could hear his voice saying, "When you see the spiracle begin to form, you will know it is starting, that these things and others will be trying to get through. You will stop them. Do you know how you will stop them?"

The children could not answer, would not; screamed. Only Alan managed to husk out a frightened, "Howwwww . . . ?" The paladin opened his eyes suddenly, looked at Alan and said in that odd voice that needed no movement of mouth to be formed, "Do this":

Together—the old paladin helped the child—they turned their eyes inward. Rushed along a sparkling silver thread, Alan felt the old paladin urging bursts of yellow light from the central fire deep inside him, out along feeders branching off the central silver thread. Each time the yellow light raced out it found a reservoir of pulsing energy; and it came hurtling back to the source purified and enlarged with power. Along and down the silver thread they raced together, the old one keeping the child in touch with the coruscating yellow power source, building it, shaping it, narrowing it into a lance of yellow light that was incredibly dense and potent. When it seemed Alan could contain no more of the yellow power, when he felt nausea bubbling up from below, far below the silver thread, the paladin *revolved* him. He (no, it wasn't like that) *turned* him, and across the scent of almonds Alan saw a gray mist. Together they *flattened* the yellow power and then the paladin *smoothed* it. The power went extruding across the sound of tin on concrete and the scent of almonds, went slicing straightaway like the horizon seen through an eye-slit. It struck against the gray mist and there was a whirling sound, as of demon winds jammed into a sea-bottle. It went on for a long time and Alan felt ill, felt

the yellow power thickening, felt it growing coarse and impure.
The old one was with him. He helped Alan keep the yellow
power isinglass-thin and irradicable. Alan trembled like a machine shaking itself to pieces. He could not feel his body; he
existed only within his own mind; trapped on that endless plain
with the horizon-line of yellow power and the gray mist and
the thrashing killing winds. Then the yellow power cut the gray
mist, suddenly, and it hurtled through into the beyond-mist-
place and was gone, and the winds died, and the old paladin
drew the child back back back into his body.

Alan slammed back inside himself, his eyes opened and he
pitched over on his side, emptying his bladder, his bowels and
his stomach—drenching himself and the wall beside him. His
eyes rolled up in his head. He went limp as death and fainted,
off off off . . .

The old paladin sent the other seven children to the primary
sensitivity sections and took Alan Pryor for advanced work.
Alan was already sensitive and potent.

This is what the old paladins taught him:

The crazing in the air was a tearing of the fabric of time.
The darkness beyond the orange spiderweb was the future.
Earth's future . . . how far ahead no one knew. Something terrible had happened up there. No one knew what it was, nor
how far ahead the disaster lay. It had changed those who lived
ahead up there. Now they wanted to escape. The disaster had
done something to the interface between the present and the
future. Frequently, without warning, those ahead up there were
able to force entrance. At such times, the paladins brought their
powers into play. The nature of the power was never explicated.
It could never be explained because it was a random talent. It
was born in rare children but some things had to be done to
them before they could exercise the full potency of the power.
They stood between the present and the future; against those
things that might be human but no one cared to find out. There
was no doubt that if they came through, they would destroy
the human race and take this Earth for themselves.

There were winds, and there were scorched places, and
people died where they burst through; but always the paladins
unleashed their power and the rift in time was sealed again and
the humping, lurching, odorous creatures from the other side

were sucked back into their own present and the Earth was safe again. For a while.

He was assigned to a ready station in Brazil. His apartment was in one of the old Bauhaus buildings fronting Leblon. He went where he chose and he was honored wherever he went. He was a paladin. The ivory and blue uniform was a badge of respect. He swam in the totally unbelievable blue of the ocean off Copacabana Beach and he stood every evening on the balcony of his apartment as the ten-minute torrential downpour eased the killing mugginess of the rain forest humidity. He attended brushup sessions in shock focus rooms like the one on the Island and he waited for his time.

One night, when he was twenty-seven years old, he attended a reception for the international crowd that had come to Rio for the film festival. When he came up the dramatically winding staircase in the American Embassy the band stopped playing and the enormous crowd turned and applauded him. He smiled shyly and accepted the individual greetings of the handsome men in their summer-weight dinner jackets and the extraordinary women in their diaphanous gowns. Then he sought a place along one wall where he could stand silently, watching them as they danced and laughed. He was alone; he was always alone; he had grown used to it.

Half of the reception story of the embassy had been wall-slatted, converting it into an art gallery; it held depth-screens on which reproductions of the paintings of American artists were projected: Rothko and Homer and Cassatt and Eakins and Bellows and Wyeth and Grooms. He stood and marveled. He had no national heritage, had never been exposed to such wonders.

After a time, he became aware of a woman watching him.

He did not stare at her, but turned slightly so he could watch her reflection in one of the polished stainless steel helix sculptures of David Lee Brown.

She was very tall and had shaved herself completely in the current fashion. Her pale skin seemed to be covered with a faint, delicate film of dew. He thought: *beautiful, I've never seen a woman as beautiful*. He remembered: the sound of a celeste, the sound of a toy piano. From long ago, before the Island.

She moved, and he turned with her movement to follow her image in the stainless steel; she slipped off the reflective surface; and when he came around to look directly at the crowded room, to find her again, she was standing too near, and she was watching him. Her expression was one of concern. He had had women, but had never approached one socially. He was about to do it, to brave it, when the spiracle began to form in the air just in front of the Louis Comfort Tiffany chandelier. One of the waiters saw it first (Alan saw it *first*) and threw his silver salver of canapes to the polished onyx floor, shouted, pointed, and ran down the winding staircase.

Then others saw the fissure widening in the air, the charred orange lips of it distending in the air, a faint rushing of demon winds already ruffling their hair. They began to scream and to surge toward the staircase.

Had he not been staring directly at her, he would not have been aware of her part in it.

Something like the rooted trunk of a tree began to slip through the spiracle aperture, its fibrous rhizomes writhing through the spiderweb threads that dangled from the yawning lips of the fissure. Droplets of moisture fell from the tendrils and where they struck the onyx floor bubbled and burned.

Alan gathered the yellow light from the wells deep inside him and, realizing the crowd would quickly shove itself over the staircase railings, knew he had only moments to seal the spiracle. He closed his eyes, clenched his fists and hurled a blast of yellow power out along the sparkling silver thread. It struck the vegetable horror emerging from the fissure and penetrated each tiniest fiber of rootling. It surged up the taproot and entered the trunk, blasting the core of life within. Then the yellow power spread outward, lapping against the sides of the spiracle. The opening began to shrink; it drew in on itself as though strings were tightening, pulling it closed like the mouth of a chamois pouch. Alan drew a deep breath, clenched his teeth and speared one last potent measure of yellow power at the spiracle. It withered, sucked back in on itself, pulled the last trailing rhizome back through the spiderweb, and then was gone.

He felt himself sliding down against the wall. He had fought off an attack yesterday, in one of the *favelas* high on the mountain overlooking the Lagoa Rodrigo de Frietas. There among the *barracos,* the tin-sided hovels, he had beat back an assault of slitted reptilian eyes that had surged out of the infernal darkness behind the orange spiderweb. And again tonight, yet another encroachment. They *never* came this close together. Was it an indication that some kind of tolerance had been built up? That it would take more frequent and stronger retaliation to beat back the shock-focus attacks? He slid down and sat with his back to the wall, feeling sick to his stomach. He never really came away from an attack unscathed: his brain felt scoured, raw, bleeding.

The crowd of silken cosmopolites had paused on the edge of riot: there was a paladin among them. And no paladin had ever failed to save them. They had paused and watched in awe and terror as this slight young man had beat back the demons. Now they crowded around him, their hands reaching down to help him.

Alan gestured them away. He sought her face in the crowd and through a momentary shift in bodies saw her heading for the staircase. He motioned in her direction and managed to gasp a command. "Stop that woman . . . the silver gown . . . yes, *her!*" And the crowd closed in across the mouth of the staircase, halting her flight. She turned and stared at him. Then she came through the crowd, her silver gown whispering against her moist skin, and she helped him to his feet.

And together they passed through the crowd of dilettanti and descended the memorable staircase.

R–40 in Bin 375.
R–41 in Bin 376.
R–42 in Bin 401.
They are so few. Never enough. But always a few to stand in the face of horror, to place their fragile bodies on the line for the rest of us. How they came to be born among us, these sanctified mutations, our children of wonder, perhaps we'll never understand. But they came when we needed them, and though they die for us, they do not die unmourned. We consecrate our lives, our world, our future, to the holy memory of men and women like Alan Pryor. Paladins . . . guardians of the human race.
QQ–42 in Bin 119.

She bathed him and he slept. She *thought* he slept, but he only rested with his eyes closed. He watched her move around the conapt's misty interior, pruning and watering her bushes; watched her through slitted eyes. And when he was certain she was not in contact with anyone else, he sat up.

Her back was to him. She was waxing the leaves of an *Alocacia amazonica*. He sat up, naked in the misty pool of warm water, and he said, "You caused it."

She did not turn. Her movements were precise and graceful. "I don't know what you mean," she said. But he knew she had caused it, and he said, "Yes, you do."

The mist settled on her hairless body and sparkled like frost. She ceased her activity and turned to him.

"How could you do that?" He heard his voice; it sounded immature and bewildered.

She sighed and shook her head very faintly, as though what he was saying was infinitely saddening to her.

Then the old paladin emerged from the mist and the shadows where he had been waiting, silently hoping this most sensitive of the sensitive children had not stumbled on the truth through the ineptitude of a judas on her first time out, knowing it was a futile hope, and prepared to do what had to be done. He was a very old paladin, who had been promised his freedom when he had prepared this woman to take over for him, and he was both furious at her misjudgment and desolate that his rest was that much further denied him.

He stepped out of the shadows, slaughtered her with a thought, and turned to the young paladin in the mist pool.

Alan Pryor looked into his face and saw what awaited him. He held up a hand. "At least let me understand why!"

The old paladin sighed. Why not.

"There are no attacks. It's all contrived."

"No, that isn't so. I—I *feel* the pain . . . I *see* the darkness coming through, the things, the spiracle . . ."

He shook his head. "All contrived. By sensitives like her, and me. We buy our lives. Judas sensitives. To keep you and others like you busy, for a cause. So we don't breed. So we don't multiply and take over. The ones who don't have the power, the nonsensitives, they knew from the first that we were the next step. They wouldn't let go; they'll *never* let go. So they contrived it all."

Alan made a sudden lurch toward the edge of the mist pool. The old paladin burned him out; there was a wisp of dark, thin smoke from the ash-filled sockets that had been Alan Pryor's eyes; and the old paladin sighed once more before he began cataloging the parts of Alan Pryor's body that could be recycled in expectation of the next child born with the power.

In that lonely place where Alan Pryor gave his life, there were no observers. The attack came in an isolated, empty place where he was burned defending us. Now we lay his body to rest, with honor, swearing that he did not go unmourned. With honor, to your final rest, Alan Pryor. Humanity will not forget.

G–64 in Bin 487.

"There are no rules. Those who are in power make up the rules. So those out of favor are bound to break them."

—JOSÉ BER GELBARD

Shatterday

INTRODUCTION

Everything that is appropriate to say about this final entry of the current grimoire has been said in the general introduction, "Mortal Dreads," with the possible exception of this:

There is a curse over the door to my tomb. It says, Beware all ye who enter here—because herein lie the proofs of observation that we are all as one, living in the same skin, each of us condemned to handle the responsibility of our past, our memories, our destiny as elements in the great congeries of life. And if you find these dark dreams troubling, perhaps it is because they are *your* dreams.

It's been nice visiting with you.

And when next the full moon rises, and the sounds from beyond the campfire are ominously semihuman, we will gather again and I'll listen to your tales and then write them up in my way, and give them back to you.

Until that time.

Shatterday

i: *Someday*

NOT MUCH LATER, but later nonetheless, he thought back on the sequence of what had happened, and knew he had missed nothing. How it had gone, was this:

He had been abstracted, thinking about something else. It didn't matter what. He had gone to the telephone in the restaurant, to call Jamie, to find out where the hell she was already, to find out why she'd kept him sitting in the bloody bar for thirty-five minutes. He had been thinking about something else, nothing deep, just woolgathering, and it wasn't till the number was ringing that he realized he'd dialed his own apartment. He had done it other times, not often, but as many as anyone else, dialed a number by rote and not thought about it, and occasionally it was his own number, everyone does it (he thought later), everyone does it, it's a simple mistake.

He was about to hang up, get back his dime and dial Jamie, when the receiver was lifted at the other end.

He answered.

Himself.

He recognized his own voice at once. But didn't let it penetrate.

He had no little machine to take messages after the bleep, he had had his answering service temporarily disconnected (unsatisfactory service, they weren't catching his calls on the third ring as he'd *insisted*), there was no one guesting at his apartment, nothing. He was not at home, he was here, in the restaurant, calling his apartment, and *he* answered.

"Hello?"

He waited a moment. Then said, "Who's this?"

He answered, "Who're you calling?"

"Hold it," he said. "Who *is* this?"

His own voice, on the other end, getting annoyed, said, "Look, friend, what number do you want?"

"This is BEacon 3–6189, right?"

Warily: "Yeah...?"

"Peter Novins's apartment?"

There was silence for a moment, then: "That's right."

He listened to the sounds from the restaurant's kitchen. "If this is Novins's apartment, who're you?"

On the other end, in his apartment, there was a deep breath. "This is Novins."

He stood in the phone booth, in the restaurant, in the night, the receiver to his ear, and listened to his own voice. He had dialed his own number by mistake, dialed an empty apartment...*and he had answered.*

Finally, he said, very tightly, *"This* is Novins."

"Where are you?"

"I'm at The High Tide, waiting for Jamie."

Across the line, with a terrible softness, he heard himself asking, "Is that you?"

A surge of fear pulsed through him and he tried to get out of it with one last possibility. "If this is a gag... Freddy... is that you, man? Morrie? Art?"

Silence. Then, slowly, "I'm Novins. Honest to God."

His mouth was dry. "I'm out here. You can't be, I *can't* be in the apartment."

"Oh yeah? Well, I am."

"I'll have to call you back." Peter Novins hung up.

He went back to the bar and ordered a double Scotch, no ice, straight up, and threw it back in two swallows, letting it burn. He sat and stared at his hands, turning them over and over, studying them to make sure they were his own, not alien meat grafted onto his wrists when he was not looking.

Then he went back to the phone booth, closed the door and sat down, and dialed his own number. Very carefully.

It rang six times before *he* picked it up.

He knew why the voice on the other end had let it ring six times; he didn't want to pick up the snake and hear his own voice coming at him.

"Hello?" His voice on the other end was barely controlled.

"It's me," he said, closing his eyes.

"Jesus God," he murmured.

They sat there, in their separate places, without speaking. Then Novins said, "I'll call you Jay."

"That's okay," he answered from the other end. It was his middle name. He never used it, but it appeared on his insurance policy, his driver's license and his social security card. Jay said, "Did Jamie get there?"

"No, she's late again."

Jay took a deep breath and said, "We'd better talk about this, man."

"I suppose," Novins answered. "Not that I really want to. You're scaring the shit out of me."

"How do you think *I* feel about it?"

"Probably the same way I feel about it."

They thought about that for a long moment. Then Jay said, "Will we be feeling exactly the same way about things?"

Novins considered it, then said, "If you're really me then I suppose so. We ought to try and test that."

"You're taking this a lot calmer than I am, it seems to me," Jay said.

Novins was startled. "You really think so? I was just about to say I thought you were really terrific the way you're handling all this. I think you're *much* more together about it than I am. I'm really startled, I've got to tell you."

"So how'll we test it?" Jay asked.

Novins considered the problem, then said, "Why don't we compare likes and dislikes. That's a start. That sound okay to you?"

"It's as good a place as any, I suppose. Who goes first?"

"It's my dime," Novins said, and for the first time he smiled. "I like, uh, well-done prime rib, end cut if I can get it, Yorkshire pudding, smoking a pipe, Max Ernst's paintings, Robert Altman films, William Goldman's books, getting mail but not answering it, uh . . ."

He stopped. He had been selecting random items from memory, the ones that came to mind first. But as he had been speaking, he heard what he was saying, and it seemed stupid. "This isn't going to work," Novins said. "What the hell does it matter? Was there anything in that list you didn't like?"

Jay sighed. "No, they're all favorites. You're right. If I like it, you'll like it. This isn't going to answer any questions."

Novins said, "I don't even know what the questions *are!*"

"That's easy enough," Jay said. "There's only one question: which of us is me, and how does *me* get rid of *him?*"

A chill spread out from Novins's shoulder blades and wrapped around his arms like a mantilla. "What's *that* supposed to mean? Get rid of *him?* What the hell's *that?*"

"Face it," Jay said—and Novins heard a tone in the voice he recognized, the tone *he* used when he was about to become a tough negotiator—"we can't *both* be Novins. One of us is going to get screwed."

"Hold it, friend," Novins said, adopting the tone. "That's pretty muddy logic. First of all, who's to say you're not going to vanish back where you came from as soon as I hang up . . ."

"Bullshit," Jay answered.

"Yeah, well, maybe; but even if you're here to stay, and I don't concede *that* craziness for a second, even if you *are* real—"

"Believe it, baby, I'm real," Jay said, with a soft chuckle. Novins was starting to hate him.

"—even if you *are* real," Novins continued, "there's no saying we can't both exist, and both lead happy, separate lives."

"You know something, Novins," Jay said, "you're really full of horse puckey. You can't lead a happy life by yourself, man, how the hell are you going to do it knowing I'm over here living your life, too?"

"What do you mean I can't lead a happy life? What do you know about it?" And he stopped; of course Jay knew about it. *All* about it.

"You'd better start facing reality, Novins. You'll be coming to it late in life, but you'd better learn how to do it. Maybe it'll make the end come easier."

Novins wanted to slam the receiver into its rack. He was at once furiously angry and frightened. He knew what the other Novins was saying was true; he *had* to know, without argument; it was, after all, himself saying it. "Only one of us is going to make it," he said, tightly. "And it's going to be me, old friend."

"How do you propose to do it, Novins? You're out there, locked out. I'm in here, in my home, safe where I'm supposed to be."

"How about we look at it *this* way," Novins said quickly, "you're trapped in there, locked away from the world in three-and-a-half rooms. I've got everywhere else to move in. You're limited. I'm free."

There was silence for a moment.

Then Jay said, "We've reached a bit of an impasse, haven't we? There's something to be said for being loose, and there's something to be said for being safe inside. The amazing thing is that we both have accepted this thing so quickly."

Novins didn't answer. He accepted it because he had no other choice; if he could accept that he was speaking to himself, then anything that followed had to be part of that acceptance. Now that Jay had said it bluntly, that only one of them could continue to exist, all that remained was finding a way to make sure it was he, Novins, who continued past this point.

"I've got to think about this," Novins said. "I've got to try to work some of this out better. You just stay celled in there, friend; I'm going to a hotel for the night. I'll call you tomorrow."

He started to hang up when Jay's voice stopped him. "What do I say if Jamie gets there and you're gone and she calls me?"

Novins laughed. "That's *your* problem, motherfucker."

He racked the receiver with nasty satisfaction.

ii: *Moanday*

He took special precautions. First the bank, to clean out the checking account. He thanked God he'd had his checkbook with him when he'd gone out to meet Jamie the night before. But the savings account passbook was in the apartment. That meant Jay had access to almost ten thousand dollars. The checking account was down to fifteen hundred, even with all outstanding bills paid, and the Banks for Cooperatives note came due in about thirty days and that meant . . . he used the back of a deposit slip to figure the interest . . . he'd be getting ten thousand four hundred and sixty-five dollars and seven cents deposited to his account. His *new* account, which he opened at another branch of the same bank, signing the identification cards with a variation of his signature sufficiently different to prevent Jay's trying to draw on the account. He was at least solvent. For the time being.

But all his work was in the apartment. All the public relations accounts he handled. Every bit of data and all the plans and phone numbers and charts, they were all there in the little apartment office. So he was quite effectively cut off from his career.

Yet in a way, that was a blessing. Jay would have to keep up with the work in his absence, would have to follow through on the important campaigns for Topper and McKenzie, would have to take all the moronic calls from Lippman and his insulting son, would have to answer all the mail, would have to keep popping Titralac all day just to stay ahead of the heartburn. He felt gloriously free and almost satanically happy that he was rid of the aggravation for a while, and that Jay was going to find out being Peter Jay Novins wasn't all fun and Jamies.

Back in his hotel room at the Americana he made a list of things he had to do. To survive. It was a new way of thinking, setting down one by one the everyday routine actions from which he was now cut off. He was all alone now, entirely and totally, for the first time in his life, cut off from everything. He could not depend on friends or associates or the authorities. It would be suicide to go to the police and say, "Listen, I hate to bother you, but I've split and one of me has assumed squatter's rights in my apartment; please go up there and arrest him." No, he was on his own, and he had to exorcise Jay from the world strictly by his own wits and cunning.

Bearing in mind, of course, that Jay had the same degree of wit and cunning.

He crossed half a dozen items off the list. There was no need to call Jamie and find out what had happened to her the night before. Their relationship wasn't that binding in any case. Let Jay make the excuses. No need to cancel the credit cards, he had them with him. Let Jay pay the bills from the savings account. No need to contact any of his friends and warn them. He *couldn't* warn them, and if he did, what would he warn them against? Himself? But he did need clothes, fresh socks and underwear, a light jacket instead of his topcoat, a pair of gloves in case the weather turned. And he had to cancel out the delivery services to the apartment in a way that would prevent Jay from reinstating them: groceries, milk, dry cleaning, newspapers. He had to make it as difficult for him in there as possible. And so he called each tradesman and insulted him so grossly they would *never* serve him again. Unfortunately, the building provided heat and electricity and gas and he *had* to leave the phone connected.

The phone was his tie-line to victory, to routing Jay out of there.

When he had it all attended to, by three o'clock in the afternoon, he returned to the hotel room, took off his shoes, propped the pillows up on the bed, lay down and dialed a 9 for the outside line, then dialed his own number.

As it rang, he stared out the forty-fifth floor window of the hotel room, at the soulless pylons of the RCA and Grants Buildings, the other dark-glass filing cabinets for people. It was a wonder *any*one managed to stay sane, stay whole in such surroundings! Living in cubicles, boxed and trapped and throttled, was it any surprise that people began to fall apart . . . even as *he* seemed to be falling apart? The wonder was that it all managed to hold together as well as it did. But the fractures were beginning to appear, culturally and now—as with Peter Novins, he mused—personally. The phone continued to ring. Clouds blocked out all light and the city was swamped by shadows. At three o'clock in the afternoon, the ominous threat of another night settled over Novins's hotel room.

The receiver was lifted at the other end. But Jay said nothing.

"It's me," Novins said. "How'd you enjoy your first day in my skin?"

"How did you enjoy your first day *out* of it?" he replied.

"Listen, I've got your act covered, friend, and your hours are numbered. The checking account is gone, don't try to find it; you're going to go out to get food and when you do I'll be waiting—"

"Terrific," Jay replied. "But just so you don't waste your time, I had the locks changed today. Your keys don't work. And I bought groceries. Remember the fifty bucks I put away in the jewelry box?"

Novins cursed himself silently. He hadn't thought of that.

"And I've been doing some figuring, Novins. Remember that old Jack London novel, *The Star Rover?* Remember how he used astral projection to get out of his body? I think that's what happened to me. I sent you out when I wasn't aware of it. So I've decided I'm me, and you're just a little piece that's wandered off. And I can get along just peachy-keen without that piece, so why don't you just go—"

"Hold it," Novins interrupted, "that's a sensational theory, but it's stuffed full of wild blueberry muffins, if you'll pardon my being so forward as to disagree with a smartass voice that's probably disembodied and doesn't have enough ectoplasm to take a healthy shit. Remember the weekend I went over to the lab with Kenny and he took that Kirlian photograph of my aura? Well, my theory is that something happened and the aura produced another me, or something . . ."

He slid down into silence. Neither theory was worth thinking about. He had no idea, *really,* what had happened. They hung there in silence for a long moment, then Jay said, "Mother called this morning."

Novins felt a hand squeeze his chest. "What did she say?"

"She said she knew you lied when you were down in Florida. She said she loved you and she forgave you and all she wants is for you to share your life with her."

Novins closed his eyes. He didn't want to think about it. His mother was in her eighties, very sick, and just recovering from her second serious heart attack in three years. The end was near and, combining a business trip in Miami with a visit to her, he had gone to Florida the month before. He had never had much in common with his mother, had been on his own since his early teens, and though he supported her in her declining years, he refused to allow her to impose on his existence. He seldom wrote letters, save to send the check, and during the two days he had spent in her apartment in Miami Beach he had thought he would go insane. He had wanted to bolt, and finally had lied to her that he was returning to New York a day earlier than his plans required. He had packed up and left her, checking into a hotel, and had spent the final day involved in business and that night had gone out with a secretary he dated occasionally when in Florida.

"How did she find out?" Novins asked.

"She called here and the answering service told her you were still in Florida and hadn't returned. They gave her the number of the hotel and she called there and found out you were registered for that night."

Novins cursed himself. Why had he called the service to

tell them where he was? He could have gotten away with one day of his business contacts not being able to reach him. "Swell," he said. "And I suppose you didn't do anything to make her feel better."

"On the contrary," Jay said, "I did what you never would have done. I made arrangements for her to come live here with me."

Novins heard himself moan with pain. "You did *what!?* Jesus Christ, you're out of your fucking mind. How the hell am I going to take care of that old woman in New York? I've got work to do, places I have to go, I have a life to lead..."

"Not any more you don't, you guilty, selfish sonofabitch. Maybe *you* could live with the bad gut feelings about her, but not me. She'll be arriving in a week."

"You're crazy," Novins screamed. "You're fucking crazy!"

"Yeah," Jay said, softly, and added, "and you just lost your mother. Chew on *that* one, you creep."

And he hung up.

iii: *Duesday*

They decided between them that the one who *deserved* to be Peter Novins should take over the life. They had to make that decision; clearly, they could not go on as they had been; even two days had showed them half an existence was not possible. Both were fraying at the edges.

So Jay suggested they work their way through the pivot experiences of Novins's life, to see if he was really entitled to continue living.

"*Every*one's entitled to go on living," Novins said, vehemently. "That's why we live. To say no to death."

"You don't believe that for a second, Novins," Jay said. "You're a misanthrope. You hate people."

"That's not true; I just don't like some of the things people *do*."

"Like what, for instance? Like, for instance, you're always bitching about kids who wear ecology patches, who throw Dr. Pepper cans in the bushes; like that, for instance?"

"That's good for starters," Novins said.

"You hypocritical bastard," Jay snarled back at him, "you ⁚e audacity to beef about that and you took on the Cum-
⁚count."

"That's another kind of thing!"

"My ass. You know damned well Cumberland's planning to strip mine the guts out of that county, and they're going to get away with it with that publicity campaign you dreamed up. Oh, you're one hell of a good PR man, Novins, but you've got the ethics of a weasel."

Novins was fuming, but Jay was right. He had felt lousy about taking on Cumberland from the start, but they were big, they were international, and the billing for the account was handily in six figures. He had tackled the campaign with the same ferocity he brought to all his accounts, and the program was solid. "I have to make a living. Besides, if I didn't do it, someone else would. I'm only doing a job. They've got a terrific restoration program, don't forget that. They'll put that land back in shape."

Jay laughed. "That's what Eichmann said: 'We have a terrific restoration program, we'll put them Jews right back in shape, just a little gas to spiff 'em up.' He was just doing a job, too, Novins. Have I mentioned lately that you stink on ice?"

Novins was shouting again. "I suppose you'd have turned it down."

"That's exactly what I did, old buddy," Jay said. "I called them today and told them to take their account and stuff it up their nose. I've got a call in to Nader right now, to see what he can do with all that data in the file."

Novins was speechless. He lay there, under the covers, the Tuesday snow drifting in enormous flakes past the forty-fifth floor windows. Slowly, he let the receiver settle into the cradle. Only three days and his life was drifting apart inexorably; soon it would be impossible to knit it together.

His stomach ached. And all that day he had felt nauseated. Room service had sent up pot after pot of tea, but it hadn't helped. A throbbing headache was lodged just behind his left eye, and cold sweat covered his shoulders and chest.

He didn't know what to do, but he knew he was losing.

iv: *Woundsday*

On Wednesday Jay called Novins. He never told him how he located him, he just called. "How do you feel?" he

Novins could barely answer, the fever was close to immobilizing.

"I just called to talk about Jeanine and Patty and that girl in Denver," Jay said, and he launched into a long and stately recitation of Novins's affairs, and how they had ended. It was not as Novins remembered it.

"That isn't true," Novins managed to say, his voice deep and whispering, dry and nearly empty.

"It *is* true, Novins. That's what's so sad about it. That it *is* true and you've never had the guts to admit it, that you go from woman to woman without giving anything, always taking, and when you leave them—or they dump you—you've never learned a god damned thing. You've been married twice, divorced twice, you've been in and out of two dozen affairs and you haven't learned that you're one of those men who is simply no bloody good for a woman. So now you're forty-two years old and you're finally coming to the dim understanding that you're going to spend all the rest of the days and nights of your life alone, because you can't stand the company of another human being for more than a month without turning into a vicious prick."

"Not true," murmured Novins.

"True, Novins, true. Flat true. You set after Patty and got her to leave her old man, and when you'd pried her loose, her and the kid, you set her up in that apartment with three hundred a month rent, and then you took off and left her to work it out herself. It's true, old buddy. So don't try and con me with that 'I lead a happy life' bullshit."

Novins simply lay there with his eyes closed, shivering with the fever.

Then Jay said, "I saw Jamie last night. We talked about her future. It took some fast talking; she was really coming to hate you. But I think it'll work out if I go at it hard, and I *intend* to go at it hard. I don't intend to have any more years like I've had, Novins. From this point on it changes."

The bulk of the buildings outside the window seemed to tremble behind the falling snow. Novins felt terribly cold. He didn't answer.

"We'll name the first one after you, Peter," Jay said, and hung up.

That was Wednesday.

v: *Thornsday*

There were no phone calls that day. Novins lay there, the
television set mindlessly playing and replaying the five minute
instruction film on the pay-movie preview channel, the ghost-
image of a dark-haired girl in a gray suit showing him how to
charge a first-run film to his hotel bill. After many hours he
heard himself reciting the instructions along with her. He slept
a great deal. He thought about Jeanine and Patty, the girl in
Denver whose name he could not recall, and Jamie.

After many more hours, he thought about insects, but he
didn't know what that meant. There were no phone calls that
day. It was Thursday.

Shortly before midnight, the fever broke, and he cried himself back to sleep.

vi: *Freeday*

A key turned in the lock and the hotel room door opened.
Novins was sitting in a mass-produced imitation of a Saarinen
pedestal chair, its seat treated with Scotch-Gard. He had been
staring out the window at the geometric irrelevancy of the glass-
wall buildings. It was near dusk, and the city was gray as
cardboard.

He turned at the sound of the door opening and was not
surprised to see himself walk in.

Jay's nose and cheeks were still red from the cold outside.
He unzipped his jacket and stuffed his kid gloves into a pocket,
removed the jacket and threw it on the unmade bed. "Really
cold out there," he said. He went into the bathroom and Novins
heard the sound of water running.

Jay returned in a few minutes, rubbing his hands together.
"That helps," he said. He sat down on the edge of the bed and
looked at Novins.

"You look terrible, Peter," he said.

"I haven't been at all well," Novins answered dryly. "I don't
seem to be myself these days."

Jay smiled briefly. "I see you're coming to terms with
That ought to help."

Novins stood up. The thin light from the room-long window shone through him like white fire through milk glass. "You're looking well," he said.

"I'm getting better, Peter. It'll be a while, but I'm going to be okay."

Novins walked across the room and stood against the wall, hands clasped behind his back. He could barely be seen. "I remember the archetypes from Jung. Are you my shadow, my persona, my anima or my animus?"

"What am I now, or what was I when I got loose?"

"Either way."

"I suppose I was your shadow. Now I'm the self."

"And I'm becoming the shadow."

"No, you're becoming a memory. A bad memory."

"That's pretty ungracious."

"I was sick for a long time, Peter. I don't know what the trigger was that broke us apart, but it happened and I can't be too sorry about it. If it hadn't happened I'd have been you till I died. It would have been a lousy life and a miserable death."

Novins shrugged. "Too late to worry about it now. Things working out with Jamie?"

Jay nodded. "Yeah. And Mom comes in Tuesday afternoon. I'm renting a car to pick her up at Kennedy. I talked to her doctors. They say she doesn't have too long. But for whatever she's got, I'm determined to make up for the last twenty-five years since Dad died."

Novins smiled and nodded. "That's good."

"Listen," Jay said slowly, with difficulty, "I just came over to ask if there was anything you wanted me to do . . . anything *you* would've done if . . . if it had been different."

Novins spread his hands and thought about it for a moment. "No, I don't think so, nothing special. You might try and get some money to Jeanine's mother, for Jeanine's care, maybe. That wouldn't hurt."

"I already took care of it. I figured that would be on your mind."

Novins smiled. "That's good. Thanks."

"Anything else . . . ?"

Novins shook his head. They stayed that way, hardly moving, till night had fallen outside the window. In the darkness,
could barely see Novins standing against the wall. Merely
low.

Finally, Jay stood and put on his jacket, zipped up and put on his left glove. "I've got to go."

Novins spoke from the shadows. "Yeah. Well, take care of me, will you?"

Jay didn't answer. He walked to Novins and extended his right hand. The touch of Novins's hand in his was like the whisper of a cold wind; there was no pressure.

Then he left.

Novins walked back to the window and stared out. The last remaining daylight shone through him. Dimly.

vii: *Shatterday*

When the maid came in to make up the bed, she found the room was empty. It was terribly cold in the room on the forty-fifth floor. When Peter Novins did not return that day, or the next, the management of the Americana marked him as a skip, and turned it over to a collection agency.

In due course the bill was sent to Peter Novins's apartment on Manhattan's upper east side.

It was promptly paid, by Peter Jay Novins, with a brief, but *sincere* note of apology.